TRANSMENTATION |
TRANSIENCE

TRANSMENTATION |
TRANSIENCE

OR, AN ACCESSION TO THE PEOPLE'S COUNCIL
FOR NINE THOUSAND WORLDS

DARKLY LEM

**BLACK
STONE**
PUBLISHING

The characters and events in this book are fictitious.
Any similarity to real persons, living or dead, is coincidental
and not intended by the authors.

Printed in the United States of America

First edition: 2025
ISBN 979-8-212-18599-8
Fiction / Science Fiction / General

Version 1

Blackstone Publishing
31 Mistletoe Rd.
Ashland, OR 97520

www.BlackstonePublishing.com

Contextual Notes and Declarations:

As a work of speculative history, *Transmentation | Transience* is not an attempt to render a perfect record of the past. It operates under the Ghanting Theory, seeking to explain present circumstances via plausible recreations of historical moments and/or personages. All due care has, of course, been taken in consulting archives of that era, however, with the Transmutation of Burel Hird Prime, such efforts are, necessarily, fragmentary. And, as the Arcalumis Society still labored under the blighted Fourth Framework during that period, records from our own history must likewise be considered suspect.

This depiction of the events of the Formation Saga should not be considered authoritative or accurate. Indeed, the instability inherent in the Simulacrum would make such claims dubious at best. The alteration of individuals, of reality, of the fundamental rules governing a universe must not only be accommodated but taken for granted in any true accounting of the past.

Though hard to imagine now, readers must recall that contact between multiversal societies was then rare, and more fraught than in our present moment, some X50 years later. Perhaps nowhere is this more evident than in the use of antiquated, society-specific terms for the bodies travelers leave behind, or enter, such as "hide" by Of Tala, "coat" by Firmāre, or "front" by Harraka. Readers may be assured that all refer to the now-standard "proxy," and can be treated as interchangeable. We have endeavored to present the terminology as it would have been used during the era.

Ghanting Admissions:

The Authors declare that this work engages with the following multiversal societies: Burel Hird, the Withered Stem, Firmāre, Of Tala, Harraka, the Arcalumis Society, the Great Society.

The Authors declare that this work seeks further understanding of Historical Trends including, but not limited to, Withered Stem isolationism, Burel Hird revanchism, the inception of the Great Society.

Published by the Authority of the College of Ætiological Ordination
A *Journal of Theoretical History* book

In accordance with Episcopal Guidelines, the Authors declare this work features:

Blasphemous Language, Blasphemous Conceptions of the Simulacrum, Concepts Antithetical and/or Heretical, Jibes and/or Japery, physical Violence, emotional Violence, Depictions of Travel lacking Suitable Reverence, References to the Vh-x, Crabs by Implication.

Published in adherence to Faculty Guidelines regarding Consequence and Responsibility
Published in adherence to all Episcopal Monitors' Recommendations
Published with the intent to achieve a greater understanding of all Simulacral Phenomena
Published with the intent to expand the bounds of Arcalumical Knowledge

—Dahr Kliearseyf and Llemykel Veydumardey
JDWI—30XƐ

The Authors aver that, to the best of their knowledge and in accordance with the *Journal of Theoretical History*'s best practices, the individuals named below were genuine historical personages. They are presented with presumed Society affiliations where applicable. All language, actions, beliefs, thoughts, memories, etc. attributed to them are the products of the Authors and in all instances meet or exceed a Plausible Behavior Assessment of 0.4.

Readers are advised to grant the figures appearing in this work, nearly all of whom were real, grace and compassion, as they were products of their era and their circumstances. The presentation of acts unacceptable to modern Arcalumical sensibilities should not be construed as endorsement of same.

GEÇIŞ LOCALITY

Malculm Kilkaneade—an intelligence operative (Burel Hird)
Ronni Deekin-Seven—an Academy student (Burel Hird)
Æthelred Æthelred—a warrior-lawyer (Burel Hird)
Haeg Vandaar-Schnitzer—a tracker (Burel Hird)
Beinir—a mercenary (Of Tala)
Shara—a mercenary (Of Tala)
Cämeel—a researcher (Withered Stem)
Laën—a researcher (Withered Stem)
Nyäll—a researcher (Withered Stem)

PRIME LOCALITY
Burel Hird Prime

Duncan Hérn—a vice-councilor (Burel Hird)

Ecklan Sammo—his husband (Burel Hird)

Yorek Dhalgrim—a councilor (Burel Hird)

Zechariah Erland—a councilor (Burel Hird)

Trystèsté Jason—vice-councilor to Zechariah (Burel Hird)

Xelia Sienna—a councilor (Burel Hird)

Priema Lirend—vice-councilor to Xelia (Burel Hird)

Iskada Bendal—a councilor (Burel Hird)

Shaddoh Shakth—vice-councilor to Iskada (Burel Hird)

Blaine Quinn—a councilor (Burel Hird)

Darmeth Tyshan—vice-councilor to Blaine (Burel Hird)

Melyssa Nandir—a councilor (Burel Hird)

Sushan Ithzil—vice-councilor to Melyssa (Burel Hird)

Zeph Estevan—a councilor (Burel Hird)

Esrisa Pirzov—vice-councilor to Zeph (Burel Hird)

Jup Hasid—a farmer, and Trystèsté's father (Burel Hird)

Reigh Climpt—a farmer, and Trystèsté's mother (Burel Hird)

Gryçan, Hÿdorå, Óphillôm, and Brènjùmyn—Trystèsté's siblings
    (Burel Hird)

Ioseun Leong—a tracker for the Council for Border Security and
    Regulation (Burel Hird)

Derrin Venksa—a recent graduate of the August Academy (Burel Hird)

Glace j•Mitchell Adzersyn—a hacker (Burel Hird)

Eria Jellisoe—sub-adjutant to the assistant to the prosecutor-general
    (Burel Hird)

Alyk Philton—a callow youth (Burel Hird)

GDERCC LOCALITY
Gdercc

Maddalena Vaish—an agent (Firmāre)

Reg Vaish—her handler (Firmāre)

Defoe—a petty criminal (no affiliation)
Frenklin—his partner (no affiliation)
Kbousch—a gondolier (no affiliation)

CALYX LOCALITY
New Darem

Mëryl—a botanist and intelligence operative (Withered Stem)
Shann—a revolutionary (Harraka)
Tre—a waiter (no affiliation)

OULRA LOCALITY
Roamers of Tala Keep

The Sibyl—a sibyl, keeper of the roamers' sigil (Of Tala)

KONRA LOCALITY
L'makor

Noah Orillo—an unappreciated youth (Firmāre)
Thaddicus Orillo—his uncle (Firmāre)
Anolia Orillo—his aunt (Firmāre)
Wolfryke—a summoner (Of Tala)

Nightingale Station

Laerd—a travel overseer (no affiliation)
A stranger—an assassin (?)
Captain Elvrii—a ~~buffoon~~ hero (no affiliation)
Uptin—a mover (no affiliation)
Chanci—a navigator (no affiliation)

ENGINE LOCALITY
Engine

Dima Tancredi—an intelligence operative (Burel Hird)

CENTRAL CLUSTER 765
Iowa District 5

Jil—wife of Milton, Malculm's proxy (no affiliation)
Padre Vikram—a Class-A summoner (Burel Hird)
Dryska Kerlik—the muscle, a navigator (Burel Hird)
Gervin Sana—a mover (Burel Hird)

RENQUEUE LOCALITY
Tekkin-Yut

Yalun Smith—Under-Vizier for Special Circumstances (Burel Hird)

Shighoa

Jenkins Jonns—a clerk (Burel Hird)
Fatima Borals—Grand Vizier for Special Circumstances (Burel Hird)

PART ONE

I

She followed them across the street, moonlight reddening the cratered pavement. Tufts of dead grass snarled up through cracks in the sidewalk and the piled sediment from a withdrawn tide. Buildings around her were bones and stalwart spars here and there, rent by explosives on one street or untouched rows along another, the remnants of some forgotten and haphazard bombardment.

Ronni stepped into an alley on the eastern side of the square. She stood in the shadow of one of the arms of the space elevator dominating the skyline and scanned the nearby vehicles. There were no signs of crabs hiding in the cored-out cars littering the street, no telltale charcoal scent darkening the night air. Only the salty, nauseating smell of decay that permeated this world. A seabird landed on a fire escape ahead and to her left. The children she followed looked back for a moment. They were dressed in the manner typical for youths in this city—clothes either too large or too small, dirty but well-mended. Ronni's own clothes had been chosen to fit in, the tan jacket coming down nearly to her ankles and its capacious pockets concealing her radio.

A cold gust of wind blew the kids' jackets back as Ronni ducked behind a car, keeping silent. She continued onto the sidewalk. Finally, they turned and rounded the corner of the apartment building.

"Lost visual," Ronni said.

She surveyed the area, looking for where the kids might've descended into the depths below. The craters that spotted the pavement weren't deep enough to conceal entrances to tunnels. She looked at the cars that lined the street and then froze.

"I think I know where they went. I've tracked them to the edge of the park, but they've disappeared. There are a number of vehicles, though . . ."

Malculm said something over the channel, which Ronni ignored. She half-ran, half-walked to the likeliest entrance, a rusted car pressed up against the side of a building, its facade little more than rubble. Carefully, she opened the back passenger-side door and peered inside. The smell of salt and charcoal hit her before her eyes adjusted. There was a distant washing, the quiet roar of the tide.

"There's a trapdoor in this car."

"Do not go in the trapdoor," Malculm said.

"I'm going in the trapdoor."

"These academy kids . . . Æthelred, do you see what they saddled me with? A literal child."

"I do, sir," Æthelred said, a buzz of feedback in the channel.

"You know I can still hear you, right?" Ronni said.

"That's the point," Malculm said.

"The People demand I take this action, Malculm."

"The People do no such thing."

"Nevertheless."

"This is training. We are training you. Allow yourself to be trained while we're stuck on this miserable slab of coral and do as I—"

Ronni flicked off the communicator.

The stars were out and bright and a breeze blew in her hair, sweat icing on her neck. Her hand rested on the handle of the car door and she pulled, leaping headfirst onto the back seat of the car. A piece of plywood lay in the footwell and she wrenched it back, revealing a ragged hole. There were boards affixed to the concrete somehow, and she maneuvered down them. She shimmied past the human-engineered layer, now carefully avoiding the sharp protrusions studding the naturally occurring tunnel below.

Underneath was a deep crater that appeared more organic than the remnants of bombing elsewhere in the city. This was more like a lava tunnel or a giant coral polyp hole. Her boot snagged in a gutter and she pulled it free, stepping farther down. She brushed against a dark line of algae on the wall of the tube as she descended, the high-water mark coming up nearly to her neck once she reached the bottom.

The tunnel was tall enough for her to easily stand, though most adults would have to stoop. A warm yellow artificial light glowed up ahead and augmented the faint, blue bioluminescence that dotted the crevices in the walls. She began to follow the light, then paused, thumbing on the radio.

"She graces us with her presence once more," Malculm said.

"She is a study in vexation," Æthelred said. "Your restraint is remarkable, sir."

"Well, I'm sorry if I got overwhelmed, *sir*," Ronni said. "There's just so much going on in this new universe. The names, the places. It's simply too much for a little girl like me!"

"Let it flow over you," Malculm said. "It can be nauseating at first, even for those of us who travel often, but focus too hard, and you're likely to give yourself a nosebleed."

"I believe that was mockery," Æthelred said.

Ronni giggled and Malculm sighed loudly.

"So," Ronni said.

"Yes?" Malculm said.

"Regarding the trapdoor . . ."

"You have prudently chosen to pass it by?"

"I have gone through it."

Malculm swore under his breath. "Today's evaluation will have some choice words about this display of egoism."

"No one reads those."

"I read all of your evaluations, sir," Æthelred said.

"No one at the *Academy* reads those," Ronni said. "They only care about the top 10 percent, and I'm in the 12th percentile, which is the reason they chose me anyway, they wouldn't ever risk—"

"Ronni," Malculm said. "Please. You are tracking insurgents—"

"They're kids!"

"—insurgents who are children, as you yourself are, need I remind you, through a heretofore undiscovered tunnel with no possibility of immediate support from any of our teams. If you persist, could you at least lower your voice?"

"I could. I will. I just get excited sometimes!"

"Nevertheless . . ."

Ronni sighed, a sharp crackle of breath over the channel. She stepped carefully along the slippery runnels which opened to more passages below, coral alcoves descending to the seafloor. The smell was briny, and amid the darkness, that faint, blue bioluminescence glowed. Ronni picked her way farther down the tunnel, shadows making it hard to see the sharp edges of the rock or coral. Her boots crunched on tiny protrusions and she trailed her hand along the damp walls, feeling the ridges and soft fronds beneath her fingertips. She had to squeeze through a tight aperture where two mounds of rock converged, and the damp saturated the shoulders of her sleeves.

Ronni turned a corner and stopped short. There was a strange flicker at the edge of her sight, a frequency that was clearly different from the ebb and flow of the shallow tide. She crouched down, her vision adjusting to the gloom. It was a small analog device made of material similar to many of the other artifacts on this world.

"Wait," Ronni said. "There's something here."

"Those tunnels are used by the insurgents. Of course there are things down there."

"That's not it."

"Little Bird, these are sewers. Where detritus ends up. It's not significant."

"It would be impossible for me to express how much I hate that code name."

"It's impossible for me to express how much I hate you disappearing into random tunnels!"

"No! Listen. It's technology. The insurgents are children, mostly, and the crabs can't use this sort of device. No one else comes down here. You read the briefings on this locality, Malculm!"

"She's right," Æthelred said. "Though I must confess I'm almost perturbed to learn that she is actually prepared."

"What is it?" Malculm asked.

"I don't know. It's small." Ronni knelt and tapped the device gently. "It measures something. The proxy I'm in doesn't know the abbreviations it uses, but there are three gauges in a single case. Needles flickering. It's active."

"That . . . does sound out of place."

"Well yeah, 'cause it's not a crab or—"

"The crabs are bad enough! If there are other people down there, you can't be investigating like this."

"I have decided I am going to investigate this."

"Ronni!"

"This is why I'm here, isn't it? To take initiative? To think flexibly?"

"This is the wrong initiative! *This is the wrong thinking!*"

Ronni picked up the device but it caught on something. A long wire snaked out from its back and ran along the wall, leading up another tunnel. The wire had been puttied into small nooks and hidden places. The work was shoddy.

"There's a wire," she said. "I'm following it." She carefully cradled the device and drew on the wire, letting it lead her through the massive catacomb-like coral head.

The sound of waves echoed as she walked, chattering like voices. All around was the smell of seawater and rot and the fungal, fecund odor of the coral.

As Ronni wound deeper into the tunnels, talk continued over the operational channel.

"I hear voices," Ronni said.

Malculm sighed deeply, the sound over the radio a huff of fuzz. "Æthelred, what's our risk level here?"

"Legally, none. We have no accord with this world, so we can presume total primacy. Potential for disciplinary action is minor but nonzero."

"And exposure?" Malculm said.

"Frankly, sir, if something goes wrong, the News Network will feast on you for weeks, and the minor channels will keep your name alive for years."

"No chance of censor intervention, huh?"

"To save *our* asses?" Æthelred said. "Not likely."

"Figures. All right, warrior-lawyer, time to see you in action."

"You've seen me in action, Malculm. I'm a much better shot than you."

"So you like to say. We'll find out. Teams One and Two, on me. Team Three, intercept Little Bird, you're closest. Secure her and get her out of those damn tunnels. Trackers on, though what good they'll do down there, who knows."

"Will you be quiet?" Ronni said. "I'm trying to concentrate. I've found a crevice that I think, if I follow it, it just might . . ."

"It just might what?"

"Oop—"

Malculm and Æthelred stood over their communicator in the abandoned building they'd made their headquarters. They looked at each other, the fuzz of static filling the room.

"Team Three," Malculm said, "Ronni's channel just switched off. Do you have a visual?"

"Negative."

"We need to go in," Æthelred said.

"True."

The warrior-lawyer pushed a sidearm into the holster strapped to his thigh and strode to the door. "After you," he said, gesturing toward the street as Malculm narrowed his eyes and went ahead into the city in search of the tunnel to the sewers below.

———

"You're not the crabs I was looking for," Ronni said, taking in the five adults in lab coats crammed into the small cavern.

"You were not in search of crabs, little girl," the man said. He held Ronni by the wrist, though she didn't struggle. The man towered above her, his armor and clothing marking him as a mercenary. His long hair was pulled back into a tail.

"She's a child, Beinir," one of the scientists said.

"Not down here. No. They are warrior pups, every one." He let Ronni go and bent forward, looking closely at her face. "And in truth, Cämeel, this one is Burel Hird."

"How do you know?" Cämeel asked.

"She has been in other universes. I can smell it."

"I would appreciate you not speaking about me as if I were a piece of furniture."

Beinir grinned. "And who else talks like that?" He turned and addressed Cämeel directly. "If she is here, there will be others. Hail Shara on the . . ." Beinir trailed off, eyes narrowing.

"The radio?" Cämeel suggested.

Beinir grunted. "The communications device. Tell her we will need her."

"I don't think—"

"Cämeel, there will be a fight, and your people will die if we are not prepared. I do not know how many of them there will be, but I doubt I will be enough on my own."

Cämeel nodded. "Laën," she said to another woman, "get them back. Pull everyone down below back up, as well." The cluster of scientists drew closer around Beinir. Cämeel checked an instrument affixed to the coral wall. "It's almost time anyway; the tides will be in soon."

"Fight?" Ronni said. "What fight? There's no fight. Who's fighting?"

Beinir turned to her and knelt down. "My hope is that no one will, but I have met your people before. Things have a way of mounting with them, do they not?"

"Well, if you're expecting a fight . . ."

"Burel Hird to your bones, girl." Beinir stood. "They are coming. Listen. Get to the back of the tunnel. They will come through here." He grabbed a bank of instruments as tall as he was and threw it to the ground across the entrance to the cavern, then pulled Ronni back around an outcropping. Seawater burbled up from the floor, pooling and receding back down. "When they come, we will talk, little girl. But you are on the wrong side of this battle line."

"Don't call me—"

"Yes, I know. Do not call you 'little girl.'"

The sound of sloshing on the other side of the barricade—the low roiling of water being dragged around by shins—silenced them, and everyone in the cavern stared at the entrance.

"We have your scout," Beinir shouted at the barricade. "She is unharmed. State your purpose."

"I greet you," Malculm said, peering through a gap between the wall and the toppled instruments. Team Three was arrayed behind him, pressed against the coral. At a glance from Malculm, they began checking the charges of their rifles. "We have no intentions of violence. However, we are more than prepared to engage with you should it become necessary. Surely it is to our mutual benefit to come to an arrangement."

"So you say," Beinir growled. "Only hold your weapons, and we may all leave this place alive. I refuse for my story to end in this stinking, nameless hole."

"Your story? Of Tala, then? And who are you working for this time?"

"He's for protection only," Cämeel said, her voice thin in the echoing of the cavern. "We're scientists; please, no violence."

"Tsst! Be silent," Beinir said.

"Working for scientists who are scared out of their minds, it would seem," Malculm said. "Who cowers behind you now? Arcalumis? Withered Stem? Certainly not Firmāre, they—"

Behind Malculm, a man interrupted, his words clipped.

"Sir, it's not just the people behind the barricade. More UFTs approaching. Five. At least. They'll be on Team Two momentarily."

"Momentarily? Momentarily, Haeg? How did you not sense them before?!"

"They're above us!" Haeg said. "Sensing in three dimensions is . . . Everything is all tangled up down here. I can't tell what's what."

"We're not trapping you," Cämeel shouted from the cavern. "They're taking shelter from the tides! This zone is safe. More or less."

Malculm turned to Æthelred. "They give us a garbage tracker to look after an Academy brat on a contested world . . . What in the People's name did they expect?" He glared at the tracker, Haeg, who shrugged.

"I was assigned a mission commensurate with my abilities," Haeg said. "If things turn out poorly, then there was a miscalculation far above us, or a failure to manage the mission effectively."

Malculm glowered but said nothing to his subordinate. "Team Two," he said into his radio, "you are unlocked; you may loose at will. UFTs on you in . . ." He looked at Haeg, who shrugged once more. "On you *momentarily*. We're grabbing Little Bird. Keep the way out clear. Æthelred?"

Æthelred nodded and then, in one motion, jumped the make-shift barricade, drew his weapon, and fired a single shot at Beinir, who peered around the edge of a wall. The coral beside Beinir's head exploded with the impact of the slug as the report of the shot echoed in the cavern.

"I missed? I miss—" Æthelred had time to say, before his head became a spume of blood and bone and brains.

Malculm leaped toward Æthelred, then froze. He cursed, ducking back behind the barricade with the same breath.

"Report, sir?" said Team One's leader over the communicator just as the three-person squad appeared from around a corner.

"Report? Well, we will be without advisement for the remainder of this mission. You are relieved of Duty Toward Restraint and can operate with autonomy. This has . . . not gone as expected. Remember everyone, the People need your lives—let's maintain possession of them."

Team One took position, the squad leader crouching behind the barricade next to Malculm, the other two members stationed on either side of the entrance. The squad leader gestured to his second, who provided cover as the squad leader began moving into the cavern.

———

Shots rang out and Beinir returned fire, the coral shattering into shrap-
nel and dust as the scientists gasped and yelped behind him in their
makeshift bunker. It was a scramble, everyone firing or finding cover.
Reports echoed off the walls, chips of coral flying in the dimness, opening new holes for water to spray and trickle in. Barely audible between
the gunfire, Ronni made out the crackle of a communicator. She crawled
behind a coral head and listened.

"This is Shara," a faint voice said over the radio. "We were beset by
three adversaries. Their lives are now spent. So, too, was one of our charges."

"Get down here, then," Beinir said. "There are five to spend before
me, and I would not carry their weight alone."

"Quick, before we all die in these caverns," Cämeel said, gesturing
to the water steadily rising. "One way or another." Hiding behind a
coral head, she pulled her knees up to her chest, breathing deeply. Water
spurted in from another gunshot beside her, just before a slug hit her in
the shoulder. The force sent her sprawling in the rising water.

"This is looking grim," Beinir said. "Are any of you sages shifters?"

"What?" Laën shouted. "Oh. No. Only Nyäll can travel, and he's
obviously already gone." She pointed at one of the scientists further back,
calmly inspecting a coral outcropping as if everything was fine. "Trust
me, if we had a mover, you'd be defending empty husks right now."

Across the room, hunkered behind a low outcropping of coral, a
Burel Hird operative leveled her rifle at one of the scientists, but Beinir
shot a volley of slugs at her before she could fire. She fell behind a coral
head, two red wounds blossoming from her side, and rolled onto her
back, groaning through the pain.

Malculm pointed his weapon through a gap in the coral, firing and
hitting one of the other scientists.

"You fire upon unarmed sages," Beinir shouted in the chaos. "If a
life must be spent, come for mine."

Coral polyps shattered in the hail of gunfire. In the air, flecks of
stony skeleton hung suspended for a moment before stippling the surface of the water as Beinir fired toward the entrance.

"If that's what you want!" a member of Team One shouted, standing in front of the barricade and firing wildly, getting off several rounds before taking one in the head and crumpling to the ground.

"I'm not trying to 'spend' any lives, you lunatic!" Malculm said. "I'm trying to save mine! Surrender and release the child and we'll all go our separate ways!"

Beinir laughed wildly, the sound booming off the coral ectoderm. Then, with a single shot, he dropped the last member of Team Three.

"No, let us play this out and see what glory awaits."

"People preserve us, why must Of Talas exist . . ."

"For the sagas!"

Still grinning, Beinir looked back to the spot where he'd left the little girl and saw a small hole right where he'd set her. Not big enough for someone his size, or any of the scientists, but a young girl could fit through there. Beinir shrugged at this new information.

Beside him, Cämeel whimpered quietly but tended the hole in her shoulder, applying a regenerative wrap of seaweed. Further back, just beyond the cavern's exit, hunkered down and safe, were the other Withered Stem researchers. The thump and hiss of rounds sizzling in coral came less frequently, the Burel Hird agents' numbers dwindling, their inexpert shots inflicting more damage to the environment than to Beinir or his charges. A low rumbling came from up ahead, beyond the cave's walls but not far off, then the muted percussion of four quick shots.

A weakened section of coral blew out at once and collapsed, shards flying everywhere and splashing among the bodies. Shara stood in the breach, the barrels of both her weapons steaming in the subterranean humidity, the living coral within their chambers still humming as they cooled.

She looked around the cavern, her gaze resting on the body of the Withered Stem scientist, and her shoulders slumped. Her eyes met Beinir's, and he nodded sadly.

———

Ronni had crawled through the tight tunnel, barely able to keep her head above the rising water. When she reached the other side, she scrambled over to Æthelred's body, wrestling the weapon away from him, then crawled over to Malculm. She checked the pistol.

"He really only got off one shot, huh?" She shook her head. "All that talk."

"Stop!" Malculm said, his voice low and steady. "We're done. Training is over. Get behind me."

Ronni opened her mouth, then saw Malculm's face and closed it again. She wriggled through the water to him, making herself small behind his legs. "Who's still alive?"

Malculm looked toward the lone member of Team One who'd still been standing. He was now slumped over in the water, not moving. "Just the two of us."

Splayed behind Ronni and Malculm were the bodies of the rest of Teams One and Three, crumpled, ravaged by the two Of Talas' projectiles. Hushed chatter came from the other side of the cavern, echoing in the gloom. Farther off, lower, was the static of the sea, its sibilant murmur a tireless attendant on this world. Water almost covered Æthelred, only his shoulder and a once-grasping arm still above the surface, small waves of foamy red sloshing around him. Shara hugged the edges of the hole she'd blasted in the wall, molded flat against its crags, already flanking them. Ronni and Malculm were exposed, utterly and wholly, and everywhere was the brackish smell of sea and blood and death.

"We offer rayita!" Ronni shouted. Beinir paused, and Malculm stared at her, bewildered.

Ronni spoke quickly, then. "We offer rayita and you are honor bound to accept or be stripped of your sagas, your name purged, your covenant broken, and the glade for you will be lost forever, lost as though burned, lost as though forgotten, the seven roads broken and buckled and never to be traveled, and there will be only ash and ash and ash for the rest of your days."

No one spoke, though there were moans and quiet gasps, the sounds of dying.

Beinir said, "Yes, girl, I do know my own laws."

"Then you must stop fighting and accept rayita."

Cämeel whispered, though in the stillness it was heard by all: "What's rayita?"

"Surrender," Beinir said. "Abject surrender. Absolute. We may take from them whatever we wish. Any price, it is ours. It is Of Tala, though. She is not. Can she—can you offer it, girl?" he said, speaking in the direction of Ronni's voice. "You lead them?"

Malculm began to speak, but at an almost imperceptible nod from Ronni, fell silent.

"Malculm is their leader," Ronni said, "but he is my bonded. I speak for them all." She emerged from behind a chipped, oozing outcropping, and Malculm followed close behind.

"They accept my judgment," she said as she crossed to Beinir, "or our rayita is void and they will lose me." She took Beinir's hand and raised his weapon to her forehead.

There was only the sound of tides, louder now, warping and echoing within the tunnels, seeming to come from all directions.

"Rayita is our rite, little girl. Not yours. How do you know it?"

Ronni smiled in response.

Beinir turned to Shara.

"She is not one of us," Shara said, and Beinir shrugged. "Has it happened before?"

"If it has, I do not know the tale."

"Can we accept?"

"We are contracted. We cannot. They must." He nodded at Cämeel and Laën. "Do you wish to accept rayita?" he said to them.

"The fighting will stop?" Cämeel said.

"Yes."

"Then we accept."

"And what do you want of them?"

"For the fighting to stop."

"Tch." Beinir rolled his eyes. "What price do you wish them to pay?"

"For the fighting to stop is enough."

Shara said, "Cämeel, you may ask anything of them and they must give it. The research you are doing here? You can take whatever they have, whatever they know. They must give it freely and happily or else be slaughtered."

"Fine. They give up their weapons."

Beinir snorted.

"And they leave this world and never return. Happy? Dramatic enough?"

Laën said, "But our research? They may know—"

"They don't know anything," Cämeel said. "They're Burel Hird."

Laën nodded curtly, and Beinir turned to Ronni.

"You have the price."

"We cannot promise to never return," Malculm said. "That has to come from a Council decision. We can only advise it."

"Then advise it."

Malculm glared at Beinir.

"Do you accept the terms of this rayita, then?" Beinir asked.

"We accept," Ronni said.

2

Duncan barely felt the change in speed as the magnarail slowed. There were windows but nothing to see beyond, except granite tunneling and an occasional marking light at set intervals. The glowing stanchions zipped by slowly, less often. And then the windows flooded with natural light as the magnarail silently came to a stop at the station platform.

He stood and exited the train, carrying his leather satchel with him, careful not to swing it. The handle was coming apart and had been for months. If it broke, he would be late for this meeting. He gathered the bag into his arms and noticed, for the first time, that the handle had been fixed. Duncan smiled as he hurried away from the train. He'd mentioned the loosening of the stitches to Ecklan last night, not expecting his husband to do anything about it, just as one of those little things in life that couples talk about. In truth, he hadn't expected Ecklan to remember at all.

With Duncan's retirement less than a month away, Ecklan had begun to fixate on their plans to move away from Burel Hird Prime. The issue wasn't Ecklan's career—his seat on the People's Council for Ground Transportation and his mechanical expertise allowed him to pursue his vocation in most any universe Burel Hird laid claim to—it was his anxiety.

Ecklan Sammo had never traveled before.

There was no hurry, they would have all the time in the world to make their decisions once Duncan aged out of his position as vice-councilor, but this assurance had done little to assuage Ecklan's feelings.

"I just don't want to be late for my first day, wherever we end up," Ecklan had said. They lay beside each other in bed, Ecklan's reading light on beside him. "I've heard from some of the others at the shop that there are real shortages in the mechanical subcommittees outside Prime, and I don't want them to think I'm a lollygagger. Or that I'm trying to take advantage of you being a muckety-muck."

"First off, I *won't* be a muckety-muck, and second off, travel takes no time at all. The space of a heartbeat."

Ecklan slept shirtless, his body made taut and muscular by his work, and Duncan was always delighted by it, so different from his own soft, round body, crafted as it was by his days of research and bureaucratic finagling. He let his hand rest on Ecklan's chest. Hair rose up between his fingers, like grass from a crack in the sidewalk, and he pressed his fingers together, making thin, scraggly hedges.

"Not now," Ecklan said.

"Is my big, strong mechanic nervous?"

"Your big, strong mechanic likes to know how things work, and his brilliant, sophisticated, intellectual husband needs to explain travel to him right this minute."

"If it'd make you feel more comfortable, I can go first and then be the one to bring you over." As a summoner, Duncan had the ability to summon those he'd marked to the universe he himself was in, but Burel Hird regulations prohibited him from using it; he was a vice-councilor, after all.

"So we'll be standing next to each other, and you'll just disappear?"

"No, Ecklan, you know I wouldn't. My proxy would still be here. You probably won't even notice it's not me, and it would only be for a moment, anyway."

"But *you'll* just disappear. And then our bodies will wander around, doing whatever they want, without us?"

"Your proxy will follow your routine. It'll do work on the mechanical subcommittee and make itself useful to the People."

"How can you talk about this so calmly?" Ecklan sat up in bed and turned away from Duncan, setting his feet on the floor and his elbows on his knees. "Our bodies can function fine without us, which means we're what? Just pilots of fleshy machinery, steering sacks of bones and blood?"

"Ecklan—"

"You're going to make me do this myself, aren't you?"

"You won't find out anything more than what I've told you."

Ecklan grunted and stood, grabbing his portable and walking to the living room to consult the online bulletins.

"Oh! My handle . . ." Duncan said to Ecklan's retreating back. He'd fallen asleep soon after, leaving Ecklan to his research, and barely had time to say anything more than goodbye that morning before he'd darted out of their home. But the handle was fixed, the careful wraps of waxed thread strengthening the worn stitchwork—a tangible reminder of how truly fortunate Duncan was.

He tucked his head down and hurried across the platform, weaving through the myriad others dressed for formal meetings. He pushed his way down into a long corridor with dark marble tile and unadorned white walls. He slowed his pace just enough so the scanners behind those white panels could get a good read. On his first day, nearly twenty-five years ago, he'd made the mistake of going too fast down this hall. He hadn't realized that it was anything more than a simple corridor and he'd been so excited to start this new phase of his career. Vice-councilor! It had been all he'd ever dreamed of, but never quite brave enough to hope for. When the uniformed attendant put a hand out to stop him, he'd initially thought it had all been a cruel joke. But no. The trackers seated behind those white walls had been unable to determine whether or not he was an unidentified foreign traveler. He was new, so no one recognized him, and that was how he started his first day—arriving terribly late after receiving a sharply worded and exquisitely thorough briefing on council house antechamber protocol.

Now, dozens of his colleagues stood at the other end of the hall, and Duncan lined up along with them patiently. He had eight minutes. Might actually make it after all. A few moments later, he reached the front of the queue, and a staffer dressed in the livery of the Committee for Safe and Congruous Egress waved him in. Duncan picked up his briefcase and continued on.

With one minute to spare, Duncan navigated the elevators and hallways to finally arrive in front of the meeting room's steel doors. He walked inside, sliding past a few of his colleagues talking and gesturing with their coffee cups. Angular cut foam protruded from the walls and ceilings, ensuring sound only traveled as far as the room. On the rear wall an embossed bronze sigil was displayed, depicting a figure standing behind a globe, encircling it with its arms as if embracing the world. And in the middle of it all stood a monolithic glass table, black as a shadow, wreathed by chairs. Fourteen chairs, and he was lucky enough to call one of them his.

They called this place the Intercessional Control and Harmony Room, or the ICHR. Here Duncan and his colleagues gathered to ensure each locality they controlled continued to be under their control—and to thrive that way. Here they hashed out impossible problems. Duncan drew great energy from the work, each member providing their unique skills, parsing conflicting viewpoints, and yet somehow they found a way to cut through it all like a lighthouse beacon. More often than not it was the unyielding focus and singular perspective of Yorek, Duncan's own councilor, that lit the way.

Before scanning the agenda on his tablet, Duncan took a moment to look the room over. There were Xelia and Priema, deep in conversation, heads close together, the former nodding in agreement with the latter, following her lead, though it was Xelia who was the councilor and Priema the vice. More and more, Xelia was taking their cues from Priema, more and more acceding to their younger colleague's insight. Something to keep an eye on, certainly. Beside them, Iskada and Zeph were loudly, ostentatiously, arguing about the accuracy of the latest episode of some historical drama, even as each was glancing at Priema. It was an embarrassing performance of nonchalance; they were growing clumsy in their dotage, though neither's term would end for several years. Toward the table's end were Melyssa and Blaine, two councilors Duncan's age who had been his contemporaries at the Academy, along with Darmeth, Blaine's quarrelsome vice. None met Duncan's gaze, though they were surely aware of it. And across from him was Trystèsté, sitting alone, a normally animated young woman whose fingers often tapped in agitated impatience even when events proceeded swiftly and smoothly.

On this day, though, she held herself in stillness, hands motionless on the table, face neutral. As he watched, her expression faltered for a moment—just a lone, dying second, but he saw it. It was his job to. She had smiled. Something about today, something about this meeting in particular, pleased her.

The room filled as the other vice-councilors trickled in once the meeting officially started, taking their seats. Only after the last vice-councilor entered did Yorek come in, taking the seat at the head of the table, right beside Duncan. Yorek sat down without a word, smoothing his gray sideburns down with a licked thumb.

Once settled, Yorek took inventory, looking everyone over, lingering over each person for a few moments, just as Duncan had, taking in any deviations from their usual demeanors. Later, they'd compare, and Duncan would help fill in any gaps. Yorek rarely had any.

Yorek nodded and cleared his throat. "Okay then, first—"

Duncan kicked Yorek in the shin, firm but carefully placed. Yorek turned to him, his eyes dark and thinned down behind his squint. Duncan stared down Yorek's glare and cocked his head toward Iskada. Yorek rolled his eyes and stood. He sucked in a breath and said, "Right. It is my honor and pleasure to recognize"—he glanced at the text scrolling on the tabletop before him—"eight years of service from Shaddoh Shakth as vice-councilor to Iskada Bendal. Happy anniversary to you both."

"Happy anniversary!" Duncan said in unison with the other members of the Chamber.

"Okay then. Now that's done. Let's start at the top of the docket. Looks like we have some reports from—"

A low, mournful tone sounded, caused by one of the vice-councilors hitting a button under the table. A thin red line glowed in front of Trystèsté, but her face remained stoic.

"You have an interjection?" Yorek said.

"Apologies," Trystèsté said. "I would like to adjust our agenda to first discuss progress on Geçiş."

Duncan loathed last-minute changes, the shift in thinking it required almost physically painful. The work they'd done in preparation the night before was wasted. The urge to argue washed over him, but he fought it. It was not his place to dissent; his role now was to see the faces and read them. Yorek would need his assessment later; too many reactions happened at once for one person to take them all in. Even Yorek.

"Progress?" a voice said. Duncan knew it was Priema before he even looked. She spoke quietly, as she often did, but her words carried in a way that demanded to be heard.

Trystèsté turned to her, nostrils flaring slightly, but Priema met the look, giving nothing up in her own face. Trystèsté's expression darkened, though, jaw visibly clenching. Duncan nearly tugged Yorek's sleeve, but he must've noticed it too because he held up his hands and cleared his throat.

"Order, Priema," Yorek said. "Trystèsté has the floor, she called a motion to rearrange our docket. Anyone against that?"

No one spoke. From what Duncan could see, no expressions changed. Shaddoh coughed but was probably just clearing his throat.

"Good." Yorek held out a hand to Trystèsté in offering. "The floor is yours. You can start with the initial report."

Trystèsté stood and ran her hands down her sleeves. Was that a slight tremble from her right hand? Duncan glanced at Yorek, who nodded. He saw it too. Trystèsté frowned and pointed a remote at the projector above the table, which whirred to life. Slowly, a large picture materialized, that of a young woman, the smile she wore like a shared joke, but one Duncan didn't understand.

Trystèsté looked down for a moment, then raised her head with a snap, her eyes wide and focused. "Geçiş. You'll recognize this face. A few months ago, we discussed Ronni's possible—"

"What's her AQR?" Priema said.

Trystèsté cocked her head. "If you recall, a few meetings ago, her AQR was recited for the record."

"Before was before. The assessment could've changed. And I'd like it for the record." Priema pointed her stylus at the black dome above the center of the table housing cameras, recording equipment, and heat sensors. She was calm, unflustered, and completely in control of her emotions and the moment; it was easy to forget she was only a few years removed from the Academy herself.

Trystèsté turned to Yorek and shook her head, spreading her hands wide, the gesture a question and grievance both. There was no forgetting Trystèsté had been part of that same graduating class as Priema, though—she wore the impetuousness of youth like a badge of honor.

Yorek sighed. "Trystèsté, please humor her. Priema, don't be an asshole."

Duncan chuckled to himself at the murmurs that followed Yorek's profanity. As if this was their first meeting with him. Priema just gave a slight nod and turned toward Trystèsté.

Trystèsté spoke with undisguised annoyance. "Ronni Deekin-Seven's most recent Academy Qualification Rank was O-2. Satisfied?"

Priema reviewed notes on her slate then raised her hand. "Good. And, for the record, has she been chosen for a specialization or is she still enrolled in general education?"

Trystèsté stared at Priema, her dark eyes falling on her like a shadow. "As the notes reflect, her seat is Deekin-Seven."

Priema nodded. "Of course. But, for the record . . ."

"For the record, Ronni is a general education student in year seven at the Deekin Academy. She will be assessed for specialization no earlier than fourteen months from now."

"Great. One more thing."

Trystèsté slammed her hands on the table. "Hey, Priema, I have the floor. If you want to request the floor so you can grill me on questions to which you already know the answers, you can do it when I'm done reporting."

Yorek nodded. "Yes, let's get on with it."

"Of course," Priema said. "I meant no offense. I ask only for the People's sake."

Trystèsté clicked the projector to show a rendering of a city on a peninsula, two red moons shining on the water. "This is Geçiş, where we decided to pilot the Initiative Initiative."

At this, there were groans and the shifting of weight from some in the room.

"Trystèsté," Yorek said, "you never cease to delight."

"Hey, we all agreed on the name!"

"I truly doubt anyone was paying attention by the time we got to naming your pet project. Not after the hour-long haranguing we endured about its alleged necessity . . ."

"Not my fault you all lack the stamina for this work . . ."

"Or the flair for snazzy names," Priema said.

"'Snazzy'?" Darmeth said, raising an eyebrow.

Trystèsté snorted. "Anyway. Fifteen percent of our assets experience some degree of analysis paralysis when released into 'live' environments, despite all the winnowing we do in simulated environments. I proposed trying to introduce live environments earlier, prior to training completion, to reduce this number and act as a further 'weeding' element, so we can see any weaknesses early and reassign before investing too much in training assets. The Initiative Initiative Subcommittee Resource Officer selected Ronni Deekin-Seven to pilot this program."

Iskada cleared his throat again. "May I intercede?"

Trystèsté nodded.

"Do you think it wise to offer her the opportunity to secure a qualitative commendation on her record? Particularly a novel one that has not yet been adjudicated or weighted? Particularly prior to specialization? It'll make it difficult for the academy to evaluate her effectively."

"The absence of these types of qualitative opportunities is exactly the point, Councilor."

"It seems to me that you would be doing her and the academy a profound disservice," Iskada said, raising an eyebrow.

"The academy does profound disservices to its students each and every day!" Trystèsté fiddled with a pen while staring resolutely down at the table's surface. "A rigid, inflexible curriculum produces rigid, inflexible bureaucrats, some of whom rise to the highest ranks of Burel Hird—councilor, even!"

Murmurs fluttered about the room, only to be silenced by Yorek's loud chuckle. "A contentious topic, clearly," he said. "Though I don't disagree . . ."

"But Ronni has—Ronni Deekin-Seven, she has room to grow," Trystèsté continued. "And she's proven to be capable, as I will show."

The next slide showed twelve faces. Trystèsté pointed with her laser as she explained each one. "Along with Ronni, there were other control assets: Malculm Kilkaneade of Internal/External Intelligence, Æthelred Æthelred of the Joint Adjudication Garrison, and Haeg Vandaar-Schnitzer, the tracker from I/EI. They were accompanied by a standard three-and-three escort. All units accounted for and recovered, following our investigation. We can skip the overview of this locality's situation, which was reviewed in our previous meeting."

A dull tone sounded, then a red light throbbed from the table in front of Priema. "If I may, could you add a brief overview? Relevant, and it should make evaluation easier should this recording need review later."

Yorek rolled his eyes but gestured with his hand. "By all means. Please keep it brief."

Trystèsté's dark skin grew darker, and Duncan could make out cords forming on her neck. "Fine. We selected Ronni to undergo a pilot training operation at Geçiş due to the insurgency presence, and due to the nature of the insurgents. These insurgents are all children, so posed little risk to Ronni, assuming no crab presence. The city, built on coral blooms, contains a rebel element that works with indigenous crabs, sized slightly bigger than personal automobiles, to fight the current autocratic regime that rules the city. Ronni's mission was to find insurgents and track them to a place of operation. Should such a place be discovered, everyone would withdraw to debrief."

"Perfect," Yorek said. "Please continue."

"Ronni discovered insurgents and proceeded to follow, using Academy trailing techniques. No one noticed her. Malculm advised against the action, but Ronni proceeded."

Another tone, another light, this time in front of Zeph. "Is this allowed? Ronni is the least experienced, but she's giving orders?"

"Not orders. She has chief agency, so she can act as best she thinks on her behalf. Malculm advises. The purpose of the program was to inculcate flexible thinking and initiative-taking. To stave off inflexibility in future bureaucrats . . ."

"Trystèsté," Yorek said. "Enough." Duncan couldn't help but notice the smile tugging at the corners of Yorek's mouth.

Zeph's own mouth was a thin line of exasperation.

Yorek kept his focus completely on Trystèsté as she spoke, so Duncan's eyes wandered the room, getting reads where he could. Zeph seemed agitated, shifting in his seat and chewing on his cheek. Most everyone else—Priema, Shaddoh, Blaine, and the rest—kept themselves composed and neutral, looking down at their tablets, then back to Trystèsté's face.

Yorek's expression could easily be mistaken for boredom. But the ways his eyes moved, quick and precise, shooting his own glance away from Trystèsté and over to the other vice-councilors, showed he was paying close attention.

"Malculm reported this was when the situation escalated," Trystèsté said. "For the record, I have a direct accounting of how that happened from a firsthand source."

A low tone and Iskada's table section lit up. "This is highly unusual." His nose was scrunched like he'd just sucked on something sour. "I must object. Firsthand accounts typically carry too many emotional indicators and tend to be very biased. If we're getting this account, I'd rather it be filtered and fact-checked, like it always is."

Yorek leaned forward, his hands tented and propped by his elbows. "Do we have the recording now?"

"Yes," Trystèsté said.

"Then play the damned thing."

Trystèsté smiled and clicked on the remote. A looming holographic face labeled *Malculm Kilkaneade* appeared over the table. Soon after came the crackle of a recording switching on, and the room filled with his voice. ". . . so, they were over there, we were back in the tunnel. I called out to Æthelred, by name . . . yeah, all I said was his name . . . an inquisitive declaration. Sure, yes, that's fair to say. My intention was to query him on the legal ramifications of the situation, as well as the optics, given the plausible potential outcomes, as any good CO should value the insight of their attached warrior-lawyer when encountering a novel scenario. I was unsure as to whether we should negotiate directly with an Of Tala agent, if they're acting as a representative of Withered Stem, or if engagement with Withered Stem is the appropriate course of action. Or, when assuming primacy, as I was informed I should, whether negotiation is an impermissible abdication of initiative when encountering unidentified foreign travelers, as the standing expectation of COs in novel scenarios with regards to UFTs is to maintain initiative by whatever mechanism deemed appropriate, which has been well-established in every edition of *Guidelines for Engagement* dating back to the third. Unfortunately, I received no guidance as to the appropriate response at that juncture, as it was then that Æthelred elected to depart this life.

"From there, things got worse. My teams were dying and earning nothing in return. That was when Ronni offered surrender. Or surrender of a sort that the Of Tala barbarians understood. 'Rayita.' I believe that decision saved our lives, and can't imagine any other outcome more positive than what occurred."

Trystèsté switched the projector off and put her knuckles on the table, then leaned in. "You heard that right. These Withered Stem externs hired Of Talas. Our agents should never be in a position where they have to combat those psychopaths, and Of Talas aren't the only threats out there. Operational attrition rates are up threefold since the 87th Turn and at least half of those incidents remain unexplained. The transmundi is getting more dangerous, and if Of Talas are willing to be hired out to the highest bidder, we need to consider them as an option. The more of this work we can off-load to them, the more of the People's lives we can preserve."

Xelia, Priema's councilor, spoke then. "Mercenaries aren't an unreasonable move—contract work is necessary sometimes, after all. We do need to exercise caution, though, lest we relinquish too much control."

Iskada's table section chimed. He turned to Yorek. "Trystèsté can't be serious. And Xelia, you know better than this! We govern our localities well because we *don't* outsource work like this. Mercenaries are one thing, but Of Talas are a completely different class. They're ruthless."

"We're ruthless," Priema said. "We just come by that quality with different aims. Hiring Of Talas could be a boon to our field assets. If done properly. Appropriate handling and demarcation between Of Talas and ourselves would provide the necessary inoculation against cultural contagion."

Duncan schooled his face to stillness, resisting the urge to roll his eyes. Priema's sop to the sensibilities of certain councilors was transparent—if not to the councilors in question.

"This is idiocy," Darmeth said, not bothering to make use of his button before speaking. "We have real issues to be addressing."

"With prudent segregation," Priema continued, "we could maintain the appearance of objectivity and distance. This could work."

Yorek nodded. "Okay. Trystèsté, are you done?"

Trystèsté nodded.

"Any other interjections?"

Duncan scanned the faces, but save for Iskada and Darmeth, whose sour expressions would've been visible from Old Earth, and Trystèsté, gleeful at Priema's advocacy, there was little to be gleaned from the neutral faces.

"Okay," Yorek said. "Seems to me we have two votes to take. First: a proposal to make contact with Of Talas, using go-betweens to maintain appropriate segregation. Do we want to impanel a subcommittee to determine if this course of action is worth considering?"

A wave of tones sounded as people hit buttons under the table, red X's or green O's appearing in the table's underlay. Ten voted no, four voted yes—only Trystèsté, Melyssa, Sushan, and Xelia. Trystèsté's glee seemed as if it was stolen by Iskada, who suppressed a grin.

"Conclusive. Next vote. Should we endorse this learning abroad pilot program and recommend continued exploration by the Board of Experimental Education?"

Another wave of chimes, another vote, even more decisive than the last. Eleven nays, three yeas. The hurt was clear on Trystèsté's face. She looked to the red X in front of Priema, then up to Priema herself. Priema looked straight at Yorek, eyes unwavering.

Trystèsté chimed and Yorek nodded to her. "This is a mistake," she said. "The intelligence we uncovered alone—"

"The intelligence is invaluable," Yorek said. "But we only got it because Ronni Deekin-Seven was reckless and failed to heed the advice of experienced team members. And yes, we would've never found out about this operation without her. But we lost ten of thirteen assets. That doesn't balance the sheets. And I worry about sending more foolish children with something to prove out there to poke around. There are a great many hornet's nests out there which may prove too tempting."

"You're all fools. This is a mistake. How do you not understand that?" Trystèsté's face fell and her chin quivered.

"Trystèsté." Yorek's tone was heavy with warning.

She took a long, slow breath. "I feel another vote may be warranted."

"It isn't. I admire your passion and rely on it. But right now, it's misguided." Yorek stood. "I concur with the vote. We can't throw people into situations like knives into the night. We're lucky it was Withered Stem. What if it had been Firmāre? The last time we ran into them was while establishing a presence in the Hyle locality. Once they were done, the stability was so bad you couldn't even travel there and expect to remain human. Or sentient. It's a dead zone and will be for who knows how long. I'd rather not have any of our other localities meet the same end."

"Does no one—"

"Trystèsté, do you know how we hold on to the 'worlds' we own?"

She sniffed. "By preparing the ground, seeding the message, and weeding the dissidents."

Yorek shook his head. "That's how we establish a presence. We hold our worlds by loving the people within them, by caring for them, by elevating them from the people we rule into the People we serve. Trystèsté, we are the People, and Of Talas are not. We cannot invite them in. And even if they somehow were, their mere presence could push those who would wish us harm into rash decisions. No, we have to maintain our order. Order above all."

"Understood, but—"

"Trystèsté, you're done. Next topic, the Asnovili locality. Oh boy, here we go . . ."

"No, no, no," Melyssa said, "you've got a decision to make on your next vice-councilor. You're dragging your feet and I'm getting it on the record."

Yorek leaned back and tapped the arm of his chair with one finger. "Noted."

"You put us all at risk when you delay this decision."

Yorek rolled his eyes. "I'll do it when I'm good and ready, thank you very much."

"You should've had a selection ready to go when Duncan turned fifty. You get a month's grace, and that's almost up."

"I get *forty-six days*' grace, and I'll make a decision when those forty-six days are up!"

Trystèsté slumped back down into her chair as Yorek and Melyssa went back and forth. Duncan let his eyes wander over the room, most everyone looking down at their tablets. Trystèsté was stoic but clearly shaken. It looked genuine enough, but Duncan knew not to assume. Trystèsté was very good at appearing genuine.

He understood her passion, but what had happened at Geçiş was very nearly a catastrophe. For the families of the dead, it was just that, and he wasn't about to support something that could lead to more bloodshed. Or worse. He hadn't been surprised at all by the outcome, and of course, his own vote had sided with the majority.

What did surprise him was the slightest, faintest upturn at the corner of Priema's mouth. He doubted anyone else in the room would notice it—almost certainly, she herself didn't realize how much she was giving away. What little game was she playing now?

3

Once the session concluded, Trystèsté waited in her seat, allowing her anger over the vote to ebb. Or suppressing it—she wasn't sure which. The other members of the Chamber idled in clusters, discussing the events of the day in hushed voices. The maneuvering never stopped, but Trystèsté had the wisdom not to be so ostentatious about it. Priema was nodding away, stuck in another energetic ramble from Iskada; one of Priema's many gifts was appearing unperturbed no matter the occasion.

Trystèsté caught Priema's eye and used the old signal from their academy days, rubbing her palms together, her right hand on top. The left hand on top was the planted nervous tic Trystèsté used for other councilors and their vices. Among all the codes and signs she and Priema had concocted in their youth, hand rubbing was the most basic: I need to talk to you.

In the meantime, Trystèsté paid attention to the paintings on the walls. A line of since-retired council members occupied the space behind Yorek's prominent desk. From floor to ceiling, there were council member faces, some memorable from history books and the period dramas her parents loved to mock, a great many forgotten by all but the most obsessive enthusiasts of Burel Hird arcana. Dhalgrim was there, of course, their genial smile and tired eyes revealing nothing of the brilliant, merciless mind that had shaped so much of their society. Estevan appeared in the same. Estevan, who had been kind, who had been forgiving, who had tempered Dhalgrim's most extreme instincts—to their detriment in the end, of course. Trystèsté's favorite, though, was Katalynn, as much for her fierce, futile stubbornness as anything else. Remembered more for her unbridled denunciations of tradition than any real legacy of accomplishments of her own, she had been a woman out of time, arriving a century and a half too early for the reforms of the 46th Turn. She had predicted them almost exactly, though, and, perhaps for that reason, received little mention in official histories—a fact that continued to vex Trystèsté.

Yorek's turn had been longer than most and so the next line of council members would be mostly new faces. Hers, possibly. Priema's certainly; her academy records alone would guarantee it, never mind her accomplishments since graduating. And the insufferable Darmeth. Duncan would almost certainly serve his tenure without his portrait ever making it to the wall. One of the faceless, a rare breed within the High Council. His mien would be committed to the book of record, but future council members would not have that symbolic reminder of who this man had been within the Council.

Duncan, like herself, had remained at his seat. Yorek never lingered after meetings, even if called out by another member. Duncan was the one who stayed behind to speak on their behalf. An odd relationship, certainly, but stable. Trystèsté glanced his way by passing over the wall behind him, letting her eyes drop to his face for a moment before moving on. He was observing Priema, or appearing to observe Priema. Here, among the leadership of Burel Hird, seeming to do something and actually doing it were rarely the same. Even voting. Even sharing confidences after votes. Priema would talk to her, but could she ever truly trust in their conversations? As much as she chose to, which was the motto everyone lived by.

Trystèsté passed back over Duncan's head, prepared to let her eyes drop, but she didn't have to. Duncan had materialized in front of her.

"Tell me something—do you really believe that your . . ." he sighed.

"Duncan Hérn, you have to say it."

"That the Initiative Initiative is the right course of action?"

Trystèsté let herself show some of the anger she actually felt. "Yes, I do. And the rest of those mildewed fools will come around to that thinking eventually. Though it'll be too late." She sighed and rubbed the bridge of her nose. "What do you want, Duncanoodle?"

"An honest assessment. This wasn't some sort of maneuver?"

What she liked about Duncan was that he was perceptive, but had none of the guile of his counterpart. If Yorek was here, asking this sort of question, then she'd be worried. But of course Yorek would never be here, asking this sort of question.

"I don't do maneuvers. I push for what I want."

"I know. Or at least I think I know. But another possibility would be that you pushed early in your career to hide maneuvers now."

Good old Duncan. If there was a transcript of this conversation (and there definitely was one somewhere), Duncan would read like a robot playing a person. But hearing the man speak was an altogether different experience. His voice was actually . . . warm, disarmingly rich, and deeply felt. And so he could say a thing that would sound like an accusation if it was anyone else, but from Duncan, it sounded like, *Well, of course, you would deceive all of us because that's perfectly natural, and I love and support your decision to do so.* Of Duncan's share of talents, this was the one Trystèsté found most disarming. Or it would be, if Duncan actually knew how to use it, which he did not.

Duncan was staring at her expectantly. She shook her head, blinking away her reverie.

"Sorry. I was just thinking . . . Did you ever listen to his album?" Trystèsté nodded at the portrait of Vikra, who glowered directly behind Duncan. He'd recorded a series of quasi-comic, almost-but-not-quite-romantic songs during his time in the Dhalgrim seat in the 53rd Turn that had been considered, charitably, eccentric. He'd acceded to the seat young, though, and by the time there'd been a "wash," all of his original contemporaries replaced by their vices, that eccentricity had come to be accepted as personality, and councilors were allowed more latitude in being who they were. Trystèsté appreciated him for that, and rather liked his album, despite its undeniably curious content.

"I did." Duncan said. "Once. That was all I could manage."

"Did you ever consider something similar? A hobby career? I've heard you at the cafés, you know, on folk nights, singing along."

"Ecklan says all the time that I should devote more time to the vocal arts, and I must confess a certain temptation toward frivolity. Perhaps after my retirement, I'll submit an application for junior apprenticeship to the Troubadours Council."

"You could never. And waste that brain of yours? You'll find another way to serve the People. Even after you've retired."

"Such flattery." Duncan smiled. "Am I a part of your maneuver? The possibility has only just occurred to me. But I only have a few weeks left in my term. Which means I'll be of no use."

Trystèsté chose her first honest thought. "Duncan, you are the only person I know that could say 'I'll be of no use' without seeming the least bit hurt by the revelation."

"Not a revelation. The simple truth."

"What will you do after this truth eventuates? Retire to a cabin in the wilds of Prime?"

"You remind me so much of Yorek sometimes." Duncan didn't wait for Trystèsté to react to the statement. "I suppose I'll take my husband to one of those synthetic beach planets in Holon and become a lounge singer. I must get going. Be well, Trystèsté." Duncan left as abruptly as he came.

Trystèsté was still smiling when Duncan passed through the steel doors. Then Priema was there. Startled, Trystèsté felt her cheeks get hot. Everyone was sneaking up on her today.

"Shall we have a tryst?" Priema asked.

This was not the first time Priema had made this joke. Because even the joke was a code for something. Trystèsté searched her mind for the appropriate response. "Yes, a tryst with Trystèsté. Less funny every time I hear it. Are you hungry? I have an hour."

"Let's sit out in the court as we eat? It is a beautiful day today."

And with that, all vital information passed between them, Trystèsté gathered her things.

———

The cafeteria was efficient, as usual, and so they were out in the court-yard within minutes. Trystèsté with an egg sandwich, and Priema with a cookie and an apple.

"You could at least pretend to eat like a normal person," Trystèsté chided. She had never figured out how Priema stayed so fit—she never ate real food in her presence. Of course, Trystèsté had considered that Priema only ate real food alone, but she could not for the life of her figure out what purpose such a performance would serve.

"Over there?" Priema asked, eyeing the familiar corner of the low brick wall that wrapped around the highest point in the courtyard before the grass sloped down toward pathways and carefully maintained shrubbery.

It was a beautiful day, the sun shining overhead in a clear sky, but with enough of a breeze to make the warmth welcoming. Good thing Trystèsté's moisturizer contained sunscreen. They sat down close enough to each other that their knees gently touched. It was not a flirtation or even a friendly gesture. That was the measurement they'd chosen for these kinds of talks. Close enough to just touch. Another code, this one disguised as companionable proximity. Trystèsté didn't have to wonder if the seeming friendship was a performance veneered over a real friend-ship. She had always known the truth.

"So it didn't go your way in there today," Priema said, voice low.

Trystèsté took a bite of her egg sandwich and chewed. She swal-lowed. "And you were a pain in the ass."

"The Chamber members must know I am not immediately on your side. Even if we align most of the time. Even if I understand your rea-soning. We must be separate enough that our friendship won't strike them as a concern down the line."

"And you voted against me."

"You knew I would," Priema said, plainly.

Trystèsté bit into her egg sandwich again.

"You didn't?" Priema said, her surprise evidently genuine. "Trystèsté, it wouldn't have passed."

"If you backed me. Really backed me. Instead of doing that bull-shit you do."

"Again—I can't always be with you. We cannot be a single unit in their minds. We just can't."

"But when you prioritized that, here and now, you put the entirety of Burel Hird at risk."

"I didn't."

"Please tell me how you didn't."

"Move too fast, move too soon, and the move will be wrong. The Chamber will think they've addressed a problem but it'll be piecemeal, insufficient. And, operating under that mistaken assumption, they won't be ready for the true challenge. Real change needs real catalysts and a real catalyst means a real cost."

"Eleven of our people died."

"During a pilot training program you designed, in a locality we had no real interest in. To the other council members, that was the result of folly. It was no real cost."

"They're wrong. We had no idea Withered Stem and Of Talas were in our outlying territories doing the People knows what."

"Contested territory. Years away from annexation. And now, with the Ray—"

"I don't need a lesson in the distinction, Priema. You read the report. We had no intelligence on their presence there. Our tracker didn't even pick up on them until after one of our academy brats found them first."

"Bad luck. It was very unfortunate."

"To call that 'bad luck' shows our arrogance. We didn't even know there were Of Talas until three centuries ago. A short span in our long history. And we know embarrassingly little of their history, their cul-ture, or their motivations."

"You mean their fables? No self-respecting Burel Hird would believe those little stories, Trystèsté. None of this is going to win an argument in the Council chamber, which, I might add, has been conservative on foreign affairs for nearly a millennium. Prime has never suffered an incursion and has seen no presence of other societies in any of our major localities. The Council needs more than skirmishes in contested territory to convince them to prepare for aggressive action. I know you know this."

Trystèsté shrugged. "You remember the Maximov Interpretation of Prime Founding, right?"

Priema had finished her cookie and taken one bite out of her apple. Trystèsté played through a list of things Priema might say after she was done chewing: "Hird History 101," or "You know the interpretation or you wouldn't be asking me, so just get to the point." But those responses sounded more like hers than Priema's.

Priema flung herself off the low wall, letting the momentum of the fall bring her body to a stooped position. She began running her fingers along the blades of grass, waiting for Trystèsté to continue.

"In the late stages of planetary catastrophe," Trystèsté began, "two thousand people left Old Earth on a generation ship called *Limitless Expansion* to settle a habitable planet many light-years away. Some things went . . . very wrong. So when the first Burel Hird traveled to this universe, *Limitless Expansion*'s inhabitants had dwindled to under four hundred people. Through Burel Hird ingenuity, they were able to turn things around and make the hard decisions the original ship inhabitants couldn't. And so, when they landed some three hundred years later, every person that stepped off *Limitless Expansion* called themselves Burel Hird."

Trystèsté jumped from the wall, but quickly stood up straight. She took a moment to watch Priema play with the grass. The grass trimmers never let it get taller than this, or there would be hell to pay from the groundskeeper council.

"Taking the interpretation as truth," Trystèsté said, "you ever consider that the inhabitants of that generation ship weren't so willing to be saved?"

Priema didn't answer Trystèsté's question. She did, however, stop playing with the grass, turning to look up at her colleague. Yes, Trystèsté knew the old interpretation back to front. Yes, this was an elaborate point Trystèsté was making. And still, even when it came to Trystèsté's elaborate points, Priema was already at the finish line, looking back at her.

Whatever. Trystèsté continued: "What if our forebears did what had to be done to ensure a Prime? They saw the promise of that new world and decided that those poor souls on that ship needed some good old Hird saviorism, whether they wanted it or not. And if they didn't . . . well, we've done worse things in the name of creating order."

"And you don't like that idea?" Not a real question—Priema was following the script, helping Trystèsté along.

"Doesn't matter if I like the idea. That's what had to happen . . . if it happened that way."

The sun had taken its place at the top of the sky. Yellow like Old Earth's. A perfect new home for the remaining survivors of that dying planet. Only it wasn't them who'd stepped off the ship and onto Prime.

"It could happen again, you know," Trystèsté continued. "Only we'll be the ones dead or dying, with travelers from other worlds arriving to . . . 'save' whoever remains."

"A bit dramatic."

"War is always dramatic. By its nature."

"You really believe that's what our forebears did? Killed everyone on *Limitless Expansion*?"

Trystèsté shrugged. "I thought you'd have my side in there. You used to say worse things back in academy. 'Better to start the war than be unprepared when it arrives.' Remember?"

"And back then, you were the bleeding heart."

"I still am. We have a lot to lose here, Priema. A world full of important work being done. I want Burel Hird to survive. The society we've built. But my greater concern is all these people."

"Like your father."

"Not the point, and you know it," Trystèsté said, her voice rising. "I will do anything to protect our own. We're a long way from making the hard choices of our forebears, back when there weren't so many councils muckin—"

Trystèsté stopped short. Priema had suddenly rolled her head around, cracking her neck. Another one of their codes, rarely used. It meant: Stop talking immediately. Trystèsté spared a moment to look around the court-yard. In front of them was mostly empty green space, the plaza of an unpopular park, but there were some other members of a lesser munici-pal council across the way talking around a row of benches. Behind them it was even less populated, except for an older woman, if her appearance could be believed, reading a newspaper, conspicuous and alone amid a vast stretch of grass. Far out of earshot, but she might be able to pick up on the conversation with the help of cybernetic enhancements. Prime had pur-posefully frozen its technological advancement for the last thousand years, though they had continued to develop advanced tech in secret bunkers in the wilds of Prime. The Council occasionally had to sign off on special op-erations using cyber-enhanced black teams, but it was a known secret that council members sometimes used the black teams for personal agendas.

Priema appeared to remember her apple and finished it, minutes passing in deliberate silence. Calmly, she stood and went back to the low wall to put the core back on her now-empty tray. She stayed there for a while longer, watching the old woman. Eventually, the woman looked up and waved at them both, the smile on her face seeming blissfully un-aware of anything amiss. Priema, for her part, also seemed at ease. Then the woman stood, stretched, and slowly walked away.

Priema didn't end the silence for another minute. "I have a story-lesson for you," she said finally. "Do you want to hear it?"

"Go ahead."

"Have you heard of Luka Dregin?"

Trystèsté shook her head, already annoyed that she was starting this lesson at a loss.

"The Dregin–Maximov Interpretation is similar to yours. Only in his, our forebears arrived on Old Earth. Through cunning and strong leadership, they brought together the smartest people from all the na-tions of that dying planet—"

"I'm sure manipulating the locality's economic market helped. I mean, presuming this interpretation is plausible."

"It is. And of course they manipulated the markets. But they still had to convince Earth's greatest minds to come together and build humanity a generation ship.

"And then they had to convince the smartest of the smartest that the transmundi was real. And promise them not just one habitable rock in their universe but legions more beyond the veil. Travel demonstrations might've been necessary to ensure the citizenry of Burel Hird Prime. And the means to get to Prime. Luka assumed there were holdouts, like in your version. And our forebears did what they had to do. Engineered a series of controlled calamities to the food system that would weaken them all, but only enough to make total starvation a believable possibility.

"Maybe a few loyal engineers had to die. Maybe one Burel Hird sacrificed themself for the cause. Maybe it was subtle enough that no one noticed that only certain people were dying. But the point was not to have to kill everyone. So, it's significantly less gruesome than your theory. However, the outcome was the same. Some good old Hird saviorism, as you put it."

"A needlessly elaborate interpretation."

"Yes. Not particularly graceful. But possibly more accurate. Progress is . . . circuitous."

"And the result of engineered atrocity," Trystèsté countered.

Priema smiled. "It doesn't have to be. Engineered, I mean."

Wisps of clouds passed slowly above them in the sky. Trystèsté wondered how the people below would look to them if the clouds had eyes—like busy specks of dust, probably, whipping about for no reason.

She pretended not to notice Priema looking at her.

Eventually, Priema came close and touched her arm. "Let this one go," she said, her expression serious. "Wait for the earthquake. Be there for the relief effort. Burel Hird will still be standing and, having paid the cost, will be ready for the change."

From a distance, a man approached them. He was holding another set of trays in his hands. A park steward, in charge of this quadrant of the courtyard.

"Vice-councilors. It would be an honor to take those from you."

"Yes, and thank you. I'll be sure to send a good word to the groundskeeper council," Priema said. "I believe the Trimming Committee handles your satisfaction reports now?"

"Yes, Vice-councilor, but you really don't have to, you are too kind. I am sorry to have given you work."

"Not at all, compeer. It is my choice."

The man smiled too long. Trystèsté couldn't help but hate such a naked show of gratitude. She looked away, feeling ashamed of herself.

"When is your next meeting?" Priema asked as the man was leaving.

"Tomorrow," he said. "But please don't worry—"

"I will worry," Priema said, with a smile. "But only enough to do my duty."

These ridiculous displays. Though Trystèsté suspected this was Priema in her truest form. Even with nothing truly to gain, Priema extended herself. And somehow she had simultaneously managed to cultivate and project a predator's cunning to the other members of the Chamber while displaying only kindness and a fixation on rules.

Impossibly, everything Priema did seemed to serve a singular, unconflicted mind.

"I have to go," Trystèsté said.

"Of course," Priema said. "Remember to tell your father hello for me."

"You don't have to worry—he'll ask about you as soon as I arrive."

4

"Well, I have good news and bad news."

Maddalena raised an eyebrow at Reg.

"Which do you want first?" he asked.

They sat in a bar, occupying a booth in the back corner. Whale oil lamps burned steadily in sconces around the room, and the bar's one electrical fixture, a glowing rendition of the owner's name, flickered behind the bartenders. At almost every table were plates of oysters and the smell of the sea, gusting in through the door when someone came in, occasionally reaching the table they sat at before being swallowed by the scent of hot sand and mulled ale.

"Give me the good news, then."

"You can come home."

"And the bad news?"

"Some more enthusiasm about the good news might be warranted," Reg said.

"What's the bad news?"

"It's tied up in the good news, a little." Reg looked away. "You can come home because you're getting pulled off the intel beat."

Maddalena said nothing.

"Don't blame me! This is so far above us I don't even know where it's coming from."

She stared at him. He continued to avoid making eye contact.

"The point is," Reg said, "your penance is over and you can come home."

"I wasn't undergoing penance, Reg."

"Everyone thinks you were."

"Everyone is wrong."

"It looked a lot like penance. To the outside observer."

"Well, I guess the key elements there are outside and observer, aren't they, Reg?"

Even with the bar filled, the chill of the outside could be felt in wisps and gasps, as when Maddalena leaned back, away from the pan of sand in the center of the table. She shivered and scooted closer, pressing her mug deeper into the sand to refresh her ale's warmth. After a moment, she took a sip. The effect was disappointing.

"Why am I being reassigned?"

"Maddalena. Stop."

"Why don't you want to tell me?"

"It's just not something that we need to—"

"Is it Burel Hird? It's Burel Hird. It's the Council, isn't it? Holy Vahanha."

"Madds, you need to keep your voice—"

"Please tell me it's nothing to do with the First Council."

"Madds, let's focus on the positives here: You can come home."

"And not the negatives: that all the slow, careful work I've been doing for years to provide us the necessary intel to make a thoughtful, calculated move is about to be thrown out in favor of some idiotic dick swinging."

"You know, *this* is why you run through handlers."

"Hm."

"Are you like this with your sources, too?"

"Like what?"

He grunted and shrugged elaborately then looked down and away from her, and she found herself both vexed and amused by the accuracy of the impression.

"No, I'm not like that."

"What are you like?"

"I'm like someone they want to be around and tell things to and give things to."

Conversation continued around them as Maddalena fell silent. The weather and the sea, the preoccupations of this city and this world, were the main topics under discussion. Evidently, the meteorologicians were said to be predicting an early cold snap before the fast ice locked the city in for the winter. Maddalena knew this distantly, the coat she occupied had known of this scuttlebutt weeks ago, but the novelty of the world rendered understanding abstract. As long as there was no ice tide, though, filling the wharves and canals, the city's daily routine would be unaltered: whaling, fishing, crime.

And it was that last item, the crime, that made this universe especially valuable to Firmāre and to her own family within the vast, fractious society that was Firmāre: Vaish.

"You've been out there, away from yourself, for a long time, Madds," Reg said. "Don't forget who you are."

"Hm."

"We wouldn't want to lose the real you. The grunting, stubborn, disagreeable—"

"Yeah, I get it. So what's Trantin's plan?"

Reg snorted. "Elevate one of the vices. One who is more amenable to cooperation than her councilor."

"Which one?"

"It's . . ." He paused, squinting. "I can't remember her name. They've all got those goofy names. The hothead."

"Trystèsté."

"That's the one."

"That's a mistake."

"Well, it's one Trantin is set on making. Remove her councilor, one way or another—I'm pretty sure the plan is assassination, as that's how Trantin thinks—and the hothead ascends. Why is that a mistake?"

"No," she said. "No, it's more than a mistake. It's terrible. It's . . . Feh! It's so spectacularly stupid."

"Hothead's councilor, Zechariah, he hates us. Brings up Hyle whenever someone mentions Firmāre, as if what happened in Hyle was all of us, not just the Orillo family."

Maddalena waved this away. "Trystèsté will be able to persuade no one, it's not in her makeup. She gets us one vote and nothing else, which doesn't tip them in favor of contracting us. No, there's a better move here. There has to be. This is the clumsiest, bluntest possible . . . Assassinating one of the seven most powerful people in the most powerful society in the Simulacra isn't just reckless, it's bordering on suicide. And Zechariah wouldn't even be the right one to deal with! Why now? What changed?"

"You've been working this angle for almost a decade, Madds, and Trantin has been pushing things with Burel Hird through open channels since you were a child. You don't think it might be time for a different tack?"

"No."

"Well, there was also some conflict in some backwater, rangat universe. Withered Stem? Casualties? We don't know the numbers, but it could be as many as a dozen. They could be more amenable to employing our services at the moment."

"A dozen? Why would that matter? The Bureau doesn't care about individual lives, it could be a thousand deaths and their calculus wouldn't change. The society, 'the People,' is all for them, it's everything. Am I the only one who grasps this?"

"Look. Papa Vaish is talking about the 'L' word."

"Don't they always."

"Well, you wouldn't understand. When a certain type of man gets to be a certain age—"

"He's barely fifty."

"When a certain type of man gets to be a certain age—"

"And here I thought it was my parentage and not my gender that was the issue."

"When a certain type of person," Reg said, wholly unperturbed by the interruptions, "gets to be a certain age, they begin to see the future not as a stage they will one day perform upon, but as the auditorium others will look back at their works from. They start to think about their legacy. So no, you wouldn't understand."

"Wouldn't I?"

"You're not a certain type of person."

She snorted. "As if anyone ever let me forget."

"Madds, you are, forgive me," he reached out and raised a lock of her hair, "the literal redheaded stepchild."

"This coat is a redhead. I'm not."

"That's right, isn't it? You're a blond back on Gora. Well, regardless. We were all so happy to see your mother free of that dreadful Haight woman."

"I have two mothers, Reg. Even though my mum left her, Enora Haight is still my moms, Reg."

"The fact remains that you are not technically, by blood or marriage, Vaish."

Maddalena rolled her eyes. Even if she hadn't been born Sylbur, one of the smaller families, heredity being not just meaningful but all-important would have struck Maddalena as absurd. They were travelers, after all, moving between universes and inhabiting bodies created for them—bodies that very much did not share the blood that was apparently so important in determining identity. Just another contradiction at the heart of Firmáre that Maddalena would have to live with.

"Ignoring the fact that this very conversation proves I am functionally Vaish, this does nothing to explain why Trantin Vaish has decided that right now is a good moment to make a move that could destroy this family."

"Well . . . It seems some have been comparing what the family has accomplished under Trantin with what was accomplished under Vaun."

"Why do they always have daddy issues?" Maddalena said. "Is a legacy of no major fuckups insufficient?"

"Trantin certainly seems to think so, yes. They all do, really, all the heads. The 'Vaun Job' hangs over Trantin. The same way the 'Loppes Affair' hung over Vaun and the 'Erryl Job' over Loppes. That's just how it goes, and that's how we keep moving forward. We need to be able to 'Do a Vaun,' or 'Plan for a Loppes,' or we stagnate. If Trantin can't join that list with an operation to call his own, he'll have failed."

"Hm."

"I can't count the number of times I myself have pulled an Iaro Job. There's a certain elegance to—"

"Have you been watching them?" Maddalena interrupted Reg, looking down into her mug and pointing with her chin toward two men in the corner of the bar.

"Madds, you know how long I've been doing this."

She glanced in the two's direction again. One sat awkwardly, his leg straight, extended out from under the table, and as she watched, he shifted slightly, unable to reposition that leg to his satisfaction.

"Full-length strapped to his leg?" she said.

"I expect so."

"Partner with a recourse?" The language of this world, its weapons and technologies, came quickly to her; the coat she wore lived within the underworld, and she had a recourse herself, still folded, strapped tight to her ribs.

"I'd be surprised if he didn't," Reg said.

Maddalena grunted.

"How long until they work up the courage to make their move, you think?" Reg said.

The two men leaned together, their heads close. They had been in the bar as long as Maddalena and Reg, but something had shifted in the atmosphere, as though they'd suddenly become visible in a way they previously had not been. Glances were being thrown in their direction, and at least one table had departed with rather aggressive haste.

"Was there no better world you could summon me to?" Maddalena said. "You know I hate meeting in these rangat universes. Why couldn't we be sitting in some quiet, central cluster coffee shop? No one ever got murdered in a coffee shop stickup, Reg."

"We've been here before, you know."

"We have? Really?"

Maddalena slumped back against the booth. The wash of worlds felt abruptly unmanageable, and she thought of exactly how long it had been since she'd seen her own face, her actual face, or her mothers'. How many coats had she inhabited, those other versions of herself? How many different universes had she traveled through? And she felt, for the first time in many years, an unwelcome, almost foreign ache: homesickness. She'd heard, from other agents who'd been gone from their original selves for too long, another term, selfsickness, and wondered if that might not be what made her feel so used up.

She breathed deeply. "Let's just go. I'm not in the mood."

"Too late for that, I'm afraid." Reg nodded in the direction of the men, and as he did, they stood, the straight-legged one tearing a flap off the side of his pants and removing the full-length that Maddalena had theorized.

"Wallets and watches!" he shouted. "On the table, with your hands, let's see them!"

His partner stood, a recourse in each hand, sweeping them across the room as he surveyed it. They were both young, Maddalena realized, practically children. The full-length's owner was small, his face flushed and glossy with sweat, the other tall and thin, almost frail.

The short one barred the front door and manhandled anyone moving with insufficient speed in producing their money, delivering quick blows with the butt end of the full-length or simply shaking them as though this would speed up their progress.

"The till," the tall one said to the bartenders, one recourse pointed at them, the other still pointing out at the patrons. "Empty it."

"What do you want us to put the money in?" one of the bartenders asked.

The tall one blinked rapidly. "Defoe?" he said to his partner.

"Just put it on the bar," the short one, Defoe, said to the bartenders. "You let us worry about how we're getting it out of here."

Maddalena sank her forehead into one hand and exhaled loudly. She couldn't help it; amateurs depressed her.

"You two," Defoe said to Maddalena and Reg. "Wallets. Watches. Jewelry. Now." As he spoke, the tall one was picking up handfuls of coins and shoving them into various pockets, dropping a fair number on the floor. Defoe walked over to their table, his stride halting, erratic, and leaned over them. His face twitched, his mouth trying repeatedly to form a grin but failing to make it stick.

"No wallet, no watch," Maddalena said, holding out her wrists to illustrate.

"How were you planning on paying?"

"I wasn't."

He laughed, a short, harsh, braying sound.

"And you?" He turned to Reg, the full-length held lazily, its mouth tracing circles in the air as the barrel drooped and drifted. "Drink and slink for you too, oldblood?"

"Me?" Reg said. "No, no. I was going to pay. Love the beer here too much not to!" He raised his glass in the direction of the bar, though the bartenders, collecting the cash in the till, didn't acknowledge him.

"Too bad—their money is my money. Let's see your coin." He tapped the barrel on the table, indicating where Reg was to place his wallet.

"Their money may be your money, but I think I'm going to hold on to mine."

"Are you, huh? You a marque? Gonna sail in on your shining corvette and save everyone here?"

"Not at all, not at all. I admire the initiative you're showing, in fact. Good to see that the youth of Gdercc remains so enterprising. Best to just leave us out of all this, though."

"Best for who?"

"For everyone, of course. I'm looking out for you, kid."

The boy slid into their booth, letting the mouth of the full-length rest on Reg's belly, keeping its barrel between them. His breath was me-tallic, his eyes dinner plates of tar.

"I don't need you to look out for me. I look out for me. I look out for us."

"Sure, sure, I understand. Still, though." Reg patted the boy's hand gently, who yanked it back, as if shocked. "Just pretend we're not here."

Beneath the table, Maddalena unfolded her recourse as quietly as she could, slotting a bolt into its chamber.

"Keep talking," the boy said, "and you won't be." He grinned, and his teeth were the color of an overcast sky.

Reg spoke on, refusing to meet Maddalena's eyes.

"We're south of Eu Bridge, right? Dixon Island? Good. So either your little escapade here is at Liszel's behest—seems unlikely, given the pot this endeavor is going to earn you—or you had to get her permis-sion. So here's what I'd like you to do. I'd like you to get ahold of Liszel and tell her that Vaish says hello."

"'Get ahold of Liszel'?"

"What is it you say here? 'Shoot her some words'?"

Reg nodded toward the bar, the bartenders looking at each other and then edging to the side. Behind them was the hole of the pneumavox, voice tubes stacked haphazardly around its mouth.

"This time of night," Reg said, "she'll respond in no time. But you know that already, surely."

At this, the standing boy faltered, but Defoe slid closer to Reg. He pressed the full-length's barrel against Reg's stomach once more and slid a knife out of his sleeve, twirling it between his fingers, never breaking eye contact with Reg.

"How about I get ahold of Liszel and tell her that Vaish says good-bye?" The knife stilled, the point digging into Reg's cheek.

"Ooh, very good," Reg said. "Initiative and wit! We'll keep an eye on you, won't we? You do that. Tell Liszel, 'Vaish says goodbye.'"

"Defoe." The taller boy finally spoke. "Shouldn't we . . . Just in—just in case?"

Defoe didn't shift his gaze.

"There is no 'just in case.' We can do what we want. I can do what I want." He drew the knife along Reg's cheek, pushing just hard enough for a single, thick drop of blood to well, sliding down Reg's chin. Maddalena primed the recourse, the springs chiming quietly, taut and ready.

"So help me," Reg said, "if you get blood on this shirt . . ."

"Defoe, please. We've worked so hard just to get here."

Maddalena had to swallow a laugh—how hard did they have to work to stick up a dive bar? It seemed a rather pitiful feat to represent the culmination of some journey. Perhaps they were even younger than they looked.

"Fine," Defoe said. "If that would make you feel better." He stood suddenly, almost toppling, and began collecting the bounty piled on other tables, sliding it into a pocket inside his jacket. "You don't go anywhere, though!" he shouted back at Reg and Maddalena.

"Wouldn't dream of it," Reg said.

"You're lucky Frenklin is a cautious man," Defoe said as he stalked through the bar, prodding the occasional patron with the full-length.

"A coffee shop," Maddalena said quietly. "Or a teahouse, Reg."

"Quiet!" Defoe said. "I love the quiet of a stickup. Do you hear it?" He paused. "That stillness? Just breathing and fear. It's perfect. It's how the world is meant to be."

As Defoe spoke, Frenklin, the tall one, slid behind the bar, prodding the bartenders to its far end with one of his recourses. He put it down and picked up one of the voice tubes, speaking quickly into it, then slotted it into the hole behind the bar.

"Don't look!" he said to the bartenders as he punched an address code into the keypad, the brass clicking and chiming with each number. The bartenders turned around, looking resolutely at the wall. With a hiss, the tube vanished, and Frenklin kneeled, collecting the coins that had fallen in his earlier collection attempt.

Defoe finished his rounds and returned to Maddalena and Reg. He jingled with each step, his coat sagging on one side with the weight of coins and accessories.

"Don't you want to keep a low profile?" Maddalena said.

"What?" Defoe said.

"Your name. You don't want to keep that . . . ?" She held a finger to her lips.

"No. Why would I want that? No, I want them to know. I want everyone to know. To know my name. Our names! Defoe and Frenklin! I've lived long enough nibbling at the scraps that sink down to the sand. I've lived long enough watching from below as the bloated, lazy, so-called leaders of this city float by unchallenged. No. No. I want this whole miserable city to know the names of the men who will—"

There was a clunk as a tube arrived in the pneumavox's mouth, slotting abruptly into place. Defoe stopped speaking and looked down. His expression was unreadable. Beneath the table, Maddalena steadied the recourse against her knee and tensioned the rod, aiming it at his midsection.

Frenklin withdrew the tube, held it to his ear, and slid its door open, tripping the coil and starting the message. At the distance she was from it, Maddalena couldn't make out the words, quiet and garbled as they were, but their fury was clear, and Frenklin winced away, holding the tube as though it would bite him.

"Defoe . . ." Frenklin's face was white, though Defoe didn't turn around or look up.

"What?"

"You need to come away."

"Is that what Liszel said?"

"Yes."

"That doesn't sound like her."

"She said you need to come the fuck away, or I need to fucking slit your fucking idiot fucking throat."

Defoe wheeled, saw his partner's ashen face for the first time, then spun back around to look at Reg, who shrugged.

"I told you I was looking out for you, kiddo. You shouldn't carry around so much suspicion. You never know when someone is trying to save your life."

Defoe leveled the full-length at Reg. "I don't recall asking for your wisdom, oldblood."

"Defoe," Frenklin said. "Let's go. Ignore him. He doesn't matter."

"No," Defoe said. "No, he doesn't." They headed for the exit, weapons still pointed back toward the bar's patrons. At the threshold, Defoe stopped. "None of you matter. Not anymore. Not now, now that we have—"

Frenklin yanked him outside, and then there was quiet. Audible was the hiss of the oil flames beneath the bar, keeping the trough of sand that ran its length hot. Chairs squeaked on the floor and someone sneezed. Maddalena became unpleasantly aware of the smell of her body, of the smell of all the bodies around her, and beneath that the faint scent of brine and sour beer and urine.

"Can we leave?" she said.

"You want to go outside? You know it's going to be colder out there than in here."

"Yeah, but it's going to be way weirder in here. The only people who didn't get robbed?"

Reg shrugged. The other patrons were beginning to talk among themselves, some shooting glances in their direction, others standing, unsure whether to try and weasel a free drink out of the bartenders now that the night was already a loss. The bartenders, meanwhile, were conferring with each other and sending pneumavox messages in quick succession, one speaking into the tubes while the other keyed in the addresses. They, too, were sending looks in Maddalena and Reg's direction.

"Let's go then," Reg said, depositing the contents of his wallet in the bar's sand as they left and nodding commiseration at the bartenders.

Outside, they saw Defoe and Frenklin down in the canal, climbing into a skiff. The propeller buzzed to life, and they shot out across the waterway and down an alley canal, disappearing.

Maddalena and Reg set off in the other direction, walking toward the seaside of the island. The stones beneath their feet were smooth, worn by decades of rain and pedestrians and the lash of the cold salt wind. The day was clear, at least, the sun sinking beyond the horizon's lip, and the air was crisp and bracing, the last pale heat of the day ebbing from the stones. They reached the water's edge and strolled along the malecón, waves curling gently against the base of the embankment fifteen feet below. Gulls circled overhead, and slipping out through the doors of the bars and restaurants facing the sea came wisps of conversation and light as passersby took refuge from the evening's encroachment.

"He was going to kill us," Maddalena said. "You know that, right? *You* he was definitely going to kill."

"He wasn't. He was peacocking for the other one."

"Yes, he was, but that was going to include killing you."

"I've been doing this for a long time, Maddalena—"

"Too long, apparently."

"I've been doing this for a long time, and I can read people."

Maddalena shook her head. "Why even play the game? Nothing in this world has value to us except our lives. He could've taken everything we had on us, and it wouldn't have mattered."

"Why even be in the game, if you don't want to play it?"

She stared at Reg. The coat he wore was old, its face ruddy and its hair gray. "How have you survived this long? You put too much faith in our name."

"It seems like I've put just the right amount of faith in it."

"You're wrong. You've grown comfortable. Comfort is not a luxury for a Vaish, it's a risk."

"You sound like my nan."

"If she lived long enough to impart her caution to her grandson, then I'd say she's worth listening to."

Maddalena grabbed Reg's arm and stopped.

"Listen to me. Yorek has lived long enough that he won't pass on to Duncan. The seat, I mean. The Dhalgrim seat. Because Duncan is now too old to accede. And he hasn't chosen a replacement yet, won't until the law says he has to."

"What?"

She began walking again, more quickly, and Reg hurried to catch up. "That's who he is. But Duncan can't take the seat starting . . . I don't know when. Soon. He'll have aged out. There's a window—no replacement chosen by Yorek, but Duncan is no longer eligible. So if something happens to Yorek, then it goes to a vote. The six remaining councilors. And they'd choose Priema."

"So?"

"She would get the votes to contract us. That's what this is all about, right? Trantin wants to be the family head who finally lands a Burel Hird contract. If he's willing to assassinate their leaders, to risk bringing the fury of trillions of Burel Hird down on our heads if it's ever discovered, to risk Vaish's annihilation for it, then he at least needs to get it right. Well, this is how he gets it. Priema is the way. She believes our needs align the same as Trystèsté, but she'd actually be able to convince other councilors."

"How do you know? How do you know they'd vote her up?"

"Because I've been doing this for a decade, remember? Priema's been . . . since when she was in their creepy academy things, she's been the golden child. Her records are flawless, off the charts. Burel Hird psychology wouldn't allow it to be anyone else. She was anointed before she even hit puberty. They'd vote her up, and they'd listen to her."

"Why are you so confident that—"

"It's Priema. Without a shadow of a doubt, it would be Priema. This is the move. She's the move. Yorek murked before he chooses a new vice but after Duncan ages out. Trantin is wrong."

"Just saying it's her doesn't make it so and isn't going to convince anybody. If you're not in the inner circle, as you very much are not, then you need more than your gut. You need proof."

"There are records."

"Have you seen them?"

"No, but I could."

"You won't be enough, Madds. Trantin will need his authenticator to confirm it."

"Reg, I've been trying *for years* to work this source—"

"You've got maybe a day before we pull you off the beat."

"Reg! I can get the evidence but I need time. You need to hold Trantin."

"Me hold him? I've met the man once, and we didn't speak. You vastly overestimate your importance if you think your handler has a direct line to the head of one of the Four."

"Then do whatever you can to slow him down."

"That will just make him want to speed things up. You know how . . . petulant he can get."

"Then call in favors, beg, threaten, throw yourself upon Lusi's feet, do whatever you can. You're a handler, so handle things. Trantin's dumbass-kill-Zechariah plan can happen at any time! Just make him wait!"

Reg sighed. "I'll do what I can. No promises, but I'll try to get you more time."

Maddalena nodded.

"Madds," Reg said, "bring me something good. Even then, it'll be hard to make Trantin change his mind."

"It's only the continued existence of Vaish and our status as one of the four chief families of Firmāre on the line, but sure. Let's indulge our man-child leader's petulance."

Reg gave Maddalena a look. She rolled her eyes.

"I'll get it," she said. "Two days?"

Now Reg nodded. "Frankie Two-Eyes meets you in forty-eight hours, whether you're done or not. Be done." They stopped walking and leaned against the short stone wall at the edge of the malecón. The sun had almost disappeared, just a sliver of wavering red above the water, and the final ships were returning home. Even before the sun had fully set, they'd almost all extinguished their lights, though whether this was a prudent tactic or old superstition, Maddalena's coat didn't know. Bells from a dozen different wharves rang, and voices called out, tattered by the wind into incoherence. She shivered. In this, Maddalena and her coat were united; the cold of this city was miserable.

"I'll bring you back here when you're done," Reg said. "However it plays out. We'll charter a ship, maybe a balloon, watch the whales at dawn. They sleep in the sky, you know. Breach and then drift, a hundred feet up. Whole pods of them. You've never seen anything like it. Throat pleats swollen as big as the rest of their bodies. Safer for a whale to sleep in the sky than stay in these waters."

"Hm."

"We're not even sure what they're afraid of. Everything in Gdercc runs on whale corpses and yet they stay as close to us as they can manage. Your coat know anything about the sea?"

"No."

"Monsters out there beyond your imagination. Truly. Tentacles long enough to blot out the sun. But sometimes you see one floating, three times as long as the biggest ship. Severed. Bitten clean in half. What could do that?"

"I don't know."

"No one does. No one in this universe or any other. Whatever it is, though, it's big enough that it doesn't have to be afraid. Or cautious. Maybe once it did. Now, though? Now it's comfortable. Comfortable in the way you think I am. Comfortable in the way Trantin wants us to be, when all of this is done. Big enough that no one can even come close enough to find out how big."

"And you were saying I couldn't understand what it meant to be a Vaish . . ."

"You don't think the job to end all jobs would be a worthy legacy?" Reg said.

"A wise man once told me that new jobs were the way we kept moving forward."

"A dirty trick using my own words against me, Madds."

"Yes, well. I'm Vaish, aren't I?"

5

Malculm heard the death chimes before he noticed the mourners entering the funeral office. Their glissando had been a daily soundtrack in the aftermath of Geçiş, before he'd been recalled to Engine and put on administrative leave for the duration of the investigation. He'd known that would be the only possible outcome, although he held out hope that the process would be swift and merciful. Doing nothing was doing nothing good for his mental state.

But even if he'd had something better to do, he would have attended the final filing for all the members of his team who'd died that day. How could he not? They were each excruciating in their own ways as he listened to the empty platitudes of the clerks and endured the blank, carefully accusation-free stares from the deceased's friends and lovers, some parents. His colleagues couldn't bring themselves to look at him at all.

Æthelred's filing had been the worst. A sizable contingent of his colleagues from the Judicial Adjudication Garrison had attended, none of them making any effort to hide their ire. As if it was Malculm's fault that Æthelred made a terrible decision. If any one person should wear the blame for what happened in that tunnel, it was the warrior-lawyer.

Malculm remained certain he could have talked their way out of that standoff if Æthelred hadn't tried to be, what? A hero? Hardly. He was a fool. A fool trying to prove himself to a man uninterested in acknowledging the work of a subordinate. A man who withheld respect too often . . .

No.

Out of all who died on that wet rock, Æthelred alone deserved what happened to him. But you can't say that, not on any world, not about anybody. Death protects a person from so much—there's no room for blame in a grave or an ash can or a ballistic sepulchre.

"You going in?"

Malculm turned to see a spry old woman dressed in an ancient but well-cared-for uniform of the masonry committee. Her stocky build indicated that she kept up with the trade, even if she were surely in retirement.

"No," Malculm said. The sign in front of the office indicated that this was the filing for Orania Jesoper, undermember of the Subcommittee for Southeast Pump Gasket Maintenance: Lubrication Division. A couple of badges were pinned to the notice, citations for service that Malculm didn't recognize, but they were the pale-colored markers of level one or two commendations. Nothing remotely impressive. "I was just passing by and heard the chimes. Are you going inside?"

She shook her head. "I just want to make sure that greasy shitspill stays dead," she spat, glaring at the door of the office.

That was the problem, wasn't it? Malculm didn't particularly want to live forever, but he didn't want to be dead forever, either. He heard a sound and noticed that the old woman was stifling tears, the wobble of her chin giving her away. What would she give to ensure the little shit stayed dead? If he had the opportunity, Malculm would murder Æthelred for what he'd done in those tunnels, how his bloody-minded, cocksure, man-of-action bullshit turned a simple training op into a slaughter. He imagined how he'd do it, how the sense of justice would feel in his hands as he squeezed the life out of someone he'd once trusted. He also knew that, given the opportunity, he'd kill this old lady for the chance to see that bastard's smug face again.

Killing was easy, he'd begun to realize. When all roads lead to one inevitable location, you either accept your destination or realize you're never going anywhere.

"I'm—" he began to say to the old woman, then stopped. He was going to say he was sorry for her loss, but there was absolutely nothing about that phrase that was right. It was what people said, but it was always wrong. What else was there to say, though?

"I'm going to go," he said, and she nodded once. The death bells chimed as he passed, their calm harmonies discordant in his ears, like an accusation.

———

He walked back to the suite of rooms he'd been allocated. They were fine—comfortable enough, but there was nothing personal about them. It may as well have been a barracks or dormitory. Malcolm's eyes passed over the blandly decorated space, wondering what he'd change if it was really his, rather than just another in a series of places he passed through. He didn't know. He'd never had a home, not really, not since his scores on the Aptitude, Attitude, and Ability Assessment sent him to the Academy. And then he was a child. For a person with so much power over others' lives, he'd never really had control over his own.

None of his parents had been Academy kids, but Malculm had tested high for intelligence at a young age, and remembered clearly his excitement about the prospect of the Academy and what might lie beyond. His early Academy years had been spent at the facility on Glitterpoint, which had felt to his young mind as if it lived up to the promise of its name—all chrome and neon and nearly magical technology. It wasn't until he'd advanced in his studies and had the opportunity to travel to a few other localities that he recognized the squalor under the shine. Glitterpoint's shabby, second-rate reputation elsewhere in Burel Hird territory was well-known, and the undercurrent of crime and bare-knuckled striving outside the Academy's walls was a useful training ground. Not to mention that overreliance on flashy technology was a marker of an adolescent society to his superiors, who exalted the controlled use of technology that marked life on Burel Hird Prime. Of course, Malculm had only stepped foot on Prime twice: once to be awarded a commendation early in his career, and now to be admonished for his biggest failure.

He sank into the functional, mass-produced armchair in his sitting room, the memory of his return to Prime resurfacing as it often had in recent days. They hadn't even had the courtesy to give him a proper dressing-down. Just a coldly neutral recorded interview for the archives, days of final filings, then it was a trip to the Movers' Annex and back to his proxy body here on Engine to wait for whatever consequences were to come.

Maybe it was because he'd grown up in a simple fourth-set locality, with its steam engines and ox-drawn carts, and his first experience traveling between worlds had been only one of many new and exciting experiences, but Malculm had never been fazed by the new and yet familiar bodies and lives that came with transmundial travel. Many of his peers in the Academy were obsessed with it—the changes that came with each new arrival and, even stranger, the similarities. Teenaged discussions lasting deep into the night about the nature of identity, self, and being.

Malculm had never given a damn about any of that. Traveling by importing one's consciousness into a new body or by riding around in some marvelous flying machine were equally implausible and, therefore, equally mundane.

He did envy those few of his fellow students who had discovered innate travel abilities, but no more than he envied the ones with an uncanny facility for language or exceptional athletic skills. Most travel mechanisms were more ponderous to use than simply finding an annex anyway, and, as an intelligence officer, Malculm would never want for access to the network of movers, navigators, and summoners who made the passage between worlds possible. And if he'd had to choose, he'd have taken his own ability to conceptualize and analyze a complex situation over any other talent.

He had assumed his intellect would never fail him. Oh, the hubris of youth.

He'd shown so much promise early on, earmarked to become a significant intelligence officer. And for a while, his promise had proven true. He'd been to over two dozen localities in his first few years, on one assignment or another, returning success after success. But then he'd been injured. It was a skirmish not even related to his mission, just some small-time conflict playing out in that locality. Some poorly armed and even more poorly organized rebels attacking the capital of a recently annexed locality. It wasn't a particularly terrible injury. He'd been caught in an explosion that had taken a few casualties, but he was far enough away from the radius of the blast to only pick up a few scrapes and bruises, a busted eardrum, and a minor concussion. But the experience had left him . . . unsteady.

He'd accepted desk jobs on Engine for a few years to sort himself out, and someone needed to consolidate and analyze the reports from all corners of Burel Hird's influence. There was always some other great mind of his generation to fill in for him. By the time he was ready for the field again, his once-promising career was a dream he had to chase. It was like he was fresh from the Academy again, only without the hunger and swagger of youth. There was a long stint of dead-end missions. A slow period of nothing at all, where he'd wasted away for a few years on a mundane world in a mundane locality with only five Burel Hird Internal/External Intelligence officers in it. They'd been there just to claim it until reinforcements arrived for the annexation. When they finally did, he was asked to stay on to get them acclimated. He'd stayed, of course. What else could he have done? This was his work as Burel Hird.

Finally that assignment ended, and he'd returned to Engine a decade older, already starting to gray at the temples, no promotion in sight. When the Ronni job landed on his desk, he'd been too bitter to consider it anything more than yet another obstacle to his already dwindled prospects. He should've been better prepared for what it actually was. He should have remembered his training, the adages drilled into him by his supervisors: Every mission is critical; take nothing for granted. And this was why he'd been kicking himself since he'd returned to Engine. He'd let his skills turn dull out of bitterness. He'd fucked himself twenty years down the ladder—all that work, gone.

Maybe he could climb his way back up, back to somewhere worthwhile. But he couldn't do it sitting on his ass in this beige monstrosity of an apartment on administrative leave, that was certain.

———

One of the perks of interlocality travel was that you didn't need to pack. The proxy body you left behind would still need clothes and notebooks as it lived its strange half-existence without you, and it's not as if you could take anything with you anyway. So, without any preparation, Malculm left the apartment and walked out onto the black and gray streets of Engine. He wandered, looking at the trees full of leaves, the squat buildings the color of industry, only a few shades off from despair, the traffic moving slowly like blood through the veins of the city, and the people—everywhere the people.

He'd never really thought about it before, but in his nearly two decades of traveling between worlds, he'd come to believe that a place was just the physical manifestation of a certain ethos. The people who made it up were its spirit, and the technology and infrastructure that bound it together was the flesh, the vessel. In the little time he'd spent there, Malculm felt like Prime was just a bit too polished, full of people who seemed just a little too well-adjusted. It was entirely too utilitarian, and even its most advanced technology were things like holographic projectors and tiny, super-efficient flying machines that did only one thing, but very well.

Engine, on the other hand, was messy. It bore the bruises of daily living openly, each street with its own palimpsest of grime. As he approached the center of town where the bureaus were all located, a perfume of hot grease began to permeate the air, the eponymous engine of the world grinding its way furiously deep underground.

He walked for a long time, letting his feet lead him where they would. Soon enough, he found himself standing at the door to the Movers' Annex. He shouldered it open and took in the anteroom before him—a comfortably functional waiting area with its familiar, pleasantly awkward chairs. Such a banal threshold to the worlds beyond and their alien landscapes.

He muttered, "Fuck it," to no one in particular, and made his way to the desk. He began to hand over his identification badge to the uniformed functionary, but the clerk held up a hand.

"Please take a number," the man said, and pointed to a ticket dispenser on the counter.

Malculm looked around. There was no one else there.

"There's—"

The receptionist tapped the dispenser without looking up.

Malculm did as he was told and retreated to one of the chairs. He was number seventeen.

As soon as he sat down, the clerk said, "Now serving . . . number six." Malculm looked up. The clerk was staring at him. "Number six. Now serving number six." His expression was impassive.

Malculm began to say something but thought better of it. In the corner, a screen was playing the Movers' Annex introduction on a loop. Malculm arrived just as it started over. Cheery, vaguely patriotic music accompanied a figure walking out into the shot.

"So, you want to travel!" they said. They were dressed to look like Dhalgrim, in the plain uniform of 1st Turn councilors. "That's great. Experiencing all of Burel Hird is a super way to see what the People can accomplish when we work together."

A couple in the video stood together, holding hands. One of them said, "Yes, we'd like to see more of Burel Hird."

"Well, you've come to the right place," the video's host said.

"Now serving"—the receptionist said—"number seven. Number seven. Now serving number seven." He had continued to stare at Malculm. No additional people had entered the room.

"But is it dangerous?" the other half of the couple said.

"Not at all!" the host said. "It may be useful to think of the transmundi as a . . . a series of islands." The artificiality of the pause, and the quality of the acting, made Malculm cringe. "Now, these seas are peaceful and easily crossed."

"Sounds great," the first member of the couple said. "Let's go, then." An implausible number of children, seemingly meant to be theirs, crowded around them.

"Well, it's not that simple, compeer. How do we cross water, kids?"

"Boats!" the couple's numerous children cried in unison.

"Ha ha, yes indeed. Well, the 'boats' are 'travelers.' There are some people who can cross by themselves, just little, one-person boats. That's the most common kind of boat. We call them mundane travelers. They can't control what island they go to—their boat just takes them to the closest island. Those who can take others with them, or send others, we call movers. Some, the very strongest, can send many people across the water. Most, though, can only send a few, and many of those movers need to travel with those they send."

"Now serving . . ." the receptionist's voice was emotionless, ". . . number eight."

Malculm cracked his neck and took a slow breath.

"And," the video host said, "as with mundane travelers, nearly all movers will just travel to the nearest island. And the islands are shifting all the time. What's the 'closest' island now may not be the closest tomorrow. If you want to go to a particular island, you need another kind of traveler to coordinate with the mover: a navigator. And they're even rarer. Here's the truth." The host stood between the couple and put an arm over each of their shoulders, drawing them in. "There just aren't that many people-boats!"

"How can we be sure we'll be able to travel, then?" half of the couple said.

"Or go where we want to go?" the other half asked.

"That, compeers, is the power of the People, brought to bear. Here at the Movers' Annex, we're able to coordinate across the transmundi, and place movers, navigators, and summoners at your disposal. Simply put, we're big enough! It may take some time for your travel request to be processed, but we promise, in no other society is cross-universe travel so simple. And that's how Burel Hird ingenuity brought the transmundi together!"

"But who created the transmundi?" one of the couple said. "I've heard that the Simulacrum—"

"Now, now, compeer, that type of superstitious, antisocial language has no place in *our* society, does it, kids?"

"No!" the couple's numerous children screamed in unison.

"Ha ha, that's right. Such talk is punishable by—"

"Now serving . . ." the clerk began.

"If you don't say 'seventeen,'" Malculm said, standing, "I'm going to lock this door and shove every single ticket in that machine so far down your throat your children will shit numbers."

". . . seventeen. Now serving seventeen." The clerk's expression had not changed, nor had the boredom in his voice.

Malculm crossed to the desk and handed over his identification badge, then laid his hand on the desktop palm-up to allow the machine built into the table to scan the chip implanted in the delta between the thumb and forefinger of this body.

The screen propped up on the desk displayed: *Malculm Kilkaneade, Internal/External Intelligence Officer III, Status—Inactive (Temp).*

"I'm looking to take a holiday," Malculm said. "A forest locality—hiking, camping, fishing, that kind of thing."

The receptionist tapped the keys on a mechanical instrument built into the desk, then frowned. "I'm afraid that won't be possible."

Malculm grunted. He didn't understand that complex cartography that allowed travel between worlds, but he did know that just because it was easy to go somewhere at one time didn't mean that it would be on another day. "Fine, fine. Anywhere pleasant would do. What have you got available?"

"I'm sorry but your travel authority is not valid." He didn't sound sorry at all. And that didn't make any sense. Malculm's position allowed free travel at any time to any locality, but even if that had been frozen, citizens of Engine were able to use a mover's service for recreational travel to an approved list of destinations. For a fee, of course.

"I don't understand," Malculm said, calmly and with authority, as he laid his credit chip on the desk. "Any recreational world would suffice. Is the mover out sick today?"

The gray little man behind the desk shook his head, and pushed the credit chip back toward Malculm with the tip of his finger. "It's not the mover. It's you . . ." He visibly searched for the best way to describe the situation. "It's your badge, compeer. There's a class nine interdiction on this identifier. No interlocality travel of any kind is to be undertaken by the authority of its bearer. You can fill out a 62/B if you're interested in appealing, but . . . I don't think they apply to C9s." He handed Malculm back the offending credential and shrugged. "Is there anything else I can help you with today?"

Malculm glared at the clerk, imagining several additional ways that violence could be employed in this sad room. Instead of exacting any of those, he turned on his heel without a word and stormed out of the office.

They intended to trap him here. To what end, Malculm didn't know, but it wouldn't be good. His superiors obviously wanted to keep him contained and that could only mean that he was done. His career, maybe even his life. Well, he wasn't about to sit quietly and wait for the axe. He still had connections, he still had a few tricks up his sleeve. He'd get out of here one way or another, and then he'd find a way to show them that they were wrong. Wrong to pin the blame for Geçiş on him, and wrong to put him out to pasture. Most egregiously, they were wrong to underestimate him. He would prove his worth to the People.

INTERLUDE

It was spring in the northern hemisphere of Calyx, and the flower was in bloom. It began toward the equator, great fields of blossoms blanketing the hills and rippling in the wind like a pale, pink surf. The ancient mountains of Kakwen were next, their crags worn to smoothness by time's rasp, now gentle enough for the flower to take hold, even the tallest peaks sporting patches of petals. It was the most potent bloom of the last twenty years—so potent, it was said, that even on the At-Saught ships orbiting Calyx, administering the planet's entry into the galactic covenant, the scent could be detected, carried up on uniforms and in landing crafts and somehow evading the onboard scrubbers.

In New Darem, it was peak season, and everywhere, the sticky, delicate sweetness was in the air, and the work of the city slowed to a crawl. Those few unlucky enough to be allergic spent their days inside or masked as they passed among the petals. For the rest of the population, it was a time of indolence and recreation. Most days were spent in a near-narcotized haze, the aroma so pleasant and soporific as to almost be an intoxicant, which was the source of the phrase "Lazy as a New Darem spring." Sheets and blankets were laid out in every park across the city, picnics being the norm for the midday meal, and some, having staked out prime spots before the sun even rose, stayed there all day, reading, chatting, and drowsing in the perfumed heat. In the café where Mëryl and Shann were to meet, a trunkline grew in the courtyard, its shrubby branches drooping with the weight of blossoms even as the stem reached up through the three floors that surrounded it. Night was approaching, the sky a pale violet, the trunkline a silhouette against the vibrancy above.

Peaches were grilling on the small tableside brazier, butter slicking their flesh and dripping down onto the coals, popping and sputtering. A server passing by grabbed each in quick succession with wooden tongs, dredging them in dried chiles and salt from a bowl he carried with him before placing them back on the grill, freshly spiced side down.

"As soon as you can smell them, like, really smell them, take them off," the server told Mëryl, who nodded. "We're a little short-staffed tonight, so if I don't see your friend arrive, just hit the button," gesturing with the tongs at a small knob on the table, "and I'll be right over."

"Of course," Mëryl said.

"Or just call my name. Tre." He grinned.

"I'll do that, Tre. Thank you."

He moved on, clacking his tongs twice, turning the peach halves at the next table with careless grace.

Mëryl was alone. She sat on the second floor, at a table beside the courtyard. The balcony was an intricate wooden lattice crafted to look like vines. A leather bag sat at her feet, slim in design but bulging, filled beyond its capacity. The At-Saught emblem of linked stars was stitched atop the flap. The table stood alone in a notch in the balcony, cantilevered over the courtyard, looking out on the trunkline and a few tables on the ground floor, all of which were occupied. Built into each table in the café was a Yio board, the ancient game played by most everyone in New Darem, regardless of age, as they chatted over tea or whiskey or at-ta, hot milk thickened with powdered tuber from the flower and sweetened with orange zest and honey. Yio pieces were fitted into the table's side and Mëryl fiddled with them, sliding out the one nearest her and slotting it into the back of the row on the other end. A cup of at-ta sat beside her, half-drunk, the orange zest still floating on the drink's surface in the pattern it had been shaken on: a crude star. Next to the grill was a jar of pickled buds, presented in the rustic style popular in New Darem, as if they had just come out of grandma's root cellar. Dozens of small candles lit the second floor, and the sounds of the café were convivial: conversation, laughter, Yio pieces clacking as they were slapped down, and whoops of triumph as someone claimed a column.

Just as Mëryl was removing the peaches from the grill, Shann appeared, squinting in the relative dark of the café's second floor. Mëryl stood up and waved, and Shann smiled as she approached.

They embraced briefly then sat.

"Thanks for meeting me," Shann said.

"It was a somewhat quicker time frame than we're normally on."

"Yeah, sorry. Things are a little . . . hectic right now. But you know how it is, work is the way we keep moving forward."

"Don't worry about it. How could I say no to my favorite member of Harraka?" Mëryl smiled gently, but Shann looked up, her eyes sharp.

"You know others?"

"No. But if I did, I'm sure you'd still be my favorite. And don't worry about the short notice. I don't have much else going on right now."

"No?" Shann said. "Isn't the At-Saught integration eating up your life?"

Mëryl shrugged. "Maybe it would if I took it more seriously, but . . ."

"But this isn't your universe, this isn't your body, this isn't your life."

"An outlook an activist can't relate to, I guess."

"Yeah, I get it."

"And it's not like I don't care. I really do love Calyx. I'm not . . ." Mëryl sighed. "That's all boring. I've been here, stamping papers while you're out there changing worlds, making the multiverse a better place."

Shann laughed. "Sure, let's call it that."

"Are you not making the multiverse a better place?"

"Well, I'm certainly trying. There's a lot going on right now. It's a little overwhelming. Things are happening. Fast."

"Ah." Mëryl looked down, extracted a pickled bud from the jar, and popped it in her mouth.

"And there is, on Calyx, a certain Withered Stem who has information that would make a difference. A big difference."

"You know everything that I know, Shann."

"Yes, you've told me, but without physical evidence. The—"

"Is that why you wanted to meet? I thought we might just have dinner. Take a walk."

"We can have dinner," Shann said. "We can walk."

"We can have dinner and walk as long as I give you material that would put my life in danger, as well as the lives of those who have *already* risked their lives for me."

"No. Mëryl, no. Of course not. If you don't feel comfortable, then you don't feel comfortable."

They sat in silence for a moment. Shann looked away and ran a hand through her hair, tousling its short curls into verticality, then took a bite of one of the peaches as Mëryl looked on.

"Oh," Mëryl said. "I was supposed to—"

"You were supposed to press the button!" Tre said, appearing beside them.

"I know, I was going to! I just remembered."

"Don't worry about it." He leaned down and spoke to them both in a conspiratorial whisper. "It doesn't actually do anything. Just makes people feel like they have some control."

Shann laughed but Mëryl pursed her lips.

"What can I get you?" Tre said to Shann.

"I'll have whatever she's having," Shann said.

"It's just at-ta," Mëryl said. "You don't have to—"

"I'll have an at-ta, then."

"Perfect," Tre said. "I'll have it right up. Need anything else at this time?" They both shook their heads. "Wonderful. Well, if you want anything, just let me know." He departed, checking on the next table in his circuit before heading downstairs.

"You don't have to abstain for me," Mëryl said. "You can drink booze if you want."

"No, at-ta is what I need right now. I just"—she looked around—"arrived. I'm still feeling a little floaty in this body. At-ta will ground me. And anyway, I think this"—she gestured around her and out at the petals floating beside them, then breathed deeply—"is enough. Don't you?"

Mëryl smiled. "I do."

"And hey, if you can go without meat for me, stick with peaches and pickles, I can manage without alcohol, I think."

"Well, when the peaches are this good, it's not much of a sacrifice." Mëryl took a bite and then winced as juice dribbled down her chin, quickly dabbing it with a napkin.

"You'll have to explain to me sometime how a tree-hugging Withered Stem is comfortable killing and eating another living, feeling creature."

"And you'll have to explain to me why so many of the perpetual revolutionaries of Harraka, seeding their insurrections throughout the multiverse, aren't."

"Look," Shann said, "if you're on the business end of an insurrection, you've got it coming."

"What tidy insurrections you engender if there are only two ends to worry about . . ."

"Yes, well. It is our specialty, isn't it?"

"That's certainly the impression Harraka wants to convey," Mëryl said. "I can't claim to have ever seen one up close, though."

"Well, rest assured, we run as tidy an insurrection as you could possibly hope for."

"I wonder if all the people being insurrected feel that way."

Shann opened her mouth to respond but Tre returned then, depositing a mug on the table.

"At-ta!" he said, then slid a small jar across the table as though engaging in an illicit deal. "Extra honey, if you need it. You didn't get it from me, though."

Shann laughed. "Your secret is safe with us, thank you."

"I appreciate it. If Erich knew I was letting people tamper with his masterpiece . . . Whoo, look out. If you need anything else, just give me a wave." He demonstrated a wave as he descended the stairs. Shann waved back, though Mëryl didn't. Once he was gone, Shann pushed the jar of honey to the side of the table and blew on the at-ta before taking a sip.

Mëryl said, "Should we talk about . . . you know," she lowered her voice, "traveler stuff out in the open?"

Shann looked around. "We're fine," she said. "No one will be able to hear us, and even if they could, they'd think it was At-Saught business." She reached out and fingered the linked stars patch on Mëryl's sleeve. Mëryl's mouth twitched and she pulled her mug closer to her, but she said nothing. Shann let her hand fall and Mëryl took a long drink of at-ta.

"I am not insensate to the suffering of nonhuman life, you know," Mëryl said, putting the mug down.

"Hmm?"

"Just the opposite, in fact."

Shann's brow furrowed.

"Regarding meat," Mëryl said.

"Oh."

"I'm not insensate to animals' suffering."

"But still insensate enough to be fine with those animals' deaths," Shann said.

"If we believed death constituted suffering, then yes, I imagine the mainstream Withered Stem outlook would likely be different."

"How could death possibly not constitute suffering?" Shann frowned.

"Because the suffering of death is in the awareness of death, not death itself. It's the knowledge of what's to be lost and the mourning of that loss."

"You don't think the animal you're killing wants to keep on living?"

"To think that, you have to impute a self-awareness and a meta-cognition to livestock that I believe they lack," Mëryl said. "I question whether 'want' is even the right word at all—it strikes me as an anthropomorphization. The suffering of a being who lacks cognizance of the future or of the self is wholly physical, not existential. Without that cognizance, without some understanding of what death will entail—its absence, its nothing, its abrogation of the future—then death isn't suffering; it's simply a lack. An absence of pleasure and an absence of suffering. Death, by its nature, is null. The tragedy is in the knowing."

"That's . . . very detailed."

"Questions of cognition, of meta-cognizance, these matter quite a lot. They help us understand the Simulacrum, understand traveling, understand morality, even ourselves."

"We don't get the classic 'nonhuman-animals-can't-travel-therefore-they-don't-have-souls' argument in Withered Stem, then?" Shann said.

"Oh no, nonhuman animals can certainly travel."

"Wait, what? *Travel* travel, like jumping universes?"

"It's not common, but there are recorded examples of it."

Shann blinked rapidly. "Are you making some joke I'm not understanding here?"

"The point is, if you wanted to drink, you could. It's not a Withered Stem thing. It's just me."

"*That's* the point?"

"If you wanted to."

"I know. And so I don't want to. Because it's just you." Shann leaned in and Mëryl smiled, looking down.

Shann said, "I don't understand how you'd be able to tell if an animal traveled between universes, though," she said. "It's not like they're going to tell you."

"No, generally they're not," Mëryl said. "There are ways, though."

"Right, but . . . how? How, actually?"

"You want the story?"

"I mean . . . yeah. This seems wild to me," Shann said.

"All right. So. There was an old musician back on Üt. He was sick. Sick beyond what our medicine could treat."

"Must have been very sick indeed!"

Mëryl nodded. "He made arrangements, traveled away, off to a universe he'd visited before, a body he'd occupied that he knew was healthy. Standard stuff, right?"

"Is it?"

"It is in Withered Stem. You can normally get another decade or so of life by jumping bodies. Sometimes more. And certainly, it's a higher quality of life."

"That is not something we do in Harraka."

"Things are a little less stable for you, I guess. Anyway. Our old musician had a pet bird on Üt. He lived alone, he fed it every day, you get the idea. They were deeply bonded. So, he taught it this little dance for when it wanted food. Not complicated, but specific. Three bobs, two spins, whatever. I don't know exactly. It ended with a couple of little gentle headbutts."

"Sounds cute," Shann said.

"Uh-huh . . . Well, the day after he travels, as he's sitting around moping in this other universe, missing his bird, a crow shows up at his window. Out of the blue. Lands on his table, hops up to him, and what do you know? Three bobs, two spins, the same set of shimmies and wing flaps, all ending with the little headbutts."

"That sounds . . . unlikely. Like a heartwarming urban legend."

"Yeah, it does," Mëryl said. "It was verified, though. Animal behaviorists said the only explanation that wasn't wholly implausible was that the bird could travel. Kicked off a whole new field of research, though it died off pretty quickly when no one could figure out a useful application."

"I suppose sending fauna or flora across the multiverse wouldn't be of great advantage to Withered Stem, dancing or otherwise."

"You know, that's actually one of the sticking points with At-Saught," Mëryl said. "One of the big things that's being hashed out."

"Teaching birds to dance?"

"Whether or not a cutting of the world flower can be taken off-world."

Shann's eyes widened. "Really? That's under consideration?"

"Have you been gone that long? I'm surprised you didn't know. I'm surprised your front doesn't."

"Hmm?"

"Your proxy. Pupa. This body. Isn't that what Harraka calls them? I thought front was what you used, at least. Still not settled in it?"

"Yes. Yes, clearly." Shann laughed. "Or clearly not. Very much not settled. Front is right. For me." She raised the mug of at-ta to take another sip.

"I don't know how you do it. Traveling as much as you do."

"I'm not sure I know how I do it either . . ."

Across the room, a red-faced man was speaking in agitated tones, his words slurred but his anger clear. The waiter, Tre, stood beside him, annoyance barely concealed, saying something that made his jaw clench. The man rejected whatever Tre said, almost bouncing in his seat with the force of his gesticulation. His voice raised, he waved angrily in Mëryl and Shann's direction, slapping his own shoulder then spreading his arms wide. Crouching down beside the man, Tre made placating gestures and said something that quieted him for a moment. Mëryl rubbed the At-Saught patch on her arm and leaned against the balcony's railing.

"Ignore him," Shann said. "He doesn't know how much you do for him."

"I don't blame him," Mëryl said. "I'd probably feel the same. And with this talk of taking a cutting of the flower?" Her shoulders drooped and she sank lower on the railing. "I don't know. It's a complicated, political thing, but . . . There are Burel Hird in the

At-Saught expedition, more than there are of us. Withered Stem, I mean. I don't know if they're driving this push for taking the flower off-world, but they're certainly helping things along in that direction. They either don't care, or don't understand, how . . ." Mëryl sighed. "Calyx would burn, Shann. At-Saught isn't popular now, but at least integration has been peaceful. If they tried to do something with the flower?" She shook her head. "There'd be upheaval. Rebellion. Maybe that's a Burel Hird strategy, I don't know. Destabilize, swoop in, rescue."

"Have there been . . . conflicts? Cloak-and-dagger stuff?"

"Between us and Burel Hird? Not here, no."

"You heard, though, about the battle?" Shann said. "On some world with crab people. Two Withered Stem killed."

"I heard, yes."

"And that doesn't upset you?"

"It does. Not in any way that's really different from my permanent level of upset, though."

"Why not? It's wrong, what they did. They shouldn't even be there. With Withered Stem, you're on worlds to research, to learn. Who even knows what Burel Hird was doing. They annex whole localities, but for what? Nothing good."

"Shann, there's going to be a fight. A war, maybe. Withered Stem and Burel Hird. It's basically inevitable."

"War? Seriously?"

"Six years ago there was an accident—four Withered Stem and three Burel Hird killed. Nine years ago, a brawl. One dead on each side. Seventeen years ago, the Iyemitch Incident. Twelve Withered Stem dead. Thirty-odd years ago was Ghith. It's kind of amazing there wasn't a war then, honestly. We've been bumping into each other more and more, and for as infinite as the Simulacra is, the spaces we occupy are not—neither society is satisfied just sitting in their own sphere. Ideology, personalities, individuals, politics, it may seem like all of these are causes. I think it's just territory. There are always new localities to explore, new technologies to uncover, new research to be done. Like here. We want different things out of Calyx, but we're both interested in it. So we're both here. Conflict isn't inevitable, but . . . basically? Yes, I think so."

"You both 'want different things out of Calyx.' That sounds a whole lot like a clash of ideology to me."

Mëryl shrugged. "Yeah, maybe. I was never a diplomat and I'm not a spy anymore, so what do I know. I'm barely even a botanist."

"Mëryl . . ."

"Most of my time is spent just throwing up whatever roadblocks I can to prevent a cutting of the flower being taken. Procedural, bureaucratic, whatever. I'm more valuable to Withered Stem as an At-Saught administrator hamstringing At-Saught than I am researching the flower."

"Why is it so important that there's no cutting? I mean, I understand the sentimental reasons for wanting to keep Calyx special, but—"

"No, it's more than that. A lot more."

"Tell me."

Mëryl took a deep breath. "There's a story about a cutting being taken to the southern continent. It may be a myth, but our research suggests that it's more or less accurate. The story goes that a cutting was taken, planted successfully, and started reaching its roots down and establishing itself, and it seemed like things were going well. But then it began flowering in the middle of winter. And not just a warm snap or anything like that. The dead of winter. And it was growing in directions it shouldn't be, that were inconsistent with its normal strategies. It started strangling itself, choking itself out of certain areas that it should have flourished in. And this wasn't happening only on the southern continent. It was happening up here too. The flower had been healthy for thousands of years, but as soon as a cutting took hold away from its central root ball, as soon as that cutting started trying to grow its own root ball, bad things started happening."

"Is there a hypothesis about why it was happening?"

"It was confused. Not about the environment—about its identity. It

didn't understand what was happening. It was split into two and didn't
know how to handle it."

"It's a plant. One that happens to be as big as a continent, but it's
still just a plant." Shann said.

"Yes, but that's not quite right. The singular is important, though.
Even though the two parts of it were separated by an ocean, by half a
world, it was still the same organism. What it was experiencing on the
southern continent affected the version on the northern continent. And
vice versa. It was still one plant."

"A telepathic flower?"

"That's too human. It's unitary. It doesn't communicate with itself,
it is itself, no matter how it's divided. That's the working theory, anyway.
That's what we're researching here. It's a truly astounding organism, one
that pushes the boundaries of what we know, or think we know, about
consciousness or awareness."

"And At-Saught, Burel Hird, they're interested in the same
thing?"

Mëryl snorted. "No. Not at all. The air on Calyx, the water, the
purity of the atmosphere, it's all thanks to the flower. It regulates the
whole planet. Development on Calyx isn't as aggressive as it could be,
but there's still pollution. There's still industrial contamination. The
flower takes care of it, though. It adapts, takes in contaminants and
pollution, converts them, and keeps the planet clean. That's what they
want: a biological, planetwide filtration system." Mëryl let her head fall
into her hands. "Sorry, can we not talk about this? I spend so much
energy thinking of ways to keep it safe, and . . . I just, I don't want to
be thinking about it now."

"No, of course."

"I'm sorry, I know you've got your own thing, and you're trying to
make the multiverse a better place, and you want to use me to do that,
and meanwhile, I'm sitting here losing my mind about a plant in a locality that's not even my own and probably boring you to tears with my
dumb neuroses, and even if you did just want to have dinner, I'd spend
the whole time talking about work, about nonsense, I—" She cut herself

off, her fingers worrying at the grain of the table's wood, and looked away.

"Mëryl." Shann put her hand on Mëryl's, stilling it. "It's fine. You don't have to apologize. Not to me. Truly. Not ever."

"All right." They sat in silence for a moment, neither moving.

"Should we play?" Shann said. She withdrew her hand and pulled a Yio piece from a slot on the side of the table, flipping it in the air.

Mëryl shrugged.

Shann caught the piece and spun it on the table. "Should we order some more food?"

Mëryl nodded.

"Then let's."

Tre was passing by then, and Shann waved him over.

"Before you say anything," Tre said, "I just want to apologize on behalf of some of our other guests. Not everyone is responding to integration with as much . . . sophistication as might be hoped for. Some of our oldsters would like to hold on to the past like screaming children. You don't need to worry about it, though. I took care of it."

"That wasn't . . ." Shann began. "Thank you. We just wanted some food, though."

"Well, I can take care of that, too! What can I get you?"

"We'll take a grilled cabbage and . . ." She paused. "Do you have those . . . The pancakes? With the leeks and the peppers?"

"Zhinch?"

"Yes!"

"Of course! We're in New Darem, aren't we?"

"And an order of zhinch."

"You couldn't remember zhinch?!" Tre said in mock outrage.

"Long day."

"I would have expected it from your friend," he gestured to the At-Saught emblem on Mëryl's sleeve. "But from a New Daremite? Maybe the old-timer was right . . . Heartbreaking what we've come to!" Tre rolled his eyes and laughed.

Mëryl said, "How do you know she's from New Darem?"

"Haircut," Tre said. "I don't think anyone else would have the courage to sport a boe except for us."

"I had no idea . . ." Mëryl said. "I think it looks nice."

"So do I," Tre said, "but I'm from here! Sexy up front, messy out back, right? So grilled cabbage, both halves?" Tre said, and Shann nodded. "And some zhinch. Sounds good."

Shann reached over and tilted Mëryl's mug toward her. "And two more at-tas, please."

"Perfect," Tre said, walking away.

Through the open window, a busker could be heard playing a traditional ballad on the Calyxian seven-string guitar. His voice was deep and strong, the words telling of the dark period after the planet's founding, as the settlers sent signals back across the vast of space, back to their original home, but got no reply. When he finished, there was scattered applause, a small crowd apparently having gathered, and he launched quickly into an upbeat dancehall tune.

Inside the restaurant, the smells were of blistered peppers and candle wax, and there was always the crack and hiss of Yio pieces slapped down on boards, then slid into position. A few tables' faces were lit by the bluish glow of personal communicators, increasingly common since the arrival of the At-Saught envoy thirty years prior. This was the contradiction of Calyx: The ambiance was rustic and pleasant, the street paved with irregularly shaped stones, but only a mile away was downtown, with its soaring, many-spired skyscrapers. New Darem was a city like so many on this planet: bifurcated. Planned out by a civilization long dead whose descendants still lived, having made do for centuries with only what the planet offered. Now, from the ruins of that civilization, a new compact had emerged—At-Saught—and slowly, the linkages were remade.

Mëryl picked up the piece Shann had spun on the table and examined it. She said, "There's another Withered Stem here. He was a Yio fanatic. Every meeting had to take place over a board while we played a game. But he had to leave, had to go back to Üt. And apparently, he spent the whole time there teaching people to play. At our first meeting after he came back, I figured we would play a game. So I showed up and started setting up the board, but he stopped me. He said Yio wasn't as fun on Üt. In his true body."

"It's the same game, though," Shann said.

"But he wasn't the same person. Yio here? It's part of the culture. It's something ingrained. He grew up with it, or his proxy did. He had fifty years of memories associated with Yio. His first crush, or his proxy's first crush, was a girl who demolished him—and that's why he first wanted to get good. All of those associations and connections bore much more of his affection's weight than he understood. Yio, even though it's the same game, even though he is, at root, the same person on Calyx that he is on Üt, isn't as fun because his love of it is biological. Without those chemical buttresses of memory and nostalgia, it's just wood sliding across wood. And when he came back here?" Mëryl shrugged. "The magic didn't. 'The spell was broken.' His words."

"Huh."

"Is that your experience?"

"Well, I never really liked Yio to begin with. This body or me," Shann said.

"Oh. Then why did you ask if I wanted to play?"

"Because I thought you might like to."

Mëryl looked away. "You're good to me."

Shann laughed. "Mëryl, playing Yio is about the smallest imposition imaginable. You need to up your standards!"

Mëryl said nothing.

"Truthfully," Shann said, "I travel so much it's hard for me to tell where I end and where the proxies begin."

"What's your travel mechanism?"

Shann raised an eyebrow and sat back in her chair. "Well, that's rather personal, isn't it!"

"Is it? It's not in Withered Stem. It's a little surprising we've never discussed it, actually."

"In Harraka, it's quite private."

"Oh. I see. I'm sorry, I didn't mean to overstep."

"Mëryl, please. I was a little surprised, is all."

"When I'm with you, I forget that you don't feel about me the way I feel about you."

"Mëryl—"

"Let's not, for a little bit, okay?"

For some time, neither spoke and in the quiet between them, the sounds of the café—laughter, silverware on plates, peaches sizzling, the busker's rich, clear voice—were loud.

PART TWO

6

Shara squinted in the morning light, a winter breeze blowing against her face in the broad courtyard. The colors were severe, the suns at midmorning painting the sky with their oranges. Greens and blues of memory in the valley below, glimpses of a past that many of her kind would speak of, mourning the mythic fullness of a rapidly fading heritage. This was her world, Beinir's world—Oulra.

Beinir clapped her shoulder from behind. "My hide was abed, though I knew yours would not be. You love the morning too much."

"I would rather not have returned here," Shara said. "They ended our contract prematurely. It's embarrassing."

"I know." He rubbed his neck, stepping in front of her. He wore a leather jerkin over a mail coat and a broadsword at his hip. A wooden shield was slung over his shoulder. His straw-colored hair was bound behind his neck and his beard was thin in this world. She had forgotten that.

"How could a Hird girl know our ways so well?" he asked.

"Spies?"

"They refuse to deal or treat with us, but they spy? For what purpose?"

"Who can say? They are as false as Firmāre, to my mind."

Shara wore a green hempen gown and a knife belt she adjusted slightly. Red curls hung in her eyes, and she brushed them aside. Beinir stared at her. He chewed a lema twig he must have found in his cell. "I forget how much I like you in this world," he said.

"What does that mean?"

He grinned. "Only that you are too lovely for the star roads alone."

"Honestly—you are the same in every world." Shara punched his shoulder and rolled her eyes. "But a better friend and partner I shall not find."

They left the courtyard and entered the great hall of the chancel. Dust hung in the air in shafts of sunlight, and the room was thick as ever with the liturgical and gray solemnity of long years. Wooden tables flanked with benches were arranged around a central hearth in which a fire burned. Stew pots had been nestled among the coals in the hearth, and meats depended over the flames from spits. There were only a few roamers about so early, three of them sitting at a bench and eating in their heavy robes, and a hide in a brown robe lit torches along the walls as another swept the stone floors with a broom. Their eyes were distant, remote.

An old, bearded man tended to the food. Just beside him was a pile of split wood and kindling moss. The smell of fish, hog, and woodsmoke filled the dark room as Beinir and Shara sat down at a table with the sibyl. She looked tired; her eyes were swollen. The dark and sagging skin of her face was beginning to reveal her age.

"Hail, Sibyl," Shara said.

"Shara," the woman answered. "And Beinir. Well met, as always."

Beinir dipped his head. "Your Glory. May I?"

"Eat, of course. Please."

"Will you have anything, Shara?"

"No," she said, but after he walked away, she called after him. "Bring me some belly."

"I was going to."

Shara smiled, returning her attention to the sibyl. "How have you been?"

"I am well enough. Some days are harder than others. It has been many years but I still feel my brother's loss, as always."

Shara looked away. "I'm sorry."

The sibyl shifted on the bench, stretching her back. "I am indebted to you and Beinir for ending that—" There came a spark of anger on her face, strange for the old woman. A moment passed, and her kindness returned, the effort plain. "For bringing my brother's killer to justice. For giving me some peace. In the end."

Beinir rejoined them with a board teeming with meat and fruit and corncakes. Shara grabbed a piece of hog belly and took a bite.

"Did you tell her yet?" Beinir said, already chewing on a hunk of fish.

"Tell me what?"

"We were dismissed, firstly. But it was not our fault."

"Not dismissed," Shara said. "Our contract was ended. Early."

Beinir shrugged. "A worthy tale, regardless. But that is not what we need to tell you." Beinir glanced at Shara, then looked back to the sibyl. "We were forced to accept rayita."

The sibyl inclined her chin, narrowing her eyes. "Rayita? From whom? Another roamer?"

"Curiously, no. It was from a young Burel Hird girl," Shara said.

"Surely not."

"We had been contracted as guardians—by sages of the Withered Stem in an iron world."

"The one with crab folk," Beinir interrupted. "We are lately come from there, your Glory."

Shara grabbed another strip of belly. "After encountering Burel Hird in these caves, we clashed. I am not fully sure why. Much life was spent, though we would have prevailed. But this young girl suddenly shouted an offer of rayita to end things."

Several robed roamers came into the hall, expecting the morning bell, which would be rung soon. Their leather pattens shushed along the stones.

"The girl was quick," Beinir said. "Something familiar about her too. A young me, perhaps?"

The sibyl scowled. "Rayita is ancient for Of Tala, from long before our many divisions. But certainly not for far-landers."

"We thought you might have heard of this happening before."

"No. Never." The sibyl leaned forward. "You accepted their surrender?"

"We did. It seemed the right thing at the time. Better not to risk—all."

She nodded. "Some of our laws are less useful than others. When was the last time you heard of anyone offering or accepting rayita?"

"It is in the sagas," Beinir said. "The older sagas. From generations long past."

The sibyl adjusted the chain of the sigil around her neck. It bore the emblem of their order, two threads unwinding from a spool—the same emblem branded on every wayfarer's forearm. The mark of the Roamers of Tala.

The sibyl lifted her chin. "We are not so bound to the old ways as we once were."

"Thanks in no small part to you," Shara said.

"Mmm—" the sibyl shrugged, smiling. "I am sorry your tale was so abruptly closed. And that I offer little more than consolation."

Beinir slammed a hand on the table. "Bah, this is good news. We may depart at once. Or—once our tales have been told, short as they are." He leaned forward. "Any—invigorating work on offer, your Glory?"

Shara thought about where they might go next. They would spend the evening relaying their accounts from Geçiş. But then Shara and Beinir would be free to avail themselves of the shifters and invokers of Oulra. They would be free to take work from the roamers or to simply travel the star roads to any world they wished. To enrich their sagas.

She could ask to visit her mother and father and brother first, in the mountains surrounding the Donar, many leagues to the north. The sibyl had changed many of the old laws in recent years—chief among them, wayfarers were now permitted to see their families. But Shara thought better of it. Her family hardened their prejudices more and more, believing that wayfarers like herself and Beinir, all roamers, were false. Or delusional. Her father believed that when a wayfarer was blessed to travel out of their body and into another world, they were in fact experiencing an episode of the mind, as though wayfarers were sick, not blessed. It was nonsense, of course. In truth, wayfarers *did* leave this universe, their hides remaining behind as they wandered the star roads. Yet falsehood flourishes where the idle are lauded. And Shara's father was ever proud of his stillness. Many on Oulra felt the same.

"As it happens," the sibyl said, "there is a nexus—the rim of a distant cosmos."

Beinir pulled a pinbone from his teeth then gulped at a mug of watered-down ale.

Shara sat very still, waiting.

"Stories are that solidity there is waning. Within it, difficult to reach, is a gathering place where wayfarers of all sorts trade. From there, one might reach worlds never before trod by roamers."

Beinir set his mug on the table and wiped his beard. "Virgin worlds mean the chance to be a source. A first account."

"True," Shara said. "But the risks—"

"Are worth it."

"And if we blink blindly into a dying star? Our sagas would be cut short, left endingless."

Beinir smiled. "I never much cared for endings."

Shara was still unconvinced.

"Ever prudent to consider the dangers," the sibyl said. She put a hand gently on Shara's. "There is something we must speak of that will perhaps guide you forward on your path."

"Yes, Sibyl."

The sibyl looked from Shara to Beinir, letting her eyes linger on his.

Shara could see the question on Beinir's lips, the woundedness in his expression, but under the sibyl's steady gaze, he relented. "I will . . . get more ale. For myself."

Once he had left, the sibyl returned to Shara. "I had a vision regarding you. A true vision."

Shara went still. "What?"

"I know."

"How . . . does this—"

"Happen often? No. Not for a generation. Certainly never to me."

"And the sigil?"

The woman touched the emblem hanging on her necklace. "Aglow with the old light when I awoke. I swear it is true."

"I believe you, of course," Shara heard herself say. "What was the vision?"

"It was . . . opaque. You were floating atop an expanse of dark water. Your eyes were closed as if asleep, but somehow, I knew you were not, not truly. And above you, directly so, mirroring your rest, was one shrouded in shadow. I could not see who lay within the shadow, and though I heard his voice, the words were indistinct. It went on like this for some time. Until you opened your mouth. And then the other being, this shadow man . . . fell into you. It was quick, like inhaling smoke. Once it was done, you opened your eyes and they were . . . they were bright as the second sun."

Shara was silent, searching for words but finding none that could meet the occasion.

The sibyl smiled knowingly, pulling her braids over one shoulder. "I'll refrain from offering a full reading. Such things need untilled soil to grow. I'll say only one thing. The vision did not feel like an ending or a death, but a transformation."

"Glory, I don't know what to make of this."

"You will," the sibyl said. "In your own time. I have already seeded the record of it, and so your name is now honored in the high annals. Felicitations and all that."

Shara blinked and shook her head, overwhelmed. "I . . ."

"You are already high in my esteem, mind you." She gestured for Beinir to rejoin them. As he approached, she gave Shara's hand one last tight squeeze. "Keep this in your heart, my Shara. Whatever this means, it is yours and yours alone."

Beinir returned, slamming a half-empty mug of ale on the table. "Now tell us, how shall we come upon this cosmos, your Glory?"

"We have an outpost in a neighboring realm, you would go forth from there." The sibyl leaned forward on the table. "In the nexus realm is a planet. One called L'makor. It is far from the congregation of wayfarers and shifters, but it is likely that you will arrive there. Star winds have a strong pull toward one world in that realm, so that whenever a wayfarer is flung from our border realm, they arrive on L'makor every time. L'makor is split into cities above and hovels below. Insurrection abounds there, as you might imagine. And as such, you might find your way difficult."

Shara was only intermittently paying attention. She was thinking about the vision, trying to picture the whole of it in her own mind. Visions were never literal in the sagas. Shara should not expect herself to be floating in water while swallowing actual shadow smoke. But by the end of those tales, the visions always held meaning, even if understanding often came too late. And if the glowing sigil was referenced—it was not always—then the vision was not just important for the one wayfarer, but for all, a foretelling of an event that would directly or indirectly lead to a great upheaval or grand change. Shara wasn't sure she believed in the old superstitions, but she did feel something of the truth in at least part of the vision: the image of her lying in dark water, rudderless, resting in false sleep. Most days she would liken herself to that image, even when she was on missions. She wanted to be that other version of herself: eyes finally open, bright as the second sun.

It was the shadow that gave her unease. The shadow with the man's voice. The dark water. The deep fathoms of the Donar perhaps? Beinir? Her father?

She was brought back to the present when the sibyl stood, letting her robes fall around her. Even in the low light the fine reds and yellows were impressive. "Go and see Melsha. She will have more details and see you off, should you choose to go." As she said this, her eyes were once again on Shara, a reassuring smile on her lips. The sibyl grabbed her wine cup and stepped around the edge of the bench. "Farewell, wayfarers. Guard and nim the sidereal ways." She dipped her head to them and left, disappearing through the dark hallway leading to her chambers.

"And what was all that?" Beinir asked.

"I'll tell you later." Shara turned willfully away from him, look-ing back to the door opening out into the courtyard. White daylight gleamed from beyond as the peal of the morning bell rang out. She could feel fate upon her like a ballast weight. It was fate that brought them to Geçiş, thrust them into conflict with Burel Hird, and it was fate that they chanced upon an outworlder knowing of rayita. It was fate, too, which would pull them toward this world rife with conflict to find some outlying waystation at the fringe of a new universe. Where it was possible that Shara might meet her true self. Or someone else, whomever they may be.

7

Noah kept himself on alert as he made his way through Sobo District, deep in the underzones of L'makor. The people not laying low down here spent their time casing marks. And everyone was a mark, potentially. The three lines under his eye marking him as Orillo would keep most of them at bay, but not all. There were plenty that recognized the family name for what it was: a big dog, but not the biggest. And sometimes it was worth the risk of going after a big dog if it could earn you favor with bigger ones.

Noah hurried along. Damp, cracked concrete lined the entire floor of the underzones, except for the brief spots where nature fought back, weeds shooting up through cracks, and vines climbing the sides of brick facades. It reminded Noah of the hunger revolts that happened decades ago, where the poor, tired people of the underzones fought back against the rich living above them in the upper cities. The inferno that followed those revolts was enough to keep everyone in their place. But once again, ferment was rising.

Noah wanted out. Not just a citizenship card for the upper cities, but away from L'makor. Away from being beholden to his uncle and his mother and maybe even the whole Orillo family. Somewhere where he could be himself, where he could be free of the constant comparisons to his brawling, banal brother and the expectations of their name. But until then, it was Uncle Thaddicus's work and the little he could skim and sock away.

Uncle Thaddicus's compound was just ahead, a concrete structure with grime caked along the edges. But power hummed inside and the lights weren't half blown out, so it looked like one of the better buildings on the street.

Noah surveilled the building, making sure there weren't any ill-meaning dregs skulking around. He headed to the back side of the compound, passing a mangy cat tackling a rat almost as big as itself. One of the basement windows had come loose over a year ago, and ever since, Noah had been using it as his secret way in. When he was sure no one was watching, he pried the window open with an old rusted nail laying in a faded plastic bucket. He had to suck in his gut to slide through the window down into the basement, softly closing the window behind him.

The basement functioned as a stock room, mostly filled with batteries and assorted electronics: flashlights, outdated chip decks, air filterers. Junk from Uncle Thaddicus's front repair business.

Noah crept between stacks of cardboard boxes, moving through the darkened basement toward the staircase. He went quietly up the stairs and would've carried on to his bedroom on the third floor if not for the laughter coming from his uncle's office. Compelled by the prospect of gathering any scrap of information that might advance his position, Noah tiptoed to the open door, keeping out of sight.

"I'm sorry," Aunt Anolia said. "You must forgive me. This grand conspiracy sounds utterly ridiculous to me."

Uncle Thaddicus sighed. "Believe what you will."

"You sure it wasn't idle gossip?"

"My source lacks that particular vice."

Aunt Anolia coughed. "And who is this source you keep mentioning?"

"All of Vaish is a leaky ship. It is a miracle they've lasted this long."

"That is not an answer."

Thaddicus laughed. "If I told you who, you'd be obligated to tell your sister, and who knows what blood debts Serena has made. And to whom. Trust me when I tell you that my silence on the matter preserves us."

An image of Noah's mother came to mind, her severe black eyes, veil of black curls, and quiet fury.

Aunt Anolia said, "And this assassination of a Burel Hird council member—"

"—will shift the balance of power in these many worlds. Especially for those in the know before it happens, who can plan accordingly. I've always wanted to get into the mercenary business."

Noah made to retreat, but the floorboard beneath his foot announced the shift in his weight. To save himself, he yelled: "Uncle! Are you in there?"

"Ah, nephew, come in, let me get a look at you."

As Noah entered, his aunt and uncle were both looking at him from where they sat in the room. He looked from one to the other in forced calm. His aunt looked distressed, but his uncle was smiling broadly. He was wearing his dark blue suit again, with the periwinkle piping, his shirt decorated with a bolo tie. Already his hair was gelled up like a wave was crashing atop his head. In total, his uncle looked like some exotic bird, which, Noah had to admit, was oddly reassuring in this context.

Uncle Thaddicus beckoned with a finger. "Come. Sit."

Noah did so, choosing the chair in front of his uncle's desk, his back deliberately to his aunt. Of the two, she seemed the more suspicious of his sudden appearance.

"Did you come home last night?" his uncle asked.

"Yes, Uncle."

He grinned at Noah. "Those Liam boys kept you out so late, I must've missed when you came in. That is what you were up to, was it not?"

"Yes, Uncle."

"Drinking, no doubt."

"Yes, Uncle."

"Don't sound so sheepish. We're all allowed our indulgences." He leaned in conspiratorially. "Relax. Your aunt isn't going to rat you out to your mother."

Noah made himself laugh. It wasn't very convincing, but thankfully his uncle's laughter swallowed his own.

Thaddicus sat back, regarding him. "Look at you, how much you've grown! Five years on L'makor have made you a man, nephew."

He looked over Noah's shoulder. "Haven't they, love?"

There was a beat of silence. "Yes, they have," Aunt Anolia said, voice low.

"You know what I think," Uncle Thaddicus began again. "I think it is time you had some responsibility."

"Responsibility?"

"Real responsibility. What do you think, love?"

His aunt said nothing.

"We've been wanting to implant someone at the sleep facility. Someone we can trust."

"My love," his aunt said, "maybe we should—"

"What do you say, Noah? Do you think you could do it?"

Noah tried to control his excitement. "Yes, Uncle. Of course."

"The real objective is to reverse engineer the sleep-swap technology so that we can reproduce it under our control. Those rangati up top have grown fat off this service, and I've grown tired of letting them. You have some engineering skills, no?"

Noah nodded. He did. All untrained, but Noah had taken to the technology of L'makor, transferring much of what he knew from Estix—the universe of his birth—though the technology here was far less advanced. That's what his mother had not understood when she marooned him here. Noah hadn't been wasting his time on Estix. He'd been developing skills that would benefit the family. Far more than if he was a slab of dumb muscle like Jacobi.

"I've been watching you, nephew. I think you can do it. Of course, you'll have to come in as a sleeper first and work your way up."

"Thad, my love," his aunt said. "Serena wouldn't approve."

"Let the boy answer for himself. You're not afraid of your mother, are you?"

"No, Uncle."

"She's a whole universe away."

"Mother has never appreciated my talent."

"Yes, that's right. Shortsighted to a fault. She wanted you to be more like your older brother. What's that boy's name?"

Noah smiled. "Jacobi."

"Ah, yes. I'd forgotten." Uncle Thaddicus opened a desk drawer and began rifling through it. A moment later, he slapped down a folder. "Here's what we know so far. Study it. I'll get you a spot at the facility before the day is done."

Noah hesitantly reached for the folder, shaking with excitement. This was what he needed. A chance to prove himself.

When the folder was in his hand, his uncle reached forward and grasped Noah around the forearm, pulling him close. "And your mother?"

"What?" Noah tried not to wince from the force of his uncle's grip.

There was a sound from behind Noah, a sharp inhale.

"She doesn't need to know about anything you might or might not have heard standing out in the hall, isn't that right?"

"I didn't hear anything. I swear."

Uncle Thaddicus watched him without blinking. "Secrets are powerful things in our world. So is trust. I am trusting you, nephew. Do I have your trust?"

"Yes, yes, of course, Uncle."

He squeezed tighter. "This is a bloody business. If you were to go off running your mouth—"

"I wouldn't."

"I'd be helpless to protect you. Though it would pain me and your aunt deeply."

Noah nodded, words failing him.

"Good man." Uncle Thaddicus released his grip, and Noah fell back into his chair. "You're all right. Why don't you get some breakfast; you look hungry."

Noah stood and left the room before tears betrayed him.

8

ENGINE LOCALITY

After his attempted vacation, people watched Malculm. From a distance, mostly, but he still noticed them. The shoes gave it away. They could remove jackets, unbutton shirts, and even occasionally change from pants to shorts to skirts and back again, but shoes, being considered "mission critical," were assigned by the agencies. So when Malculm saw the same scuff marks on the same bluchers (oxblood leather, welted construction, cork nitrile sole, standard issue for any field operative level 4A or higher) or the same frayed aglet on the same left sneaker (high-tops, popular since the 87th Turn and required on any surveillance, infiltration, or contra mission in second set Burel Hird environments) each day on his SDR, no matter how meandering he made it, he knew he was being tailed. Which meant Burel Hird knew he knew about their extra restriction on his administrative leave.

Malculm returned to the familiar blandness of his beige apartment, its institutional homeliness now grating, and he fought the urge to explode and rage. He was a professional, after all. So he went to his bedroom, pretended to forget to hang up his jacket, and then went into the kitchen and made a bowl of hominy porridge with milk, his usual afternoon ritual. He sat at the kitchen table with his meal and took out a novel he'd read once before.

He tapped his foot and turned the page regularly, even made his eyes move from side to side. But he wasn't reading. He was searching at those moments when his eyes hit the edge of a page. Quickly, so as not to tip his hand. He reminded himself to eat, which let him drop his eyes away from the book. He counted at least three cameras, two in the dining room, one in the kitchen, and a microphone concealed in the hinge of his refrigerator. There were certainly more, though. He was out of practice.

In his early days working with I/EI on smaller localities, Malculm spent a lot of time running op centers on backwater annexations, gathering intel that was briefly reviewed once by some minor committee member and shelved, waiting for the unlikely moment in which something happened, and proof of due diligence was needed. Still young enough in his career to believe working hard and well would get him noticed and appreciated, Malculm did his job thoughtfully and meticulously. One common tactic was to leave a few cameras out intentionally, so they would be found. Others were hidden much more thoroughly, sealed and shielded so that even with detection instruments, nothing would be picked up.

This had a couple of effects. One was that it unsettled the target, making them more likely to make mistakes that could be seized upon. The other, and more important, was that it spurred action. When conducting external operations, Burel Hird was typically a muted presence, unknown and unheard by the target, so those under Malculm's surveillance would rip out the cameras and mics they found and begin to ask around. Who was watching them? Why? How had this happened?

Such speculation, recorded by those cameras not meant to be found, garnered actionable intel quickly and efficiently, and had led to myriad connections: who the target feared, saw as rivals, and sometimes led to the discovery of organizations yet unknown.

Malculm hoped that his efforts were successful here. Because the only reason to employ visual surveillance was to let him know I/EI was watching. Which meant, more than anything, they saw nothing threatening in Malculm. They figured he would grow terrified knowing that such a vast and powerful organization watched him and be cowed into meek compliance. And, they were half right. He was worried. This had all the hallmarks of an administrative defenestration, and he was not particularly interested in being drummed out of the intelligence service. But more than that, he was insulted. Did they truly think so little of him?

So, while chewing his porridge and staring at the words on the page, Malculm decided he'd get out of Engine, out of this locality, and figure out why things had gone so wrong at Geçiş. And, when he uncovered the truth, they'd let him back into the fold.

Even Malculm had his secrets, unknown to Burel Hird, and one of them was his ticket out.

———

Malculm understood that Burel Hird didn't make mistakes, but mistakes *did* happen. When these "momentary oversights" took place, course correction was rapid and effective; the issue was remedied before any "unexpected complications" could result.

Basically, the opposite of Geçiş.

Before Malculm started packing the duffel bag, he seeded things appropriately. He called his old boss, a woman he called Mom, and had a banal conversation. It meandered, but eventually got to the point.

"Did you get a chance to read *Life in Vermillion* yet?" Malculm asked.

A pause. Long enough to signal that she knew what he meant. "You know, I didn't get the chance. I've heard good things."

"It's great. I highly recommend it."

Another pause. "Are you saying I should put it on my reading list?"

"Definitely."

The conversation continued on, but that was the important part.

The woman, in fact, was not his mother but someone he worked with closely and someone whose life he once saved. And with that had come an offer for a favor down the road. A favor he was calling in. He had been young, full of bravado, and *that* Malculm had loved the feeling refusing said favor gave him, selflessness a satisfaction his work rarely offered. She'd insisted, though. And now the *current* Malculm was grateful she had, his younger self revealed to be naive and cocksure and deeply, profoundly mistaken about how life was going to progress—as younger selves so often are.

Mom arranged a book trade for a few hours later at the park. He spent most of the time staring at his book and trying not to sweat, going over every step he'd need to take once their meeting ended. Rationally, Malculm knew that no one in I/EI could read his mind, but that didn't stop his brain from going over the branching possibilities and unpleasant outcomes as though they could.

But once it was time, he grabbed *Life in Vermillion* from his shelf, donned his sunglasses, and headed outside, making for Resiliency Park. Along the way, he glanced around the periphery without moving his head, keeping tabs on familiar shoes. The day was pleasant, the sun offering a gentle warmth, a steady breeze bearing Engine's diesel perfume. From exhaust ports came the ceaseless clanging and grinding of the eponym's operation, life built directly atop the planet's grand machinery. Densely packed buildings lined the street he took, and running all around him were swarms of children not yet old enough to descend into the machine, none taller than his waist. It was as idyllic as days on Engine ever were. But the fear that I/EI would pick him up before he ever reached the park clawed at him until Resiliency's deep green finally came into view.

Dima Tancredi sat on the agreed-upon bench, wearing short pants the color of turmeric and a linen blouse, its sleeves rolled up, a large blue cloth flower adorning the place over her heart. Dima was only five years older than him, though she dressed much older. Light clothes that showed a lot of skin, proof that the wearer no longer toiled among the great machines underground. Which was how the "Mom" nickname came. The name had stuck because she also fussed over her subordinates. Malculm was no exception. He made a show of waving at her as he approached.

"You're getting fatter, compeer," Dima said.

"And your outfits are getting older," Malculm said.

She smiled and patted the bench next to her. "How've you been?"

Malculm sat, setting his book next to him. "Oh, you know. Had an operation go bust, probably my last chance at a promotion, but I'm alive. So that's something."

She smiled, causing her eyes to turn up slightly with her mouth. "You could always come back to work for me."

Something Malculm had considered but dismissed. It would be easy to do that, lick his wounds, fall into familiar patterns. But then, that would be it. He'd die working for Dima, and there were certainly worse fates, but that didn't make it a desirable one. Not when there was a chance of turning this around, proving that he could still provide true value to Burel Hird.

Malculm grunted. "I might take you up on that in another life."

Dima nodded. "I thought so." An expression crossed her face that Malculm couldn't read, and she placed a green book on the bench. "It was good to see you, Malculm."

"Likewise, Mom."

Dima snorted and dismissed him with her hands. "You know I hate that."

"Once you modernize your wardrobe, I swear I'll drop it."

Dima picked up *Life in Vermillion*, turned, and walked away, wagging her finger at him without looking back. "Never."

Malculm remained on the bench as Dima left. The book she'd left, titled *No Time but the Present: How to Unlock Your Hidden Potential*, felt heavy in his hands. He remained on the bench, not to ponder his choices or chances, but because, once more, he expected agents to descend upon him. They would keep him hidden from sight until some committee formed from the Geçiş Incident Retrospective Report decided the best course of action. More than likely, that would mean reassignment, a spot on the Inter-Bureau Cleanliness Committee, on "Toothbrush Detail," scrubbing moldy grout in subbasement bathrooms for the rest of time with no opportunity for advancement. But no one came.

———

Malculm cradled the book under his arm as he walked out of the park. He counted between each step, footfalls tapping out a smooth, steady rhythm on the pavement. Nothing suspicious about this stride. Nothing for a field operative to notice at all. How many assets had he instructed on just this technique? How many agents had received his tutelage in spycraft?

Æthelred was one, though unofficially. They'd worked together half a dozen times before Geçiş, small-bore stuff, early-stage observations, pure reconnaissance without intervention, part of his fallow period of dead-end missions. Nothing that was likely to require advisement, Æthelred present only because the Joint Adjudication Garrison had managed to weasel out a statute that required one of their warrior-lawyers accompany every operation of three or more people. Their third op together, both deeply bored as they awaited another meaningless report on a slow-motion coup from a doddering archduke, Æthelred had asked Malculm to show him some techniques.

He demurred, such a thing being an inappropriate cross-contamination of operational specialties and well outside I/EI regulations. Æthelred had insisted, though, producing and signing several documents acknowledging that Malculm held no liability, and Æthelred assumed all bureaucratic risk should their actions be found in breach of their respective agencies' guidelines. Malculm laughed and gave in, then told him how to set an effective surveillance detection route, how to identify useful bottlenecks, how to observe without looking, and how to measure his steps so that he gave nothing away.

Had Æthelred's interest been genuine or had it been a technique to ingratiate himself with Malculm? They'd never grown close enough for Malculm to ask. They never would.

According to the shoes around him, only two agents remained in observation.

The day was warm, the sun hot on his neck. Across the street, an old arcade stood on the block, part of an Engine-wide push for civic improvement some years back. It was two floors, and its exterior showed the building's age. Paint was chipped and worn, revealing the rusted alloy beneath. It had been abandoned long ago. Malculm thought that there was comfort in the run-down, in the familiar. The rhythm of his footsteps was steady.

The bakery was a mere fifteen paces away. Nothing to do now but keep moving and walk through the door. After that, he would be gone.

But a man stepped from an alley just before the bakery door—the third set of shoes. He grabbed Malculm by the elbow and led him a few more steps, then turned toward him, taking time to tip his cap and smile at some of the passersby.

"What's in the book?"

"Chapters, I hope," Malculm said. They'd made him comfortable, made him think they'd made a mistake, but the third man had backed off to circle around. He supposed he should be flattered.

"Very funny. Look, we can't scan inside, the binding is blocking the signal. So we need to know what's in that thing."

"There's nothing here except words and dog-eared pages."

"Okay. Open it." The man motioned with a quick wave.

Shit.

Malculm's chest thrummed. He had spent most of his life as a rule follower. Well, at least a follower of Burel Hird's rules. He'd broken plenty of laws from other localities but always in the interest of furthering Burel Hird's aims of expanding its holdings. Of spreading its firm, responsible governance. A bus arrived at the stop behind him, its brakes sighing, a pneumatic squeal coming as it knelt, letting off its passengers. The agent glanced over Malculm's shoulder. The man had a twitchy left eye, and a nebula of burst blood vessels darkened his cheek. A 6B—Malculm would lay money on it. Past his prime. Just like Malculm.

One thing stood out to him. They must not know about the baker.

A 6B wouldn't dare question him just outside the door if they had. Malculm could even try and run for it, bar the door amid boules and baguettes, and make his escape. He might even have a shot at pulling it off. Just not a sure enough shot to actually try it. But it did give him a window to try something.

Before he'd been an agent, before he'd been one small mechanism in an apparatus of state control, he'd been a troublemaker on Glitterpoint. It had been only two years, between the ages of thirteen and fifteen, but a mischievous streak overtook him. He snuck out of the Academy and spent time with some of the rougher Glitterpoint youths. Thinking back, the Academy staff probably allowed little rebellions like those he was involved with, letting kids blow off steam.

He couldn't say many of the things he learned while causing havoc there would ultimately help him later in life, especially stealing appliances from kiosks, but the South Street Shuffle might just save him here. He'd have to be quick, though. Only one agent threatened him, but the other two would be circling fast. He waited until he heard the hiss of the bus behind him preparing for departure.

Malculm made like he was going to open the book, but before 6B could react, he used the heel of his right foot to scrape down the agent's shin, grinding his heel into the man's instep. The agent howled and recoiled, doubling over. Malculm grabbed the back of his head with his free hand and kneed him in the face with all the force he could manage. Something popped. 6B collapsed, and Malculm ran toward the bus, hopping on just as it started to leave. The self-driving AI didn't even slow, just gathered speed until it moved at a decent pace along with city traffic.

It was the No. 32 bus, heading straight for the city center. The next stop was Fountain Plaza. Good. A subway station was beneath the plaza, with three intersecting lines. He kicked off both shoes and balled up his socks, putting them in his shoes, then tucked his footwear underneath one of the seats.

At the next stop, Malculm pushed through the people and headed for the subway. As he descended the stairs, he froze as he spied another agent on the sidewalk mouthing something. He looked toward where Malculm stood, then toward the bus. Malculm steadied himself and walked on, unhurried, unperturbed, just another commuter in the crowd. Just another shoeless, sockless commuter. Malculm willed the agent not to look down, not to notice the one person on Engine evidently willing to expose their bare feet to the industrial grime that covered every public surface. The agent glanced back at the subway entrance, his eyes passing over Malculm, then ran after the bus, hand on his earpiece.

Once inside the subway, Malculm scanned his transit card, wincing as he did so, realizing that would tip off the agents. They would be here soon. He ran to the nearest train and hopped on, working quickly to unbutton his shirt as a child stared at him, her upper lip curled in disapproval.

Malculm threw his shirt on the floor as the train slowed to the next stop. The child's mother tried to give it to him, but Malculm waved her off, shirtless, telling her to keep it.

Once out of the station, Malculm jumped into the nearest autocab.

"Where would you like to go?" the AI said.

"Take me in a big circle," Malculm said.

"Closest match: the Circle Plaza, midtown."

"No, just drive in a circle."

"Please use clearer instructions."

Malculm sighed, checking for any sign of the agents. "Just take your next four right turns!"

"Acknowledged."

The car started forward in a lurch. Malculm scanned outside both windows, keeping his bare shoulder low and watching for any sign of his pursuers. He loosened his belt and pulled off his pants.

"Sir, please remain clothed."

Malculm grunted. His clothes were I/EI issue, and he couldn't trust them now. "I'll pay a hundred more."

"Acknowledged. Property and security fee is accepted."

Malculm pulled his underwear off next, and flung those out the window.

"Okay," Malculm said. "Please change course and take me—"

"Where would you like to go?" the AI said.

"As I was saying, please take me to the bakery on Felstar Street."

"Oodles of Caboodles Bakery. Acknowledged."

The car lurched off again, and Malculm watched out the window, his skin prickling. It was unlikely they had installed subdermal trackers, but not impossible. This proxy had been sitting on Engine for years, after all, and they would've known he'd be sent here after Geçiş. If this body had been chipped, they would know where he went as soon as the cab stopped. Malculm used breathing exercises he had learned in training—deep in, hold for four, deep release—but his hands shook.

"Are you injured?" the AI said.

"No injury."

"I am glad. We have arrived. Property and security fee deducted. Please exit on your right."

Too many people were on the sidewalk, too many. Malculm had gone skinny-dipping once in his youth, but he had felt embarrassed the entire time. And that was with other nude people.

"Sir?"

"I'm going."

He decided to jump out as fast as possible, the book positioned over his crotch. A few gasps escaped the crowd, but no one moved toward him. He saw no agents. With a grimace, Malculm hurried inside the bakery.

The shop looked like something out of an old rustic film, with no AI, flour-dusted wooden cutting boards, and glass displays for all the freshly made treats. A wide-framed woman stood behind the counter, her face knotted with confusion. Malculm said nothing. He simply handed her the book. She took it and opened it. Malculm didn't know what was inside but remembered Dima's words. *If you ever need to fly, I have a ticket for you.* For all he knew, it was a literal ticket.

The woman stared at whatever it was, and Malculm grew anxious.

Could this be the wrong bakery? Or worse, had I/EI already discovered it? Was this baker one more of their agents?

The woman smiled. "Ready to go?"

———

The woman in the bakery led the man through a door in the back after flipping her "open" sign to "closed" and down a dark set of stairs. She took the man past looming bins of flour and sugar to a heavy oak door. The baker opened the door and ushered the hesitating man inside, but his sad, naked form still found a way to move, finally crossing into the room.

Years before, the baker discovered, quite by accident, that when she ate a certain concoction created originally by her assistant, she could send other consciousnesses through localities, but only if she consumed it in complete darkness. So, she closed the door behind the man and turned off the light. He yelped, no doubt scared, but the baker already had her hand in a tub to the side of the room, where she grabbed a fistful of fermenting dough and started chewing. The over-salty, too-runny dough caused her to wince, saliva rushing into her mouth, and with it came a tingle of energy building from her toes.

The man asked questions that the baker ignored, focusing instead on the energy. Once it reached her waist, it had become unstoppable, the point of no return reached. The feeling rolled through her and rushed away into her hands, which she brushed as lightly as possible down the man's arms.

Turning the lights back on, the baker waved at the man's body, which stood staring. His mouth was a straight line. She took one of his hands in hers and spat the dough into it. The body looked down, then at her, curious. She patted it on the arm, then guided it upstairs, its steps light, without urgency.

Once they were back upstairs, she told the man to go home, and he turned, but she reconsidered, asking him to wait. The man's body placidly obeyed while the baker entered her closet and returned with a pastel yellow and green sundress. One of her favorites, but worth losing for what she gained from the book: more than enough to bribe (or blackmail, depending on one's perspective) old Waltir in BSR for the rest of her days. She put the dress over him and pointed to the door. It hung loosely on his bony frame, but oversize had been the style a few years ago. No one would look twice at him. The body gave a single nod, turned, and headed for wherever home was.

The man would have another body knitted for him when he lands at the next locality, a place to house his thoughts and dreams and fears and wishes. A body which, once he arrives, will have always been there, will have lived its full complement of years, will have parents and siblings and friends who all will—immediately, retroactively, permanently— remember their lives with a man who, the moment before, had not existed. The one he left behind would go about its routine, doing the same mundane things the body did before the man was inside it. Perhaps the dress will be returned when the man comes back to the body.

9

The train out to Maynard took over an hour. Trystèsté usually spent this time sorting through the catalog of music her auto-curator had culled from the airwaves and new-release bulletins. An hour to relax, to catch up on songs that had passed her by while keeping her head down in Burel Hird's work. She dared to look forward to this trip and the return for its stupid, wonderful lack of catastrophe.

She'd switched the music off only ten minutes in, not because she wasn't enjoying the sludge-punk synth that tumbled into her ears like a slow-motion circus troupe, but because she couldn't get Priema's words out of her head. Her little allegory. Wait for the earthquake.

Had she been so calculating back in the Academy, so attuned to the arithmetic of human lives and value? Much of her remained familiar from those days when competency assessments and morality tests were the most important things they could possibly imagine. She still liked her riddles, the story-lessons she was so fond of collecting and reciting whenever a favorable convergence of opportunity and circumstance occurred. She led you to her thinking sideways, waltzing you there so that you never saw her point coming until you'd already agreed with its principle. Priema had always navigated the political theater much better than Trystèsté.

She seemed more ambitious now. Ambitious wasn't quite the right word, but it was close enough for Trystèsté's thoughts to move forward. Trystèsté had no ambitions of her own, not really. Not anymore. She did when she was younger, vying for top spots in the August Academy—which meant second, behind Priema—fighting for every ounce of respect her young self could wrest from their instructors. If her compatriots thought she was fiery now . . .

And now there was an increase in transmundial tension. Of Tala and Withered Stem. Not a combination she would've expected, and not one that sat well. She still couldn't see why the Council voted her down. How could they miss the threat? It wasn't just those two getting cozy. Other travel-capable organizations lurked within the transmundi, and if they joined with Withered Stem and Of Tala, Burel Hird's power wouldn't be enough to save them. Unlikely, perhaps, but none of their models had predicted Geçiş, and if such a union did come to pass, any action they could undertake would be little more than failure mitigation. She sighed. Priema's earthquake better come soon.

The town of Maynard didn't have much. As the train slowed, the golden blur of prairie gave way to a few dilapidated farmhouses and then, very quickly, the cluster of low-slung buildings that was downtown. Barely longer than the train itself, Maynard was three blocks by three blocks, a time capsule from the 85th Turn—quaint or depressing, depending on one's perspective. Trystèsté gathered her things as the train stopped and walked to the middle car—the station was only big enough for a single platform. Few others were disembarking.

The scent of magnolia greeted Trystèsté as she stepped from the train, nostalgic and ominous; the smell told her she was home.

She registered with one of the community automobiles parked by the tracks, scanning her ID and settling into the driver's seat when the vehicle had unlocked. Opportunities to drive in the city were rare, and she relished these moments. They also provided an excellent chance to see exactly how little changed between her visits. The town replacing the stop sign with a traffic circle at Fork Creek and Vinyard seemed to be the only thing, an addition that almost certainly had produced gnashing of teeth and bitter complaints at the Traffic Safety Council's planning meeting. Trystèsté could hardly blame the Maynardians. Familiarity usually comforted her, as well, but as she reached the intersection, all she had were jumbled thoughts and a pearl of dread in her stomach.

She knew her childhood friend Glace still lived nearby, one of those few old relationships whose power hadn't been dimmed by Trystèsté's time away at the Academy. Trystèsté could still remember their arguments together, slurping milkshakes in the summer heat, Glace railing against gendered pronouns as individualist exaltation and unjustifiable deviations from Burel Hird principles as established by Dhalgrim Dhalgrim ninety turns ago. And Trystèsté, back on a break, proclaiming the value of allowing the People productive opportunities to express themselves.

She thought about a quick detour. She wouldn't go, though—she knew it as soon as the thought occurred. Too much time had passed. The awkwardness of a visit with her parents would be more than enough.

A left onto Vinyard took her away from Maynard's downtown stretch and out into open fields on either side, fields that once were populated with crops and people tending them. Most farmers had been moved closer to the city in the 85th Turn, around the time Maynard had been frozen in time, where vertical ranges supplied more food with less water and could be transported with less pollution. It was the correct decision, objectively, but Trystèsté still missed the smell of fresh-cut plants. Now, the fields all grew wild. Except for those tended by a few holdouts. Like her mother and father.

She turned into the gravel driveway, one her father insisted be left unpaved, as gravel deterred rabbits and moles—so he claimed. Even after Trystèsté showed him article after article debunking that particular folk myth, her father remained unswayed and even ordered more gravel, widening the drive.

Trystèsté's mother tended the herbs out front, her hair tied up with a bandanna. She ripped unwanted vegetation in quick jerks and tossed it beside the box garden. She didn't stop even as Trystèsté pulled into the driveway. When her mother was set on something, she didn't allow distractions until it was finished.

Finally, her mother stood and turned. Sweat beaded her forehead, and she pulled one of her gloves off and wiped it with the back of her hand. "Oh. You're here. It's been a while."

"It's only been a few months. It's been busy," Trystèsté said.

Her mother nodded. "Our Trystèsté. Ever ready to serve the People." "Yeah, well."

"Your father's inside, cooking. He started last night, so however it is, tell him you love it."

"I'm sure it'll be delicious."

"Good. So tell him that." She slid the glove back on and knelt once more, leaning forward to peer beneath a rosemary bush, her face hidden from Trystèsté's gaze.

At first, her trips home had been the result of guilt, messages from her father hounding her about when she might come back. She'd come to enjoy the visits, though, and made the trek every other month, not only because she liked the decompression time the train ride provided but because she still felt a connection to Maynard—not just to her parents, strained though that sometimes was, but the place and the memories. Aside from connecting with the past, she was able to be someone her life rarely allowed for, as well. Her test scores had earned her admission to the Academy at age five, just as her older siblings' scores had before her. But it was only Trystèsté who sat in the Chamber. In Maynard, though, she didn't have to be a vice-councilor, or committee chair for Asset Development and Cultivation, or the occupant of the Jason seat. In Maynard she was just Trystèsté, Trys, or sometimes simply Try.

"How's Priema?" a voice called from behind her. Her father stood on the porch, wearing the same simple clothes he'd worn since her youth: a monochromatic T-shirt with beaten jeans.

Trystèsté forced a laugh. "She's fine, Dad."

Her father waved her inside. "Come on, I'm making some lunch."

Memories of her father were clearer, more crystalized. While her mother spent long hours outside, her father tended to the inside, fixing broken toilets, mending walls, cooking meals, sweeping. Always in motion. Always present.

She followed her father toward the kitchen, the floor creaking in expected ways, the same decorations up in the hallway—pictures of her sister and three brothers, three porcelain cats on a table, each waving its left paw—the artificial flowers hanging from a basket above the threshold to the kitchen. They were enduring talismans that loomed monumentally in her earliest memories, before she'd even left for the Academy, knickknacks somehow both trivial and mythic. There were new photographs—Hÿdorå on the wheels of a tractor, Gryçan peering out from within a cornfield—but the cats, the faded petals, the twist of the cane in the wicker basket that reminded her of crossed fingers; these were unchanged.

"The soup's almost done," her father said.

"What's in it?" Trystèsté said.

"Carrots, celery, lentils. Some tomato. Cilantro. Parsley. Salt."

"Sounds good."

Her father sighed. "That's a load off."

"It's okay, you couldn't have known that I love celery now. Ever since I had the celery relish at Bosco's."

"Right." He grunted and looked out the window. "How could I have known."

She cleared her throat. "How are Óphillôm and Brènjùmyn?"

"Good. Good. Well, I can only guess about Brènjùmyn. He hasn't been home in almost a year. But the SCANCs moved him to some senior position within Supply and Distribution over on one of those worlds of theirs, so I guess he's doing okay."

"That's not funny, Dad."

Her father threw up his hands. "Sorry, I forgot I had one of our top SCANC boosters in my kitchen."

Trystèsté rolled her eyes. "Okay, okay." She reached into her bag and removed two packages. "Where are Hÿdorå and Gryçan? I brought them something."

Her father's jaw worked, and she could almost hear his teeth grinding. "Gryçan's in the playroom. The Subcommittee for Child Abduction and Neural Control took Hÿdorå to the Academy in the spring."

"Really? I thought her testing went poorly."

"It did. Looked like she wouldn't qualify. I guess they loved her qualitative day, though. So they took her as a late entry."

"Well—that's exciting, Dad. I should make a trip down to Gryxport to congratulate her."

Her father stared at the table. "That's a good idea. She'd love to see you." He got up and went to the pot simmering on the stove. Rich, pungent smells filled the room as he set the lid to the side and ladled soup into two bowls. Twin wisps of steam curled up from the bowl, conjuring more old memories, long past meals shared with her father and brother and sister and mother. Longing, like an ache, pricked the skin of her neck, its heat trailing down to the small of her back, and she closed her eyes. "Gryçan?" her father called. "You hungry?"

From the adjoining room came Gryçan's response: "No. Thank you, though."

Trystèsté stood and walked to the doorway. Gryçan lay on the rug in the den, playing with disconcertingly familiar colored blocks.

"Were those mine?" she asked her father.

He scratched his head. "Uh, yes. I think so." He handed her a bowl, and she returned to the table.

Blowing on the soup would do little, she knew, but she did it anyway. It was part of the process. Of the performance. She ate a spoonful, scalding the roof of her mouth. As she always did. She would regret it later, as she always did, but the soup was best this way. Why deny herself the pleasure?

"How have you been?" her father said. "Anything new with you or Priema?"

"Not much that I can share. Still eating. Still drinking. Still ensuring prosperity and security across nine thousand worlds."

"And are you still quilting? Painting?"

Trystèsté shook her head. She thought again of what it was that begged to replace her tempered ambition. Her father seemed to have opinions. "Not lately, not enough time."

"You should make time."

"I can't lengthen the days, Dad."

"Sure, but you can maybe make some room."

Trystèsté sighed. "Dad, this isn't a . . . a day job. It's unending. Everything comes second. It has to. For all our sakes."

"I just wish you had some space in your life for something that wasn't 'the Council.'" He made his eyes wide and wiggled his fingers, mocking. "You love art."

"I did," Trystèsté said. "A while ago."

"You're saying you don't want to paint anymore?"

"Not really. I don't—"

"—have time. Right."

She slipped her spoon into his bowl and stole a spoonful. He rolled his eyes but smiled and plundered a spoonful of his own from her bowl. Behind them, the screen door creaked, and her mother appeared in the doorway. Smudges of dirt marked her cheeks, and a sprout of hair had escaped the bandanna and hung over her forehead. She bent down to kiss Trystèsté's father and tousled Trystèsté's hair, then filled a glass at the sink, downing it in two gulps. Before she even finished ripping a hunk of bread from the loaf, she said, "Well, back to work," and, after dipping the hunk once in the soup, she proved as good as her word. Quiet rushed into the space where she had been, the only sound Gryçan and the blocks in the other room. Her mother had always been like that, a presence that found its way inside only a handful of times during the day. When Trystèsté was five, every night they watched historical dramas on the EN. Back then, Trystèsté had no use for the programs' melodrama or their patriotism, much less her parents' running commentary on both, but the warmth of her parents on either side of her kept her on the couch as she sewed, all the way until it was time for bed.

"How're things here?" Trystèsté asked once her mother left. "How's the farm?" If her mother had been there, she'd say the same thing she always did: that plants grew and got pulled, so who can complain? But her father could manage more nuance—and honesty.

"Better than last year. Eggplants had a good yield. We brought enough to market to hit the three-year SGT, so we're set for a little while. Could you see about lowering it, though? I feel like one really bad year, and we're screwed."

"I have absolutely no control of social good numbers, Dad. If you want to see them changed, talk to the Independent and Hobby Farmers Council. Sit with the local subcommittee."

"I already have a seat name, kiddo."

"You haven't been I/EI since I was a kid."

"And thank goodness for that. We really could use more land to expand our soybeans, though. Be a whole lot easier to hit that threshold with another three parcels to work with. We put in a bid for a plot, but we're not sure if it's—too fast, Gryçan!" Her father pushed back from the table. "Excuse me."

He marched over to Gryçan, who looked up, frowning. Her father squatted down next to the boy, patting his back. Trystèsté grabbed the gift she brought him and joined her father in the den.

"You know how important this is," her father said.

"I know," Gryçan said. "It's hard."

"Hey, kiddo," Trystèsté said. "Is everything all right?"

Trystèsté glanced at her father. He studiously avoided her gaze.

"You know what, buddy?" her father said. "How about we take a break? Let's visit with your sister, okay?"

"Okay!"

As Gryçan put the blocks away, Trystèsté opened the box and pulled out the toy inside. It was one of the new action figures with interchangeable parts, complete with ten alternate heads, arms, torsos, and legs. "I got this for you."

"Thank you! It's great." He began to open it, then stopped. "I should wait, though." His face was solemn, and he looked up at Trystèsté. "I can't play with this until after the tests."

"Tests? What—" She squatted and picked up one of the colored blocks. Recognition came slowly as she turned it over in her hands. They were used in one of the Academy Aptitude Assessments. She remembered it vaguely but well enough to know Gryçan had failed; every arrangement was wrong. But her father hadn't said, "Wrong column." He said, "Too fast."

"Is he failing these on purpose?" Trystèsté said. Something in her clenched, and her palms were abruptly damp.

"Dad," Gryçan said.

Her father patted him on the back. "It's okay. Trys, can we take this into the kitchen?"

Trystèsté stood, her jaw clenched so hard she could hear a thin, high note in her ears. Far below her, the floor creaked with each step she took, vertigo making her totter as she went. Her father turned to face her, leaning against the sink, and Trystèsté sat down at the table. They stared at each other. "What do you think you're doing?" she said, breaking the silence.

Her father shook his head. "Saving my son."

"Oh, stop. Every child must be evaluated for service."

"He will be. But if there is any goodness left in this world, he'll fail."

"That's not for you to decide. You could be imprisoned for this. You understand that, right? And then he'd be taken anyway."

Her father sniffed. "Of course I know that. But who knew your mother and I had a DNA recipe perfect for little bureaucrats? Most families give one or two children to Burel Hird. Some three. But five? Why do they need five of my kids?"

"Because we make Burel Hird better. Because the People need us. Because all the prosperity and plenty and safety and justice that we get to enjoy are a direct result of the Academy's work. You know what life is like outside Burel Hird. Fear. Hatred. War. Deprivation. We have none of that. Your comfortable, boring life, this little farm, that's all owed to what we've built. And the kids that go through the Academy. Kids like Gryçan and Hÿdorå. Kids like me. I can't believe you'd be so selfish that—"

"You can't ask me to pay this price again. It's not . . . It's not right. I've given them four kids, four wonderful people that I was honored to know until they passed those damn tests. What were you, five and a half? I was just getting to know who you were, and they took you from me.

We saw you occasionally when they let us. Maybe once a month? But so much happens in the span of a month. You can't cram that into a day."

"Dad . . . I was never yours to hold on to."

"Trys—"

"I am the People's. We all are. All of us."

"And now that horseshit . . ."

"Dad!"

"You can believe it if you want! You can believe anything at all. I just wanted your beliefs to be your own."

"They are."

"Come on, Trys. You act like I don't know what the Academy is, like I didn't get the same education you did. I'm not sure I made a choice of my own at all until I met your mother."

"Well, I have. I'm doing what I want to do, the only thing I can imagine myself doing."

"I don't doubt it—because they worked very hard to control what you could imagine." Her father ran a hand along his cheek. "You had no choice at all."

Trystèsté felt a tear fall from her eye. "Dad, I make the lives of trillions of people, *trillions*, better. I'm honored to be a part of that."

Her father turned from her, put his hands on the sink, and hung his head. When he spoke, his voice was unsteady. "We should've gotten to know you. We never had that chance. Priema knows you better than I do."

"Is that why you always ask about her first?"

The silverware jumped in the drawers as her father pounded the counter with his fists, then spun to face Trystèsté. "Why I always ask about her? Trys, for years, you'd visit, and the first words out of my mouth were, 'How have you been?' or 'What have you been doing out there?' And when you were six or seven, you'd have something to say. Not much, but something. Before too long, those somethings turned into a grunt or a shrug, and by the time you were eight, you wouldn't talk about much other than the weather and how great Burel Hird was."

"Dad, I—"

"And then one visit when you're ten, you tell me that you hate some-one called Priema. And it was like the floodgates opened. The next time back, she was your best friend and you were going to name your firstborn after her. The next time you love her but she's your biggest competi-tion, and you don't know how to reconcile those two things. Trys, you wouldn't talk about anything else, and I certainly wasn't going to stop you." Her dad rubbed savagely at his cheeks with the heel of his palm.

"Why do I ask about her?" he said, his voice incredulous. "I ask about her because I've been asking about her since you were ten. Be-cause for the twelve fucking years the Academy stole from us, she was the only topic I could get three words out of you on. Because I don't know you well enough to ask about anything else."

Trystèsté turned to the window and saw clouds darkening over the field. "I've got to get going."

"You just got here. Why don't we at least take a walk around—"

"Dad."

He opened his mouth to speak but said nothing, then nodded. From outside came the sound of the tractor, its electric hum a thin, pure over-tone atop the cicadas as her mother headed out into the fields. After a moment, it was gone, and Trystèsté could hear Gryçan playing with the blocks again—practicing. She knew he would remember this day, would remember what she'd said, what their father had said. He would have been listening. He wouldn't forget.

Her father spoke. "Please don't say anything about . . . about Gryçan."

"I have to go."

"You'll come back in a few months? For the apples? I'll have pies waiting."

Trystèsté looked at her father, then past him. "If I have the time." He nodded again, and didn't follow as she walked from the kitchen.

In the hallway, Trystèsté paused. The sink ran behind her, her father washing up after the meal. Dishes and silverware clattered, suffering under his rough labor. She took a slow, shuddering breath and closed her eyes. When she opened them, she was looking at the photographs that lined the wall, crowding against each other, a tapestry of her family's history. In the center was the picture of Hÿdorå and the tractor. Trys-tèsté blinked and leaned closer. It wasn't Hÿdorå who sat on the tractor's wheels, though—it was Trystèsté. She was smiling and waving, her skin bright and brown in the summer sun. She had no memory of it, of the picture being taken or the photograph itself. How long had it hung there? How many years had she walked past it, not recognizing herself?

She shook her head and stepped back. She hadn't said goodbye to Gryçan. The den lay through the kitchen. Smells like incantations hung all around her, the soup, wood warmed by the summer's heat, the faint scent of her mother's sweat and deodorant, lingering, curled like a question mark. As she left, the screen door hung open for a moment, its spring voicing the slightest complaint, before it swung closed, slapping back into the jamb.

10

Duncan smoothed the front of his suit jacket as he passed a young aide in the hall, her heels clacking along the polished marble floor. The stone pillars of the upper chambers buttressed arches carved in a style popular during the 76th Turn: ivy and joined hands running the great width of the vaulted ceiling. Moonlight, soft and white, reached in from hundreds of windows and skylights, casting the terrace in a sepulchral glow.

Rounding the corner, Duncan reached the stairwell leading up to the roof, but paused before continuing, glancing behind him to see if anyone was around. He had pinged Yorek's home but there was no answer, so he checked his office. The suite was empty and so he looked all over the council house—the library and archives, the cafeteria, the laranette courts, the massage annex even, but Yorek was nowhere. That meant—

Duncan ascended the stairs and pushed the heavy door open. The nearest moon was full and it was bright out despite the hour, only a few stars visible, dim amid the blinking air traffic and the red lines of space drops. He walked along the gangway rimming the massive colmer-alloy roof, famous for its bronzing over the centuries. From afar, the coloring was seamless, but up there, one could see the segmented replacement sheets, even the engraved soldering dates, the oldest dating back to the

60th Turn. The People's Architectural and Sheet Metal Council provided regular upkeep, and their good work showed.

Duncan found Yorek on his cot, hidden on a maintenance platform in the shadow of a heating and air cabinet. He sat, saying nothing. Duncan remembered when he'd first learned of Yorek's secret. He had found the man's proxy up there on the roof staring at the sky. The thing had turned to look at Duncan with glassy eyes, the deep reservoir of Yorek's identity absent in that shell, and Duncan knew immediately. Of course, he did. Duncan and Yorek had been friends and colleagues for many years by then, and Duncan had met plenty of travelers, had seen their bodies going about their day without them, remnants of their personalities present, but you could tell when one was . . . empty. Too even-tempered. Unflappably content.

Without either of them acknowledging it, Duncan had taken over the work of bribing the on-duty tracker from the Council for Border Security and Regulation in his sector, ensuring that the record of a traveler's departure—and arrival—was scrubbed from the ledger. They'd never spoken of it, and Duncan had never inquired as to what it was Yorek had exchanged to originally purchase the indulgence. Over the years, it had cost Duncan: thirteen letters of commendation to border security, six letters of endorsement to the National Housing Committee, three personal visits to Prime parish schools, seven letters of support in vocation transfer applications, and one awkward conversation with a very confused administrator of the Council for Effective, Reliable, and Courteous Metropolitan Travel about a change in bus routes. The current tracker, Ioseun, was a man Duncan's age with whom Duncan had a solid rapport. He was satisfied with occasional cash contributions, which perhaps explained the rapport.

Yorek had pushed the Council once for expanded traveling rights for councilors, but he'd been outvoted. It was a risky thing, considering.

He'd always been reckless.

Some years ago, when Yorek left this universe from his office, Duncan had been forced to entrap his proxy there. It had banged and begged from behind the linwood door, but Duncan wouldn't allow it out.

Eventually, Duncan had been forced to use his own power—properly registered with the Committee for Appropriate and Reliable Transmundi Traversal, but ostensibly, never to be activated—to summon Yorek back. A young man had pinged from the suite entrance to see about the commotion, and Duncan had told him that the councilor enjoyed violent holo-streams but that he was getting older. The volume was becoming a problem. The young man laughed at the mundanity and left.

It wasn't so much Yorek's traveling itself that unsettled Duncan, though he did agree with policies restricting councilor travel. Nor, in truth, was it that Duncan had to do the bribing to keep the secret safe. More often than not, leadership meant a certain degree of moral compromise, and Duncan had done the grubby work of subordinating his own beliefs to what was good for the People more than once. No, it was the corruption *itself* that rankled—that it was even possible. It was disheartening to know that amid the plenty of Burel Hird, there were some who would always want more, whatever that meant. However much the Council worked to ensure equality, however ingeniously devised the policies Burel Hird bureaucrats instituted, there would always be a weakness their systems couldn't protect against: human frailty. And Duncan contributed to that frailty. Cultivated it. Used it. None of it sat well with him.

Perhaps more distressingly, it meant that infiltration was possible. If the borders of Prime could be made porous, then certainly more distant localities would be even more vulnerable. Which meant the People were vulnerable. And, of course, he was hardly in a position to crack down on abuses in the various councils overseeing border security and transmundial travel or push the Subcommittee for Equity, Rectitude, and Compliance for more vigorous oversight. Which meant, again, that Duncan was contributing to the People's vulnerability—a thought that made him physically ill.

However much trouble Yorek could be, though, he was a great man as well—one Duncan had loved for the better part of his life. It was nothing romantic. Duncan's husband, Ecklan, had never had cause to be jealous, though the relationship did cause marital strain in the early years. It wasn't that Duncan prioritized Yorek over Ecklan, but Yorek needed him a great deal more. Duncan filled in so many of his gaps. Duncan always caught what Yorek would miss in the Council chambers. And Duncan supposed the reverse was true. Yorek gave him strength and confidence that he might have lacked in his absence. They worked well together. A perfect union of intellects, Yorek called them, whenever he felt theatrical.

Duncan had just about had enough and was preparing to summon Yorek back when Yorek's body suddenly shot up from the cot, his feet swinging down to the ground. The soles of his wing tips raked on the old cement slab.

"Where are you back from this time?" Duncan said.

Yorek turned, his face awash with relief. And it was him, Duncan could tell. "Where were you?"

Yorek stood up from the cot and folded his blanket, not looking at Duncan. "Would you believe I was a knight in shining armor?"

Duncan snorted.

"A real spears and spells world. I've never really seen one like it. I mean, there was that colony on the rim of the Nightfar Nebula—the crystalline overlord, remember? Shit, that was a weird one."

"Nothing about your traveling makes any sense. You should've ended up in Holon this time; that's the next proximate locality right now."

Yorek pushed his fingers through his gray hair, short and well oiled. "Got me. All I know is that I tend to find myself in positions of power when I travel. Makes sense, I suppose. I've been at this for long enough, after all."

"And in all that time, you'd think you would have learned that—"

"Let's not do this, Duncan." Yorek picked up his cot and pushed the front legs down into their housing.

"You're the one doing this. More and more, it seems." Duncan placed his hand on his forehead. "Honestly, I don't understand it. Councilors cannot travel. Must not."

Yorek stepped closer to Duncan, towering over him in the night. "Oh, I've got it! Just leave me a note to keep in my pocket from now on. It'll read, 'Councilors must not travel!'" He returned his attention to the cot, putting away its rear legs. "You'll be duly noted in perpetuity."

"You're so—"

"Careless, I know." He slid his cot on its side behind the cabinet. "And again, duly noted."

Duncan stood up, wiping dust from the seat of his slacks. "Is it the stress? Is there something I'm missing? You didn't have to serve your full term, Yorek. I'd have gladly stepped up."

Yorek buttoned his suit jacket, rubbing his hands together from the cold. "I do what is best for the People. Always."

Duncan stepped in front of his old friend, his mentor, gripping his shoulders. "Then why the traveling, Yorek? Why keep putting yourself at risk?"

"Why do people drink or gamble?" Yorek said.

"Come on."

Yorek pulled free of Duncan's grasp, stepping around him to gaze out on the city, the wilds hardly visible in the distance. "No. It's not even that. It's who I am." Yorek's silhouette was wide and tall. A breeze blew around him, mussing his hair a little. "Why should I be forbidden from doing all that I am able? Even if I were to retire and go live somewhere out there, alone in a cabin, I'm still not allowed to just be what I am. A traveler."

Duncan joined Yorek near the edge of the roof. "The Council must be constant, present. And travel must be regulated. You know this."

"Not every fucking second of it, Duncan. I'm given family and friend time. I'm allowed a balance, aren't I? The People can't control everything."

Duncan said nothing, tired of the old arguments.

"When I travel," Yorek said, "even if only for a moment, I can feel the wind of worlds rushing by like cold water on my face. It's plunging into an icy river after too much wine, that proof of life that keeps me going. I would die without it."

"A little melodramatic, don't you think?"

"I am who I am."

Duncan took a deep breath and exhaled slowly. "Trystèsté's not wrong, you know? Nor is she alone."

Yorek nodded. "The worlds they're inheriting, the growing societies—it's all so different from when we were coming up. We're bumping into fucking Of Talas out there now, for People's sake. Just by chance!" He shook his head. "Change is on its way whether we like it or not."

"So why didn't you back her?"

Yorek didn't answer, just looked out again at the horizon. Duncan did too. The city lights were pink and bright white rings, the green glow from the streets and silver towers, thousands of them in the lower district, the rolling skybridge with its purple traffic lamps, and always the undercarriage of the spaceport to the north, hovering from orbit and sending red trails of light down to the surface. They flickered and flared and vanished in threads.

"I don't know," Yorek said at last. "Maybe she's wrong. Maybe all of this is a good thing. Maybe we should embrace change, for once, open ourselves up." He drew in a deep gulp of air and exhaled, his breath smoking away from him. "I've seen so many worlds, so much fluctuation. Maybe it's time for us to stop all this planning. To just wait and see."

"Wait and see?"

"I know. Deviant, right?"

Duncan laughed.

"And the Geçiş op was a shit show," Yorek said.

"It was."

"She has to take her lumps for that."

"She does."

Yorek stretched his shoulders back, lifting his chin to the breeze. "I suspect Priema's with Trystèsté, whatever she says in the room."

"No," Duncan said. "She's got much more on her plate. I doubt hiring mercenaries is a higher priority than Silnur Seven. Priema's overseeing Echtonian scopes in that locality that can just begin to see into neighboring worlds when the right conditions are met. So she says."

"I remember. They'll never work."

"Of course not. But if they can shift just a little of that work from humans at CARTT to machines . . ."

Yorek nodded.

"Priema wants Burel Hird supremacy," Duncan said, "in a way that Trystèsté may not have yet fully reached. I find it hard to believe her pushback is calculated."

"I'm rarely wrong about these things." Yorek turned from the edge of the roof and began walking back to the stairwell. "Come," he said. "I'm hungry."

"I haven't slept yet," Duncan said.

"You wouldn't force me to eat alone."

———

They moved into the hallway, which was empty, though footsteps could be heard from the floor below, echoing out into the cavernous core of the building. Yorek and Duncan made their way to the cafeteria, where the night crew prepared steaming bowls of anise soup, the fragrant basil filling Duncan's nose, ram tripe pooling fat on the surface of the broth, and green onions perfuming the air. "So good," he said hungrily, even though he'd eaten only two hours before.

"Good? It's fucking great! No better travel food. I'm starting to suspect this body starves in my absence."

Duncan slurped several noodles then sipped broth from the rim of his bowl, reveling in the scent of ginger, cardamom, and cloves. "I assume you've not seen tomorrow's agenda?"

"No." Yorek talked around a hunk of meat.

"The conflict on Noll, in locality 8XE9-VW."

"Remind me."

Duncan leaned back in his chair. "The one with the blue-skinned queen," he said, sighing.

"Ah, yes. What of it?"

"Melyssa is going to push to intervene."

"We know this?"

"We're confident of it. She hasn't exactly made a secret of her intentions, and Chel doesn't think it's a smoke screen."

Yorek sucked up a noodle, broth slapping into his beard. "Why now? We had no reason to interfere before."

"Firmāre."

Yorek raised an eyebrow and sat back in his chair. "No. Doing what, why? Out in the open?"

"I don't know. But it looks like a full challenge."

"They don't want to start a transmundial war, Duncan. What's the play?"

"I'm not sure. We have to presume they see some way to profit, but . . . there's really not a lot there. We must be missing something. And with Trystèsté looking to reach out to Firmāre—"

"Priema too, trust me on that. People help me, it'll be a long day. And one that will end with even more bloodshed if we're not careful."

Duncan yawned and set his napkin on the table. "Whatever we think about societies like Withered Stem or Arcalumis, they at least have beliefs. And limits. If Firmāre sees some advantage in out-and-out opposition, who knows what manner of havoc they might wreak. Trystèsté knows it, Priema too. A working relationship, even a radically constrained one, might not be a bad solution."

"It's a question of principle, Duncan. I've never been an ends-justify-the-means man, you know that."

"No. But a hostile Firmāre wielding lunatic Of Talas is a dangerous enemy. And should Withered Stem ever feel the need to approach them, ally with them first—our morals and our righteousness may well be lost to history."

Yorek smiled but it was halfhearted, Duncan knew. "Now who's being melodramatic?"

Duncan shrugged.

"So you think we should do what?" Yorek asked. "Reach out over this local coup to start a dialogue?"

"Maybe."

"Or should we oppose it outright, beat them into an accord where we dictate terms—bridle Firmāre and Of Talas both, teach them the People's wisdom?"

"There'll be votes for both. Count on it," Duncan said.

"And what if we go hands-off altogether? Let things play out? How many votes for that?"

Duncan had no answers, not yet. They would need the deliberations, though there could be no real consensus. Duncan was sure that Yorek would argue against the move to intervene because it's what his nature demanded. Burel Hird must expand, everyone knew, but that directive came with rules. Precepts. If Firmāre wanted to play the upstart, then so be it. The ideals of Burel Hird would prevail and shepherd the People into the future, while Firmāre would ultimately fall, replaced by some other upstart. And maybe they would prove more amenable.

"I'm going to head over to the office in a bit," Yorek said. "Play catch-up on all of this. You go home, get some rest." He reached across the table to slap Duncan's shoulder. "I'll get these dishes. And please apologize to Ecklan for me."

"He's used to it by now," Duncan said. "But, yes, I'll do that." He made no move to go, however.

"What?" Yorek said.

"There's still the other thing . . ."

"What other . . . ?"

Duncan looked at Yorek, unblinking.

Yorek scoffed. "Oh, fuck off."

"Yorek."

"You're done when I say you're done!"

"I'm done forty-six days after my fiftieth birthday."

"It's absurd."

"It's the law. You need to pick a new vice-councilor—your forty-six days are almost up. Have you looked at the prospectus I sent over? There are some interesting candidates in there."

"It's an antiquated by-law and very nearly superstition. Frankly, I'd go so far as to call it anti-Burel Hird."

"Derrin Venksa's academy scores are spectacular, and—"

"Absolutely not. Kid's a pushover. Can smell it a mile away."

Duncan smiled. "Well, I'm glad you read it, at least."

Yorek crossed his arms and said nothing.

"I'm sure the People would appreciate it if we could skip the sulking, Yorek. We both know you'll make a choice, and a good one because we both know you respect the rules Dhalgrim laid down. So choose my replacement, and let's dispense with the melodrama, shall we?" He stood up from his chair and turned away, hiding some sudden emotion. He would be replaced. Retired. How did *he* feel about that?

Duncan pushed the thought away. "See you in the morning," he said, walking out of the cafeteria. It was a suitably dramatic exit, but Duncan nevertheless felt distantly forlorn. For all his brave talk, he could not imagine a world in which he did not see Yorek in the morning or eat midnight soup in the Council cafeteria.

II

Malculm arrived at a stop sign in the "East Wastes," the name his wife had given to this part of the sprawling suburbs of Iowa District 5.

Two things from the last time he'd been in this body were new. Iowa now had five suburban districts. And he had a wife. And, yes—he was abruptly remembering—he'd promised to be home by six, in time for the dinner she was making. It was five 'til. He swore to himself, his proxy's frustration simmering within him, and drove through the intersection, headed home. He'd hit traffic entering District 3, adding thirty minutes to what would've been a ten-minute drive on the late Freeway 17. Would've—if it hadn't been demolished to build more residential homes with minimum setback requirements and mandatory off-street parking.

He was angry about this added drive time, or, more accurately, his proxy was. His proxy, who was called Milton—was just the sort of man to get upset at obstacles to his commute. Malculm hooked a finger over the knot of his half-Windsor and yanked, then threw the tie on the passenger seat of his SUV. It was too much car for a married couple without children, but Jil hadn't given up hope on having a daughter. It was too much car for any human, but then, Milton was a certain type of man, and Jil was a certain type of woman, and this was a certain type of locality. Malculm glanced over at the tie sitting in the passenger seat. Taupe with mauve polka dots. Taupe. Mauve. The words leaped to him unbidden.

"Jesus," Malculm said. This world was going to eat his brain if he wasn't careful. Trivialities writhed in his head like a sack of ferrets set ablaze. So, too, evidently, did folksy aphorisms. Milton couldn't keep his mind empty or his thoughts still, which meant neither could Malculm. Sometimes it was like this. Traveling meant meshing with a proxy, and there was no way to know how comfortable that fit would be until it was happening. In the field, they called it either "going down easy" or "the back end of a shovel." Milton was the latter.

Malculm quieted his mind, pushed his other self to the periphery, and continued the slow crawl home.

In this locality, the United States of America (it wasn't always called by this name, though there was a nation like it in most central cluster localities) had made itself fat on its eponymous dream. White picket fences crowded out cities, nature reserves, and highways. Suburbs sat along the shoreline and extended into the bay on stilts stretching out for miles. Office jobs became remote jobs if you were lucky, or you worked for yourself and employed people who'd show up to your house to work. More often, though, you were the employee, your boss instructing you to take your shoes off when entering their home. The boss's kitchen was your office kitchen; your food from your house was labeled in your boss's fridge.

As a result, corporations no longer defaulted to skyscrapers. Instead, a family could turn their house into a franchise extension of Doobl or Nile River and transform half their square footage into office space. In New Dakota, entire neighborhoods had been convinced to franchise by Gryftr, trees cleared and homes expanded to setback limits. Driving through those neighborhoods was like passing through an eldritch primary color nether realm: chitinous vinyl siding sprouting above double-hung windows, gable roofs ominously steepled, and crew-cut lawns aligned in scaly, fertilized patchworks. The great, bulging centipede of the suburbs coiled across the land, split-levels upon bungalows upon craftsmen, stretching over the horizon and off into infinity. In those places, the lack of trees was causing dust storms.

None of it made sense, of course. The Simulacrum had done its work here and turned this locality into someone's version of a dystopian nightmare. The citizenry's demand for single family homes had made everything else impractical, travel especially. It was easier to buy a home down the street from your parents than to attempt a cross-country trip during the holiday season.

Milton/Malculm's wife had her own small business and her own employees. She was the successful one in their marriage, able to clock out by three because her assistants finished out the day replying to lawn care requests. If he was lucky, he was home by six. He was rarely lucky.

Malculm arrived at his little island in tract housing hell at 7:15.

Jil came out and stood in the open doorway.

"Traffic," Malculm said, playing his part. "Slow as molasses in January." He winced. Jil didn't notice.

"The food is cold."

"I'll have to grab a sandwich anyway," he said, waiting for her exasperation to pass then deploying the excuse he'd practiced in the last five minutes before arriving.

His sister, Ulna, had gotten drunk and crashed into someone's mailbox again, which carried a fine and a night in Foley's Garage and Jail if the bail wasn't met. Malculm was bail.

"Shit," she said. "Just stop by Marigold's drive-through on your way out of the cul-de-sac, then. I'll pack up the food. Can you take it for lunch tomorrow? The fridge is already full and Madge is bringing Jell-O salad for Garry's birthday."

"Of course."

"And that reminds me, if you're going to sit up all night with your stamp collection, could you put it away before morning? Stanley almost used your 1899 postcard as a coaster."

"Okay."

"The franked one, Milton. Chinese Imperial Post. Two cent carmine."

Malculm nodded again, foot tapping. Jil looked at it pointedly. With great effort, Malculm stilled his foot.

"Fine then, go."

Malculm waited for the front door to close behind Jil before he sprinted to the shed in the backyard, where Milton had stashed several yards of packing rope. And a can of gasoline. And some gardening shears. All of which could be employed for a variety of purposes. Turned out his proxy was good for something beyond inexplicable idioms, after all.

Hopefully he wouldn't have to use any of it, but considering his luck so far, it was better to be prepared.

Malculm stuffed everything into his gym duffel and placed it up front for easy reach. He got back into his car and continued to District 4, his real destination. Houses slid past as he drove, houses beyond counting, houses with driveways and mailboxes and lawns and smooth, unbroken sidewalks. He kept to the speed limit and rolled the window down, the summer air warm, ripe with the smell of grass clippings. And all of it was lit by the diffuse, sodium orange of streetlights, casting the entirety of Iowa and the midcoast region beyond in its unearthly glow.

Malculm arrived at Padre's house at 8:30. It was a Foursquare, with an addition in the rear running all the way to the property line. Every light in the house was on, and Malculm hoped that was just Padre's aversion to darkness at work and not an indication of the house's occupancy. He rang the doorbell.

Padre was distracted when he answered the door, looking back over his shoulder and yelling something to someone deep inside the house.

"About time you showed up. How much I—"

Padre only had a moment to register alarm before Malculm punched him in the face. There was another moment after when Padre stood there, stunned. Malculm caught him in a bear hug before he could fall and dragged him out of the house. It was a short walk to the SUV, but Padre's front light flooded the lawn. Fescue, Milton knew. And so Malculm did. Beautifully maintained. He shook the thought away. No one was around to see them, the houses along the street lit from within, curtains drawn. Malculm hoped they would stay that way.

It occurred to him that this was the first time in a while that he'd punched someone. True, he'd not shot at anyone in a while, either, not until the Geçiş Incident. But he'd actually shot people with far more regularity than he'd punched anyone. He had not been sure he'd be able to knock the man out, but his training held.

Malculm wrestled Padre into the back seat. He shut the door, got into the front, and pulled out of the driveway. Someone was standing in the doorway, a lanky man. He had a cup in his hand. He didn't yell but stood there backlit, his body in shadow. Malculm waved and smiled. The man rushed back into the house.

A patrol car or two would be dispatched, a simultaneous call to all the neighborhood watch in a fifty-mile radius. That was fine. Malculm wasn't going very far. I/EI had purchased a bungalow in the neighborhood and had tended to it as a safe house. They'd also built a drive-in garage on the property in the event that something like this happened and cover was needed.

Well, perhaps not this specific situation.

In under fifteen minutes, Malculm was pulling into the driveway just as Padre woke from his involuntary slumber. He hoped Padre would still be useful. "Hey," Malculm said, "you got the key to this place, right?"

"What?"

Evidently, Padre was still waking up. Malculm asked a different question. "There was a remote for the garage on the porch the last time I was here. You didn't move it, did you?"

"Jesus, my nose is bleeding."

Malculm really liked how the Christian-themed localities took their Lord's name in vain. "I'll take that as a maybe," he said. He turned to look at Padre as he was dragging himself up into a seated position. "I'm going to get the garage remote. Your head is likely still spinning so I'm going to trust that you won't do a silly thing like running off when I'm trying to get us inside safely. I'm not going to kill you or anything. But if you run—"

"The thought hadn't even crossed my mind—"

"Well, good—"

"—that you would kill me. Now it has."

"It's mostly a threat," Malculm said and exited the car. He ran up the short flight of stairs and lifted the potted plant near the door, which had a hollow beneath where the key and garage remote rested, linked together with a key chain. He pressed the button on the way back to the SUV.

Padre was still there, but now he was glaring from the back seat. "You are going to have your traveling privileges revoked as soon as I/EI finds out about this."

Malculm put the SUV in drive and let it roll into the garage without touching the gas. "Too late for that." Malculm didn't elaborate and Padre didn't ask for a follow-up, but Malculm could see the wheels turning.

Once the garage door closed behind them, Padre got out of the back on his own accord. Slowly, he walked over to the bungalow's interior door and waited.

Malculm grabbed his duffel with the rope, garden shears, and can of gasoline and made his way to the house. It smelled of rubber and grease in the garage, and for some reason, ham. Nostalgic smells, for Milton. Distracting smells, for Malculm. Smells that could get him killed. It was the back end of the shovel, for sure. He took his eye off Padre to fumble with the lock but kept half his awareness on the man.

"I'm not going to do anything," Padre said. "Now I'm just curious." He wiped at his nose with the sleeve of his shirt. The bleeding had stopped.

Malculm pushed the door open. "After you."

Padre sat on the couch in the living room, releasing a relaxed breath. Malculm took the love seat.

"So," Padre said. "What are we doing now?"

"You're going to summon me a mover and a navigator."

"Why?"

"That's for me to know and for you to . . . not know."

"You have no idea what you're doing, do you?" Padre said.

"I've been trained for this."

"I mean, sure, you know what you're doing, but you don't have a plan for how this'll play out. Get yourself to a new locality and then what?"

Against his better judgment, Malculm said, "Find a backwater locality, where I'll—"

"Move yourself beyond Burel Hird space? You're too smart for this bush-league bullshit, Malculm. You're I/EI. You know how this goes. 'A head full of secrets has one cure,' remember? They won't let you go. We have enemies now."

"And that's precisely what I'm going to find out. Who our enemies really are."

Padre shook his head. He'd spread out on the couch and had leaned his head back ever so slightly, looking down at Malculm as he smiled. "You must've fucked up extravagantly to think you can shit show your way out of trouble."

Malculm straightened. "I've been nice so far, Padre. But as you have so clearly surmised, I'm desperate. And, People help me, I'm willing to do whatever it takes to change my situation, which is why we are here. And in about thirty seconds, I'm going to be deciding whether you're a better whistler without toes or with your toes on fire." He held up the shears in one hand and the gasoline in the other. "You can render judgment on my tactics all you want once I'm gone, but right now, it's time for you to give me what the fuck I want."

Padre stopped smiling. He wasn't the kind of intelligence Malculm was. He wouldn't be able to win in a fight.

"Who do you want me to summon first?"

"The mover. Gervin."

"Smart," Padre said.

Padre was a Class-A summoner—anyone he summoned would appear beside him, rather than entering the locality at random or into the body they'd occupied if they'd been there before. Malculm wouldn't have to go searching for Gervin; he would be in the room with them in moments. Padre slapped his hands together and started whistling a tune through his teeth. He had never confided to Malculm the name of the tune or how he'd discovered that it would trigger his summoning mechanism, but it was one of the strongest summoning abilities Malculm had seen in the field. Padre was also one of the biggest assholes Malculm had ever encountered, so perhaps it balanced out.

His ability did have shortcomings, though. It worked more predictably if existing proxies in the locality were within a hundred miles of his location, which was why all the Burel Hird agents in this suburban misery lived in Iowa. It also seemed to work in only a quarter of localities, but tract housing hell was one of the lucky ones. This was only part of the reason he'd been stashed here, though.

Padre occupied the Vikram chair of the Committee for Regular and Special Exfiltration. He and the other summoners on the committee marked high-value members of Burel Hird society, which allowed those VIPs to be summoned at a moment's notice. Padre had to be ready at all times for an order. Of course, Malculm suspected that it was defection, rather than kidnapping, that the committee was most often called on to address, which was perhaps why the Subcommittee for Post-Exfiltration, Reeducation, and Training existed. Thankfully for Malculm, at no point in his life had he been important enough to be marked, so he was unlikely to find himself on the business end of a SPERET "lesson" any time soon.

Padre was still whistling his tune when Gervin appeared. "What in the People's shitship . . ." He looked around to Malculm, just in time to receive a right hook to the jaw. He fell just as fast as Padre had, but this time Malculm's hand pulsed with pain.

"Good one," Padre said.

"Old man," Malculm said, reaching for the shears, "I am fit to be tied."

"Right, right," Padre said quickly. "Who's next?"

Malculm rubbed the bridge of his nose. Fit to be tied? Had this proxy always been like this and he'd just never noticed? Or had these sorts of things crept in once Jil entered the picture? He hated how natural the words had felt as he'd said them. This world was a nightmare.

"Malculm."

"What?"

"Who now?"

"Dryska."

A quick expression crossed Padre's face. "When's the last time you saw Dryska?"

"Does it matter?"

Padre shrugged. "I suppose it doesn't." He pursed his lips once more, repeating the tune.

The woman who popped into existence did not look surprised. She was, however, about twice as large as when Malculm last saw her, muscled in a way Malculm had never been at any point in his life. It took Dryska only a moment to assess the situation, which meant Malculm had only a moment to ready himself before she lunged at him.

He stepped back from her grasp but stumbled against a side table, and that was all it took. Dryska seized his momentary clumsiness and punched him twice, once in the gut and once in the chin, the second blow sending him tumbling backward, his vision blurred. He had barely righted himself when she planted her boot in his chest, and Malculm tumbled once more, toppling a love seat in the process. Dryska vaulted over the fallen sofa, and for a moment, she seemed suspended and weightless above it. Malculm, sprawled on the ground, took in the tautness of her forearms' muscles, the swell of her thighs, her balletic, gravity-defying grace; she was in her prime and Malculm, clearly, was not. He rolled away as her heel crashed into the spot his face had been the moment before, and he pushed all thoughts of forearms and thighs from his mind.

"I probably should've mentioned," Malculm heard Padre say, "Dryska is Dryska Kerlik now, on the Committee for Close-Quarters Conflict Resolution. A little different from her academy days."

"The Kerlik seat?" Malculm managed to say, ducking into the kitchen. "Christ, Dryska."

Dryska smirked a little and shrugged, but her pursuit of Malculm didn't falter. She followed him through the transom window between the kitchen and living room, over the love seat once more, and back into the kitchen. Malculm made to dive through the transom a second time, but she blocked his path, spinning him back against the sink. He raised his fists, knowing she wouldn't be going down with a single punch but with few other options. He blocked a series of blows and, seeing an opening, kicked her thigh with all of his strength, trying to create some space between them. She moved a little. Malculm moved a lot, flying backward, his head snapping against the corner of the fridge. The pain was numbed by the adrenaline, but not nearly enough. Dryska winced at Malculm's groan. She straightened and lowered her hands.

"Whatever you're doing here, Malculm," she said, "we can talk about it. After you surrender."

There was not an ounce of smugness in her expression, but that didn't stop Malculm from feeling condescended to. Nonetheless, she'd assessed the situation correctly. He would not be winning this fight.

"All right," he said, trying to catch his breath. "All right. I'm just trying to get out of Burel Hird. That's it."

Dryska shook her head. "There's a process, Malculm. Kidnapping agents is very much not part of that process. You don't get to just walk out knowing what you know."

"I told him that," Padre said.

Gervin, still unconscious on the floor, shared no opinion on the matter.

"Something is happening, and the high-ups on Engine are too lazy or stupid to figure it out." Malculm had to pause to breathe again.

"So you are Burel Hird's last hope?" Dryska said. "I hadn't taken you for an individualist or an egoist. How depressing."

Malculm leaned on the kitchen top, but his hand slipped, slick with sweat and blood and, probably, though he tried not to think about them, tears and snot. It came to rest against the polished chromium of a toaster.

Dryska put up both hands. "Why don't I give you some time to get sorted and we can have a chat in the living room? We have history and I haven't forgotten it."

"If you walk away from me, I'm going right through that front door."

Dryska shook her head. "Now why would you say a thing like that?" She stepped forward.

"I'm not letting you take me back to Engine."

"'Let' has nothing to do with it."

Again, she lunged at him, which Malculm was banking on. As she came close, the sound of the toaster's plug popping from the wall earned a glance from her, but it was too late. There was a terrible crunch when the toaster made contact with her jaw and a ringing from the toaster itself that stayed with Malculm even after Dryska had crumpled.

"Shit," Padre said. He stood up to flee, but Malculm had a clear line through the transom to his stupid little face if he threw the toaster just right.

And so he did.

———

Getting out of tract housing hell had not been easy. Malculm did end up using the rope he'd brought from the shed. He'd gotten creative with the garden shears as well. The gasoline, though, had thankfully remained in its container. Such unsophisticated methods of persuasion were of no use on Dryska, however, so Malculm offered a secret he'd picked up about the Committee for Covert Annexation Activities, which proved to be a sufficient enticement to cooperate. A secret that, if used wisely, could be used to ascend even further up the ranks of I/EI. Malculm hadn't pegged Dryska as particularly invested in career advancement, but during their negotiations—conducted with Dryska bound in restraints he was fairly confident she could've escaped from—he realized that she had grown into someone who might occupy the highest rungs of I/EI power within a decade. He now understood that he would not. Would never, no matter how successful he was on this mission. At best, he would save himself from being retired disgracefully. Likely, he would be pushed out no matter what he did. But perhaps he could engineer a defenestration without dishonor.

"This won't end the way you think it will," Dryska had said. "You're a decent agent. Could've been great if the right things happened at the right time. But even if you unravel some great conspiracy, even if you perform an undeniable boon for the People, you've embarrassed the agency. Twice. That you can't buy your way out of. Authority is ungrateful when it comes to maintaining its power. Burel Hird will never encourage an outlaw, let alone an individualist one."

Was she right? Maybe for the powers at Engine. But he had faith that someone somewhere would see what he'd done and why he had to do it. That would have to be enough.

INTERLUDE

Deep in Mëryl's bag, her communicator buzzed, a complex rhythm muffled by the bag's contents.

"You can check that," Shann said. "It's all right."

Mëryl looked down at the bag, its flaps distended, the leather lighter where it bulged, and shrugged. "I'd rather not. I've been going on and on about myself . . . I'd rather hear about you. How you've been doing."

Shann closed her eyes and breathed deeply. "I'm feeling a little ragged lately. I know we don't get to see each other often, and I don't want to drag it down when we do get the chance. I just start to get, I don't know, patchy. Tattered. I've had to travel a lot recently. More than normal. Burel Hird is . . ." She leaned in, Mëryl leaning closer as well.

"Things are escalating," Shann said. "Not just Withered Stem and Burel Hird, but us. There are plans being put in place to . . ." She looked around. "There are worlds that aren't happy under the Burel Hird yoke. Worlds that are teetering. Worlds that are ready to choose freedom. And with certain pieces of evidence . . ."

"Ah."

"Mëryl—"

"They'll kill me, Shann. You understand that, right? If Burel Hird gets wind that so much as a hall pass has been leaked, they won't stop looking until they've found the source of the leak as well as the person who engineered it."

Shann didn't respond.

"And that means I will die, and that means the people who trusted my discretion will die too." Mëryl leaned back and shook her head. "You push me on this like you don't understand that it's my life on the line."

"Mëryl, it's possible the evidence you have of how Burel Hird's academies function could liberate as many as a dozen localities from their despotism. That's how many universes we're looking at. That's how big this operation could be."

Mëryl crossed her arms but said nothing.

"They forcibly take children from their parents for those academies," Shann said. "You do know that, don't you?"

"I do . . . I've only been following their damn schools for twenty years. And you do recall that of the two of us, I'm the closer to an expert on the matter, don't you?"

"Yes. I'm just saying—"

"And it's not quite right to say they 'take' children. From the outside, it might seem that way, but that's not how it's viewed inside Burel Hird. That's not what it feels like to the kids."

"They have to leave their parents and live with strangers," Shann said. "How is that supposed to feel?"

"It's not every Burel Hird child, just those who are recruited. And I can't really explain how different childhood is, and parents are, in more collectivist societies."

"You sound sympathetic to Burel Hird." Shann leaned back and crossed her arms. "I'm shocked."

"Not sympathetic, necessarily. I just understand it. This part, at least. I was raised more . . . communally."

"With the Withered Stem?"

"No," Mëryl said. "We also raise children more communally than some, but I wasn't Withered Stem originally. My original body . . . I don't know anything about that universe aside from what I remember. I've never been able to find any trace of it. I don't even know if we were on a moon or a planet or a colony ship. We just called it 'the Settlement.'"

"Sounds sinister."

"It might have been. I really don't know. I only have fond memories of it. In day-to-day life, it was preindustrial. We did quite a lot of work in the garden and a fair bit of candle making, for some reason, but there was certainly advanced technology present. Some of the adults had wireless communicators and there were buildings children weren't allowed in that I imagine had similar material. The things that seemed strange then—that some kids didn't like the same things that I liked, that older kids had more freedom than I did—are not the same things that strike me as strange now."

"Like?" Shann prompted.

"The religious rituals. The mantras when we planted something. The way I couldn't seem to get more than a couple stadia away from the Settlement before I would 'coincidentally' run into an adult who took me back."

"Huh."

"But the child-rearing seems normal, rational even." Mëryl paused for a moment, nodding slowly. "There was almost no possessiveness among us, for toys or for people. I knew who my biological parents were. These things weren't a secret. We lived communally, though, so I was rarely alone with them. And they didn't particularly like kids. Or at least weren't good with them. So . . ." She shrugged. "They didn't have much of an effect on my life."

"I'm sorry."

"It wasn't a bad thing. There was a woman, Miss Sae. She was what I imagine parents were like for other people. She was one of the teachers but a parent to all of us. She was who we came to when we needed comfort or advice or for someone to rub our backs while we cried. There was no sense that she was mine, though, or that I was hers. She was just an adult who seemed to understand young people, who operated on the same frequency that we did."

"She sounds like an excellent mother."

"She wasn't, though." Drumming her fingers on the table, Mëryl shook her head. "That's what I can't convey. She wasn't a mother because there were no mothers. We didn't have a word for mother or father. In the Calyxian language it would be something like 'birther' and 'seeder,' only . . . you know, not gross. But they weren't common, everyday words because those weren't significant roles. There were just adults, all of them with different parts to play in raising the kids. Some of them had big roles, like Miss Sae; some of them had small roles, like my biological parents. But none of them were parents. They were just adults."

"That is . . . difficult for me to imagine."

At a table across the way, a small crowd had gathered, standing and watching an intense game of Yio reach its conclusion. The board was nearly full of pieces, the final battle having stretched over several turns and sprawled into multiple points of contact. As one of the contestants began placing his pieces, the crowd responded with a sort of low moaning as they saw his stratagem. The moan crescendoed with each piece that slid across the board, climaxing as he slapped down a double piece to initiate the battle with hoots and hollers. His opponent sunk her head into her arms, thoroughly outflanked, and the onlookers laughed and cheered, clapping both participants on their shoulders and congratulating them on the quality of the game. The commotion had drawn Mëryl and Shann's attention, and as the crowd dispersed, they turned back to each other, each taking a sip of at-ta, Shann digging around in the jar of pickles to extract the final, reluctant buds.

"Your experience was rather different from mine, I suppose," Mëryl said.

"It was. I was raised as part of a small, tight-knit family. We traveled often, before I knew I was a traveler myself. There were seven of us, the five of the team, plus my sister and myself. Experience was my education—we worked advancing a number of causes, and though my role was minor, I did have a part to play. I'm proud of what I did in my childhood, and I'm proud to continue the work that my parents taught me."

"I see," Mëryl said. "That sounded . . . suspiciously well-rehearsed."

"It was rehearsed." Shann winked.

"How much of it was true?"

Shann laughed. "Some of it. We're not supposed to tell too much about ourselves."

"Since when did the Harraka start following rules?"

"Since we decided we didn't like getting found out, tortured, and killed if something went wrong."

"Oh." Mëryl looked away.

"That's something we rehearse saying, as well. Mentioning torture tends to keep people from asking any more questions."

"I can imagine it would. Because it did."

"It's not something I'm really concerned about with you, though." Mëryl paused. "Dare I ask?"

Shann laughed again, popping a pickled flower bud into her mouth. "Also part of the script, yes. Meant to build trust."

"Ah."

"But!" Shann said. "But, it's a line that's generally meant to be deployed prior to spending years getting to know someone. At this point, it really isn't something I'm concerned about with you."

"Well, I should hope not," Mëryl said, her lips pressed thin.

Tre came up the stairs then, bearing three plates on one arm and holding two mugs with his other.

"Half a cabbage here," he said, setting one down in front of Mëryl, "and half a cabbage here, and a platter of zhinch in the middle. Plus, an at-ta for each of you. Does this all look good?"

Shann breathed deeply. "It certainly does. Smells good too."

"Well, I'm delighted to be the bearer of good foods. I'll leave you to it." He produced his tongs, clacked them twice, and headed for a table in the corner, the peaches on their grill filling the floor with the scent of charred sweetness.

Shann and Mëryl began pulling apart their cabbages, steam perfumed by vinegar and mustard seed escaping with each leaf. On their plates sat small dishes filled sloppily with a creamy sauce of crushed nuts, fruit juice, and herbs, and they both dredged the leaves in the sauce as they ate. In the middle of the table, the zhinch sizzled, crisp, oil-seared edges curling against themselves, tawny shells still glistening.

Shann said, "How many Withered Stem are here with you?"

"You probably know how many of us there are better than I do."

"How could I?"

Mëryl snorted. "I'm not quite so credulous as to believe you don't have any other sources on Calyx."

"None like you."

"Well." Mëryl looked away. "I certainly don't know how many of us there are. Not precisely. I'm . . . not exactly known for my collegiality. And the researchers cycle in and out. Not like I was really one of them anyway."

"Oh?"

"Honestly, I think I was more or less forgotten about when the operation shut down. I have more autonomy than a lot of Withered Stem agents just because no one seems to care what I do. I'm not even sure if I care what I do . . ."

"Which part of it? It seems like you do quite a number of different things."

"All of it, I guess. Maybe it's because I'm not native Withered Stem, but I'm less optimistic about . . . everything. Burel Hird. The future. Our work in this locality." Mëryl sighed. "There aren't many of us here. Twenty at most. I'm not sure we can do all that we need to before something terrible happens."

"All that you need to regarding what?"

"The flower. I just . . . There's a feeling in me, Shann. Nausea. Tension. I don't know. I just have this sense that something bad is coming."

"I can help. I can help you."

"After Ghith, there were moves made to try and understand Burel Hird better. Some officially, some somewhat less so. Like my operation. I had already spent time on Calyx for the flower, so this seemed ideal. Calyx is, simulacrally, not far off from a Burel Hird locality, and that relationship has been fairly stable. Since we've known about it, they've never been more than two or three universes away from each other. So I've learned more about Burel Hird than most in the Withered Stem, certainly more about their academies than anyone . . ." She trailed off and sighed.

"Mëryl, truly, if you let me—"

"We're not built to deal with something like Burel Hird. We're not built to deal with war."

Mëryl raised the mug of at-ta, now cool, to her nose and breathed deeply. From where they sat, glimpses of the night sky could be seen above the courtyard, the underlit trunkline of the flower bright against the darkness. It rose just higher than the balcony Shann and Mëryl sat on, gently pink petals fluttering in the breeze beside them. The trunkline's green skin shone as though burnished, a deep, solemn shade of olive. On the ground floor, petals lay where they had fallen, superstition demanding they not be disturbed until midnight. The busker had departed, and music was being piped in, though only the ground floor had speakers. Evening's calm lay draped over New Darem, the hour late enough that the first wave of revelers had retired but not so late that the coming, inevitable raucousness had yet found purchase.

Mëryl grew solemn. "I'm afraid, Shann. I'm afraid of what will happen on Calyx. I'm afraid the flower will be split apart, driven mad, that Calyx will die without the flower—the whole planet, every life it supports, gone. I'm afraid of what Burel Hird will do. I'm afraid of what the Withered Stem won't be able to do. I'm afraid all the time and I hate it. I hate being afraid so much. I hate, so much, being afraid."

The cabbage had grown cold and Shann pushed her plate away, the last few leaves limp and glistening. In the bowls of sauce, the fat had begun to separate, small slicks of oil rising to their tops. Nothing remained of the zhinch but flakes of char. On the walls, small torches burned heatlessly with chemical flames, their tongues a dark, dusty red that sent shadows skittering across the floor as breezes blew through the open shutters. The night's air was warm, the smell of the flower heavy, but atop it was the anise fizz of Calyxian liquor, bubbling and seething when ice cubes were added to it, and the spicy scent of spiked at-ta.

"You don't think Withered Stem can deal with Burel Hird?" Shann said, leaning back.

"Deal with? You say that so easily. I don't think we have the language to articulate what dealing with Burel Hird would even mean. And, if we did, I don't think it would change anything. The way that the Withered Stem—" Mëryl stopped, breathed deeply, and took a long, slow sip of at-ta. "I've been studying these kids for so long now, how they teach them, what they learn, how they think. They're . . . they're not like us. You and me. Withered Stem or Harraka. It's not that they're smarter. They just see the multiverse, life itself, in terms of advantages and disadvantages. Everything—everything—is stripped down to their brutal, naked calculus: Does this advance Burel Hird's ends? Does this inhibit them? And they're so good at making that judgment. It's frightening. They're so good at paring away meaning, paring away morality, paring away life. If you can reduce the totality of existence, the unmeasurable infinity of the Simulacra, to that basic equation—this serves the People, this hurts the People—then there's nothing you can't do. Nothing you would be unwilling to do."

"A society without boundaries."

"And that way of thinking . . . We don't understand it. We can't conceive of it. No one in Withered Stem understands what Burel Hird is and what conflict with them would mean. I can't make them understand. They won't let me."

Mëryl hung her head for a moment and Shann said nothing.

"They left me out to dry," Mëryl said, looking up. "I was supposed to have a full team, but that was cut even before I arrived. So I did the work more or less by myself. For eleven years. And it was a struggle the whole time. Sometimes it seemed like they were going to expand the operation, or get me some more help, at least, a proper team. Other times it felt like they were about to cut even the pitiful support I did get. And then they did. No warning, no explanation. The wording on the plebiscite was bad. I think people didn't understand the value of what I was doing here, so . . ."

"So no more intel."

"That was four years ago."

"Four years ago?" Shann's eyebrows rose.

"I've been doing occasional data collection since then recreationally, just keeping my network up, in case . . . Well, I don't know. For you, I guess. For the hope that maybe some good will come of all this."

"It can. It will."

"Once, I knew what this was all for. Why we did it." Her chair creaked as Mëryl slumped backward. "Or I thought I did. It felt like it was all leading toward something, that there was some single purpose that we all shared. I thought it was what separated us from the other societies."

"And now?"

"And now I don't know. And now I feel like I'm getting pulled in three different directions at once. And now I confess my doubts about my existence and my purpose to a Harraka spy, betraying the society that welcomed me into it. Which is maybe the best answer I can give."

"Betrayal seems strong, I think. Don't you? Harraka, Withered Stem, we're not so far off from each other. Look how well the two of us get on, after all." Shann reached out to touch Mëryl's hand, but Mëryl pulled away and looked down at her plate.

"Sometimes I think about defecting," she said without looking up. "To Harraka, I mean. I can't really imagine going anywhere else."

"You don't want to do that."

"I don't, or you don't want me to want to?" She raised her head and looked steadily at Shann.

"You were just complaining about being pulled in three different directions. In Harraka, it will feel like two hundred different directions. Every movement, every cell, every family, each with a different ideology, a different goal. Not dissimilar goals, of course, but not the same."

"Do you think there's room for a closer tie between Withered Stem and Harraka?"

"Do you want the agent's response or Shann's response?" Shann said.

"I'll always prefer you. You know that."

"I want there to be. I don't see it, though."

"How come?"

"Because you think it's a question you can even ask," Shann said. "Because you think it makes sense. I don't mean that as a criticism, I think it just illustrates how different we are. Withered Stem and Harraka. There's no 'Harraka' to ally with Withered Stem because there's no 'Harraka' at all. Not as a single thing, anyway. We are . . . diffuse. Like I said, there are hundreds of movements within it, thousands of ideologies, millions of families, each one different enough that they don't get along quite as well as they should."

"That really does sound an awful lot like what everyone else says about Harraka."

Shann shrugged. "Sometimes what everyone says is true."

Neither spoke, and in the lull were the sounds of the restaurant, the voice of one of the bartenders on the ground floor loud enough to carry as she extolled the virtues of their peach cider. A wind blew down from the roof, through the courtyard, and across their table. Two small leaves of cabbage fluttered on their plate momentarily, and then were still.

"Have you ever considered it?" Mëryl said. "What life might be like outside Harraka?"

"Outside Harraka . . ."

"Yeah. Maybe you felt tired of everything that you did, everything you have to do, and decided to leave. Alone or with somebody. Whatever."

"I have. I have considered that. It's appealing. Because I do feel tired.

All the time. All the time, I'm tired of the work and the people and the bullshit and the danger."

"So why not leave? You have a choice, don't you? That's what Harraka is all about, isn't it?"

"It is. And I do have a choice." Shann sighed. "But what I'm working on now? I have to finish that, at least. It's too important. Ten, twelve universes, liberated from Burel Hird? What kind of person would I be if I chose my happiness over those billions?"

"The human kind?"

"That takes a rather low perspective of humans, I think."

"At a certain point, altruism becomes just a slow-motion suicide. You are allowed to rescue yourself, too," Mëryl said.

"Is that the Withered Stem talking?"

"That's your friend talking."

"Mëryl, I don't need you to rescue me. I've lived my whole life this way."

"That sounds like a confession that you do need rescuing."

"You're very sweet," Shann said.

"And you're very young."

"Younger. And not really by that much. You're barely older than I am, aren't you? You certainly don't look older."

"I'm old enough," Mëryl said, her shoulders sagging. "Maybe I'm not. Maybe I just feel that way."

"After all this is over . . . I don't know. We could have more time. More time together. You wouldn't have to defect. You wouldn't have to do anything. You could stay here. We could stay here, maybe. No societies, no traveling, just . . . Calyx. The flower. Zhinch."

Mëryl laughed. "No societies, huh? In a locality already occupied by two of them?"

"After I'm through with Burel Hird, there's no guarantee they'll even have the resources to stay here."

"Oh my. That sounds like a high-quality insurrection indeed."

"It will be," Shann said.

"Perfect for putting a target on your back."

"At this point, I don't think there's room on my back. All new targets have been appearing in the armpits or around the elbows."

"Rather cavalier for discussing a society of billions, maybe trillions, wanting to murder you."

"As though they'd be the first trillion people who wanted to murder me."

Mëryl's face contorted. "This does not comfort me. Shann, this does not reassure me."

"I don't know what's going to happen. Not with Burel Hird, not with Calyx, not with the future. But whatever does happen, I'd keep you safe. You understand that, right? You know I'd keep you safe."

PART THREE

12

Noah walked into his workspace and dropped his duffel onto the iron bench near the door. He unzipped the duffel, pulling out the necessary items inside: an eye mask, sound-dampening headphones, a small pair of pliers, a translucent rubber mouthguard, and a camera. He'd finally managed to sneak the last item in once he figured out a way to conceal it within a hidden sleeve in his bag, which he'd lined with a deflector he'd devised himself.

Into the duffel went Noah's pants, jacket, and T-shirt, leaving him in his underwear and socks. He looked up at the security camera as he scooped the other items from the bench, wrapped his own camera in the eye mask, and made his way over to the bedpod.

These rooms were all linked up to central security, where he'd show up on some bored desk rat's screen as one box among many. But, as long as he remained calm and kept his movements normal, his little act of espionage would skirt by as not suspicious or worth later review.

Sleep transfers had only been released to the public three years prior, and Refresh Inc. held the patent. It had been an overnight revolution. Production in all industries soared, health and well-being increased, and sleep technicians on the platform enjoyed prestige for the societal benefits their service wrought. Technicians were paid to sleep for the tired and the sick, the overworked, the ragged from below—if they could afford it. And the sleep given was somehow improved, more concentrated. The transfers offered euphoria in most cases, as well as strength and vitality. The solar proximity of the platform had something to do with that. But it wasn't the bedpods or the silra wiring or the nano-effuse technology that was critical for all of it to function properly; it was the filters. The other things would be difficult to replicate but not impossible.

Noah tugged the bedpod lid open, blue light spilling out onto the white, antiseptic floor, the mirrored walls, and his pockmarked face. He flipped open the control panel near the bed's joint, and with his pliers, he managed to locate the coupling filter and pried it out. He quickly snapped several pictures of the filter, pressed the transmit button on the camera's side—another bit he devised—jammed the filter back in place, then closed the panel. It took seconds, but Noah was already sweating. He tried not to shake too much as he positioned himself over the top of the closed bed to take one final image: himself, smiling stupidly, holding up two fingers in an ancient peace sign. Unlike the other image, already wiped once he'd hit the transmit button, this image would remain on the camera's drive to explain its presence in the room, just in case it was discovered at any point during his shift.

Noah walked swiftly over to his duffel and tossed the pliers and camera back in. He wiped his face of sweat. That was it, over a month of effort done in moments. He listened for any sign that he'd been caught, but the room hummed on, the muffled noises beyond typical of any other day since he'd taken the job. He wouldn't celebrate until he left, but he allowed himself a sigh of momentary relief. He'd done it just like he said he could.

He fixed his expression back to placidity and returned to the bedpod, donned his eye mask and headphones, bit into his mouthguard, and sat down on the thin cushion of the pod. He spun, pulling his legs up onto the pod like he'd done dozens of times now, laid back, the cushion molding around him. The material was unique to the platform, something that would never appear down below. What he'd done could change all that. He pulled the bed closed over him.

Technician 31. Clocking in?

"Clock in," Noah said.

Loading transfer, please wait.

Noah heard the system scanning for his day's loaded transfer, the sound reminiscent of some bird call. But something was different this time, the call coming louder and louder in his ears, shrieking and morphing into something like a child's cry. Behind the sound: the spooling and whirring of the cogs from within the bedpod's interior.

Transfer CF971.8 loaded. Bed hatch is secure. Initiate?

The crying died off, falling to an incessant whimper.

Initiate?

Noah blinked behind his eye mask before shutting his eyes again. "Initiate."

Then came the slow creep of slumber, heaviness in the pod as warm ionized air stippled Noah's bare skin, coaxing him to the edge of consciousness. Then the blissful moment right before sleep where an hour might skitter away in a blink and night might become morning. Noah balanced there, for moments or longer, until he was dragged down into the realm of sleep.

Something was wrong.

He felt it first as a charge, something raw entering him, swelling, growing—

—an arc of caustic fire rose to consume Noah's nervous system, his mind, synapses raking forward and colliding with . . .

With . . .

He was flailing. His mind was mixing together with some other foreign thing, the thing with him, in the same soup, and they were tearing at each other, his self and this other self, like two beasts, flayed to their foundations and then fusing back together, every flaring cell engulfed by this new compound consciousness, this new—

Noah rolled from the bedpod and onto the floor. When did he open the lid? Lying there, he gulped and shuddered on the floor like a goldfish, the pain of falling mixing with some deeper unnamable pain.

Noah tried to collect himself. Noah, he thought. My name is Noah. Why was he thinking that? Stomach acid billowed up into his throat and Noah didn't have time to turn; it came out hot and violent from his mouth. Somehow this was better, a terrible sensation anchoring him to his own body. And yet, in the same moment, he was seeing a man kneeling down over him, saying words he didn't understand. Noah tried to use his mouth but it felt like the action was happening elsewhere.

"Are you okay?"

"I—do not know. Where am I?" Not his voice. Not his mouth.

Again, he vomited, but there wasn't much left in him the second time, mostly dry retching. He was alone, sitting on the floor, his back against the bedpod.

He was Noah. He pushed the other one out of his mind, but could still feel her there, at the edge, and just beyond that edge, he felt it: memories, someone else's memories, her—

Noah reflexively rubbed his eyes, a smear of the heavy black liner he was wearing to obscure his tattoo coming off on his fingers.

He had to find her, this woman. He heard his uncle's voice in his head, his warning . . . Noah was exposed. If she knew half as much about him as he was coming to know of her, if she acted on that knowledge . . .

Noah braced against further vomiting. When it didn't come, he stood up from the floor and pressed his palms against either side of his head, trying to quiet the remaining panic, then walked over to his duffel. He retrieved his clothes and redressed. It was a wonder that no one had checked in on Noah, that no system had flagged his bedpod for follow-up, considering how long he'd been out.

He pressed his thumb against the terminal on the wall and the door hissed open. He stepped into the hallway and avoided the eyes of other technicians going by. The air was charged with nanites and the hairs on his neck stood up as he passed a bank of rooms where active transfers were in session.

He had to find her. It couldn't wait. He poked at the space where she resided in his own mind and found her there. He knew just where she was. In a way that wasn't very far from the truth, he was there already.

———

"You'll be fine, just stay hydrated and get some rest." The doctor smiled and wrapped her stethoscope around her neck, making for the door.

"Is this commonplace?" Shara asked. "Have you heard of this happening before?"

The doctor didn't answer the first question. "Well, not personally. But it's covered in the waiver you signed, that everyone signs."

Shara shook her head. "So, I have no recourse."

"The platform corps, they're—"

"Above the law," Shara said, thinking of her father. Only it wasn't her father, not really. This life, this body—it was all new to her still. She did not yet fully know her hide. "The man I was with . . ."

"He's in the waiting room," the doctor said. "Big one, nice arms. And that lovely long hair. Is he your—?"

"Certainly not." Shara slid down from the cushioned table. The whir of the imaging bot filled her ears as it hovered back toward the doctor, its internal fans puffing her black hair. "Will these effects go away? I can feel this person in my head."

With a puzzled expression, the doctor was looking down at the tablet in her hand. "It'll take time, but yes. Like I said, get some rest."

"How long?"

"Hard to say." She was still not looking at her. "A week maybe? The records vary."

Shara watched the woman with suspicion. "How many cases of this have you heard of?"

The doctor lifted her face for a moment, and her eyes told Shara everything. If she had heard of this happening, it was not an instance this severe. A transfer of a memory, perhaps, but nothing like Shara's case. Nonetheless, the doctor had no intention of discussing the implications with her. These platform corps were above the law, and everyone was in their pockets.

Shara pulled the hood of her sweatshirt over her head and thanked the doctor. She passed her medicard over the sensor on the wall and left the room. Thoughts from the man in her mind bloomed and swam with her own, and Shara struggled to make sense of anything. Two nights prior, Wolfryke, their Of Tala contact, had arranged a job for her and Beinir. If they hoped to reach the wayfarers' gathering place, they would first need to leave this planet, and in this world, that meant they would need money. She hadn't slept properly since the conversation with the sibyl, and finally, desperate, she had stolen the sleep transfer voucher. Though the work had been trivial—small-time enforcement, without so much as a single fight—she had collapsed, drawn into whatever mental episode she seemed to have signed up for. Beinir must have carried her to the hospital. She dreaded his inevitable boasting.

She walked into the waiting room.

Beinir stood up from his chair at the sight of her. "Shara," he said too loudly. "Whole and hale and—"

"Do not," she said.

"Come, please. A little gratitude." Beinir moved through the row of chairs and people waiting, nudging legs from the aisle. "Think of it. Imagine. Me carrying you, as though dead, cradled in my arms like a babe through the night and the rain for miles." He shoved one man backward in his chair, nearly toppling him. The man looked up with a grimace but said nothing. "The streets were thick with malcontents, doubt it not. But I stayed my course. I delivered the stricken Shara to those who might save her. And just look at you. None the worse."

Shara took in the faces of those in the room, all staring. Of course, they were. Beinir's insistence on keeping to his particular manner of speech tended to mark him, though whether as an Of Tala or simply an unemployed actor depended on whether their order was known to the world. As the roamers maintained only an outpost—and that only being the single, ancient invoker, Wolfryke—Shara suspected it was the latter. "Let us away," she said.

"Och, well. There is my thanks." He slapped her back as he joined her at the exit doors. "I warned you about shortcuts. Sleep is not a thing to be trifled with."

"Stop. I know. This hide, this—" She lowered her voice and pulled Beinir's arm, leading him out of the waiting room and into the daylight. The noise of traffic beside them was welcoming. Shara led Beinir along the sidewalk. "This world, it is strange—and now that little man is in my skull."

"What little man?"

"The one who slept for me. Noah. A sleeper."

"And?"

"And now he knows our plans to reach the nexus."

"So, what is that to us?" Beinir said.

"There is more."

They crossed the street, and a shuttle flew by, its side plastered with Shara's father's face. Her hide's father. Another ad for his upcoming election. In all the star roads she had traversed, she had always found herself on the edges, an unknown. This was most peculiar, but not nearly as peculiar as the dual . . . no, triple identity she was now inhabiting.

"I know this Noah now too," she said. "He knew of our order before we—collided."

"Of Tala people all worlds, it is said."

"By fools. Not even Hird touches all worlds."

"Still. It is no surprise we are known here."

Shara looked behind her. Hovering traffic slid along the light-roads of the platform before countless buildings reaching up into the sky. Lower, though still towering, rose statues and monuments that shifted for reasons neither Shara nor her hide could comprehend.

"He is coming for us," she said.

"He will find his death."

"Perhaps, but—" Shara stopped Beinir on the sidewalk, turning him around to face her. "He too is a wayfarer. Firmāre."

"The sibyl told us they rule from the shadows here. What of it?"

"Yes. Only—it is something in this man's head. I do not yet understand it all."

Beinir reached out and touched her shoulder. "What is it, Shara?"

"In moments, I feel like I am this man. Or he is me. And I know our ways have crossed. Or will cross."

"What ways?"

She turned from the confession begging to be spoken. Instead, she said, "He knows of an assassination plot."

"Of Tala?"

"Burel Hird."

"Then it is a sad tale for whomever is slain, but not of our concern."

Shara frowned. Beinir turned from her then, gazing up at the yellowing sky and the sun behind a screen of clouds. She knew what he was thinking. That their story had gone ahead of them. Fate had taken over. To her, it meant something more.

"I suppose you're right," Shara said. "We have enough now to get off-planet. Let us go. And quickly."

"Do not worry over this little man. If he comes for us, he will die."

Shara struggled to contain the lives within her, the memories of her other selves mixed with Noah's, and the already difficult task of acclimating to a new hide. She looked into Beinir's eyes, grateful for him but terrified for herself, of herself.

"Fate follows," Shara said.

13

Trystèsté's desk flashed like the floor of a Glitterpoint casino. She hated it, even before the morning's inevitable headache. It had been like this for days—an endless stream of urgent reports, demands for appeals, policy submissions, and decision reviews. The noise of notifications from various platforms chirruped in the room like insects from the wilds. She'd never seen anything like it, and every councilor's office was equally inundated.

Trystèsté had exhausted herself and her staff for most of the night, attempting to filter the legitimate work requests from the dross. She'd initially set up a number of programs to scan the incoming data and rank them based on some of the more likely indicators, but she could tell that they were missing something obvious. She wanted to script in some kind of triage that could sort the deluge, but it was all too random, too haphazardly encoded to identify correlations. She'd turned to the techs in her department, and they'd used their experience and intuition to narrow the pool further, but it was still only a little better than reading each report manually and making a determination, which was a numerical impossibility.

Another screen popped up, its vaguely blue glow adding to the visual din. She'd disabled audio notifications days before, but the desk was hardwired to surface any new communication coded "urgent," and she didn't have the skills to modify the hardware. She was seriously considering reaching out to the underground Infotech Engineering Commission for help. She didn't think she could last much longer if this kept up.

"Trystèsté!" Zechariah's voice boomed from their workroom. With relief, Trystèsté turned away from the strobing desk and walked into the sanctuary that the shared space between their offices had become. Absent the intrusions of technology, they had a modicum of peace and could speak without interruption. Mostly, they'd been talking about the intrusions of technology.

Zechariah was already waiting on the two-seat couch he preferred, his back against one armrest and his feet up on the other seat. He held an enormous, oddly shaped mug, the creation of one of his grandchildren. It was certainly filled with bitter, black coffee, steam curling under his nose.

"Something has to be done," he said, without preamble. "It's a fucking nightmare."

Trystèsté nodded. "Whoever is doing this, their plan is working. We're all buried under this flood of submissions, there's no way to know what's a legitimate filing and what's . . ."

"Bullshit," Zechariah finished her sentence. She shrugged. "I just got a petition, in my personal inbox no less, from the Outplanet Persimmon Growers Cooperative in the Vahnt-6 locality."

"What did they want?"

"Fuck knows." Zechariah caught Trystèsté's bemused expression. His curiosity was the source of his vast diversity of knowledge, but it also meant that he could rarely pass up an opportunity to delve into a new topic, even when he knew better. "Okay, fine. They're asking to get three new planets added to the berry export quota. They're arguing that their product is superior to anything in the local supply. I'm sure it is, too. But . . . Look, the growers' cooperative is the largest single stakeholder in persimmon exports in Vahnt-6, and the locality is already in the fold. They don't need an addition to the quota, they can send their stock anywhere. It's not a competitive industry."

"So it's just another waste of time."

"Exactly. Every single thing I've looked at for days has been just that. A waste of time."

Trystèsté poured a cup of tea from the samovar on the sideboard and let its aroma envelop her: clove, sappan wood, cinnamon. "Is a persimmon a berry? Doesn't it look more like a tomato?"

"Tomatoes and persimmons are both, morphologically speaking, berries. But that's not what's important here."

"Right. The question is, how do we weed out this junk?"

"No. The real question is, how do we get it to stop."

"That too." Trystèsté sipped her tea. "It must be some kind of co-ordinated effort."

"Of course it is. But from where?" He leaned his head back on the armrest of the couch and closed his eyes, rubbing the bridge of his nose. "You think it might have something to do with that Geçiş business? The Withered Stem people making an end run? Using our own strengths against us? They aren't known for direct conflict."

Trystèsté thought about it. There was something distressingly elegant about using the very committee system that brought order to all the worlds Burel Hird managed against them. It was the kind of thing she could imagine might appeal to the lab coats in Withered Stem and their aimless, abstract ideals. They'd want to keep their hands clean, and this was a bloodless attack, at least on the face of it. She knew, though, that if things carried on as they had been there would be real-world casualties—a lifesaving medical transfer lost in the onslaught of phony requests or something like that. She hoped it hadn't happened already.

An attack from another society was not something she'd ever seriously considered before, not something anyone in Burel Hird thought about much. She knew her history. All of Burel Hird's significant conflicts had been small-scale, local, and internal. The People did not take localities by force of arms, but by force of will, by force of rectitude;

they demonstrated the superiority of the Burel Hird ideology. They offered the comfort of order in the midst of chaos. What they did not
do, what represented a failure of the justice of their ideology, was fight
full-scale wars.

"Maybe," was all she said aloud. She knew her councilor shared
the same worries, and mentioning them wouldn't help them solve the
problem. "Whoever it is, they'd have to know an awful lot about our
low-level processes to pull this off."

Zechariah nodded. "They'd have to have someone on the inside."

Trystèsté stared at him. It was obviously true, and yet nearly unthinkable.

"I don't like it either," he replied to her unstated question, "but there's
no other way we'd get something like . . . like this." He waved a hand.

"So we're looking for a traitor. A mole."

"Yes, potentially," Zechariah said, "but we need to head off this flood
of fake requests or we won't be able to do anything." He took a final
swallow of his coffee then peered down into the mug's depths, pursing
his lips at its emptiness.

"How?"

"I think the answer is in the requests themselves." Zechariah nodded.
"Those files are the key, they have to be, but we haven't been looking at
them right." He kicked his feet off the end of the couch and stood in
a fluid motion, then strode into his office. He left the door open and
began swiping on a light screen, drawing up a set of heat maps of the
most recent requests.

"What are you doing?" Trystèsté asked.

"I thought I'd have a look at them visually: submission time on the
x-axis, locality population on the y-axis. See if I can spot a pattern." He
frowned at the display, then zoomed in on one corner.

"I already tried scripting, and that failed. There are almost no agree-
ments from one data type to the next. Believe me, I looked."

"Hence, the visual approach. Maybe whoever is sending them is
doing it from the same location or in batches. They are all coming
from somewhere, after all. There might be a common time stamp or

originating desk. If we can identify something in the structure of the requests, we might at least be able to identify the bulk of the chaff."

Trystèsté nodded. "That would be a good start. If we could at least pull out the legitimate work, then we can worry about who's behind this at our leisure."

"Maybe not leisure," Zechariah said, but the barest implication of a grin flickered at the corners of his mouth. "But not a panic, at least."

Trystèsté stood. "I think I know someone who might be able to help."

———

Metadata. People always forget about the metadata.

Glace's fingers danced over their desk, and the screen filled with the image of a middle-aged person, frozen in time halfway through a casual smile and wave. They weren't particularly attractive, at least not to Glace's taste, but they did have a great smile. The display flickered, and the image was replaced by a scroll of text in a tiny font.

Most people didn't think about the metadata, even when they were trying to hide something or to plant fake information. They thought about the vids, the pictures, the audio, the numbers. They thought carefully about the substance that their little package of deceit contained. What they often didn't think enough about were the file handles, the creation dates, the modification times, or any of the other minutiae that made up the digital representation of the file. They didn't think of just how much information was hidden in that gibberish embedded in the container when they were so deeply concerned about its content. And that was where they gave themselves up.

Glace skimmed the details—the file size, bit rate, coordinates where the vid had been taken, and upload location. Most of it didn't matter, and any or all of those elements could have been falsified, but given that the details indicated that the footage was created in content farms rather than the pleasure beach on Carmelean, Glace figured this was from one of those cheap, commercial rent-a-friend operations as opposed to an actual candid shot. The client would probably be annoyed, but they must have had their suspicions, or else Glace would never have gotten involved.

Just as Glace was sending off the report, a new notification popped up. Official, direct from the First Council's communication server, but marked personal correspondence. It had to be from Trystèsté j•Reigh. No, Trystèsté Jason, they mentally corrected themself. Well, that was unexpected. Glace hadn't seen them—her—in years.

She'd certainly made it far from home, all the way to a Chamber seat. Everyone in her hometown knew that, even those who cared little for the individuals who held those august positions. Her family was modest about it, but there were only fourteen Chamber seats for all of the trillions of People of Burel Hird. It was an honor to be able to say, "I knew her when."

And, of course, Trystèsté would have kept tabs on a childhood buddy from her old hometown, even if Glace still lived in Maynard, a town so many thought of as the conservative hinterlands of Prime. And Glace was unusually traditionalist, even for Maynard. But Trystèsté knew well enough that just because a person kept to the ancient ways, that didn't mean the individual was of no use to contemporary society. It's not as if Glace was a proselytizer; how other people chose to describe themselves was of no concern to them. Still. Glace figured the probability that this was an actual personal correspondence was more or less nil. It had to be some kind of off-the-books request for their services. But what could they offer that the entire mechanism of bureaucracy that supported the Council couldn't provide? And why the circuitous approach?

Glace chuckled as they read her note. It was addressed formally, to Glace j•Mitchell Adzersyn, in the style they preferred, but the tone was warm and personal, cognizant of the many years since they'd last spoken, yet assured of their continued connection. She mentioned a few of Glace's recent accomplishments and congratulated them on their recent ascension to the Adzersyn chair. No wonder she'd gone so far. And when they reached the meat of her letter, there was no wonder why she'd reached out. No one was quite as good as Glace at finding signal in the noise, and it looked like Trystèsté—and the rest of the Council—was utterly drowning in a sea of noise.

"Of course I'll help," they wrote back. "Send me a sample of your data."

14

Once the negotiating was done, Dryska could offer only three potential destinations for Malculm. Might as well have been only one, given his needs, but Korlifor was the last place he wanted to go. Why that was, though, he wasn't altogether certain. At first, there was just a feeling, a disquiet whose source he couldn't identify. But, as neurons fired and connections formed, he quickly realized why he wanted to avoid that locality. Still, it was his best chance forward. So, through gritted teeth, he gave Dryska the word then she and Gervin did their things.

After his stomach dropped and his consciousness folded away, he blinked against the midmorning brightness of a Korlifor back alley, the movement of his hands uninterrupted as they passed deftly over five different colored, upside-down cups. At least seven onlookers stood around the torn panel of a refrigerator box functioning as his table. His concentration stayed on the cups, but his peripheral awareness was better than it had ever been, even after years of field training. His hands, too, were quicker, vipers snapping out to strike and move a cup, arms weaving around each other in a blur.

Each motion came from instinct, allowing his attention room to take in his surroundings. He sat cross-legged in a damp alley, the sickly-sweet stench of rot wafting from the dumpsters that flanked him. The seat of his pants—wet from a puddle of what he hoped was water—rubbed against the asphalt as he rocked back and forth, moving his cups. The crowd was enthralled, a few other onlookers arriving to throw money onto the already-substantial pile.

A sudden, monstrous itch overwhelmed Malculm while his hands did their work. It had been lurking beneath the surface, just below consciousness, since he'd arrived and had passed some threshold, manifesting into maddening life. He'd experienced addiction and withdrawal—the most miserable posting of his life had been in the Triptych locality: a week of vomiting, seizures, and not infrequent hallucinations as he attempted to combat a proxy's alcohol addiction—and this was not that. The awareness of physical itches came to Malculm then. Bug bites that had been scratched into oblivion, capped with pinprick scabs, sores still gummy and tender.

Just thinking about it was enough for his hands to twitch, to hesitate, to break the enchantment he'd so carefully cultivated. The red cup tipped over when his left hand came away from it, revealing the white stone he was only a few moves away from sleighting into his sleeve. All twelve of his onlookers pointed at the red cup.

Malculm bowed his head and paid everyone, leaving him with nothing but his life, five cups, and a useless white stone.

He abandoned his cardboard station and bent paper cups and headed out from the alley, only then aware of his lack of shoes. Luckily, this proxy came equipped with calloused feet, and he felt nothing.

Malculm emerged onto 43rd Means and everyone on the street hustled along the sidewalk and across traffic. The bus lanes—one for onboard/offboard, one for moving—allowed for a continuous flow, and the bicycle lane beyond that was wheel-to-wheel yet moving at a steady pace, four bikes wide in some places. Pedestrians swarmed the sidewalks, moving with great and terrible purpose, jostling any who walked with insufficient haste. The grumble of Malculm's stomach confirmed that it was, indeed, lunchtime.

Malculm made his way eastward, hoping to find his bearings. He'd never been to this city before but knew that a large lake lay in its center, and from there, he could get a good sense of where he needed to go. He shuddered, thinking about what would soon come.

———

Had he attempted an unsanctioned travel such as this to a locality like Prime, Border Security and Regulation would have been on him almost immediately. Luckily, Korlifor had been stalled out at stage four of the Vorren Protocol for at least a century, and so, while it was wholly administered by Burel Hird, it had not yet been wholly acculturated to it. A certain latitude could thus be expected in the monitoring of the populace, and so Malculm hoped he might arrive in a proxy that would skirt immediate detection. Malculm clenched his jaw and balled his fists, trying not to scratch as another bout of the itchiness passed through him. This hadn't been what he expected, but a street magician on society's periphery certainly fit the bill. If he moved quickly enough, he could perhaps evade BSR altogether. Thanks be to whatever gods governed the transmundi. He balked at the unexpected thought; apparently this proxy was also a closet mystic.

A finger tapped at Malculm's shoulder, and his heart jumped. But, turning, he recognized the blue uniform and the gold, circular badge pinned to the chest and rolled his eyes.

"Hey, compeer," the resource officer said. "No need to get testy. Just wanted to know if you needed any aid."

"I'm fine," Malculm said.

"If you don't mind me saying, you don't look very fine." The officer exuded genuine concern, as any representative of the Committee for Public Safety and Wellness ought to, but Malculm had no time or use for it.

"Well, looks can be deceiving."

"Would you submit to a tox scan? No requirement to, but I'd feel much better if you did."

Malculm scratched himself. He could, but if a positive test came back higher than the Appropriate Public Intoxication Limit, they'd whisk him to a well-being facility. His name would be entered into the grand machinery of Burel Hird's systems and, slowly but inevitably, would be flagged by I/EI.

"No thanks," Malculm said.

The officer nodded, then inhaled deep. "Okay. I get it. But I'd at least feel better if you'd listen to my spiel."

Malculm spread his arms. "By all means." His right hand returned to his side, but the left made its way toward the officer. For no reason at all, an urge to swipe the officer's badge came over him. Malculm stuffed his left hand into his pocket and tapped out an anxious rhythm against his thigh. "Substances can be fun, but if you take too many, it can start to wear you down. You're more than the chemicals you take. You deserve more. You're worthy of a better life, neighbor." They stared at each other for a moment before the officer said, "Oh! That's it. I keep it short and sweet."

"Right. Well, I'd better be off."

"Let me at least help you get where you need to go. The transient dorms are back thataway. Opposite from the way you're heading. Unless you're trying to get to the Velmon Dorms, obviously."

Malculm ground his teeth but kept his voice even. "Not heading for the dorms."

"No? You should. They're doing a series called 'Find Your Fit' that would be most helpful, I'd wager. Not to be presumptuous, but I think a person in your circumstances might benefit from the services that—"

"You know what? There is a place I'm trying to get to. Could you help me?"

The officer smiled, big and toothy. "What are neighbors for?"

———

Malculm had satisfied most of his itches by the time he arrived at the Deekin Academy, though he found that one lingered, one he couldn't

scratch away. His fingers longed to fidget, to find use for their nimble-
ness. Four times on the bus he had to sit on his hands to keep from
lifting things from the passengers—books, pens, even a sandwich. Useless things; still, his hands yearned for them.

He got off early and walked the rest of the way to the academy's
campus, a perhaps too-grand word for a single squat building made up
of white bricks and dark windows. A fence ringed the grounds, each
post crowned with bent spikes that discouraged but didn't altogether
eliminate, he guessed, students from slipping out—or in, depending
on the time of night.

Could he climb it himself? Surely he could, and it might even calm
his wayward hands, getting to work at a problem that didn't involve pil-
fering someone else's property. But once inside, then what? Ask where
the students were? Just another opportunity to get IDed and flagged
for I/EI pickup. As any Academy brat would be happy to let you know,
they were Burel Hird's most valuable resource, and however genial the
resource officers might be outside the walls, inside there was no room
for error. Simply being this close to the Academy, even beyond its borders, was dangerous.

"Hey!" someone called. A guard dressed in a white jumper walked
up. He wore a shock rod and a radio, holstered on either side. "This
isn't a dormitory. You need to move along."

To Malculm's horror, his right hand shot out and touched the guard's
shoulder. "Sorry about that, I must be lost."

The guard shrugged away from Malculm. "Must be. Keep moving.
Now." He flipped the safety off the shock rod's igniter and fondled the
button with his thumb. "I better not see you skulking around here again."
A small man aroused by the scrap of power he'd been lent. He did a disservice to the People simply by existing—with any luck he'd be ERCed
before the year was done. Malculm withdrew, casting glances backward as he did, the guard following him with his eyes until he was out
of sight.

Around a corner, Malculm squatted against a wall. A block away
was the bustle of 18th Will, lunchtime aromas and the sounds of traffic

carried on the early afternoon heat. The street where Malculm hid was residential, though, three-story apartment buildings crowded up against the Academy and each other. In truth, the street was little more than an alleyway, barely wide enough for a pedicab, let alone a bus. Malculm slumped further down and held his head in his hands, his feet almost touching the opposite wall.

None of his options were good. Climb the fence? Suicide. Fill out the official visitation forms? Dead of old age before receiving approval. Parachute in? Suicide again. He laughed at the thought of himself, dressed in this tattered khaki jumpsuit, falling from the sky, steering a parachute fashioned from stolen items lifted off bus passengers.

He went to scratch at his waist when he felt something bulky and stiff. He reached into his pocket and pulled out a radio. The guard's radio. While worried about what his right hand was doing, his left had gone rogue. Malculm risked a peek around the corner. The guard hadn't noticed his missing radio and he was some way down the block. He would soon, once it came time for him to report in. And Malculm was sure to be the only suspect.

Malculm held the radio, index finger on the transmit button, tapping it lightly enough not to transmit, sweat collecting underneath his joints. He had to find a way to get to the students in the courtyard, but also to disperse the guards. Fire came to mind and was immediately dismissed. Surprise inspection would work, but the inspection might take place indoors. Should he order pizza? He hit himself in the head with the radio's antenna as soon as the thought occurred.

But then something came to him, an old incident he remembered from his own time at the Academy. He closed his eyes, switched the transmitter to the direct line for facility operations, and cleared his throat, adopting his best impersonation of an ERC officer.

"Facilities?"

"Facilities here, go ahead."

"This is Rankin Dodh, of the Subcommittee for Equity, Rectitude, and Compliance. Please ready the grounds for inspection." Malculm pitched his voice as flat as he could possibly manage.

"I'm . . . say again?" came the response. "You're on radio twelve. Where's Leighton?"

"We cannot comment on ongoing investigations and your inquiry into your coworker's infractions has been noted."

A quiet, breathy "Fuuuuuck" emerged from the radio, followed by a brief silence. "We had an unscheduled two weeks ago. This is just real soon for a follow-up."

"Yes. That is the point of an unscheduled," Malculm said. He began walking in the opposite direction of the guard, following the fence of the Academy.

"I just . . . I need a case number and an ID. Not that I doubt you, but this is a little atypical, so for record-keeping purposes, I want to make sure all my—"

"As is only appropriate. This is case Dhalgrim Quinn Lirend, five three nine aught six. Again, DQL, five three nine aught six. And the ID is sixty-six nine, four seventy-two, eight eight, eight eight."

"I'm sorry about this, but none of that is lining up with previous inspections. Can I check the logbook? That is, I have to check the logbook. I'm sure it's fine. I just need to cross-reference. Okay? Can you hang on?"

"If you feel that to be a necessary step, that is your judgment, but the inspection has begun, and the time of response is being noted. Unwarranted delays to conceal or dispose of contraband, bribes, or antisocial propaganda can be surmised even in the absence of any discovered materials."

"That's not what I'm—Look, I know all that, I just—"

"Please vacate the building and have the student body and staff assembled at the gate. My team will meet you there."

"Right. We don't really have what I'd call a 'gate,' though, so—"

"ERC out." Malculm clicked off the radio, tore off the antenna, then tossed it all in a nearby bush.

If his ploy worked, he'd be greeted by hundreds of students and dozens of staff, most annoyed, some anxious, a few pants-shittingly terrified. If it didn't, he'd have to keep on running, as it would only be more guards greeting him. He walked unhurriedly through the plaza.

At the square's other end, the fence began again, and it was true: There was no gate. Instead, the academy's building formed a grand U, the courtyard abutting the plaza. Malculm loitered around the fence as inconspicuously as he was able. The evacuation of the grounds was in process, a riot of motion, uniformed students filing out through the building's double doors then scattering across the courtyard like blown leaves, gathering in varied assortments on the lawn where they whispered and tittered and looked around them.

Malculm's guard, the one without the radio, was the last one inside, drawn in from the commotion in the courtyard. Given time, he would likely ask around and eventually discover the ruse, but for a while, all the students were outside without guards, and Malculm had a few minutes to get a message through.

Malculm's gaze fell across the assembled students, some isolated, some in small groups, chatting, gossiping, poking at screens. None appeared to be Ronni. He had only spent a short time with her, though. It was possible he wouldn't recognize her—not here, not in whatever body she had now.

Soon, those guards would come pouring out, and he'd need to be long gone before that. Malculm wanted to shout the girl's name and watch for a head to turn, but instead, he focused. And he spied a tall girl with purple hair so dark it was nearly black. He pushed the noise of all other conversation from his mind, focusing on her words.

"I'm telling you," the girl said, "Bastion Away is amazing. It's impossible to express how much I love that band."

That turn of phrase wasn't altogether uncommon, but the way she said it, how she stressed the first syllable from "impossible," and the cadence reminded him of how Ronni said something very similar back on Geçiş. Malculm approached the fence and motioned to her, eventually getting her attention. The girl scrunched her nose but walked over. It wasn't Ronni.

She stared at him, an eyebrow raised. "You all right, Uncle? You're looking rough."

"Do you know Ronni?"

Her expression changed, and her brow relaxed. "Who's asking?"

"I *am* her uncle."

"Fuck off."

Malculm snorted. "Fair enough. I'm . . . Well, she's waiting on a little something from me."

"Oh shit, you're her mover!"

". . . Yes. Yes I am."

"Hey, let me get your information, she never shares."

"Get her a message for me and we can talk."

"Sure. Yeah, she's inside. Trying to get rid of . . . well, whatever she was going to use to pay you, I think. You might want to be careful—we're having an unscheduled."

"Good to know."

"I'll let her know her usual guy wants to meet at her usual place, yeah?"

"No. Tell her to meet me at the park on the corner of 25th Means and Deveko Way."

"Why?" The girl crossed her arms.

"You're having an unscheduled, aren't you? That means we change things up. And tell her it's her uncle. Her uncle Malculm."

———

Ronni didn't show up until three days later. By then, Malculm had gotten pretty good at finding patrol paths that mostly avoided all the jovial officers admonishing him for not staying in the transient dorms and learning valuable skills. The chiding irritated him but he endured. Worse were the children with their questions, followed by the disapproving looks from their parents.

He circled an old well in the center of the park, preserved from times long before Burel Hird found—liberated—this locality. The well, the plaque read, served as a town square of sorts, where folks of all walks gathered and traded gossip and goods. He wondered if that well would still function if Burel Hird had kept their fingers out of this place. Likely some other group with something to prove would've taken it and left it disheveled. At least Burel Hird preserved the well, keeping it as it was, so people in the city could see it and reflect on how far they had come. A disquieting reminder for some, perhaps.

"You still have that odd shuffle in your step," someone said.

Malculm turned and knew it was Ronni without any need for scrutiny. Same freckles across the nose, though her complexion was darker and her eyes narrower.

"And your presence still pains me, Little Bird."

She blinked twice, fast, then nodded her head to the side. Malculm followed her, taking the long path around the well.

"Things must be pretty bad for you to come here."

"Only 'pretty' bad?" Malculm said. "I'm burned. Doubly so now that I've evaded tails and assaulted fellow agents to get here."

Ronni's eyes widened. "What happened?"

"You happened. After the Geçiş Incident, I got flagged. I could either accept my fate or make another. I chose the latter."

"I feel like half the Academy blames me for what went down—"

"As they should."

Ronni smirked. "But the other half sees what I salvaged, and I retain value from that. It's well on its way to being a story-lesson."

Malculm fought to keep from grinding his teeth. "Had you stayed on mission, we would've never encountered Of Talas. We all could've gone home happy, alive, with a success on our records."

Ronni looked away. "The People have benefited from—"

"Fucking don't. Not with ten dead." Ronni said nothing more. Malculm plucked leaves from a nearby bush. The wind blew in the trees, and he heard the tides of Geçiş, rushing through the coral tunnels.

"Malculm?"

"What?"

"Was it my fault?"

He looked at her, her face open.

"No. No, Little Bird, it wasn't your fault. None of us will earn plaudits for that day, but it wasn't your fault."

She nodded and looked down. "Good."

For some time neither spoke.

Eventually, Ronni said, "Why did you want to meet?"

"A good question." Ronni began to respond but Malculm sighed and shook his head. "I don't feel safe. I've been running for days."

"Running where?"

Malculm threw his hands in the air. "Anywhere. Out of Burel Hird territory. Somewhere neutral, where I can take the time to figure out a way to clear my name . . . or . . ."

Ronni looked at him askance. "Or?"

"Or nothing. Clear my name."

Ronni bobbed her head, coming to stand beside him. "I liked working with you, Malculm. I really did. You did everything right."

"Someday you may understand how profoundly wrong you are about that."

When she placed her hands on her hips, Malculm couldn't help but notice how narrow they were, how small her fists, how she was well and truly just a kid. "I can't do much for you."

Malculm nodded. "I know, Little Bird." He sat, back against the well, enjoying the cool and the grit of the stone against his neck.

"What I can do is tell you about the Slinger."

Malculm rubbed a finger in his eye. "Slinger?"

"I thought that's who I was supposed to meet. Until Brina remembered my 'Uncle Malculm's' name."

Malculm smiled. "Watch out for her. She's gunning for your connections."

"She'll be dealt with." Her voice was so solemn that Malculm almost laughed. "Well, the Slinger could theoretically get you out of here and to a neutral locality. We use him all the time."

"He's a mover?"

"Yup. Underground, though I'm sure he does some work for Burel Hird. Still, he brags that he is 'Beholden to himself alone.'" She bugged her eyes out and waved her head side to side in imitation. "He actually says that. A lot."

"An unaligned mover. Here. How's he manage Border Security and Regulation?"

Ronni shrugged. "Hell if I know. Look, you'll need something to trade."

"Not money, I hope. That would be a . . . challenge for this proxy."

"I can see that. It doesn't have to be cash, though."

"I have some secrets." The lie was accepted as easily as it was proffered.

"Good. I would expect nothing less from my old Uncle Malculm." Ronni took out a piece of paper and wrote down instructions. "This should get you to him."

"Thank you." Malculm stood and leaned in to hug Ronni, who accepted it with arms stiff at her sides.

"I was joking about the uncle thing. You smell real bad."

He pulled back and squeezed her shoulder. "Well, I really do appreciate it."

"Yeah, yeah," Ronni said, backing away, looking at the ground. "I kinda owed you. I guess."

"Debt paid," Malculm said.

Standing, facing her, he felt something like affection, or maybe heartburn.

"Do you want to say goodbye?" Ronni asked.

"Do you?"

"Is that what this is? No, don't answer that. I'm deciding it's not. I'm deciding that this is 'I'll see you again,' when I've graduated and been named councilor and you've . . ." She waved a hand, indicating all it was he was meant to accomplish in the intervening years. "And you've showered, and cleared your name."

It felt good to smile. Malculm didn't try to stop it. Best to enjoy it while he could still find something to smile about. "Until you're a councilor and I've showered, then."

Ronni gave a low wave and jogged off, leaving him alone by the well with the wind and the heat and the disorder of his thoughts.

He waited till the count of three hundred before opening her wallet and cataloging its contents. He was out of secrets, out of assets, so this was all he had: a child's wallet, pilfered from the only person he could maybe have called an ally in this entire universe. It was a paltry haul, but it would have to be enough.

15

"I hope your contact is as trustworthy and discreet as you think, Trystèsté," Duncan said. "Going outside the Council's in-house engineers was risky. Perhaps it would have been worth it if you'd gotten useful information, but this . . ." He waved his portable in front of Trystèsté, showing the report on the metadata that Glace had anonymously supplied. "This is nothing."

Duncan wasn't wrong. If there were any connections linking the reports, Glace had been unable to identify them. And, even worse, they were all from verifiably legitimate Burel Hird sources. Trystèsté was unwilling to concede that her plan had proved unfruitful.

"I disagree," she said. "We did get something." What that was had yet to reveal itself to her.

"Oh?"

"Yes. Yes! We did. We know that whoever is behind this has access to actual subcommittees all over Burel Hird territory." She felt almost triumphant until the actual implications of that fact settled in, another feeling replacing it. Something unfamiliar. Something upsetting.

"Well," Duncan said. He pursed his lips. "That's not ideal."

The Council was not naive. They knew that no place was

impenetrable, and spies from one society or another surely worked in Burel Hird space. But they had convinced themselves that their trans-mundial borders were, if not impervious to penetration, deeply resistant. The Council for Border Security and Regulation maintained teams of high-ranking trackers posted to every transit point across Burel Hird's sphere of influence, and travel between localities was strictly regulated. The faith of old-timers in S&R was near absolute—Zeph and Iskada could never pass up an opportunity to publicly proclaim their esteem for that council's work, nor, in truth, could Zechariah. And, as Zechariah and Trystèsté's surveillance team had discovered, Duncan felt similarly; he'd sent multiple glowing commendation letters for S&R agents. This faith was yet more evidence of their blindness. Trystèsté was willing to grant that Prime itself was locked up tight, though; unidentified foreign travelers may exist in the outer territories, but Prime's borders couldn't be porous enough to allow externs to infiltrate so many different sub-committees.

"There must be something we're missing," Trystèsté said. "Even if border security is failing, there's no way that outside operatives are en-tering Burel Hird space completely undetected."

"Yeah." Duncan looked down and rubbed the back of his neck. "It seems unlikely."

"There has to be something in the logs."

Duncan nodded. Around them, staff wheeled and pivoted in spontaneously choreographed movement, delivering reports from sub-committees and intra-council communiqués, where normally only the murmur of hushed greetings echoed from the high ceiling. Duncan led Trystèsté to a narrow hallway, the soft moldings installed on the ceiling during the 74th Turn slightly dampening the sound behind them in the Central Atrium. When they reached his workspace, Duncan began swiping at screens and pulling the reports from S&R, the din from the Atrium following them. As there had been for weeks, there was a steady roar of activity in the cavernous space: conversation, debates, arguments, notifications, footfalls as aides darted in and out, the constant shuffling of documents—a roiling surf of human sounds. Trystèsté closed the door.

"Here," Duncan said. "Let's start with the inbound travelers for the Renqueue Sovereignty."

"Why there?" Trystèsté wrinkled her nose. Renqueue was a large, galactic empire, a nightmare to administer, which only barely upheld Burel Hird's tenets.

Duncan shrugged. "It's where I'd go if I were sneaking in. It's on the edge of our territory, close to other stable localities, large enough to get lost in."

Trystèsté leaned over his shoulder to look at the list of names and their corresponding home localities. Most were from other parts of Burel Hird space, as one would expect, but there were a handful from other societies. It wasn't unusual for members of other societies to visit Burel Hird, though, on business or diplomatic missions, and the number of non-Burel Hird visitors looked to be correct.

She pulled up the files on each one, searching for anything out of the ordinary, but they all seemed aboveboard.

"There's nothing here," she said after a few minutes. "These are all legitimate visits with proper documentation. If anyone snuck in under a false identity, they did a good job of covering their tracks."

"Anything unregistered?" Duncan asked.

"There were two unscheduled arrivals for the week, but R&S sorted it out. An accidental traveler who got sent right back and a mover mix-up. Both resolved within hours." Once again, an unfamiliar feeling stirred in her. Everything she was looking at was quotidian and appropriate. The normalcy was off-putting.

Duncan nodded, swiping at his workspace again. "There's a different story on the outbound side." He looked up at Trystèsté, and pointed at the list of travelers. "This is too much movement for such a short time frame."

Trystèsté made a complex gesture with her fingers and the workspace adjusted to show a three-dimensional tree of the data Duncan had pulled out. "These all originate from Academy worlds." She pointed at lines of travelers who had left from Renqueue recently, then zoomed out to forest view. "And there's more, from some of the Academies directly." She laughed. "You know what this is, yeah?"

Duncan looked at her blankly.

"I remember my Academy days," she said, grinning. "We thought we were so clever, sneaking out to those leisure localities."

Duncan nodded, and blinked several times. His expression could possibly be construed as a smile, in a certain light. Twilight, perhaps. In a cave. "You never did that, did you?" she said.

Duncan shook his head. "I did not. I never believed they wouldn't get caught," he said. "And there are no exotic shopping opportunities or drugged-out parties that could ever be worth the cost of my future career."

He was so matter-of-fact about it that Trystèsté felt a flush of embarrassment at her own youthful indiscretions, mild and tacitly sanctioned though they may have been.

"And," Duncan continued, "compromising border integrity for personal pleasure strikes me as a rather flagrant display of egoism. A trait I have worked hard to combat, as all Burel Hird should."

"Well," Trystèsté said after clearing her throat, "some things don't change, it seems."

"No, they don't."

"Individualist though such acts perhaps are, I don't think these transfers are meaningful. Maybe we want to follow up on the outgoing transfers, make sure there's nothing real there, but it's the incoming travel that's actually relevant for our purposes."

They spent a few more moments poring through the data without speaking. The seashore hush of work continued between them, comfortable and familiar. The smell of coffee reached her, and Trystèsté's stomach grumbled, reminding her that a piece of fruit was not a sufficient breakfast. She pushed the reminder away—work first, then food.

Finally, Duncan said, "I don't see any signs of unusual activity here."

"Neither do I." Trystèsté's head snapped up abruptly. "That's it!"

Duncan arched an eyebrow and waited for her to explain.

"That's the pattern," she said. "There is no pattern."

"Okay," Duncan drew the word out.

"No, it most definitely is not okay. It is the precise, exact opposite of okay. Duncan, this isn't the Withered Stem or anyone else sneaking across our border and infiltrating our committees. It's exactly what it looks like."

"But it looks like a coordinated effort of our own people to overwhelm the Council with frivolous demands. It looks like . . . well, it looks like an administrative insurrection."

Trystèsté nodded slowly. Her insides twisted and she knew, suddenly, painfully, what that unfamiliar feeling was. It was fear.

"Exactly."

16

The effects of the transfer sickness were fading, but slowly, and Shara could still feel Noah's identity blurred with her own. She sensed him following them. Shara and Beinir had paid the toll for the liftline into orbit, where they'd taken jobs on a small cargo barge. Two weeks of sedentary travel across the Konra galaxy, an attempted boarding by pirates who had been easily dispatched, several days through astral static streams, and then nothing. For days.

Shara sat at a table in the mess hold, looking out into the black void of space. There was a nebula out there that looked like a pink and blue flower. A wash of beauty in a cold and lifeless sea, saturation against the vacant, dead waste. Space reminded her of the Donar on Oulra, where her father was a fisherman, with its unyielding darkness. Beinir had come to love space, but not Shara. She preferred the horizons of solid ground, solid worlds.

Beinir stooped through the hatch and opened the cold box, pulling a bottle from its door. He popped the top off the bottle and gulped down half of its contents before setting it on the table. He looked at Shara. "What?"

"You've only been awake two hours, and already you're drinking?"

"My throat is dry."

"From how much you drank before bed."

"Do not scold me! I am bored, and this captain is insufferable. He spoke to me of hyperdrives for the glade knows how long. I hate waiting."

Shara nodded. "Not hyper enough, this drive."

Beinir leaned against the bulkhead, crossing his arms. "After we unload the cargo on Gedlon, then what? Honestly, I cannot suffer another trip with that man. Do you see how he picks his nose?"

Shara thought about that. The station they traveled to was as far from Wolfryke's planet as it could be in this realm, light-years away, full galaxies. There were vessels that could span the distance in no time, her hide knew, but they were only for the very wealthy in the planetary confederacy. There was talk of the technology being used one day for public transportation, but her hide knew, as well, that such talk existed only to placate the masses. "How flexible are we morally?" Shara asked.

"What do you mean?"

"If we keep to barges, with labor as our currency, it will take months to reach the nexus. And I am being optimistic."

"Och, and if every captain is as dreadful—it will feel like ages."

"And Noah is still following us."

"What is the alternative?"

Shara looked behind her through the hatch to the cabin and saw the captain hunched over in his seat. "When we get to port—we could commandeer an arcdrive ship."

Beinir frowned. "An arcdrive ship?"

"An arcdrive ship."

"Just steal an arcdrive ship?"

"That is what I said."

Beinir shook his head. "We may need to spend lives for that, Shara. For a theft."

"Hence my question about flexibility. This tale has had me steal once already."

"Your sleep voucher, yes. That was a necessary theft. Still, someone sleeping for you, ridiculous." He wrinkled his brow and chewed on the inside of his lip. "How long of a voyage with an arcdrive?"

Shara smiled. "Days."

Beinir took a long breath and ran a hand through his hair. "I suppose I am feeling flexible."

———

The Gedlon port was dark in the gloaming of the rainy season, but the cathodium lights of the city kept it warm and shifting like firelight, the sound of the downpour against the great dome above them like the hum of a ship's engine, that dull din so comforting and ever-present, Shara could almost forget it was there. The smells of food along the dockside alley were intoxicating. Something oniony and smoked, fried doughs and meats and the perfume of cooked fish.

She walked with Beinir beside her, having unloaded and reloaded cargo for the captain they would never see again. He hadn't been very understanding, but he would have no trouble finding other hands needing passage. Ports on all confederacy worlds were filled with people seeking transport, seeking escape.

A man in a red suit stood beneath a glowing awning, smoking from a steel contraption. His dark hair was piled atop his head. "Looking for fun?" he asked Shara.

"We're fine," Shara said.

Beinir threw up a hand. "We are grateful for the offer."

They continued down the street. Around the corner and past a warehouse with a sign for Enthor's Boat Works and Saley's Shipping rose several slip alleys lined with parked hovering vessels, some with spooled-up power units, preparing for launch. The dome walls were lit up, and Beinir and Shara kept moving through the streets of a city they had never seen.

"This way," Shara said, moving to their left and down a slip alley past where several workers were filling fuel ships.

"How do you know this place?" Beinir asked.

"My hide has been here before. Knows the ship."

"Do you think your hide worked the streets here? As that gentleman does?"

"I swear—"

"I jest, I jest."

In the dark, Beinir and Shara could be taken for late-shift dockers or captains or mates. They walked to the end of the alley, where a bright and beautiful ship rose up before them.

"Stop," Beinir said, pulling Shara backward. They crouched behind a line of freight containers. "Guards." He pointed to the portside and aft of the ship, where two people in black suits stood. "Do they look armed?"

"They're armed."

"Then what is the play? There is too much light over there to board without being seen."

Shara took in her surroundings. Several streetlamps bathed the end of the alley in orange light. "Feels like a wildering situation to me."

Beinir frowned. "And now *you* jest."

"No," she said. "You're right, there's no way aboard without going through the guards. And if they have weapons, which they do, we cannot allow them to fire, or risk being set upon by marshals."

"Why not pull the woman-dispatches-fools-who-cannot-see-beyond-her-beauty routine?"

"Because they will know me."

"They will?"

"The father of my hide is a consul of the confederacy."

"A consul—are you telling me we could have used your hide's family this whole time? Why did we work on that barge with that awful man? You could have simply used your father's name and money."

"No. My hide is a part of the insurrection the sibyl mentioned. It is arrayed against men like her father, working to topple the confederacy. If he found her, he would imprison her."

Beinir rubbed his jaw. "Fate, draw me in. What a tale your hide here weaves, eh?"

"Hence—wildering. This could actually help my hide as much as me."

"But I have no—"

Shara held her hand up to Beinir, silencing him. She opened it to reveal a single, delicate mushroom.

"How did you—"

"It is of this world, obviously. This hide apparently enjoys visions as much as insurrection. But I think that this will suffice for our purposes."

On Mitgun'ja, not far from their homeworld, Beinir underwent a year of training in the forests with the Shamans of Far Rake, learning the way of the wildering. He ate mushrooms and drank herbal potions to bring him the fury of the wild, where he slept and trained with other wilderings, fought with beasts of all kinds—goreboars, rivens, nightbears, and great mawks. He wore their skins and blood and stayed out of his own mind, allowing himself to be carried by madness alone, instinct and muscle and bone. Wilderings were deadly in battle, dangerous to themselves as much as their enemies. Shara didn't like to put Beinir into that state unless it was necessary. But Beinir loved it. If he were permitted, he might be lost to it. Which is why he trusted her to govern him. On this one thing, at least.

"Have I told you that I love you, Shara?"

"Stop."

"No, no. I do, I love you. Take that how you like." He grabbed the mushroom and put it into his mouth. "Och, a worse flavor I have not had."

"I'll be right behind you," Shara said.

Beinir took his coat off and his black shirt. He began tugging off a boot. "Try not to ogle me, madam."

Shara shook her head. "The same thing. Every time."

"I do not always—"

"You say it every time. Every. Time."

"Well—still." He pulled his trousers off and stood up naked before her. "Do try."

He gave her a last withering smile before she could see the madness take him. It happened quickly in some worlds, slowly in others, and neither of them knew why. The wildering was inside Beinir's consciousness. It was merely activated by hallucinogens. But why the nudity?

She shifted farther behind the containers to wait as Beinir walked toward the ship. She could hear his feet slapping the concrete and his terrible snuffling. The guards would take him for a drunk or a lunatic, someone with an illness perhaps. It didn't matter. His speed would be too much in the end. She heard speaking, raised voices, then the stumbling noise of struggle before a sudden silence. She waited. If there were any aboard, they would be dealt with soon enough. Beinir would need to be asleep for hours once they were free and he came down. Shara would take it from there. But from behind her, she heard a voice.

"Stand up," a man said. She stood with her hands raised and turned to see Noah aiming a pistol at her.

Shara took a deep breath. "There's no need for this," she said. "Noah, I know you do not want to do this."

"Shut up," Noah said.

"I am still in your head."

"This shouldn't have happened."

"No. But it did. Whatever it is you think I mustn't know—"

The rain sounded louder, or her breath came heavily, or the air had grown thick along the docks—she could feel her head throbbing and maybe that was the sound that was getting louder because she had been close to death before, many times, but this was new, this vertiginous fear, for Noah *was* her, just a little, and she was him as well, so it was like turning a weapon upon themselves, which Shara had never done, Noah had never done, and as he lowered the pistol to quiet the throbbing of his own head, or was it her head, Shara batted it away. She punched his face, and he fell to the ground, unconscious. She felt his mind quiet like a candle snuffed out.

Shara picked up the gun and aimed it at Noah. And that baleful sensation came again. She swayed, unbalanced, the world tilting around her, and threw the gun into the space below a service barge. It fell onto the force field holding out the vacuum of space. The field hummed against the pistol, being scanned for signs of life, before allowing the thing to slip through. It fell into the black as Shara fled.

————

Shara left Beinir in the lower hold of the ship to sleep off his stupor. She sat in the pilot's chair in the cockpit and dialed in the coordinates for the small planet where her hide's unit was based. The windows of the ship whitened from the speed of the arclight engine, a smear of space-time around them folding and thinning out, strings being stretched to their limits as they punched through the firmament. The lip of reality could almost be seen, like the edge of a map going over into nothing, the yawning abyss of their tale becoming legend, myth, forgotten. But then it was white and black and still. They would go on.

They arrived at a blue and green planet and entered its atmosphere. Shara was impressed by the ship's inertial dampeners, dazzled and non-plussed at once, still enduring the waning sleep transfer sickness.

The ship soared through a blue sky above rolling hills and great white mountains, a smattering of blue lakes and rivers, green heather, and flowering fields. Three angular sunlets were interposed near the horizon as the ship sank down toward an airfield nestled in a small valley. The docking gear could not be felt when they landed. A twinkling sound came from the navigation panel, and a gentle, feminine voice said, "We have arrived at the destination."

Shara unsnapped her shoulder belt and ducked through the cabin door. She walked down the gangplank to a waiting group of vaguely familiar people. Several of them began unloading the crates of foodstuffs she had packed in the cargo hold. A woman handed her a credit wand in exchange for them.

"Enough to keep you going another six months," the woman said. "Stay alive out there."

Shara nodded and thanked her. But her hide would be creditless once they paid the shifter at the nexus. She would be stranded at the edge of the universe. Shara found it hard to care.

She could feel Noah in her mind, now light-years away from her. But he followed. He was a fool and he could feel her thinking that he was a fool, Shara knew. He would get himself killed in the end, but what could she do? He was not a man who listened when it mattered. Noah wanted to belong in his family, to be a person of consequence, someone like his uncle perhaps, a schemer. Shara could feel his want. But next to his ambition was fear. His despair, his isolation. Would he only ever be a single story to his family, his superiors? The failed brother, the disappointing son, a petulant minor note in a wider history, waiting to be sloughed off by the eddying current of his family, a weakness excised, and Noah was weak, was he not? He knew what his family would do. His uncle had told him as much.

What choice did he have?

You do not want to do this, Noah. Stay.

What choice did he have?

———

"Where am I?" Beinir had only just opened his eyes.

"You are in the cargo bay of the ship we took."

"How—why did we—"

"Remember our tale? The nexus, Beinir. We are speeding for the nexus of this realm."

"If—who is flying the ship?"

"The ship is flying itself, Beinir. Remember that they can do that?"

"That is astounding, Shara. Truly."

"Yes, you love it. I know you do." Shara held a hand in front of his face. "Can you see me? Can you see my hand?"

"I think so, yes."

"How many fingers?"

"Um—seven?"

"No, but that's fine. You are fine. You have been sleeping for some time."

"Sleeping?"

"Yes. More than a day now. Are you hungry?"

"I can see your hand. It is five fingers, forgive me."

"That's right, yes. Good. Good."

"I am hungry. Yes. I am hungry." Beinir shifted on the pile of blankets, slowly sitting up.

"Well, you're in luck. The mess on this ship was stocked with fineries, let me tell you."

"What fineries?"

"Tins and tins of Benara milt, Beinir. The stuff of dreams. Eel noodles from the Nevering Coast. Glow truffles, piles of nera, pearl melons. There was a tank with fifteen lobsters and hundreds of shellras. And light-preserved bread. So much bread. It was as though someone was showing off."

Benir wrinkled his nose. "My hide is repulsed by some of those things."

"I am sure. I sold all of it anyway."

"But—"

"Worry not. I kept a few things. And something special just for you."

"You did? Oh, Shara. What?"

"Beef, Beinir. Aged and dried beef."

"I like beef," he said.

"In every world, you do. Yes. Can you stand?"

"I think so."

Shara slipped an arm around Beinir's waist. "Try to stand. Take my hand."

"What is wrong with your hand?" he asked.

"This? Oh, nothing."

"It looks like something. Like you punched something. Someone. Did you punch someone?"

"I did, yes," Shara said. "There you are. Do you feel stable?"

"My head is all swimmy. As though I took—"

"You did, Beinir."

"I did?"

"We have you to thank for the ship."

Beinir took a tentative step, then stopped. "Who did you punch?" he asked.

"The little man in my head. Do you remember?"

"The little man. Yes. Yes, I remember. He was following us."

"He still follows."

"But you—"

"I'll explain everything later," Shara said. "Let us get you some food. Come. Up the ladder."

"The little man follows. Fate follows. Why?"

"I don't know. He thinks that we will use information from his mind. He is afraid. Very afraid."

"He should be afraid," Beinir said. "Why did you not slay him?"

"Let's go. Through here. Sit, sit."

"I want beef."

"Yes. I will get it. Sit."

"I will slay him if he comes again."

"Here. Eat."

"We will slay him."

"I know."

17

Ronni's directions took Malculm on a journey so circuitous he wondered if she had played a joke on him. The feeling crept in on his third bus change, but after the cab ride and ferry, his suspicion had graduated to almost certainty. She had played him for a fool. That eased his mind about the theft of her wallet, at least. But with no other leads, fool or no, he had little else to do.

Malculm walked the rest of the way once his boat docked, straight past the tacky merchandise stands peppering the docks of Raker's Isle. He walked until the sidewalk ended, then proceeded into the dense undergrowth. Pushing through prickled feather vines, slowbrambles, and slasher ferns, he ignored the cuts that soon marked his palms and forearms, trying to comfort himself with the hope that he would soon be leaving this body behind, anyway.

He wondered what sense of humor would be required to find amusement in this joke. Ronni couldn't see him. Would she simply imagine him, then? The only clothes on his person—rags, really—were now shredded, his skin pricked and sliced by ferns. Would she laugh when she pictured this?

Abruptly the foliage gave way, and Malculm nearly fell. He stood at the edge of a field, though calling it that was probably too generous—it was about the size of one of the dive bars back on Engine. Just a small grass patch, really, with nothing but two men wearing helmets—one shaped like a smiling cat, the other like a frowning demon—standing to either side of a black door that seemed to go nowhere. Malculm walked toward the door. Act like you belong. That had worked for Malculm in more situations than, by rights, it should have. He could count at least six times when—

"Ticket, please," the guard with the cat face said.

"I left my ticket," Malculm said.

"No ticket, no entry," the guard with the demon face said.

"I need to see the Slinger."

"Lots of people need to see him. You can come back when you have a ticket."

"I've got something better than a ticket." Malculm glanced to his left, attempting intrigue. "But if the Slinger isn't interested, I can find someone else who might be."

He knew he had to commit. He turned and left the way he'd come. His eyes were watery. He thought about having to wade back through the brambles and vines, enduring another assault from the plants, enduring another round of cuts and scrapes. Enduring this body for another day.

He was across the field, carefully pulling the first slasher fern cluster back when the guard in the cat helmet yelled after him.

"What kind of better-than-a-ticket do you have for the Slinger?" Cat said.

Malculm let the fern fall. "Let me in, and I'll show him."

"No way. Show first."

Malculm crossed the field once more and pulled Ronni's badge out. It danced through his fingers, over his knuckles, and under his palm before he presented it with a flourish.

The guards whispered to one another, and then Cat turned around, speaking into a radio. A few moments later, they motioned for Malculm to come closer. He went with them, cautiously, until the branches over the door hung over him as well. Cat opened the door, and Demon went inside. Malculm followed, the door leading to a stairwell descending into darkness at a rather steep angle. Before he had a chance to react, the cat guard came in after, closing the door behind him.

The door at the bottom of the stairs opened into a long hallway. Neon tubes ran down both walls and cast a dim glow, throwing pale shadows over the ceiling. In the gloom, Malculm's hands grew antsy, the back pocket of Cat's pants alluring in ways that remained inexplicable—and undeniable. He worked to keep his hands still.

Turgid bass filled the hallway, its beat regular, heavy, a thrum reverberating in Malculm's core and in the hall, growing louder as they went. A small, pink square seemed to float before them as they marched on. It grew and Malculm realized that it was a window, chicken-wired and frosted, hiding a pinkly lit room beyond. The demon guard opened the door, and music rushed out, the volume causing Malculm's ears to pop. It was loud and harsh and bounced in his chest. There was a kid in their twenties in the room dancing feverishly, flecks of sweat flying whenever their hair bloomed out.

The cat guard passed Malculm and the other guard went with him, marching to the stage where a man with a mixing deck and keyboard stood fingering controls. He pulled his headphones down around his neck. The music played on but when the dancer noticed the DJ abandoning his post, they stopped, their face sullen. They walked over to the bar, where a fox-helmeted bartender stood, zesting lemons.

The guards spoke with the DJ, who nodded and said something, then hopped down and strutted, half-dancing, toward Malculm. His movement was confident, determined, and fluid, and Malculm found himself unnerved. He folded his arms across his chest, widening his stance.

"Ooh, look at compeer over here," the DJ said, "the very image of square-jawed, Burel Hird competence. Knock it off with that shit. My friends say you're looking for an exit."

"I need to talk to the Slinger," Malculm said.

"Okay, Drama—you are. I'm the Slinger. You need to relax, though. I can't have all of this," he swirled a hand, encompassing Malculm, "in here."

Malculm lowered his arms.

"Much better. My friends say you have something for me?"

Malculm pulled out Ronni's badge and handed it over. "All yours if you can get me out."

The Slinger examined the badge and clucked his tongue. "Oh, Ronni, Ronni, Ronni. What a little scamp she is." He shrugged and returned the badge. "Still, I have no need for Burel Hird accoutrements down here. If I take this from you and get caught, do you know what happens?" The Slinger leaned close. He smelled of sweat and incense.

"I don't."

"Neither do I. But I'm sure it's nothing good. We may be in the borderlands out here, in this universe, but . . ." He spoke in a hoarse, conspiratorial whisper. "I think you know we're still very much in reach." Beneath the scent of cloying, perfumed smoke was something curdled and sour. The Slinger stepped back and made a gesture of dismissal.

The guards walked over and seized Malculm's arms at the elbow. They dragged him toward the door.

"Please! Wait!" Malculm struggled free of their grasp and stood, for a moment, by himself. Desperation made his mind vibrate; the room around him had become very small, and he'd become very large. If he had any thoughts, he couldn't find them amid the tumult within himself. There was only the swirl of the music, the shudder of the lights, bass rumbling the air in his lungs, stomping like the heartbeat of the world. He had nothing to say. The dumb elation of panic had robbed him of words. He was alive. The guards were beside him, and once more, they grabbed his arms, and once more, they dragged him away. He was alive.

"Anything!" Malculm shouted. "Anything!"

The guards didn't stop, but on his way to the stage, the Slinger did, and the demon-helmeted guard turned.

"Anything!" Malculm shouted again, his voice ragged as he tried to lift it over the music. "Whatever I need to do. Anything."

At a sign from the Slinger, the guards dropped Malculm, and he fell. He sat there, the floor sticky beneath his palms, the cuts along his arms throbbing, and breathed, the air fetid and delicious. The Slinger waited as Malculm stood and crossed the room once more.

"Will you now?" the Slinger said. "Whatever you need to do?"

"Yes."

"Hmm. Well then, here's what you need to do. Part one: Answer me. What are you running from?"

"I just need out of here."

"Not an answer."

"I'm running from . . ." Again, the room shrank, and Malculm swelled. It shivered, or he did, and he plunged into the tumult for a response. "Fuck! I'm running from myself."

The Slinger sighed, heaving his shoulders dramatically. "Tsk. That's just something people say. Let's try again. What are you"—he tapped Malculm on the nose with a finger—"running from?"

Malculm recoiled straight into the chest of the cat-faced guard.

"I don't know. I started, and now I can't stop."

"Not running from, perhaps? Perhaps, running to?"

"I . . . Maybe. I don't know."

"And look at the sight of you. Do you even know? You're wearing scraps for clothes, Drama. Scraps!"

"I didn't even have clothes when I started running."

The Slinger slapped the cat guard. "No clothes! It's charity, then. But we're due for some, aren't we?"

The guards exchanged glances but said nothing.

"Charity it is," the Slinger said. "Your lucky day."

"You'll help me?"

"Well, here's part two. A dance. Can you dance, badge man?"

"Dance?"

"That's what I said."

"Yes," Malculm said. "I can dance."

"We'll see. If you can dance, we're gonna send you into orbit. And if you can't, well, gravity, you know . . ."

The Slinger grinned and shrugged, then walked back to his booth, and the dancer at the bar returned. The guards took their place on either side of the Slinger.

"Get ready for it!" the Slinger said, and the music exploded, twice as loud as it had been, shaking the bottles behind the bar, the glasses, every fixture in the room rattling. Malculm fell, the force of sound overwhelming him, but the dancer stood over him, offered their hand, and helped Malculm up. He got close to them, and they to him, and they moved together, shivering, rolling, sinking to the floor, and rising again like flags whipped stiff in a steady wind. Malculm couldn't remember the last time he'd danced. At first, the music felt strange, like he was learning another language, but the dancer leaned in, their smell sweet and musky, like an aura around them, mixing with Malculm's own.

The music continued to build, a cacophonous crescendo, and Malculm moved with it. He didn't even mind the cuts anymore, stinging with sweat, their pain transmuted into something glorious, something exalted, as though they'd always been there and he'd simply never noticed the hurt. The dancer shimmied close, put their arms over his shoulders, and shouted in his ear no louder than a whisper.

"The beat eventually drops for us all."

Malculm cocked his head, and the dancer simply smiled then slid away, water across the floor. He followed them, wanting to ask a question, wanting to ask a thousand questions, but the beat finally did drop just then, and the world melted away from him.

18

"This is a serious accusation you're making," Priema said.

"Obviously," Duncan replied, and beside him, Trystèsté nodded. "That's why we're talking to you, not Yorek or Zechariah. We need another opinion. It's possible we're wrong. But all three of us . . . less likely."

They stood in the annex linking the Old Hall with the ICH building, a cramped, dour space with the dark, polished wood floors of the mid-80s turns. Diagonal wood beams rose from the walls every few paces, bracing the ceiling—a severe, geometric arbor. Perfect for clandestine meetings, though that wasn't why Priema loved it. No, it was how precisely out of step the low ceilings and long, narrow hallway were with modern, airy Burel Hird architecture, a reminder that even so staid a committee as the Council for Consonant Design was subject to the inexorable gravity of changing human preferences. Though the fact that anyone entering the annex from either side could be seen well before they'd get close enough to overhear a conversation certainly didn't hurt.

"Have you shared it with your teams?" Priema said. "Chel? Griftyn?"

Duncan and Trystèsté glanced at each other.

"No," Duncan said. "I have not informed the Subcommittee for Internal Clarity and Opacity for the Dhalgrim seat, no."

"We've opted for discretion," Trystèsté added.

Priema nodded. "How about any of the other vices?"

Trystèsté snorted and crossed her arms. "I'm not giving Darmeth shit."

"Trystèsté, this is exactly the sort of thing he's good at."

Before Trystèsté could respond, Duncan cut in. "They're all dealing with the same issues. I've had Chel . . . monitoring things."

Now Priema and Trystèsté exchanged a glance. Acknowledgment that councilors surveilled each other was rare, an open secret that decorum demanded go undiscussed. But then, decorum offered no guidance on the situation they found themselves in, so perhaps it needn't hold sway.

Duncan continued. "I thought it better to allow each investigation to proceed in parallel. Slower, perhaps, but less likelihood of confirmation bias. We won't compromise their perspective, nor will we let theirs compromise ours."

Priema nodded and pursed her lips but said nothing. Her eyes flicked over the report Trystèsté had prepared: conjecture, negative correlations, and a persuasive, nightmarish implication.

"Treason," she said, finally.

"That is the correct word, yes," Trystèsté agreed.

"A supposition, currently," Priema said. "Nothing more. Let's not forget that." It was difficult to come to a different conclusion, though. If the Chamber was being deliberately overrun with garbage requests, which was almost certainly the case, then it must be for some purpose. To obfuscate a legitimate request? That was doubtful—a request had to be sent to be actioned. To cause a breakdown in administration? Maybe. That had certainly been Priema's operating assumption when she'd believed the attack came from outside Burel Hird. But if it was true that this all originated within the chain of bureaucracy . . . That was hard to reconcile with everything she knew and believed about her society.

"So how do we test it?" Duncan said.

"Are there any connections between the subcommittees forming these requests?" She already knew the answer.

"Nothing," Duncan confirmed. "They are coming from tiny little satellite localities, from Prime, from everywhere in between. The petitioners are all members in good standing, many of whom have been in their positions for years with no previous issues. And none of the individual requests are objectionable in any way. It's more the timing than the content that's the problem."

Trystèsté nodded. "The only thing that's certain is that it must be a coordinated attack."

"It's the coordination that is the attack," Priema said. "What about Legal? Have these all been properly signed off by the subcommittees' attachés?"

"All double-stamped and fully legitimized," Duncan said. "Which is better than average, as you know."

Priema nodded, then tapped a finger against her chin. The smell of varnish hung thick in the hall, another reason their conversation had been undisturbed: Few wanted to push through the unventilated annex and its atmosphere of resin and shellac. The Custodial Commission had not stinted in their labors, even for so neglected a hall. The visible sections of the exposed wood beams were smooth and glossy. Priema did wonder, though . . . She reached above her head and ran a finger over the back of one of the beams. Her skin caught on the rough surface, and when she examined her fingertip it was dark with grime. Even with the Custodial Commission's diligence and commitment, some corners were inevitably cut.

"These petitions . . . They're all certified by the Joint Adjudication Garrison? Every single one?"

Trystèsté pulled up her report from Glace and bobbed her head. "The Garrison has duly countersigned all of them, yes."

"Mm-hmm. So there is a common element, after all."

"That is hardly revelatory, though," Duncan said. "Every subcommittee has a legal attaché certifying inter-bureau communication. It's all as it should be."

"This is true," Priema said, "but things are not always as they should be, are they?"

"No, they aren't," Trystèsté said, comprehension dawning on her face. "These are all technically correct, which individually is, well, correct. But as an aggregate . . ."

Duncan placed a hand on his forehead. "It's actually anomalous."

The three of them stared at each other for a long moment. From somewhere came the sound of a buffing machine polishing marble, though Priema couldn't tell whether it was from the ICH building or the Old Hall. It was a steady whir, its frequency just high enough that she couldn't tune it out. She'd have to check the Custodial Commission's sensory accommodation parameters and make sure they were being consistently applied. Wiping her palms on the thighs of her pants left twin small, damp smudges.

"This has to be coming from the Garrison's counsel-generals," Trystèsté said finally. "Is every warrior-lawyer on every subcommittee in on it? There's no way. This has to be originating with the Garrison steering committee."

"Members of the Garrison are known to be fiercely loyal to each other," Duncan said, "from the counsel-generals all the way down to the most junior private-intern. If the steering committee issued a decree, everyone would follow it without question."

"Sure, but their plan is what?" Priema said. "Extort the Council? They're weirdly, I would argue inappropriately, hierarchical, but they've always functioned comfortably in the Burel Hird ecosystem. They play an important role in maintaining legality in contact zones, in applying the law with all appropriate force, yes. But they're still only a committee of soldier-jurists, a Rank 2 committee, nothing more than that. They can't possibly think themselves so insulated from consequences."

"We could just wait," Duncan suggested. "See if they issue demands. They'd have to expose themselves then."

"I don't think that's their play. If they make a move, it would be to swoop in and act as savior, magically make this all go away."

"They have already made a move," Trystèsté reminded her. "There's no percentage in making the nuisance but never following up."

"It would be a balancing act," Priema said. "They'd want to wait until we're desperate, until the Council is on the brink; the greater the pain, the greater the gratitude, the greater the reward. But not wait so long that we're able to work any of this out, that we consider them as potential culprits. Which means either they've miscalculated and waited too long already, or they've got something else in mind, and we're barking up the wrong tree. Again."

"Maybe it's bait," Trystèsté said. "They could be expecting us to shut down the lines of communication to the subcommittees? Sow discontent?"

"That is possible," Priema said slowly. "So we don't do that."

"Then we wait," Duncan said. "We can manage a little longer." He didn't sound entirely convinced. "As long as we're able to present a facade of normalcy, they might push things, get desperate. And they might give us something real we can use."

"I would prefer a strategy beyond doing nothing," Priema said.

"So you want to confront the Garrison?" Trystèsté said. "With nothing?"

"They'll put up a fight, whatever we opt for," Duncan said. "They are soldiers as much as they are lawyers."

"You're right, we're going to need proof," Priema said. "None of the attachés have actually done anything wrong. There are no examples of untoward behavior from anyone at the Joint Adjudication Garrison at all. We can't just accuse them."

"I can't think of a way around it," Trystèsté said. "We need evidence that's not circumstantial, and we don't have it."

"Why?" Duncan said.

"Why what?" Trystèsté asked.

"Why do we need hard evidence?" He continued without waiting for a response. "We're not in a courtroom drama on the Entertainment Network. We don't need ironclad proof, or an eyewitness, or a dramatic confession. Real cases almost all rely on circumstantial evidence." He blinked several times. "And this isn't even a legal case. We have no jury to convince. We'd simply be sharing our concerns with the Garrison regarding certain troubling patterns involving their rank and file. A courtesy before forwarding our report to the Subcommittee for Equity, Rectitude, and Compliance." Duncan smiled, the expression awkward. "You know how much they hate ERC poking around."

Priema nodded and rubbed Duncan's arm. "That's a great point, Duncan. Circumstantial evidence is all we need as long as it points clearly to our interpretation. That should be enough to buy us some time, at the very least."

"I'll talk to my contact," Trystèsté said.

———

It was early morning, and the sun had not yet risen above the horizon when Priema arrived at the Joint Adjudication Garrison headquarters. The ground floor café was already open, so she ordered a pot of tea and a pair of pastries and sat down at a table near the window.

Through the rear doors could be seen the capacious expanse of the foyer hall, with its finely dressed people going in all directions, up and down the lift rails connecting the many floors of the building. She wondered who among the throng out there was aware of what was happening. The long-haired man checking his wristboard? The two women rounding the fountain? Maybe all of them. Maybe none. In time, the truth would come out, and the People would know.

The tea had barely cooled to a drinkable temperature when a short but wide figure joined her at the table. Eria Jellisoe was sub-adjutant to the assistant to the prosecutor-general, which made them more or less equal in stature to Priema's own position in the Council, if the Garrison and the Council were comparable. Which they most certainly were not.

Priema exhaled slowly, letting tension melt from her shoulders, and offered a soothing smile, pushing one of the pastries across the table. Her notable sweet tooth was not as consummate as she let it appear, but she'd long ago learned that dessert put people at ease, even when they weren't the ones eating it. And she did like sweets—her trademark dining choices were no hardship, though her own kitchen was nearly devoid of sweeteners. She got her fix easily enough when she was in public.

"Cup of tea, adjutant?" she said.

"Please." Eria undid the clip of their immaculate suit jacket and sank smoothly into the chair across from Priema as she poured. Their biceps bulged under the tailoring, but they delicately lifted the pastry to their lips and took a demure bite. "These are so much better when they're fresh," they said, dabbing at their lips with a cloth napkin. "Usually, I don't get down here until midday, when they've gone just a bit dry. Of course, I eat one anyway. I can't resist cinnamon and clove."

"They are delicious," Priema agreed. They each took another bite of the sweet rolls, and then Priema said, "Have you had an opportunity to review the files my office sent over?"

Jellisoe nodded once. "There was a great deal of material, all of it circumstantial, as you yourself have admitted," they began. "But I fear that your interpretation has some merit."

"I'm glad to hear that," Priema said, "and concerned as well. The People are not served by dissension across bureaus or factionalism within Burel Hird leadership."

"I quite agree," Jellisoe said. "Unfortunately, however, it may well be that dissension is precisely what we are dealing with. In fact, I believe we are very close to uncovering a conspiracy against the Council."

Priema kept her face neutral, but couldn't stop herself from leaning forward. "Tell me more."

Jellisoe took another sip of tea. "We will have to undertake an internal investigation, but I suspect that there is a connection some-where within the Garrison to the nuisance reports the Council has been receiving."

"I see. That is troubling. I'm comforted to hear you admit it, though. I'm certain Equity, Rectitude, and Compliance will similarly appreciate your transparency."

Jellisoe laughed, the sound booming in the small room. "Oh, I'm admitting nothing. I have suspicions, that's all. As I said, we will have to conduct a proper investigation. *Without* ERC interference. But the Council should expect to hear from us soon."

"We appreciate your prompt attention in this matter, and I feel confident your report won't fall behind a filing cabinet to be lost forever."

"We haven't used physical cabinets for anything save triplicate backups in a dozen turns," Jellisoe said. "And I wouldn't be here talking to you if we were likely to 'misplace' our findings."

Priema leaned back in her chair, wondering about Jellisoe's loyalties. Thanks to their martial legacy, the Garrison had a reputation for being just slightly more committed to their own chain of command than to society as a whole.

"The People thank you for any help you can provide," Priema said.

"We serve the People," Jellisoe replied then stood, straightening their suit jacket fastidiously and fastening each of its four clips. "You'll hear from me soon."

"You won't stay to finish your tea?"

Jellisoe smiled. "You know how this works, Priema."

"How unexpectedly transactional, Eria."

"But, if I linger . . ."

Priema nodded. "Who knows what might slip out."

———

Soon, as it turned out, was less than a week later, the torrent of nuisance reports stopping abruptly.

"Does this seem a little too easy?" Trystèsté asked, after joining Priema and Duncan in a vacant meeting room on the mezzanine floor about as far from the Council chambers as one could get while remaining in the same building.

"Well, we can do our jobs properly again," Duncan said. "That's a boon, at least."

"Darmeth sent over messages of appreciation and gratitude," Priema said.

"Did he now?" Trystèsté raised an eyebrow.

"He said, 'Fucking finally,' which I think counts."

"That's his way of saying his team had made no progress at all," Trystèsté said. "And I suppose I wasn't expecting them to admit it so quickly." Gesturing toward the three countersigned confessions on the screen between them, she flopped back into a rolling chair and spun in circles.

"I did have to dump rather a lot of evidence on them," Priema said. "Evidence we likely wouldn't even have if your mystery contact hadn't done whatever they did to make the connections so clear."

"I suspect a person doesn't become pro-gen without having the ability to induce a confession from any one of their subordinates." Duncan's voice was mild, though the implication made the skin on the back of Priema's neck itch.

"Is that what we think this is?" Trystèsté said. "Three sub-adjutants going rogue?" She waved at the names as if they were meaningless. "Or are they taking the fall? For the . . . the Garrison itself." She blanched saying it, and Priema felt the same discomfort.

"It beggars belief, doesn't it?" Duncan said. "Three functionaries, acting alone."

"If it is the Garrison," Priema said, "then we're still waiting for the other shoe to drop. If it's rogue underlings, then this is how they'd have to handle it; the Garrison serves at the pleasure of the Council, just like every committee and subcommittee and lesser assembly in all the nine thousand worlds." The idea that a lower body would hold anything back from the Council was ludicrous. Unless they were planning a coup, which was unthinkable in a different way.

Trystèsté shrugged. "I guess so. This felt like a coordinated end run against the Council all along—I don't like that we're just going to let this be the end of it."

"I'm not sure we do need to let this be the end of it," Priema said. "But the petitions have stopped, and that's what matters. We can function normally again. Once we're fully caught up, we can pursue things further."

"That could be a potentially dangerous complacency. *And*"—Trystèsté cut Priema off—"it looks bad regardless for the counsel-generals that it came from their people."

Duncan nodded. "Although they aren't their people anymore."

"No, I suppose not." The three saboteurs had been found guilty of several counts, stood down from their positions, and dishonorably discharged. The Council could order additional penalties if it wished, but Priema couldn't see the point. If they truly were to blame, the punishment was just; their careers were done, and whatever it was they were trying to accomplish had failed. They were disgraced, dishonored, and disbarred. And if they weren't to blame, they'd be needed when the Council made its own move. A calculated magnanimity was the canny choice.

"Is there a rationale anywhere in those confessions?" Priema asked. "Anything beyond attention?"

"There's nothing in here one way or another," Trystèsté said. "It's just a lot of legal admission of culpability. There's no explanation as to why they did this."

"I realize the Garrison doesn't care about motivation beyond its mitigating influence or evidentiary value, but I find it hard to believe that they didn't even ask. Out of curiosity, at least," Duncan said. "If the counsel-generals know, they've chosen not to share that information with the Council. A conscious decision."

"Now, that is the kind of circumstantial evidence that won't get us anywhere," Trystèsté pointed out.

"We may never know," Duncan said. "And, if we doubt the authenticity of these confessions, perhaps Priema's meeting with Sub-adjutant Jellisoe was sufficient. Perhaps they will, as Ecklan is fond of saying, back the fuck off."

"Heads need to roll," Trystèsté said. "You both know that, right?"

"Those heads aren't going anywhere, Trys," Priema said. "If we so choose, they'll be available to send rolling when the time is right. Sometimes the prudent course is the passive one. The patient one," Priema added as Trystèsté began to speak. "The People would praise our efficiency." The barest hint of irony brought a welcome warmth to Priema's chest, and she smiled. "I suppose we should be pleased for that."

INTERLUDE

On Calyx, evening had purpled into night, and Mëryl and Shann walked through the Park of Eight Saints beneath a sky of layered blackness, a dozen shades of dark. They had left behind the more manicured expanse of the South Lawn and were wandering through the untamed paths west of it, a swath of preserved forest and dimly lit paved trails. While trees encroached on the view of the sky, stretching out above the path, stars were still faintly visible, despite New Darem's glow. And, of course, the At-Saught ship hung above New Darem, geosynchronous, the brightest star in the sky. Occasionally a spark sank down from it or rose up to meet it, skiffs running their ceaseless errands between the planet and the expedition, even at this time of night.

"Do you think there are any travelers elsewhere in this universe," Mëryl said, "or are they just in this system, around Calyx?"

"I think that's a question for someone in Arcalumis."

"I've always wondered about it, though. There's a whole universe of people here—At-Saught is more than sixty worlds, with another nineteen discussing integration and who knows how many more in the process of being contacted. This is a crowded universe, one of the most crowded I've heard of. And an old one. But Calyx is where Withered

Stem showed up. Calyx is where Burel Hird showed up. Calyx is where Harraka showed up." Mëryl gestured at Shann. "Why? Why are we all here? Isn't it an impossible coincidence that the first travelers to this locality all showed up in Calyx, or the At-Saught expedition above it?"

"Mëryl, that's really an Arcalumis question."

"You don't think about it?"

"I don't think about things I have no control over. I don't see the point."

"So I'm just neurotic, then." Mëryl sniffed.

"I didn't say that."

"But I am, though. I know it, you know it. You only put up with me because of what I have access to."

"Mëryl, that's—"

"And you're right. Of course. Why do I care about the reason we all ended up here? I have no control over it and I'll never know the answer. Why can't I just accept that fact? Why can't I just let things go?"

Shann spoke slowly and evenly. "Mëryl, I wish you didn't talk like that. Your inability to let go of things is one of the best things about you, one of my favorite things about you. It makes you who you are."

"It's a pretty noxious way to be."

Shann exhaled loudly and looked away.

"I'm sorry," Mëryl said. "I'll stop."

They walked without speaking. Many of the world flower's blossoms had closed for the night, but its scent still hung in the air, less intense but still potent. Night birds called out to each other in the darkness, cackling and swooping through the trees, making vines creak as they alighted upon them. Athwart a small stream, a stone bridge looked east, the South Lawn distantly visible as a splash of vibrant green through the trees, lit by the floodlights ringing it. Mëryl and Shann walked to the bridge's edge and leaned on its railing. Invisibly, the brook rushed beneath them, the sound of water on rocks a ceaseless whisper.

"Do you know much about this universe?" Mëryl said. "Does your front?"

Shann shook her head.

Mëryl said, "Calyx was one of the Last-Settled. The Regency was already in decline when the first settlers shipped out, and by the time they arrived here, it had functionally collapsed. Can you imagine?"

"I don't think I can."

"You go to sleep, wake up hundreds of years later, and spend the rest of your life building a city and assembling a transmitter so that it doesn't take those who came after you the hundreds of years it took you to arrive. But no one shows up. No one even responds to your message. It's like you went to sleep, and everyone else in the universe died before you woke up."

"A morbid thought."

"Maybe. Maybe a liberating one, too."

"I'm going to be honest, Mëryl. All of that Simulacra stuff? Geography and cartography and whatever else? It's not for me. I'm interested in people. Their lives. Their condition. I can't understand all that six-dimensional, multispatial nonsense. What I can understand is suffering. Injustice. Power: the ways it's abused, the ways it's kept from those who deserve it."

"I see."

"Which is why—"

"You weren't going to ask for my files again, were you?"

"No. Definitely not."

Mëryl pushed away from the bridge's railing and resumed walking, Shann following soon after. The trees around them were impressions of darkness, shadows of sooty blue before the depthless black beyond. The sound of human voices came from ahead, and as they rounded a bend in the path, a couple appeared before them—two men, one berating the other in caustic tones. The reason for the argument was unclear, but that it was recriminatory was evident. The berater slapped the back of his hand into his palm, punctuating his words with each blow. The berated man, meanwhile, looked to Shann and Mëryl, rolling his eyes and spreading his arms slightly, seeming to appeal for some camaraderie, but whatever he was looking for, he didn't receive, and frowned, turning away, and then Shann and Mëryl were beyond him, the upbraiding continuing in their wake.

When the sound of the argument had been swallowed by the night, and there were, once more, only the noises of the trees and the birds and the insects, Shann spoke again.

"So what is your travel mechanism?" she asked.

"I thought that was very private."

"Yes. Maybe. So?"

"I'll tell you mine if you tell me yours."

"Of course."

"All right . . ." Mëryl paused. "Don't laugh."

"I won't."

"I have to sing."

"That's it?"

"I'm not a good singer."

"As in, this body isn't a good singer?"

"As in, none of my bodies have ever been good singers," Mëryl said.

"How is that possible?"

"The Simulacrum has a sense of humor?"

"I have not found that to be true," Shann said.

"Well, making a traveler sing for nineteen seconds to travel and then only giving her bodies that can't carry a tune seems like a cosmic joke to me."

"Does it matter what you sing?"

"I don't know. Probably not. Whenever I've had to travel, I just use whatever my proxy knows best."

"Can you, like, whisper-sing? Do people around you know you're doing it?"

"Shann . . ."

"I'm just thinking, if you were in some situation that you had to escape from, would anyone notice?"

"Why were you thinking that?"

"Because that's how I think!" Shann said. "Escape is often on my mind . . ."

"Well, I don't know. Probably there is some minimum volume. Probably. It's never been an issue, as I've never had to 'escape.'"

"You must have traveled very young. Nineteen seconds? That's not very long."

"I don't know." Mëryl laughed quietly. "Is it not long? I don't really sing to myself in day-to-day life."

"Or maybe your traveling power just wasn't active yet."

"Well, I was young, but not so young. I don't know. I was in the Eighth Expectancy, which is aggrandizement."

"I recognize that those are words but I have no idea what you're trying to say," Shann said.

"Yeah, we were . . . It was weird how I grew up."

"Right, the 'Settlement.'"

"Yes," Mëryl said. "My first time traveling was . . . traumatic. No, that's not right. Less than traumatic."

"It can be traumatic. If you don't know what traveling is. If you don't understand what's happening. That's trauma-inducing. The first time I traveled, I thought I was losing my mind. The meshing alone . . . My moms had me summoned too young. Even though I knew what traveling was, even though I knew I was going to enter a new body, and that that body, and all of its history and memories, would be created in the instant I entered it, trying to untangle my front's memories from my own, not knowing what was me, what the Simulacrum had created for me, was difficult. And if I didn't know what was coming?" Shann shook her head.

"Yes, well, all of that. But also . . . So I was in a music education class. We had to sing hymns. That was part of the education. And I never did. Because I'm not a good singer. I mouthed them but didn't actually sing. Which worked fine for years. But there was a girl. Magdie. She and I were . . . we weren't allowed to have rivals. Every conflict had to be voiced publicly and resolved, and it simultaneously made everyone more open and more secretive. I can't explain it. Everything being public meant nothing festered. That was the idea. And we absolutely got called out. 'Hey, Tahmi, you're being very awkward with Ghie. Why is that? Ghie, why are you and Tahmi being awkward?'"

"Yikes."

"It certainly helped in making you aware of yourself and your own pettiness."

"In a good way?" Shann asked.

"That's another question entirely. But me and Magdie, we were rivals as much as we could be rivals. We each wanted attention from Miss Sae, we each wanted to be the best and most devout little settler. We were probably just too similar. We weren't popular kids but we also weren't—you know what? I can't explain the dynamics. They were just too weird and specific to there."

"I'm still stuck on the singing. How did you manage to avoid singing for that long? Were there no children's songs? Lullabies? No schoolyard taunts?"

Mëryl shook her head. "No."

"Nothing?"

"The hymns *were* music. Singing itself was worship. There wasn't music that wasn't also worship."

"Well, then, what was it that you were singing when you first traveled?"

"A good question. What was it? Oh. It wasn't in music education. It happened during service. That's what it was called. We had just come from the school, from music education, to sing during the adult service. It was . . . Wow, I haven't thought about this in so many years. It was called 'We'll Feed.' Something like that. But feed as in offering food to someone, not as in we ourselves will eat. Those were two different words."

"Do you remember it?" Shann asked.

"Yes? Kind of? Language is weird when traveling, right? Because the words weren't in the language we're speaking now; this body doesn't know that language. And my mind sort of does, but only sort of. So I know roughly what the words of the hymn were, but I also know that those words aren't exactly conveying the right meaning."

"Well, what are the not-quite-right words?"

"Well, there's a lot about the Lord, which . . . That word here comes from the Regency period. It was the . . . the God-king? That's what's coming to my mind. But that's not really right, either. It's conveying the same general idea, but there was a, it was a more unitary, singular thing, the Lord, the God-king, baked into the word was that he was the only—"

"Mëryl."

"What?"

"The words."

"Yes. The words. Right. The words . . ."

Mëryl looked down and closed her eyes for a moment, then looked up, her eyes still closed, and began reciting.

"'Our flesh will taste the air, oh Lord, our soiled flesh, its seed unclean, our flesh will taste the air.'"

"Why 'soiled'? Why 'unclean'?!"

"Umm . . . And then, 'Our bones will greet the stars, oh Lord, our ragged bones, stripped bare, oh Lord, our bones will greet the stars. Our blood will wash the dirt, oh Lord, our fouled blood, spilled carefully, our blood will wash the dirt. We'll feed the worms, oh Lord, oh Lord, oh Lord, we'll feed the worms. We'll feed the worms, oh Lord, oh Lord, oh Lord, we'll feed the worms.' That bit repeats."

"Wow," Shann said.

"Hearing it now, it sounds worse than it felt back then."

"Does it?"

"The melody was pretty cheerful, actually."

"You were 100 percent being raised in a cult," Shann said.

"Was I?"

"Was human sacrifice involved?"

"I don't think so . . ." Mëryl said.

"'Our fouled blood, spilled carefully'? Yeah, there was human sacrifice."

"You're making it sound bad."

"If quoting what you said makes it sound bad, then I think the problem is in what you said and not me quoting it."

Mëryl said nothing.

"I'm sorry," Shann said. "I wasn't trying to upset you about your childhood."

"No, you're right. It does sound like a cult. One that may well have involved human sacrifice."

"Mëryl, I was joking."

Mëryl didn't respond, and they walked without speaking for a moment.

"Well, you're not part of it anymore," Shann said. "That's over now. You're free."

"I know . . ."

"What?"

"It's just . . . I traveled a lot when I discovered what was happening. Because I was scared. Because I was lonely. Because no matter where I ended up, it didn't feel right."

"I understand."

"Do you? You grew up traveling with your family. I was a kid. I didn't know what had happened. What was happening. A lot of people, if they're not born into a traveling society, can get back to their world the first time they travel because it's still the closest locality to them. I couldn't. When I traveled, I didn't know what was happening, but I knew it was the fault of my singing. So I started singing again. Immediately. But . . ." Mëryl shrugged.

"But the Simulacrum had shifted," Shann said.

Mëryl nodded. "Or, while the Settlement was close to the universe I ended up in, there was another one even closer to it, which is where I wound up. Like I said, I traveled frequently then, but it was always . . . It was always scary. I didn't want to keep traveling. I was always worried wherever I went would be worse than where I was. But I just couldn't—" She stopped herself and took a breath. When she spoke again, her words came slowly. "The reason it's upsetting to think there was something rotten at the core of the Settlement? When I finally wound up in a Withered Stem proxy, it felt familiar. The way everyone thought of life, of existence, it wasn't the same, but . . . it felt like home."

"Mëryl."

"Yes?"

"Does the Withered Stem practice human sacrifice?"

"Very funny."

Shann put a hand on Mëryl's shoulder. "I'm being serious," Shann said, her mouth twitching into a smile.

"Then no, not to my knowledge, we don't practice human sacrifice."

"How about cannibalism?"

"Cannibalism?!"

"I just want to make sure you're safe!"

"No, there is no cannibalism, and no, there is no human sacrifice. And I'm not trying to say there was immediate recognition for me or anything like that. There was just—" She gestured with her hands, making circles. "I'd been wandering for so long." She stopped herself and took a breath, then turned away, looking out into the darkness of the park.

She said, "There's a five-hundred-year burn coming up on Üt. If I could get approval, I'd go back. There's no room, I don't think, and after the burn, there will be even fewer accommodations."

"You burn your own cities?"

"It's not quite as simple as that, but sort of."

"Is it to get rid of all the bodies from the human sacrifice?"

"Shann . . ."

"Sorry."

"I saw a fifty-year burn not long after I arrived. I was still new to Withered Stem—I couldn't have been more than twenty-three, twenty-four. When Sëlwyn explained it to me . . . Well, I didn't understand. I didn't understand Withered Stem yet. Didn't understand the Settlement. I didn't understand myself. I'd been thinking about the Settlement a lot. About life. Death. Withered Stem felt familiar, and so I didn't trust it. I was a kid, is what I'm saying. I was having doubts. And then . . ."

"And then?"

"And then the burn. Almost half a continent. It's a communal thing. Not the burning—there are people whose job that is, rangers who tend the forests, who keep them healthy. I thought it would kill them to see their forests burning. We gather around the edges. It's important to witness, to help you understand. And fire is mesmerizing, of course. Even this," she gestured at one of the lamps along the path, burning with the same heatless red of the chemical flames at the café, then made the flame above flicker by knocking the post with her hand. "Fire is beautiful. I can watch it for hours. We all can, can't we? A flame is arresting. But to see a forest burn? It's . . ."

Mëryl stopped.

"It was only a fifty-year burn. Most of us will see at least one. Many of the trees come through just fine. It's a lot of underbrush management, really. But even still, thousands gather. You sit around the edges and watch and talk and watch. It's solemn, but it's also a celebration. I'm not sure the mood is something I can really convey. We eat, we sing, we dance. Schools devote whole units to it, the ecology of the forest fire, the chemistry; classes are held outside for a couple of days. You can see the flames from Caëmvërn—the city is part of the forest, and the forest is part of the city. From fifty stories up, it looks small, but when you walk along the river, and the smoke is above, reflecting in the glass, and you can hear the fire, even from as far away as you are, the way you can hear a . . . Afterward, once it's passed through an area, we tour the woods. There are still little fires burning. Here and there. Nothing dangerous, and the rangers are with you the whole time. But still. Pockets of embers, some stumps still smoldering, isolated flames. The smell of a forest after it burns . . . I still didn't get it then. Not yet. It was a tragedy, I thought, so much destruction, so much waste."

She fell silent, and they both listened. New Darem could be heard faintly, as an ocean can be from behind dunes, a slurry of city sounds compressed into a wash of human static. Mostly, though, there was the sound of the park, of trees, wind, and the stream they walked along.

"I took another tour. Three months later. There were still signs, of course. Blackened bark. Charred logs. The smell was faint but present. But there was such growth, such new growth. The forest wasn't just still alive, it was vibrantly so. Ferns and flowers and saplings and moss. Animals feeding on the sprouts, making homes. Trying to stave off death, viewing it as anomalous, an aberration, something to be cured, it's . . . Deny death and you deny life. That's what I didn't understand. Death to me felt like the end because I could only conceive of myself as myself.

It took me until I walked through those fields . . ." She stopped and collected herself. "It took me until the fire to understand I wasn't just me. I was everyone, and everyone was me, and that's a comforting, beautiful, astounding thing to realize. We'll feed the worms, Shann, and the worms will feed us."

Shann handed Mëryl a handkerchief, and Mëryl wiped her eyes and blew her nose.

"You still believe that we'll feed the worms," Shann said, "and that they'll feed us, yet you want to defect."

Mëryl laughed and knuckled her tears away. "I don't know what I want."

Again, the communicator buzzed in her bag. She rolled her eyes and reached inside, stilling the device without looking at it.

"It's really okay," Shann said. "You can check. I don't mind."

Mëryl waved the idea away. "I don't want to."

"I won't be offended."

"Shann, do you not want to talk to me? Would you rather be doing something else?"

"No, I'm just saying I don't want you to miss anything. Anything that might be happening in the world."

"I don't want to miss anything that's happening here. With us."

Shann nodded but said nothing, and they walked in silence for some time. Mëryl spoke first.

"I don't know if I'd ever actually leave Withered Stem, but . . . Isn't it possible that the ethos is right, but the execution isn't?"

"I've yet to find a universe in which the execution is right, regardless of the ethos."

"Well, that's Harraka right there, isn't it?"

Shann snorted. "I didn't know I was so easy to peg."

"We're all products of where we're from. No matter how many bodies we inhabit, it's impossible to escape who we are, right?"

"Hmm."

"I'm Withered Stem, so I'm a neurotic overthinker. You're Harraka so you're restless and independent and wonderfully, heartwarmingly loyal."

"I didn't realize categorization was so simple," Shann said.

"Oh yes. If studying the Burel Hird academies has taught me anything, it's that it's very difficult to be something other than what your society makes you. It's why Burel Hird are inflexible authoritarians, Arcalumis are impractical fantasists, and Firmāre are liars and betrayers."

"I see." Shann looked away and kicked a loose branch off the path. "You still haven't told me how you discovered your travel ability."

"Right. Yes. Singing. The Settlement. The wretched Magdie."

"I don't know why she's wretched yet."

"Because she outed me," Mëryl said. "She backed me into a corner and made me sing."

"So is she wretched because she made you sing or wretched because she made you travel?"

"I don't know. Both, maybe. Probably. It happened, as I told you, during service. We filed in during the sermon and were standing on risers, waiting. And then, out of nowhere, during a lull: 'I have to make Admission.' She announced it to the whole congregation. This was normal enough—public admissions were looked upon positively. 'Myriel and I are feuding.' This is what she said."

"Myriel?"

"That was my name. That girl's name. That's how it's always been with me—similar names in each of my bodies but never quite the same."

"But Mëryl is your name here?"

"I first had it on Üt. But it's what I feel most comfortable with, so it's what I use everywhere I can."

"Names are weird in the Simulacrum . . ."

"Yes," Mëryl said. "Yes they are. Anyway. Magdie."

"Magdie."

"In her admission, she said we were fighting about the nature of death and the destination of souls. This is what I remember. I also know that it's impossible, as the soul's destination was known to us in the Settlement: It was one of the universe's stars. All good souls were burned up in a star forever, and it was the greatest bliss to be joined with others in that eternal flame. This was foundational for us. It wouldn't have even occurred to us to doubt it. It would be as though she'd announced we were fighting about what our names were. There was simply nothing to fight about. But that's what I remember. 'And what should your punishment be?' Mr. Rhaett asked. We were meant to name our own punishment."

"Of course."

"Who better than the sinner to know the depth of the sin? Magdie said we should sing the next hymn alone, the two of us. That was a just punishment. Mr. Rhaett said, 'And why would it be punishment to praise the Lord, Magdie?' And Magdie said, 'Because we don't like singing.'"

"Devious."

"I was outmaneuvered. Outflanked. It was a surprise attack, a stroke of tactical genius that I never would have credited Magdie with. Deny it, and I'll be made to sing to prove its falsity. Accept it, and it becomes a just punishment. I don't think I was impressed then, but I certainly am now."

"Did she actually not like singing?" Shann said.

"I don't know. If she didn't, I was unaware of it. All I remember thinking then was that I had no idea how she knew that I didn't like singing because I was sure I'd been so careful in how I hid my not-singing. Apparently, I wasn't quite as careful as I'd thought."

"Apparently not."

Mëryl looked at Shann expectantly, her eyebrows raised. "So?" she said.

"So what?"

"Now you have to tell me your first time."

"I do?"

"Shann . . ."

"Are you whining?"

"Yes! If you want to be fair, you have to tell me. Now," Mëryl said.

"Who says I want to be fair?"

"I give you all of my history and personal tragedies, and you give me nothing?"

"I give you nothing?" Shann said. She stopped walking and turned away. A zeppelin passed overhead, low enough that it could be heard. Its lights marked it as a floating club, the gondola likely glass-bottomed in at least one room, the better to heighten the thrill of the dance. None of the club's music was audible, though—only the smooth, electric thrum of the propeller as the zeppelin finished a circuit of Eight Saints and moored to one of the skyscrapers that lined its edge.

"Have you seen the pitcher here?" Shann said. "They light it up at night. It's a big one."

"I haven't."

"This proxy likes the flower a lot. A lot. She's visiting all the major pitchers. Wants to get down to Kahoeckee to see the pitcher there before she dies, but, you know." Shann shrugged. "Musician."

Mëryl laughed. "They don't make vacationing easy here, do they?"

"It doesn't seem that way, does it? Anyway, come on, it's just this way."

They continued on the path to a curve where it doubled back on itself, wending toward the South Lawn. Sprouting from the curve was a second path, though this one was unpaved, a trail of well-packed dirt leading through the underbrush. Branches closed in around them as they walked, long boughs drooping over the path, the feathery leaves of the addle-bark tree grazing their foreheads and hair.

Several minutes down the trail, they reached a clearing with a small gully at its center. Bright lights illuminated the clearing, directed toward the center of the gully, where a wide hole was present: the flower's pitcher. Surrounding the pitcher were pink and yellow petals, their surface visibly slick, a glossy, glistening coat that gave the colors a metallic sheen. Faintly, spiny hairs could be seen within the pitcher, pointing downward, their bristles black shadows within the darkness of the hole. A low fence ringed the clearing, with signs posted at regular intervals reading:

STOP. GO NO FURTHER.

IF YOU FALL IN YOU WILL

NOT BE RETRIEVED AND YOU *WILL* DIE.

YOUR LIFE IS WORTH MORE THAN A PHOTOGRAPH.

"Well, that's aggressive," Mëryl said.

"It was a trend a little while back. Taking pictures posed over the mouth. Making it look like you were about to fall in. Or were falling in. Six people died in New Darem in one summer. Kids, mainly."

"Thus the sign."

"I'm surprised you hadn't heard."

"So am I," Mëryl said.

"It would've closed up small enough that only an infant would fit if that hadn't happened. There aren't any animals big enough here anymore for it to stay open, and the Botanical Authority doesn't feed pitchers. This one was closing up, actually. After it got the six people, though . . ." Shann shrugged. "It'll be open another hundred years now."

They stayed there, looking down into the gully for long moments.

"It really is very slick," Shann said.

"How many of the pitchers has your front been to?"

"All of the twenty biggest, except for Ganly's Maw. And Kahoeckee, obviously. The Maw is planned for next summer if I don't muck things up."

"And how could you do that?"

"You know. If I end up being here a little more." Shann raised her eyebrows. "On Calyx."

"Uh-huh. And which has been your favorite?"

"The Great Hole outside Trivetna has been closing for centuries, but it's still remarkable. It was apparently once the size of a New Darem city block, which I can't even really conceive of."

"What's it like now?" Mëryl asked.

"Still big. Maybe ten times bigger than this?"

"And is it your favorite or your front's?"

"Can you tell the difference?"

Mëryl shrugged. "Sometimes? Maybe. I don't know. I've probably been here too long, in this body too long, to have any sort of distance."

"Well, it's a good body to occupy, at least." Shann smiled and Mëryl leaned forward over the fence, looking deeper into the pitcher, before settling on her heels. Shann reached out and touched the back of Mëryl's hand, their knuckles brushing against each other. Her gaze resolutely forward, Mëryl said nothing.

"Mëryl . . ."

"Hmm?"

"What are we?"

Mëryl shrugged and turned her back, walking down the dirt trail, away from the lights and the hole and the clearing. Shann came behind, and once more branches swept over their faces, depositing leaves and seed pods in their hair and on their clothes. They emerged onto the path, but Mëryl stopped, Shann almost running into her. Mëryl took a deep breath and turned to face Shann.

"You know what I want," she said. "And I know what you want. They're not the same."

"Aren't they?" Shann said.

"You know they're not."

"Do they have to be different, though?"

"They do. You made that very clear last year at the Palladium after I told you how I felt. Or had you forgotten our very quiet, very awkward ride back into New Darem?"

For a moment, Shann said nothing. Then, she said, "Could you be with someone who didn't care about the things you care about? Who didn't share your values?"

"And I don't? You seriously think that . . ." Mëryl drew closer to Shann as she spoke, her voice rising, but she stepped back as she trailed off. The wind blew, her hair falling across her eyes. "I need to be getting back. You've heard my communicator buzzing all night long in my bag, which means tomorrow will be a long day."

She continued on, Shann opening her mouth but not speaking before following at Mëryl's heels, a step behind. They walked in silence, accompanied only by the sound of leaves scuffling beneath their feet and the chirruping of insects. The path widened as they walked, the lamps growing more frequent, and a small stone wall emerged out of the dirt, running on both sides of the trail. Gradually, the city returned to them as they returned to it. Smells were carried on the night air, food and garbage and hints of mildewy vapor from the buses, along with the noises of New Darem. They reached a fork in the path and both stopped, neither looking at the other.

"I'm heading back to the South Lawn," Mëryl said. "I'll catch the bus from Kalathis."

"Let's go this way, up to Peace Fountain."

Mëryl shook her head. "I have to head home. I told you, tomorrow will probably be rough."

"It'll add ten minutes, and we'll get to walk across the plaza. The view of the city down the concourse is amazing at night."

"I can't."

Their eyes met, and they stood facing each other for a moment, neither speaking. Not far off, down the path to the right, the lights of the South Lawn turned the canopy into a kaleidoscope of greens and blacks. Shouts of triumph and despair were audible, though whether from one of the pickup games of tend-let or from a game of Yio, it was impossible to tell. Mëryl looked away from Shann, gazing in the direction of the sounds, holding her bag close to her and thumbing the At-Saught patch on its flap. The zeppelin, having completed its circuit, was visible, moored to the CosLife building, floating above the cityscape like a technicolor pill, where it let off the least hardy of its revelers and took on a second wave. A bell sounded and Shann turned her head in its direction: an elevated subway arriving at the Parkside East station. Soon it would depart, skirting along Peace Plaza and cutting across the corner of the park, north into the hills. The train's announcement reached them, the words garbled, and the bell rang once more.

"To be honest," Shann said, "I don't really remember my first time beyond what I said: the disorientation, the confusion, the fear. I was young enough that I can't say anything more than that for certain. I know some societies have prohibitions on traveling with kids, but Harraka doesn't. That's kind of the point, I think." She laughed, short and quiet.

Mëryl hesitated for a moment, starting to gesture to the right, but looked down at her feet. "And?" she said.

"It passed. The feelings, the disorientation. Truthfully, it could have been much worse. I don't think about that time much."

"You don't think about that time?"

Shann started up the left path, toward the fountain and the sound of the bell and away from the South Lawn. She spoke without looking back to see if Mëryl was following her; she was.

"The second time I traveled, that is, the third world I was in . . . It was challenging. We were fleeing, my mother and I. I didn't understand that's what was happening at the time. Or, perhaps I did, in a broad sense, but not truly. I didn't understand a lot, back then. I knew it wasn't good, whatever it was that was going on with us. Up to that point, it wasn't like our lives had been . . . We hadn't lived in luxury, but we'd been secure. Safe. I hadn't been afraid, not of anything real. The dark, drowning. The Simulacrum sending me into a gross body that I hated. You know: kid stuff."

Mëryl had caught up to Shann, and they walked side by side, Mëryl watching Shann's face and Shann watching the ground.

"I don't know how long we were there, in all," Shann said. "I don't even remember arriving. Maybe they moved me while I was sleeping. We had traveling pass phrases, so parents could let their kids know who they were if the Simulacrum dropped them into fronts they didn't recognize. I don't remember any of that, though. I remember the food, which I hated, and the body, which felt puny and pathetic, and the overwhelming sense that something was chasing us that I was absolutely powerless to stop. Three or four Calyxian months. That's probably about how long I was there. Half a year."

A group of young people approached from the opposite direction, heading into the park, and Shann fell silent. They were singing a song, popular among the youths just then, about a man who falls in love with Death, only to find that Death is wholly uninterested in him, and so he is made an unwilling immortal, waking each morning hoping for a visit he's doomed to never receive. They broke around Shann and Mëryl like a stream around a rock, not acknowledging the pair's existence—or their youth preventing them from even noticing they were not alone in the park.

When they had passed, Shann resumed her story, though her voice was quieter, and she kept her head down.

"Before we left, I spent the night in a train tunnel. I couldn't travel myself yet, or didn't know I could. Perhaps I could have, had I known. My mother left me there and went out to find someone, a mover for me. The tunnel was supposed to be safe as long as I didn't move. She'd used it as a hiding place herself when she was younger. We were journeying at night then, hiding during the day, so when we got there, it was dark. We felt along the wall and found the same nook my mother had hidden in however many years before. She left me there with what was left of our food. Said she'd come get me in two days."

Shann took a breath.

"Four days I sat there. The food didn't last past the first day."

"Oh, Shann . . ."

"In the tunnel, there were bodies and sounds, and I wondered if it was the train, but it was rats eating the bodies. They never bothered me. They crawled over my feet, and I shifted, but they left me alone. I don't know if the bodies were people who died trying to pass through the tunnel or if they were dumped there, or if they fell off the train. I don't know what happened. When day came I could see some of them. I was deep enough into the tunnel that everything was dim, but there was enough light to make out faces. Or their remains. Some split open by the trains' wheels, others nibbled at. Coming apart. I wanted to push them away so they weren't looking at me, but I was too scared."

"I'm so sorry."

She stopped walking, Mëryl pausing beside her. "Could we sit?" A bench stood back from the path, shaded during the day by long, swooning branches, its outline only barely visible in dusk's murk. The sounds of bats came from above—quiet, leathery flutters as they wheeled around the lampposts.

"Of course," Mëryl said.

They sat, Shann hunching forward, her elbows on her knees, looking down at her feet. She began speaking without looking up.

"There was soot over everything. The walls, the bodies. Me. The planet was nearly postindustrial, but there were still pockets where steam locomotives were in regular use. Progress had not been distributed evenly. I still remember the taste of the soot on my tongue. I couldn't breathe without tasting it. And when a train passed, I couldn't breathe at all, the air was too thick. And after it passed, all the smoke and ash would just drift down, and I could feel it landing on my arms like hot snow. But it didn't melt. It just stayed there, piling atop itself each time a train went by. Fourteen per day. I counted them. Counted down the time between them—fourteen each day and three each night. We got lucky that first night. A train had just gone by. The nook was half a mile into the tunnel. If the timing had been wrong, we would have been hit."

Mëryl nodded but didn't say anything.

"The trains were crowded. Always. I could never make out faces in the windows, but I could see people in them. They were just dark shapes backlit by yellow light, but they were there. Sometimes, people clung to the sides of the trains or crowded on the back platform well beyond what it could hold. Not often, and not many, but I wondered if that was how some of the bodies wound up in the nook. No one fell off while I was there, though."

Shann stopped and leaned back, kicking her feet out and tapping her heels in the dirt. Shifting, she slid her hands beneath her so she was sitting on them and bobbed her head up and down before continuing.

"One night, a group of people passed by. They must have waited for the train; they showed up not long after it passed. They weren't silent—I heard them coming the whole way—but they didn't talk. There were maybe twenty of them, coming from the same direction we had come. I thought they might be the people who were hunting us, though now I think they were probably just rebels. One of them looked right at me. I couldn't see well, but I could see they were gaunt, dirty, but well-equipped. Large packs on their backs. Weapons. The one that looked at me, I thought they saw me. Were deciding what to do. I didn't move. Couldn't. I'd been sitting there so long . . . It was the third night. I stared back at them. Our eyes locked. They clucked once, the sound was loud in the tunnel, and kept walking. They didn't see me at all. They just saw a pile of filthy corpses."

Mëryl put her hand on Shann's back, rubbing gently back and forth.

"I don't know what it says about me that I waited for four days. I don't know how long I would have waited beyond that. Or what it says about who I was. The me now wouldn't have waited that long. I would have ventured out. Died, probably. I don't know if the current me would have even managed to wait a day."

Shann stared off into the darkness, her mouth slightly open and her eyes wide, then shook her head.

"What happened?" Mëryl asked.

"My moms came back. With a mover. A weak one, though. We had to get to a particular waterfall for him to be able to move us. It took three days of hiking. I coughed the whole way there, wiping ashy blood from my chin. If that coat made it to fifty years old, I'd be shocked. When we finally did make it to the waterfall, I just wanted to sit in the pool at its base. They wanted to travel, though, and said, 'You'll feel clean as soon as you're in a new body.' But I didn't think about traveling in that way. Not yet. The idea that what I was experiencing was tethered to the front I was in? I just couldn't conceptualize that. Even though I myself was in my third body. Everything still felt so permanent."

"Did you get to take a bath?"

"No. We traveled—no navigator—and ended up in a pastoral world. Farming. Hand tools, draft animals. Clean air. It was just luck. Even there, though . . . I felt the soot for months. In my nose, on my tongue. Every breath I took, I tasted it. And no matter how often I bathed or how vigorously I scrubbed, it was still there, an invisible second skin. I couldn't shed it. Like a . . . a hangnail. Like my whole body was a hangnail, something I just needed to grab hold of and strip off. But, of course, I couldn't. So I just went through each day feeling like I needed to be peeled."

They sat close to the edge of the park, the stairs up along the East Wall starting not far down the path. While Peace Fountain itself couldn't be heard, the crowd gathered near it could, a muted murmuring of people-sounds, pitched just below coherence. Another elevated arrived, outbound once more, and once more, the station bell rang. This time, the train's announcement was clear, the automated voice cheery and loud through the trees: The next stop would be the South Hills–Eight Saints station. With another ring of the bell, the doors clunked closed, and the motor whined to life, an electric keening, as the elevated slid north through the park and into the night. In its wake, the night was quiet once more, its absence noticeable in the sighing of the breeze in the branches and the rasp of Shann's boots on the pavement as she shifted, hunching forward, making herself small.

"People say residue is a myth," Shann said, "that you can't carry sense memories between coats, but it's a lie. It took almost a year and three more travels before I could feel clean again."

Mëryl nodded, looking off into the distance. "Did you escape?" she said.

"What?"

"What you were fleeing from. Did you escape it? Are you free?"

Shann sat up, her back straight, and put her hands on her knees, her eyes widening slightly.

"If I find out, I'll let you know."

PART FOUR

19

"Congratulations on your escape."

"Who says I'm escaping?" Malculm asked.

Laerd shrugged. "Exfiltration, expatriation, whatever you want to call it. People who leave Burel Hird territory generally aren't doing so because of their deep bonds with Hird society."

"I'm going back," Malculm said. "I'm going to return."

"Well, let me know when you plan to, and I'll be happy to accept your money and send you right back to where you came from. They're your credits to waste."

That had been four days ago. Four days spent draining the small account he'd set up in this universe a decade prior. Four days spent playing the pauper's slots in the bar and drinking their cheapest draft. Four days spent realizing that he had no idea what he was doing and no idea how to proceed.

The few connections he had on Nightingale Station—a remote, frontier speck in an expansive universe—could offer him no insight that might provide him some direction. And could he blame them? His inquiries were comically vague: Had they heard anything about Withered Stem expanding their territory? They had not. Was there talk of anything potentially significant about the Geçiş locality? There was not.

What significance was there in Withered Stem contracting Of Talas? No significance at all; they'd been doing this for centuries. Why don't you know this? Aren't you supposed to be an intelligence officer?

Malculm's training had been designed to weed out distractions and noise from analysis as brutally as possible and to pare down the extraneous until all that remained was evidence. Theories are simply preconceptions by another name, as Bearshen was fond of saying, and preconceptions can only cloud judgment. Yet all he had were theories, so how could he rely on his judgment?

If he were to rely on only evidence, the conclusion was unavoidable: Malculm was lost.

Sitting at the bar, drinking alone, he was forced to confront that fact, and that confrontation was going poorly. The vertigo of despondency held him tight and made him doubt things he was shocked to learn he had the capacity to doubt: the nature of his work for all these years. The nature of Burel Hird. Even his commitment to it. He couldn't tell if these thoughts had been with him his whole life but only now, in the forced stillness of his exile, were audible, or if he himself was changing. To be pursued by your own people, restricted, controlled? How could he *not* change?

But then, he had always been controlled. Sometimes, the chain was loose. Other times, its weight was overbearing, but it had always been there. This was the point of Burel Hird: what allowed it to function, what allowed it to bring goodness into the transmundi, what allowed it to bring peace, safety, and justice. Once, he himself had been a link in that chain, restrained and restraint both. It had given him purpose. Meaning. In all his actions, he had felt righteous, for he acted on behalf of a righteous cause: Burel Hird.

Why, then, the change in his feelings?

Pare back all preconceptions until naught but evidence remains. The evidence suggested he was not, in his heart, Burel Hird anymore.

His thoughts were ugly, and he despised them and despised himself for having them. He sat alone and drank until he had them no longer.

———

The screen above the bar usually streamed some spectacle—human sports or alien pornography, Beinir had difficulty distinguishing—with an overlay of the day's arrivals and departures at the port. Now, though, for some reason it was tuned to a dead channel, its picture the precise color of the sky on Orva Noxal on a stormy day.

Beinir looked around at the few people sitting at tables and the seemingly abandoned serving area.

"Is there no one on duty?" he growled at the empty space behind the bar. "What kind of taverner is uninterested in currency? Do they fancy themselves beyond the necessity of coin?"

"I don't think so," Shara said as a harried-looking face popped up from behind the bar.

"Sorry," the barkeep said. "Just dealing with a minor . . . infestation." She stomped a foot down hard and there was a crack and a squelch, the sounds of a boot being scraped against the floor grating. "What can I get you?"

Beinir ordered something that claimed to be ale and Shara gestured toward a bubbling neon green liquid on tap. She handed the bartender a small console to pay and they carried their drinks to a table bolted to the floor near a bank of electronic games of chance.

"You want to try your luck?" Shara asked Beinir, as he eyed the machines carefully.

"Perhaps I shall," he replied. "There won't be any problems if I leave you alone?"

Shara cocked an eyebrow.

"Noah," Beinir said, by way of explanation.

Shara nodded. "He's here. Somehow. I think. Things are a little fuzzier. Perhaps because the way is thin. So many wayfarers about."

"Should I remain?"

"No. It won't be a problem. And if it is, you won't be far." She smiled and squeezed Beinir's arm.

"Indeed, I shall not be. For though I away to untold riches, the heroism of a roamer is never distant! And also, this establishment is quite small, so I would certainly notice any foolishness." He gathered his drink and stalked over to a particular terminal with flashing lights and an annoyingly strident ping. Shara watched him play for a few moments, but the repetitive game didn't hold her interest long. She glanced around the room, playing her own game—wondering if the patron was there for conviviality or was, like her and Beinir, awaiting a meeting with the shifter who could send them to further worlds. For a tidy price, of course.

Time passed, and either the ping grew more strident or Shara's tolerance waned. She moved back to the bar for a refill—the drink had proved tasty, if oversweet—and settled in on a stool, anticipating another wait as the infestation, whatever that meant, was dealt with.

A stranger sat down beside her. "Where are you off to, then, traveler?" they said.

Shara shrugged.

"No destination in mind? Leaving it up to the Ol' Wryneck? See where it spits you out?"

"Perhaps I shall."

"You travel for pleasure, then?"

"Maybe."

"Brooding and mysterious! What a delight."

The two sat in silence for a moment. Shara felt unmoored. She had difficulty focusing. Sense impressions played around her, ghosts of sounds, tastes, an empty room, a desolate gangway; Noah was close.

"This is the part in the conversation where you ask me about myself," the stranger said.

"And do you travel for pleasure?"

"Oh, does anyone find pleasure when they're surrounded by Burel Hird?"

"Some do."

"Talk my ear off, why don't you! Two words? You think I have all the time in the world?"

Shara laughed. "I think you might talk enough for us both."

"Nonsense. I talk enough for at least six."

Shara laughed again but didn't respond.

The stranger leaned closer. "You seem muddled. Not that I blame

you. Around here? Who knows what might happen? Snake-bird's muddled up more than one job on this sorry hunk."

"Snake-bird? You talk in nonsense."

"Snake-bird! The Ol' Wryneck. The Twisted Jynx. It's all just the
Simulacrum, looking every which way at once, making trouble. I thought
for sure all you Talons would know this stuff."

"I do not recall saying I was Of Tala. In fact, I do not recall either
of us discussing traveling at all."

"Doesn't matter what coat you're wearing, I'd make you as Of Tala
from thirty yards in a sewer at midnight."

"Would you now?"

"Those fingers, itching for a trigger, muscles twitching, ready to
brawl, how could you be anything but?"

At this, Shara did tense.

"See!" the stranger said. "There you have it."

"Is it so obvious?"

"For those of us whose lives depend on not picking the wrong fight,
I'd say it is."

"If your life depends on picking fights at all, you may need a new
living."

The stranger sighed dramatically. "Well, I need a new something,
that's for sure. The spark is going out for me. Sure do wish I had time
to pick your brain because I might be running out of interesting ways
to kill people."

Shara blinked rapidly, and the stranger continued on, unperturbed.

"I imagine there are some stories you could tell, eh? Not short on
variety, the life of an Of Tala! I'll confess, I'm about this close to just
shoving people off balconies. How do you keep it fresh after so long?
How do you find your inspiration? Probably don't need any, do you?
Just remarkable."

The stranger finally fell silent, their smile small and genuine. Shara
found herself unable to respond. Unease warred with distraction, and
her thoughts bristled with intrusions. She was looking at herself even
as she looked down at the bar, a kaleidoscope of images and moods

playing across her mind: the grain of the bar's synthetic wood, the slump of fabric around her waist, a weary, murderous resignation. A man sat down beside Shara, and the world came into focus as though a series of lenses were finally aligned—her senses were her own once more. Before either she or Noah could speak, though, the stranger did.

"You two know each other? Astonishing. Adorable. The Talon and the Orillo pup. How delightful!"

"I'm not—" Noah began.

"Come now, I'd recognize that little Orillo tattoo anywhere."

Noah blinked and shook his head before reaching into his suit, his fingers fumbling for a weapon they failed to withdraw, and he gave up, sighing. The stranger's eyes widened, amusement playing on their lips.

"What knotty nests Ol' Wryneck constructs. What curious worms we make." The stranger laughed, the sound rich and melodious. "It seems my part here is finished. Well, good chatting with you, Talon. These in-between worlds, they bring out the malaise in me. I'll get those stories out of you next time. And you, little Orillo . . . I imagine there won't be a next time. A small twig, I suspect."

"What are you—" Noah began.

"And there's Laerd, giving me the sign. Another day, another world, another life." They slid away, toward a private office behind the bar, leaving Shara and Noah alone.

"What was that?" Shara said.

"Don't. Don't make this h-harder than . . ."

Shara looked down at the weapon poking from Noah's speed suit.

"Kerst! How did you even—that doesn't dissipate, Noah!" Shara lowered her voice. "You'll kill yourself and everyone in here."

His gaze followed hers and he looked down at the weapon strapped to his side, his expression uncomprehending. He was intoxicated. Deeply. The smell of indigo spirits hung in the air around him, a noxious veil. Shara put her hand over his and pressed the weapon back inside his suit. He did not protest, and looked up at her expectantly.

Shara pitied him. She saw herself and saw him and they saw each other. Motherly feelings arose in her, and then disgust, roiling, like bile.

Noah felt that disgust, slumped, stared straight ahead. Between them, reality was rippling.

"Whatever needs to be done," Shara said, "can we do it in private?"

Noah didn't respond. She stood, pulling him gently upright, and guided him toward a bathroom. His gait was uneven, and she could feel eyes on them. Her heartbeat quickened, anticipation heightening her senses. She noted those who observed her, those who pretended not to, those who looked away, committed them all to memory. The cameras in the room, the doors, the thickest machines, these too she made note of. She hoped none of it would matter, but circumstances demanded preparation. She sought out Beinir with her eyes, but the most expedient path out of the bar took her in the opposite direction from him, and he had not, in fact, noticed the foolishness.

In the bathroom were two stalls and a sink, and once Shara shepherded him inside, the door slid shut. A half-quiet descended, the sounds of the station still audible but muted, the indeterminate humming of every space station a burr on the edge of consciousness and a buffer. It provided distance, and Shara knew they would not be disturbed. Calm came to her then, and her body was relaxed, ready. Noah felt it as well and stood straighter, shrugging out of her grip. He turned to look at her.

"You came alone," Shara said.

"I had to. You got here so fast. I couldn't . . . I didn't have the resources. I burned everything to get here at all. How did you do it?"

Shara shrugged, Noah laughing bitterly in response.

"It was that easy for you? You can't imagine what I've given up to make it to this moment."

"Why did you come here?"

"You know why."

Shara sighed. "We're leaving. Beinir and I. We're going to a world far away, far from your kin, far from whatever it is you're planning. None of it matters to us."

"It matters to *me*. You're my mess to clean up. You know because I know, and I'm not supposed to know. No one should know anything! Not my family, not my uncle, not me, not you!"

"I don't! I don't know anything."

"You do! You fucking do! And when they find out—"

"I know you, Noah. That's all."

And she did. She felt his yearning for contact, his loneliness. She felt his family, the word vaster and more weighty than what she conceived it to be, a complex web of resentments and affections that touched every corner of his psyche. She felt his responsibilities, the grim work of Firmāre, its twin pillars of profit and violence holding up enterprises that spanned universes. She felt his mother, her absence, her disapproval, a great mountain whose shadow he dwelled beneath, chilling him even when he managed to forget, for a moment, its looming expanse. She felt his inadequacy. Failures real and imagined. The greatest: to be who his mother wanted. To be someone she loved. Or were those her own feelings? The confluence of Shara and Noah was muddy, the waters of their lives running together, and Shara was adrift upon them.

Noah shook his head. "You spend a few weeks in my head, and you think you know me? You don't know me. If you did, you'd understand what they'd do to me if they ever found out how . . ." He trailed off and looked down, then shook his head once more. "If they ever found out how badly I fucked up."

"Noah, what you're saying, it's absurd. How could anyone—"

"They'd find out. They always do." He smiled sadly and stood up straight. "They always have." Shara could see the decision being made inside of him. She watched his body go taut and his weight shift. She knew what was coming.

Noah reached into his speed suit, and the world tilted on edge, the station jolting and groaning with some far-off impact, and they both stumbled, stumbled into each other, and Shara's wrist-blade was out, and then it was in Noah's gut as she held his hand away from the gravitun's trigger. He shuddered and she shuddered and he began to speak and she wished to speak and she wrenched the blade upward, and Noah did no more.

They fell, and she lay there, across him, for long moments, his heat beneath her.

When she rolled off him, her breath was still ragged, her heart still pumping a torrent of panic beneath her skin. She stared at the ceiling, observing its institutional blandness, the repeated tiles shared by every major station in every major system and waited for the world to steady itself around her. It did not. She stood and tried to remain upright.

She needed to hide Noah.

She pulled him toward the stall, a calligraphic swipe of blood staining the floor behind his body. The room was so small. She'd be unable to conceal him, let alone clean the room. This was not how roamers fought. This was not how roamers were meant to fight.

Propping Noah against the wall, she staggered upright, but his body slumped to the side and then toppled, the sound of his skull meeting the floor both loud and dull. Nausea seethed within Shara, and she walked slowly out of the bathroom, trying to keep her vision clear and her stomach settled, the two necessary steps tentative and intentional. The door hissed closed, the mechanism catching, then hissed again. Existence telescoped upon itself, the space between Shara and her extremities growing long, even as the distance to the edge of the universe dwindled.

A woman stood before Shara, eyeing her and the bathroom behind her.

"Out of service," Shara managed to say. "Being cleaned."

"Is it now?"

Shara looked down and saw Noah's foot in the doorway, the door endlessly hissing back and forth as it attempted to close. She nudged his foot back into the bathroom with her own. The door whispered shut. "Yes," she said, "it is."

"Why was he on the floor?"

"Very thorough." A manic giggle escaped Shara's lips, and she punched the door's console, shattering it.

She made it only halfway down the corridor before she had to slump against the wall, her limbs shaking with something between laughter and sobs. Her training told her that hysteria was taking hold, that she needed to get back to Beinir. Her body told her she'd just slid a knife into her own gut but hadn't properly finished the job. Against her wrist was the blade's pressure—rosantan bone, to evade scanners—normally a comfort for this hide, now a dark temptation. It belonged inside her, as it had been in Noah, opening a hole from navel to sternum. She shuddered. Weightless emotions floated past and some distant part of Shara observed them with detachment. Remorse. Anticipation. Exhilaration. Fear. Her mind slid over her actions, and, their surface slick with aversion, she could find no purchase, could not judge them with any clarity.

She saw his face, its shock and its horror, and it was hers, mirrored back with terrible symmetry. She'd killed him, her double, herself. It hadn't been her, though. Their bodies had come together, and he'd fallen on her knife. That was all—a clumsy choreography. Surely she'd made no choice. Surely she hadn't driven the blade deep into Noah and then held him still as she—

Stop. Shara stilled her mind. She focused on the wall she leaned against. Its cool against her cheek. The smell of its alloy. The texture of its grime. She breathed. Deliberately. Patiently. Her hands found the blade's strap, and it fell from her sleeve to the floor. She stepped away from the wall and her feet carried her down the corridor, back toward the bar. Her arms were bloody, her clothing stained. Had the woman at the bathroom seen this? Nothing for it. They would be leaving this universe soon, anyway.

At the precipice, she waited, breathing still. The process occupied her. Inhalation. Exhalation. A bank of gaming machines stood before her, their cheerful chirrups far off in her ears, their lights garish and hot. A gambler noticed her and looked away. The mechanics of her lungs' operation required all of her attention. This was a blessing. Her ribs expanded and grew tight. And again. The world was askew, though in what direction she could not say. A rumbling was all around her. It was only as she observed a commotion at the far end of the room that she understood it was not within her mind. Security officers clustered, making motions and gathering weapons. She became aware of an emergency message, looping on the sound system, and of how the lights were low and every entrance was closed, blast doors down, and she was reminded of the way the station had shaken in the bathroom, was reminded of how she had—

Inhalation. Exhalation.

She would find Beinir. But for what purpose? She could tell him nothing because she could name nothing because she could trust nothing. Especially not herself; waiting patiently at the edge of her thoughts, oblivion and obliteration hovered, demanding that she join Noah.

20

"Another triple sparks?!" Beinir leaned in toward the machine, eyes narrowing. "Which is it, friend? Have you been tampered with, or were you born false?" He thumped the side of the console but this failed to elicit a response, only more grating, cheerful chimes. "So be it. Your secrets are your own. Yet should I learn I have been dealt with poorly, I will return for my quanta." He stood and headed back to the bar.

The patrons and attendants of the Seven were all wayfarers or somehow engaged with the traversal of the star roads. There were no veiled words here or secret handshakes in the Seven, though—only a carefully maintained reputation as the most dangerous, disreputable, and unhygienic watering hole on the totality of Nightingale Station. This, and a cozy relationship with the station rulers, ensured that Licensed Hostelry #7 was frequented almost entirely by those aware of what far-landers called the Simulacrum. And, when some unlucky soul stumbled into the Seven, unaware of its cosmic significance as a favorable nexus, they were made to understand their presence was unwelcome.

At the bar, Beinir gestured for another drink. Laerd, the travel overseer, arrived along with the beverage.

"You're headed to the Pinter'reyk universe, correct?" Laerd said.

"That is our plan. We have been tasked with—"

"I can have Chanci, our navigator, send you there now, or you can wait three days, and we'll have Uptin move you natural by himself."

"Summon Chanci, then, and let us be about it."

"All navigator-assisted travel incurs a premium of 50 percent or 32 percent for parties of six or more."

"Fifty percent? You jest."

Laerd regarded Beinir, his face blank. "I haven't jested since '32."

"A grim thirty years it must have been."

"Yes. Have you set up payment for proxy maintenance yet?"

"My hide?"

Laerd rolled his eyes. "Yes, Tala. Your hide."

"Why would I pay for—a hide requires little governance."

"This is a space station. Resources are limited. If you want to return to this universe, or at least return to this body, you need to pay us so we can keep it around."

"But why? Do they not simply wander? There is nowhere they can go."

"There most certainly is. They can take a swim in the black if it suits me."

Beinir straightened, sitting taller on his stool. "Say that again."

"He means," a man said from beside Beinir, "that he'll boot them out the airl—"

"I see you, rat. Your stink is in my nose. You would ransom my hide? Charge more for travel in good time? Are you a man of business or a bidstand?"

Laerd shrugged. "Find alternate arrangements if you'd like. The rates are the rates." He walked away.

Beinir sat, having risen to his feet during the quarrel. The trills and chiming of the machines behind him had taken on a sinister pitch, as though they were laughing at him, and he now felt confident the machine he'd played had, in fact, cheated him. He considered whether it would be worth it to return, to vent his spleen and engage in some therapeutic mayhem, but elected for commiseration instead.

"You witnessed the same behavior I did, yes?" Beinir said to the man beside him. "The odious profiteering? I did not hallucinate?"

The man took a long, deep drink. "That's life out here, I suppose."

"Small wonder you would side with that blackguard. What else to expect from this place and its folk."

"I side with no one."

"At least there is honesty in your churlish mood."

Beinir took a long gulp from his drink. He smelled the fermentation, the sweetness, and old rindy funk fortifying.

"Had a bad experience with a Tala recently," the man said. "Not really looking to make friends with one now."

"Not a roamer, to be sure. They are my kind. Perhaps a butcher or a binder. They can be vexing."

"I don't know what any of that means."

"There are many ways to follow Tala. To roam, as I do, is one of—"

"I'm not interested in your cult's superstitions."

"Cult? No, it must have been a butcher you encountered. Roamers work only in defense of—"

The man crossed his arms on the bar and put his head down on them. "Please stop," he said, his voice muffled. "Please, please, please stop."

Beinir rested a hand on the man's shoulder. "I shall," he said solemnly, "I shall stop for your benefit, friend, for that is the calling of a roamer such—"

"That wasn't you stopping." The man's head remained down.

"I confess, I often struggle to . . . calm my passions. I have been chided for it."

The man raised his head, blinking. "You work hard against yourself."

"Against my—I do not follow, friend."

"Your language. It's not of this universe."

"I speak how I speak. Would you have me speak as another?"

"You are another. Your proxy. Your hide." The man rolled his eyes, the same as Laerd had. "It didn't speak the way you're speaking now. Your words don't come naturally to its tongue."

"A curious accusation."

"No accusation, just an observation. Your hide is of this universe, and so the way it talks, or the way it would talk, the way you would talk if you let yourself, is of a piece with the universe. You make sure that doesn't happen, though. You swim against the current of yourself."

"Why would I do that?"

"Because you're afraid."

Beinir began to speak but the man held up a hand, stopping him.

"You're afraid of losing yourself. You're afraid that maybe the you that you think is you is just chemicals and meat in a particular time in a particular place, and if that place or time or meat or chemicals were to change, well . . . Well, then you might find out the things you thought you believed were another set of chemicals' beliefs."

"Absurd. Ridiculous."

"I've been doing this a lot longer than you, big guy. Trust the truth of misery." The man laughed quietly. "Trust the honesty of a churl."

Beinir glowered as the man returned to his drink. After such a bright beginning to their time in this realm—carrying Shara through the night, a sportive spirit-swap—events had conspired to sour his mood. The miserably long journey to this station, the strangers critiquing his diction, the rigged gambling machines, Laerd wringing every red quantum out of them.

That Laerd should turn a profit, Beinir did not object to. Beinir and Shara were compensated for their services, after all. Why should shifters and mappers not receive recompense for their own labors? No, it was the predatory, wresting manner that so aggrieved Beinir. Rarely were they forced to travel off the Tala roads. This sort of grubby dealing was acceptable for more mundane work, to be sure, but for wayfaring? For bridging the fractured path? This was an affront to the glade as much as anything—there was no story to be had in profiteering, only lucre.

Or perhaps Beinir had been too long ensconced in his own sagas. Perhaps he expected too much of those who did not share roamer beliefs. He had traveled the star roads long enough to see cultures nigh incomprehensible to him, to be confronted with mores and customs so alien that to even call them mores or customs stretched the meaning of the words. But this was what it meant to be a roamer: to nim the side-real way, to protect, to feed, to clothe the innocent and damned alike. So perhaps he should not judge too harshly a man who merely walked a different path.

No.

No, it was Laerd who was wrong. Beinir looked forward to sharing the galling affair with Shara. No doubt she would be as aggrieved as he was. It occurred to him that he hadn't, in fact, seen Shara in some time. Before he could seek her out, though, Laerd returned.

"You have come to apologize?" Beinir said.

"No," Laerd said. "Why would I do that? What would I be apologizing for?"

"For your stench, say?"

Laerd looked around himself. "What?"

"Knave."

He shook his head. "Listen, the station's scanners are picking something up, so odds are good that in less than three minutes, we're going to be up to our skivvies in kwepi."

At this, Beinir brightened. "Kwepi? Well. Something to occupy our time then, given we are captive to your—"

"What about you?" Laerd said to the man beside Beinir. "If you don't want to find out what it smells like when space scorpion acid dissolves human flesh, then we offer expedited traveling services for double the arranged fee. Otherwise, you're riding this out here."

"You know I have nowhere to go, Laerd," the man said.

"Still, we could send you off to Pinter'reyk for a couple of hours, pull you back as soon as—"

"I know what kwepi are, Laerd. I know they show up at least once a year, and everyone makes a big fuss about them, but they do no meaningful harm, and by the next week, everything is back to normal. I'll be fine."

Laerd shrugged, moving down the bar, surely planning to bully other patrons into spending more of their hard-earned quanta. Beinir returned his attention to the man beside him.

"You seem to know more than I do, friend. I have but the memory of my hide to go by, but I suspect we have a storied night ahead."

"I guess so," the man said.

"This hide clearly recalls watching a hive-cluster arrive in low orbit on a distant moon and fending off a swarm of these kwepi. And, of course, tales of Captain Elvrii's exploits in defense of this station are legendary in this place. It is as though every year brings a grander tale than the one before. I wonder if we'll fight alongside this Elvrii."

The man's shoulders sagged, and he dolefully raised his empty mug, examining the foam popping in the dregs.

"Still and all," Beinir said, "I won't press you. I will say that you are more calm than I would expect. This station may hold under regular assault, but folk will die. I hear kwepi venom is quite painful, friend."

"People preserve us. Why must kwepi exist?" The man hung his head, resting it in his palms.

"For the sagas," Beinir said, clapping the man's shoulder.

"For the—?"

Malculm and Beinir each paused and looked at each other, Malculm's eyes widening and Beinir beginning to laugh, when the station reeled from some far-off impact; the aliens had arrived.

They each tumbled off their stools, Beinir catching himself on the bar while Malculm fell to the floor. He scrambled upright again, wild-eyed and unsteady.

"It seems fate is upon us," Beinir said. "Our tales are joined. They go on. Are you called 'Malculm' in this world as well?"

"I'm taking you back," Malculm said.

"Back?"

"To Burel Hird, yes."

"I admire your confidence. Have you forgotten our last meeting?"

Malculm was reaching around inside his clothes, clutching at something that wasn't there.

"You have no weapon," Beinir said. "Your hide prefers a reverse cant cross draw, but there is nothing there." He tapped the hip Malculm was favoring, indicating the missing holster. "You are unarmed."

Malculm ignored this. "You have crimes to answer for and conspiracies to unravel."

"Do I?"

"What Withered Stem is doing in Hird territory. What it was they
wanted from Geçiş. Why Of Talas have thrown their lot in with those
pencil necks."

"You . . . are a very confused man."

Malculm put his hand on Beinir's shoulder. Beinir regarded the
hand with some amusement.

"I fear I have other engagements," Beinir said, "and so decline this
invitation."

"There was no invitation."

Beinir raised an eyebrow. The man was drunk, but his gaze was focused. "You do not think there are greater concerns upon us?" Beinir
looked around for a weapon he might wield against the kwepi but
found none.

"There is no concern greater than the People's will, and I shall see
it done."

A sudden stillness in the bar stopped their conversation. Every
face was turned toward the entrance, and Beinir turned as well. A
blood-splattered woman stood in the doorway. Her uniform, the bur-
gundy and gold of the station's security, was torn—one sleeve wholly
missing, the other smoking slightly. Her eyes were wide and her shoulders heaved.

"It's not kwepi," she said, and turned to the console at the bar's entrance, keying in commands with shaking fingers. Doors slid closed, the
lights changed to a lurid red, and the station-wide emergency message
began to play. "It's rosantans!"

At this announcement, there was chaos, shouts and screams inter-
mingling, security clustering together, access panels opened, and weapons
distributed. In the corner of the room, Laerd tried to be heard over the
clamor as he informed the room that, due to recent market shifts, the
cost of expedited travel had quintupled. He was mobbed as the Sev-
en's patrons tried to flee the universe, the cost irrelevant, as any and all

currency was offered up if only to escape the impending arrival of the rosantans.

In the midst of it, Malculm and Beinir sat, Beinir laughing as Malculm hung his head.

"Nothing in this life can be easy, can it?" Malculm said, running a hand through his thinning hair.

Beinir rubbed his hands together and cracked his knuckles. "No story to be found in an easy life."

"Lunatics," Malculm said. "Lunatics, all of you." He stood. "This conversation isn't over."

"Circumstances beg to differ, friend."

Malculm ignored this. "Don't die. I need you alive. One way or another, I'll clear my name, and you'll answer for—"

A rosantan alpha burst through the wall, its tusks stained already with blood and ichor, chunks of metal flying through the air, the floor groaning and cracking beneath the beast's weight. With it came the smell of battle, flesh crisped by acid blood, the ozone of laser fire, and the odors trapped for decades within the walls, released in an instant.

It shook a head nearly the height and breadth of Beinir himself. The creature roared as guards opened fire, the strobing of their lasers casting vibrant shadows against the remains of the wall. The alpha turned to them, tusk-blades scissoring and scraping against each other, even direct hits of weapon fire doing little to slow it, and prepared to charge.

Leaping over the bar, Beinir wrested free a keg and hurled it at the rosantan, the impact resounding in the room, a clattering, dissonant gong. Annoyed, if uninjured, it wheeled on Beinir, laser blasts still breaking harmlessly against its side.

"Come then, you great fiend," Beinir said. "Let us see how you fare against a roamer."

Chitin rattled as the alpha lowered its head, neck plates locking into place, and barreled forward. Beinir tumbled to the side as the rosantan careened through the bar, tusk-blades scything, kegs bursting, and liquor splattering. It crashed into the far wall, making jagged rubble of the steel and wiring within, and slowly began to turn around.

As it did, Beinir grabbed for a bottle high up on the one shelf that had somehow survived the chaos and uncorked it, soaking a dishcloth that lay on the ground with a liquor so foul and potent it could be smelled over the stench of the rosantan. He cast about and grabbed a handheld torch from the shelf, its days of setting drinks alight over. With a press of a button, a small flame sparked to life, and Beinir lit the rag in his hand, stuffing it in the bottle. It blazed as it arced through the air, Beinir's throw proving true, and exploded on the alpha's flank, the accumulated liquor and rosantan blood a caustic fuel, a wave of heat washing over Beinir as green-blue flames swayed sinuously before him. The alpha seemed not to notice, though; the fire did not perturb it in the least.

"I see." Beinir took a step back.

The rosantan reared up above Beinir, supported on its four hind legs, forelimbs wiping its tusks clean, flames blazing along its scales, and prepared to charge once more. It took a step forward and the floor gave way. The rosantan tumbled through it, its legs scrabbling at the edges of the gap for a moment, carving six trenches where they struck, then they too disappeared, the sound of the alpha crashing through the station's sublevels coming at intervals.

Beinir walked to the edge of the hole and peered down. There was only wreckage and darkness.

"Coward!" he shouted down into the void. "Fleeing before the battle has even begun . . ." He looked for Malculm but found him nowhere among the crowd milling around Laerd as he negotiated ever more exorbitant prices to send people out of the universe.

Quills whistled past him, embedding themselves in the wall behind the bar, and someone grabbed the hem of his nanofilament armored tunic. "Get down!" Shara said, pulling him behind a toppled table.

"Ah, there you are," Beinir said.

"Here I . . . am."

At the bar's entrance, there was a cluster of rosantan thetas, thrust sacs engorged and quills quivering. They hissed, ducking their heads and lifting their tails, then shrieked in pain. More quills thudded against the table, their tips protruding out of its back, sizzling gently only inches from Beinir and Shara's faces, barbs still slick with the lubricating pyorrhea that allowed the thetas to discharge them so violently.

Beinir leaned in close to Shara.

"Are you well?" he asked.

She closed her eyes and took a slow breath. "Later. We'll discuss it later."

"You are not well. What can I—"

She put a hand on his arm to still him and pointed at a quill that was particularly close to his eye. "Later, Beinir. Truly. This isn't the time."

Another alpha arrived, widening the hole in the wall as it crashed through, a half dozen thetas keeping up their quill fire, heads ducked low and bristling backs arched above them. The sounds in the station were strongly masticatory as station security agents were rent and chewed by alphas and thetas alike. Human screams were cut brutally short, replaced by the rosantans' melodious grunts.

"This is not the quest we were charged with," Beinir said, "but it is ours, no matter. This station needs our aid."

At that, a squadron of security agents arrived from outside the Seven, taking the rosantans by surprise. The alpha was knocked to the ground, stunned but still very much alive. The station security agents swarmed over it, blasters and shock prods firing. A gout of green blood splashed against the bulkhead and the alpha roared, its forelimbs throwing off the guards as though they were insects, their bodies twisted and broken when they landed. The alien eyed the remaining humans, snorting and emitting a low, rumbling grunt.

"This thing's nothing but teeth, blades, and claws," Shara said. "A formidable monster."

"It is, at that," Beinir said. "A legendary battle awaits." With a foot, he stretched out to a fallen guard, pulled a blaster to him, and opened its side panel, beginning to overclock it. "Something of the Svyslahk, eh?" he said to Shara without looking up. "Brings me back." Quills zipped by above them, slicing through glasses and pinging as they struck the Seven's walls, their hum like a thousand deadly tuning forks. "The

Svyslahk, yes? Recall? Shara?" He looked up. She was holding her hand before her face, regarding it with some fascination. "Shara!" She shook her head and blinked rapidly.

Before she could speak, the alpha tossed off the last guard and stomped the ground twice, shaking the room. With a great, shivering roar, its scales rippled, aligning into an unbroken sheet that glistened like an oil slick in the gloom of the emergency lights. A sizzling hiss cut its bellows short, the thetas arrayed around it falling in turn.

Standing, then, amid the fallen rosantans, his cape swaying gently, his hair impossibly, impeccably coifed with rakish curls, a sword of crackling light in his hand, was a man of heroic mien and noble bearing. A cheer went up from the still-living crowd.

"Ha *ha!*" he said, planting his foot on the alpha's head and rolling it out of his way. "Only a pulse-blade can penetrate this beast's neck plates. Surely I've taught you all that by now! Ha *ha!*"

The crowd began to chant: "Captain Elvrii! Captain Elvrii!"

Beinir sighed. "Again I am robbed!"

"Perhaps this is not our story," Shara suggested. "Perhaps we are side characters here."

"Well, he certainly has the look of a hero," Beinir said begrudgingly.

"Or a clown."

"Pshaw! He reminds me of me."

"Indeed."

"You are feeling more yourself! Ha ha!" Beinir grinned and waggled his eyebrows at Shara, who smiled despite herself.

From the corridor came rumblings, and a moment later, more rosantans burst through the wall, alphas and thetas in numbers and a roiling mass of zetas.

"Ha *ha!*" Captain Elvrii shouted as he rolled to the side, slicing a zeta in half.

"Truly, why does he keep doing that?" Beinir said.

"To me, my friends, to me!" Captain Elvrii called as he slid beneath an alpha, disappearing within their ranks.

"We will have to return," Shara said, "so you can interrogate him on his technique. For now, though, this is surely his story, and these are surely his foes—we should leave him to it."

Beinir sighed once more. "You may be right. To steal a saga would be . . . I do not enjoy being a side character, Shara."

"I know," Shara said, "but we have our own tale to tell. There are matters to discuss, and this is neither the time nor the place for such a discussion. This way."

They scrambled across the floor toward an alcove in the corner of the room. The battle raged around them, a rosantan alpha buckling under the onslaught of laser fire from a phalanx of helmeted station guards. Other guards fell, screaming, their chests pincushions, their light armor no match for the thetas' quills. The emergency message broadcast came through only as garbled nonsense, static-like sibilance hissing through every word. Even the alert siren was failing, its sharp edge reduced to a mournful keening as its pitch fell until it, too, became only background noise for the chaos.

"Should we find a shifter?" Shara said. In the private room, they were shielded from the fray, though grunts and groans could still be heard, along with sporadic laser fire and the steady, humming slash of Captain Elvrii's pulse-blade. "Leave this station to its fate and this captain to his tale? Quickly, as well, lest all the shifters be slain in this assault."

"Perhaps. There is something we must weigh, though: We are pursued."

"Hardly anomalous."

"By agents of Burel Hird."

"I see . . ." Shara said slowly.

"The man we fought among the crabs, who offered us rayita, Malculm. He is here. He aims to take us back to Burel Hird territory with him."

"He recognized you?"

Beinir grinned sheepishly. "He recognized my enthusiasm for the sagas, I believe."

"And for what purpose does he wish to apprehend us?"

"We did not get that far."

"Well, no good purpose," Shara said.

"No good purpose," Beinir agreed. "He may not have survived the attack, but where one Burel goes, the herd follows; there will be more."

"That does complicate things . . ."

"Och. You also? Noah still?"

Shara winced and looked away. "He'll trouble us no more."

"What then?"

"I understand why he pursued us. I think. There's to be an assassination. In Burel Hird. Not long from now. He believes—believed, I knew more of it than I do, as though that mattered."

"Assassination? Unusual but hardly anomalous, either. They tend to dispose of each other, do they not? Outsiders not required."

"That is what we are given to understand, yes. Perhaps you are right. And perhaps it is no concern of ours. Still. That there is Firmāre involvement, that Noah seemed to think it was of such importance . . . Feh. I've always found these sorts of entanglements tiresome."

"We have our own tasks, set to us by the sibyl. Away from Burel Hird and Firmāre."

Shara nodded.

"To the shifter, then?" Beinir asked.

Shara stood. "To the shifter."

21

A jar of pickles greeted Beinir and Shara, flying through the air and bouncing off Beinir's armored tunic. A man stood in the stock room, the pickle-thrower, cowering between shelves, but at the sight of them, he relaxed, relief clear on his face.

"Am I glad to see you," he said. "That was my only jar. It would've been bags of pretzels next, and I'm not sure they would've done much."

"I'm not sure the pickles would've done much either," Shara said. "Or did much." She looked at the jar, still rolling harmlessly on the floor.

"You're the shifter," Beinir said. "Uptin?"

The man sighed. "Shocking, it's not my humanity that matters to my rescuers, but my utility."

"That's not what—" Shara began.

"It's fine," he said. "You haven't split me open and started chewing my bones yet, so you're already an improvement."

"Excellent," Beinir said, "as we have a job for you. Our plan was to reach the Pinter'reyk realm. Is this within your abilities?"

"Are the rosantans gone?"

Beinir and Shara looked at each other.

"We haven't seen any for some time," Shara said.

"Your Captain Elvrii appeared to be delivering great battle upon them," Beinir said, "much as I might. Something of me about the man, I must say."

"He's a clown," Uptin said. "Vainglorious and absurd."

Shara hid her smile.

Beinir said, "What we saw was a display of—"

"And his ridiculous little laugh?" Uptin said. "He practices that, you know. Go by the gym and you'll hear him working on it, just so it comes out the same each time, whether he's winded or not."

"It is a . . . curious affectation," Beinir allowed. "Nonetheless, he had the situation in hand."

"We can hire you, then?" Shara asked. "You can send us to Pinter'reyk?"

"Well, I can move you to the proximate universe, but it's not Pinter'reyk. Not for another three days or so. It's Renqueue."

"That is not where we are tasked to go. Is there no mapper who might aid you? This . . . Chanci? Laerd spoke of her. Surely she can . . ." Beinir trailed off at Uptin's face.

"We were together when they came," Uptin said. "I made it in here. She didn't." He scratched at a box of soap powder, worrying a hole in its side.

"I see. Peace and solace to you."

"I hated her, and she hated me. That doesn't mean I enjoyed watching her be sliced in half."

"Of course," Shara said, bowing her head. "This has not been a good day for any of us."

"It was a worse day for Chanci."

Beinir shrugged. "Better disemboweled than enthralled." Shara gave him a look, and he hastily added, "Though both are quite bad, obviously."

"Both quite bad," Uptin agreed, laughing bitterly. "So no, if it's Pinter'reyk you want, there's nothing to do but wait."

"Renqueue is a Burel Hird realm," Beinir said. He tapped a foot and looked up, considering. "Not under their total reign, but . . ." He turned to Shara. "Is fate yet guiding us?"

"You could send us there?" Shara said to Uptin. "Now?"

"I'd have to find my pants," Uptin said, "but they're around here somewhere."

They both looked down. He was, in fact, wearing pants already. "You are, in fact, wearing pants already," Beinir pointed out. "Does your traveling gift require a particular sort?"

"It does not. I just have certain pairs that I prefer to be wearing."

"And this has no effect on your abilities?"

"Do you Talas have no sense of decorum at all?"

"I am decorous in the extreme," Beinir said heatedly. "I am well-known for my—"

"Then don't ask travelers how they travel. Just shockingly rude," Uptin said.

Shara gripped Beinir's arm. "Uptin, could you excuse us for a moment?"

The man nodded and gestured deeper into the storeroom. Beinir and Shara strode to the corner, stepping behind a shelf stacked high with jugs of degreaser and battery cubes. Thumps came through the walls and floors, rattling the shelves, signs that the battle, though farther off, persisted.

"It would seem we have a decision to make."

"It would," Shara said.

"We know there is to be an assassination. Within Burel Hird itself, though the target is a mystery."

"But someone important—whatever that means in the mess that is the herd—if Noah's paranoia is any indication."

"Should we bother ourselves with these machinations?"

"It could come back to us," Shara observed. "They pursue us already, and if an assassination were to occur, the pursuit would intensify. Threefold. More."

"And what a chronicle that would inspire. Beinir and Shara, holding against the arrayed forces of an entire civilization."

"It could come back to Oulra."

Beinir sighed. "You are right."

"It is this that concerns you?"

"It would reflect poorly on us, surely. Can whatever glory is to be earned in so novel a tale be worth the price? It may be that we should warn the Hirders and attempt some parley. We may not know just what is planned, but if Noah thought this was so important, then neglect may purchase an ending to our story, to Oulra's, worse than any death."

"Perhaps. And yet . . ."

"And yet you wish to throw caution to the wind, to strike out into the unknown, as we were bade, come what may of Burel Hird, of assassinations, of their absurd suspicions and conspiracies."

"I don't believe I suggested that."

"You did not have to."

Shara looked past Beinir, through him, into nothing, her gaze suddenly distant.

"Let us do it," he said. "Let us wait for the shift and take the star roads to Pinter'reyk. Let us leave all thoughts of Burel Hird behind."

"Oh?"

"To seek out the unknown was the task set to us, and that path runs through Pinter'reyk. It is not for us to play these political games, to fret over who lives or dies within a far-off hegemon. No, the farther from this universe, from the sorry business with Noah, from Burel Hird, the better. We deserve adventure, you and I."

"That Elvrii got under your skin."

"No. He did not."

"He did, but I am grateful. I don't know if I would have been able to come down on one side or the other; I fear ambivalence would have overwhelmed me. I appreciate your decisiveness and trust your instincts." She smiled, and Beinir smiled at its loveliness. "Let us inform the shifter of our choice."

"I shall finally battle a rosantan. A small blessing to pass the time of waiting."

"Yes," Shara said, "let us call it that."

They walked once more into the center of the storeroom, finding Uptin muttering to himself. What the rosantan's assault hadn't dislodged, he had. Detritus was piled around him—cartons, jugs, and empty pallets stacked on their sides, leaning against each other.

"We will remain with you," Shara said. "Until Pinter'reyk is the closest realm to this one."

"I thought you wanted to go to Renqueue," Uptin said, rooting around among the now-almost-bare shelves.

"We decided otherwise. We await the realm's shift."

Uptin stood up, tossing empty boxes aside. "It's just as well. I couldn't find my pants."

"Have you checked your legs?" Beinir said.

"Hilarious. You're Talons, right."

"I fail to see the import of that."

"We are Roamers of Tala, yes," Shara said.

"Good," Uptin said. "Stay with me, keep me alive if there are any rosantans still around, and I won't even charge you extra. Just the normal rate. Paid direct. To me."

Beinir rolled his eyes. "Is nothing in this universe more important than one's share?"

"Spoken like someone whose survival has never depended on their share. How nice it must be to live like—"

A tusk-blade thrust through the wall, the bulkhead tearing like paper, and Uptin screamed, clutching at Beinir and Shara.

———

Malculm had fallen through three levels of the station, finally coming to rest in a service shaft on one of the waste levels. Unfortunately, this particular shaft had been infested by a nest of zetas that had swarmed Malculm almost the instant he crashed through. A lone rosantan zeta was no bigger than his forearm, but there were more than a dozen of them, and their mouthparts were certainly strong enough to rend flesh.

There had been a moment's hesitation as they regarded him, and he regarded them, their lantern eyes dim in the gloom. Wincing, he'd sat up, groping about for a club or a blade without ever dropping his

gaze. His hands found none, and he stood just in time for the first zeta
to throw itself at him.

Only three were left when they finally gave up the fight and fled,
leaving Malculm to his triumph in the desolate shaft, a dead zeta in each
hand and a half dozen other broken bodies on the ground around him.
Their mandibles proved rigid enough that they functioned as piercing
weapons, and, when his hands had grown too slick to properly grasp
his chosen corpse anymore he had simply beaten them to death, flailing
wildly with a rosantan in each fist.

In the sudden quiet, Malculm could hear the sounds of battle elsewhere, screams and blaster fire echoing in the shaft, tremors as the whole
station shook, shipworms grappling with it, disgorging their contents
through their maw-docks. Maybe Nightingale Station would survive,
maybe it wouldn't; the outcome was irrelevant to Malculm. He had
found the Talas, found the first piece that he needed, a piece of syn-
chronicity that would be suspicious if Malculm allowed himself to fully
consider it. He did not, for to consider the working of the Simulacrum
on one's life was superstition, was primitivism, was simply not appropriate for a man of Burel Hird such as himself.

For that is what he was: Burel Hird. He had questioned it, he had
doubted it, but now the Of Talas would provide a path forward. A path
back. Where exactly they would lead, where all of this would lead, he
didn't know. He would pursue them, though, and uncover the truth.

Malculm stood in waste, some human, some simply trash—had his
nose not already been assaulted by the reek of rosantan ichor, he would
have had a difficult time managing the stench. There was nothing for it,
though; if this was the price of redemption, then so be it. His body was alive
with the elation of pain and purpose. The zetas fell from his grasp. Their
blood was already doing its work, the tingle of its poison making his fingers
twitch and curl. This body would not survive. No matter. He would soon
depart this universe, glory awaiting his pursuit, deliverance close at hand.

Malculm took hold of the ladder and began to climb.

———

Uptin was going to die. The knowledge brought a calm that surprised him—he'd figured he'd be the panicky type.

He was cowering in the corner of the storeroom, fallen boxes all around him, while the rosantan noisily ate the two Talas' corpses. It knew he was there, though. They'd locked eyes after it had felled the woman and, evidently deciding Uptin presented no threat, elected to feast instead. It was nearing the end of its meal, rib cages pried open and internal organs slurped up, and Uptin understood that he was soon to be slurped himself. He was face-to-face with his death, and it was to be an ugly and chitinous one. Not at all what he'd expected.

He thought of his sister, Treeni, struggling in her dead-end revolution, hoping to bring down the great galaxy-spanning corps with pinprick guerrilla actions. She'd warned him he would come to no good end. Being lectured about responsibility by a wanted rebel had felt like delicious irony once. She'd been expecting bookies to airlock him, after all, or smugglers to toss him in the recycler. That would have been fitting, perhaps—a hedonist's end. It had been a favored topic for her lectures: There's more in life than just the pleasures you can wring from it.

Treeni, you don't know the half of it.

He'd tried, once, to explain travel to her, to explain the multiverse. She thought it was drug talk. He'd offered to send her to another universe. It would just be for a moment—he'd have a friend summon her right back. Just for long enough to blow her mind wide open and see that there was more in existence than she could imagine. She said that even if he could, she wasn't interested. There was more than enough fucked-up shit in this universe already. Why go looking for more?

That had been four years ago. They hadn't spoken since.

The slurping had slowed, replaced by the occasional crunch, bones snapping like twigs between the alpha's jaws. Uptin shifted slightly on the ground, his butt going numb, his pants still damp, clinging uncomfortably to his thighs. Was it fitting that only now, waiting to be prized apart by an alien marauder, could he summon the self-reflection necessary to say he was unhappy? Freelance mover had turned out to be just another job, no more glamorous than working the docks, and only slightly more remunerative. He was a stevedore of souls, shuffling impossible cargo between realities. Sure, he knew more about the true nature of reality than almost all of the trillion people of this universe, had even been to a half dozen worlds beyond the veil, but for all that extra-dimensional knowledge, the average Avancorpo junior executive still lived a better life than he did.

The alpha rose. A torso was impaled on its radial tusk and it shook its head, blood splattering the walls. The room was too small for its bulk and the ceiling buckled as it stood to its full height. It made a sound disturbingly close to a chuckle and its breath filled the room, the smell harrowing.

His sister wasn't wrong in her convictions. She wasn't wrong in her fight. A revolution was just so much *work*, though.

Metal groaned as the alpha spread its forelimbs, the walls bowing out like cloth.

His quest for riches had proved just as fruitless as the better future she sought. They were each failures. She, at least, would have the luxury of failing for some years longer. Uptin's run would end here. How disappointing to find that all he felt was disappointment . . .

The rosantan raised its head and roared, triumph and bloodlust and dominance, a sound that began with thunder and ended with a gurgle. It blinked, something like confusion in its eyes. Uptin became aware of a humming, a humming that the alpha was very much not producing. Its arms moved toward its neck, or maybe simply twitched, and then its great head fell from its great shoulders. The sound of a pulse-blade crackling filled the room as it seared itself clean.

A man stepped forward, passing through the gap between head and shoulders. If it was even possible, the smell in the room got worse.

His hands were purple-black, rosantan necrosis creeping up toward his elbows like bloody stalagmites. If he lived, he would become a thrall. If not, he would die in even greater agony than he was surely in already.

"You're the mover?" he said.

Uptin could only nod.

The man took in the scene in the stockroom. His gaze fell to the remains of the Talas, little but their heads still intact.

"You sent them before they died?" he asked.

Uptin nodded again.

"You sent them to Renqueue? It is still the closest?"

Once more, Uptin nodded.

"Then send me after them."

Finally, Uptin spoke. "That's . . . That's Captain Elvrii's." He couldn't stop staring at the pulse-blade. "How did you—"

"He was under the mistaken impression that he needed it more than I did."

"Oh."

"Send me after the Talas."

"I can't. Not yet." Uptin stood, leaning against the wall, not trusting his legs to bear his weight. "Talk to Divonta. He can have you summoned into Burel Hird space."

The man shook his head. "Dead. Why can't you?"

"My mechanism, it's . . . I just can't. Not for a little while."

The man looked at Uptin, then looked down at his pants, as Uptin himself did, a dark stain in the crotch streaking down toward the knee. He grabbed a bottle from the shelf and twisted the cap loose with his teeth. Beer bubbled down its side, hissing and steaming as it touched the man's flesh. He handed the bottle to Uptin.

"Then drink up," Malculm said, "'cause I'm going home."

22

Beinir walked along a dirt road toward a city forged of stone and metal. A hot wind sang down from the far peaks behind, fanning sand up from the dunes to spray and sparkle in the moonlight. A veil of pollution shrouded the sky, a new moon just shining through. An array displayed distance, wind speed, air quality, nearby weapon signatures, and power percentages. His hide understood it all without thought, and Beinir turned to his partner.

It was Shara, of course. He knew her in every universe, here even, where each part of her was covered in bright orange armor. A reflection of his green armor shone in her faceplate. Kardoral armor, marking them as members of the famed warrior caste. Kardoraa were permitted to go where they pleased, albeit grudgingly.

"This is no uncharted world," Shara said, her voice modulated through her helmet to a flat monotone.

"That pissy stockfish shifter sent us off early," Beinir said.

"Must you always be so coarse?" A hint of sadness carried in her voice.

"That is indeed what happened," Beinir reminded her, his fingers dancing on the buttons set into his gauntlet, an intricate map display coming into view. "He pissed his trousers and now we are on Tekkin-Yut, as far from virginal realms as one might be."

"We decided to leave the Hird to fend for itself, and yet we find ourselves in a Hird world," Shara said. "Perhaps fate has intervened."

Beinir wished fate were a tangible thing. Something that could be throttled. It was fate that had brought that little man into Shara's head and so muzzied her.

Beinir grunted. "We journeyed to the nexus for a chance to become a source."

"To the city." Shara aimed her cannon down the road toward the buildings ahead.

"Indeed, where else would we go?"

"Just move."

Beinir made no reply. He knew Shara needed time, and so they walked on, two jots of color in an amber desert, toward the gates of the city.

———

Two guards flanked the gate to the city. They wore the bright blue and silver standards of the watch, their long robes swaying in the breeze, soft and opulent, yet Beinir knew that the fabric underneath could stop a blade, and their invisible shimmershields would repel most energy weapons. Still, only two guards. The city was open to travelers, and the guards waved Beinir and Shara through after a surface scan.

Just past the gate, scrubbers cleared the air of sand and other impurities. Perfectly cut stones paved the roads, worn by centuries of sandaled feet, hooves, and leather boots. The buildings and people were a riot of color—royal functionaries in their violet and gold, city workers in blue, and off-planet merchants in the liveries of their guilds. Other citizens favored bright patterns and various prints. Paint schemes on the storefronts and homes ranged from garish to artistic, leaving little natural stone or sand to be seen anywhere apart from the streets and alleys. Flare-up light displays hawked merriment, meals, handicrafts, and other services across Beinir's heads-up display. He grunted and thumbed off the overlay.

"These folk clearly never learned that brevity exceeds."

"I enjoy it," Shara said. "All this color—it's water in a desert. Life in a wasteland."

"Honestly, I could do with a wasteland right now," Beinir said. "But this tavern will suffice."

The light inside the taproom was low, yet the walls and the bar, the mugs and glasses, and the great miresilk ribbons festooning the upper reaches of the rafters were also loudly colored. The patrons ignored Beinir and Shara as they entered—obviously accustomed to seeing Kardoraa.

Once they found a table in a dark corner, a boxy, mechanized serving unit rolled toward them, lights blinking, its facescreen displaying a menu.

Shara entered their order onto its face and it rolled away. She reached up and unclasped the fastenings at her collar, lifting off her helmet. She had dark hair here, cut short to her scalp, and her pale face shone with sweat. Her freckles seemed brighter as if this locality somehow imposed bright colors onto their hides' skin. It reminded Beinir a little of home.

He removed his own helmet, shaking loose long braids, some dyed a vibrant green to match his armor. He sighed. "Fate, deliver me from these worlds of wood and iron."

Shara sniffed at that. She did not laugh, a sound Beinir enjoyed more than most things. He hoped she would laugh again soon.

"You love them all," she said, her voice flat. "The many worlds along the star roads. Don't jest, you'd never suffer stillness back home."

Beinir grunted, and the sound of hard wheels over stone distracted him as the serving unit returned with two large mugs. The thing beeped once, and Shara reached over to take their drinks, depositing several coins into the unit's receptacle. The server rolled away. Beinir grabbed a mug and drank deeply.

A bipedal humanoid with a bulbous blue head and several antennae strolled over to the table, dressed in skirts of a swirling sea blue and streamers the color of dried clay. It carried a bouquet of putrid, stinking leaves.

"An edoh for your love?" The creature addressed Shara, plucking a leaf from a posy and waving it in Beinir's direction.

"Do not even think it," Beinir said to Shara, turning away at the stench.

"I'm afraid not," Shara said.

The alien made a gurgling noise, then wandered off to the next table.

"The reek of those things, och!" Beinir inhaled deeply from his mug to rid himself of the smell.

Shara nodded, sipping her own drink in silence. After a moment, she looked over Beinir's shoulder.

"What is it?" Beinir said.

A vaguely familiar form silhouetted in the doorway. At first, Beinir did not recognize the tall, cloaked man, but as he walked into the bar, something in his gait struck Beinir's memory. "Fate, draw me in," he groaned.

"I fear it already has," Shara said, leaning back against the wall and almost smiling. Almost.

"Well, well, imagine meeting you two here." The man's voice had an accent that Beinir could not place, and his face was older, fuller. Yet it was unmistakably him. "Told you I'd bring you in."

"Malculm."

"I'm afraid so." Malculm sat without invitation, his robe dangling open just enough that Beinir could spy the free-firing cannon trained upon him, mounted to Malculm's waist. "It seems your escape from Burel Hird was short-lived." He gestured vaguely around him. "Good that you did, though, for however long it was—you probably don't want to know what became of your proxies." He grimaced as though in jest, yet Beinir glimpsed a hint of true abhorrence.

"That way lies madness," Shara said without irony. "It would be impossible to function if one bore responsibility for the actions of every hide a person inhabited."

"That it would," Malculm agreed, shivering slightly. "Best not to think about it."

"How did you find us?" Beinir said, his eyes narrowing.

"I didn't," Malculm admitted. "Or rather, I wasn't trying to. I had no idea you were here. I just came in to get my bearings and a cup of galck. And what do I see but a couple of familiar-looking Kardorans." He looked at the two helmets perched upon the seat next to Shara. He laughed. "What else could two Of Talas possibly be here but Kardorans?"

"It's Kardoraa," Shara said. "The repeated final glyph makes the plural."

"Yes, of course," Malculm said. "I'm still acclimating. The galck should help."

"And it's Of Tala," Beinir growled.

"Is it?" Malculm said. "Huh." With that, a different serving unit appeared at his side, and he tapped in an order before the machine moved on.

Shara shifted on the bench seat, placing her booted feet upon its edge. "For someone threatening to apprehend us, you don't seem to be in much of a rush."

"He mentioned that, did he?" Malculm glanced at Beinir.

"We are a team," Shara said, waiting for a response that never came. "Are you not concerned about how one man with a cannon aims to over-power two professional, heavily armored warriors?"

Malculm shrugged. "This body doesn't seem to be concerned about much."

Shara's face twitched. "In my experience, it doesn't really work that way."

"Maybe it's not just the body," Malculm allowed. "In truth, I am en-joying this. This moment. I've lost . . . so much. I've been chased naked through the streets, I've broken my oaths, assaulted colleagues, stolen, lied, crawled through dirt and shit and blood, and felt myself dying. All to lead me here. To you two. Let me savor this moment. And if the Trimming Committee bursts through the door right now and splatters my brains against the wall, at least I'll die feeling triumphant."

"So, it is real," Beinir said, interested finally in the conversation. "Your assassins guild."

Malculm laughed. "No, it isn't real. The Trimming Committee are groundskeepers, for the People's sake. They mow the lawns. It's just a, you know . . ." He waved a hand in the air. "An inside joke. A bureau-cratic boogeyman."

"A secret hidden in plain sight?" Beinir said.

"Sure." Malculm raised his hands as the serving unit returned with a steaming cup of gray and clotted porridge. "You know what, if you want to believe the Trimming Committee is all that, it's probably for the best. Keeps you lot on your toes." He dipped a spoon into the thick stew and blew on it several times before slurping it up.

"Galck," he said, swallowing. "It looks absolutely revolting, but it tastes like home."

"Home . . ." Shara said, her face taking on that look she had in every dodgy world. The one Beinir knew meant she contemplated something foolish. "Your home. Prime."

"Shara?" Beinir said.

"I know we agree that this is none of our concern," she said, ignoring Malculm's curiosity. "We chose to avoid this providence, and we failed."

"You think fate has other plans for us?"

"I would not presume to know the coming verses of my tale, but this is a Hirder outpost," Shara said, "and I cannot unknow what I've learned. Noah—" She bowed her head, teeth showing in a grimace, then shivered and looked up again. "My actions must come to some good. This doesn't need to be a part of your story, Beinir. I can do this on my own."

"You are more than capable, to be sure," Beinir said, placing his mug on the table. "But I have nothing better to do."

"I don't mean to intrude," Malculm said, "but what are you two going on about?"

"It seems we find ourselves at a fortunate confluence," Shara said, "where your aims and our aims happen to align."

Malculm's hand stopped partway to his lips, the spoon's haul of galck jiggling like a worm. "You wish to be detained? Is this some Kardoral kink I don't really want to know about?"

Beinir slammed a fist on the table, causing the near-empty bowl in front of Malculm to fly into the air. It came down and landed upright, spilling a little. "You will take this seriously, Hirder." Shara laid a hand on Beinir's arm, likely recognizing the flush of clan pride that blazed within him. But it was more than that. Whether she knew it or not, Shara's pain was his pain.

"I seek an audience with a ranking member of the Burel Hird . . . Security Committee," she said to Malculm. "Or whichever of your people's innumerable committees is appropriate. That is what you aim to effect as well, is it not?"

———

Malculm looked at her, considering. At last, he popped the spoon into his mouth and chewed. "What's going on here, exactly?"

Shara took a deep breath. "I think there is going to be an assassination," she said. "Someone highly placed in your society. They're going to be killed. For what purpose, I do not know, by who, I do not know, but an attempt will be made. I caught wind of it when my mind melded with this man—Noah—during a sleep transfer. I could feel him, before. Parts of him whispering at me from within. He's gone now."

Beinir crossed his arms. "You're troubled."

"He's gone."

"You must've driven him off from within when you dispatched him from without."

Shara nodded, but she didn't look convinced.

For a moment, Malculm stared at her, then returned to his galck, scraping the bottom of his cup. "This is a distraction. You're trying to throw me off the trail of whatever you and the Withered Stem were wrapped up with on Geçiş."

"All they did during our time on Geçiş was study rocks and fish."

"It was quite dull," Beinir said.

"This plot, though," Shara continued, "is real. Noah believed it enough to try and kill me, to keep it secret. Someone is being dispatched to Burel Hird Prime. They may be there already."

"That's absurd," Malculm said. "The layers of security, the background checks, the body scans . . . Prime isn't one of your earthwork forts defended by spears and stockades. And who would carry it out? The likelihood of even a junior subcommittee page being suborned by outside forces is, at best, slim. The likelihood of an extern infiltrating Prime is even slimmer. No, it's not absurd, it's farcical."

"You were alone on the station," Beinir said. "You are alone here. Did you cross the star roads with the approval of your clan?"

Malculm tapped the table with a finger. "You're smarter than you look," he said.

Beinir shrugged.

Shara leaned closer to Malculm, her voice urgent. "If you were able to slip through your people's security, who's to say no one else could."

Malculm looked at her again. "You really believe this."

"I do."

"And you're sharing it because . . . ?"

"Because fate has made it clear that I must."

Malculm nodded slowly. He couldn't pretend it was fate that had brought them together; he had worked too hard and given up too much for that. But now, sitting across the table from these two mercenaries who had killed Æthelred and his other agents and who had so thoroughly derailed his life, he was actually considering listening to them. Perhaps there was some providential cosmic joke at Malculm's expense.

A disquieting feeling to have, one unbecoming of a Burel Hird. He looked at them, Beinir and Shara, at the dents in their armor and the dust on their faces, at the Kardoral tattoos their proxies sported, darkening their cheeks and necks. He believed that they believed they were telling the truth, and however farfetched an assassination plot might be, he couldn't dismiss it. Not when he remained a man alone, exiled, at the very fringe of Burel Hird territory, still hoping to prove he could be of service. Whatever triumph he had felt moments before had vanished, and all that remained was the firm pressure of responsibility, making his sternum ache. Malculm sighed. The things he did for the People.

23

For the second time that night, Yorek stepped out onto the balcony of his councilor house. He had a drink in one hand, something mixed by one of the staff. The name of the concoction had the word "Dusk" in the title. Dreamer's Dusk? Dusk Dreamer? A heavy layer of blue rested at the bottom of the glass, then a line of pink before the vibrant colors merged into a liquid as translucent as water. Pure alcohol, Yorek had confirmed. The acknowledgment of it actually unsteadied him.

The house, lofty by Prime standards but not by much, was given to him when he acceded to the councilorship. It was the same house that Dhalgrim themself had been given ten years into their term, the same house that every councilor of the Dhalgrim seat had lived in.

Accession wasn't quite right concerning Dhalgrim. Those seven original members had created the Council and then stepped into that freshly made body. Acceded into the thing founded by them.

What did Yorek know of this person, the first of their line? The person whose name he'd been granted?

A path that lifted and fell over crests of small hills lay beyond the balcony, lampposts casting wide spreads of orange light out onto the stoneway, stippling a line over the nearest rise and disappearing in the dark. Yorek could make out the outline of Councilor Nandir's house, though the lights were all off. Because she was here, inside Yorek's house, getting drunk. He could hear her laughing, a distinct, slurred staccato.

Yorek could hardly speak. He was drunk himself.

He wondered what Dhalgrim might think of him, if he was worthy of this most-cherished seat.

If the Maximov Interpretation of Prime Founding held true, his predecessor had been one of those who had stepped onto Prime. There'd been no record of those early days before the charter. Like the charter itself, these great figures of the past sprung into existence fully formed, already granted powers to build and govern Burel Hird. Dhalgrim was a sharp-witted, shrewd thinker who had been the most prominent councilor of their generation. It was Dhalgrim's ingenuity that established the Vorren Protocol, the method by which a locality might be quietly assessed for complete control, or, conversely, influenced by a secret guiding hand. It was they who had settled the first non-Prime world: Isigar-3. And it was the Dhalgrim seat that most acceding councilors hoped they'd occupy.

To carry their name was a marvelous honor. He truly believed they would approve of his work. He hoped so. Yorek had been so lucky. He'd held that seat for longer than most—twenty-nine years, nearly a full term. And now, during the Dhalgrim ascendancy as chair of the Chamber, he'd seen it all come full circle. Someone else would accede, soon, taking his place. But not Duncan. This night was the occasion to mark his retirement. Yorek, despite being at an age where stepping down was expected, still held his seat. Whenever nagging thoughts of his own retirement came, he pushed them away. It wasn't the right time. But what about now? Perhaps now was the right time. And perhaps that was the Dusky Dream talking. Fuck. That was it: Dusky Dream.

The lights beyond Councilors' Hill flickered. He hated that name— it was a neighborhood, like any other, with shops and parks and dorms and schools. And homes for five councilors. He hated the name and loved the feeling walking the streets gave him, the way people nodded as he passed, the way children punched each other's arms and pointed, casual conversations struck up at the market and the deli with those who had the courage to approach him. And yes, the deference. Duncan would tell him such feelings were improper, were egoism. Duncan was right. He often was. Duncan: proper, uncompromising, and Burel Hird, through and through.

Why hadn't Yorek resigned and given Duncan his shot at the small table?

Because this was the arrangement, unspoken but understood. Because this was their relationship. Because the People needed Yorek Dhalgrim. Yes, all of that, certainly. But. But also.

Because he hadn't wanted to. Because his instincts told him not to. Because he rarely denied his instincts, and they rarely let him down. Why were his instincts now telling him it might be time to call it? Why were they telling him it now when it couldn't be Duncan?

Storm clouds lit up in the distance, and thunder carried across the city, a lethargic, erratic drumroll. Below, attendees spilled onto the lawn, holding glasses and speaking in small gatherings. Not for the first time, Yorek wondered if there was a way to control how people flitted about at parties and what such a study might teach someone wanting to manipulate a group of people without them knowing. What variables could be tweaked to loosen lips or gain favor from anyone he wanted it from? Music? Liquor? Seating arrangements? But as Yorek's mind wandered, reaching for more specificity—what other things could a host manipulate?—he realized he wasn't lucid at all. Whatever accident of decisions had been arranged, this party (his party, he needed to remind himself) had managed to make him so drunk he couldn't even track his own thoughts. He needed Duncan.

What was he just thinking about? Right. Dhalgrim.

Someone stepped out onto the balcony and Yorek was thankfully still aware enough to hear the person and respond gracefully.

"Need some fresh air as well?" he asked the stranger, not bothering to turn. He didn't want to ruin the illusion of confidence and security.

The wind blew in his hair and he liked that.

The person that sidled up to him—too close; were they too close?—said, "I wanted to thank the host." They extended a hand. "Alyk."

Alyk had short-cut hair and a face smooth with youth. They were very tall but broadly built. Beautiful, in the way only the young can lay claim to. "Well, you know who I am. But I'll introduce myself anyway. Yorek."

He didn't know Alyk. They weren't on any of the committees he'd invited to this party. Certainly weren't attached to any of the councilors; he'd know it. Unless—

"Did you recently arrive on Prime?"

"How could you possibly know that? Is it so obvious?"

Yorek laughed, losing track of his hand for a second while he turned fully to face Alyk. Luckily, he found the railing. "No, no, you fit in just fine. Maybe you don't carry yourself with as much self-importance as anyone here. But I just know that I don't know you. And I know everyone."

Usually, he'd have played up his performance to unsteady the other person—the loquacious Yorek Dhalgrim, holding forth, once again—before swooping in with a compliment of some kind, a crude but effective ingratiation. For him to be so direct, here with this stranger. But he somehow knew it wouldn't work on Alyk. They seemed perfectly confident on a balcony with one of the most powerful people in all of Burel Hird. Or he was too drunk to be clever. A bit of both?

A bird called from the darkness beyond the domed roof behind them. Yorek gazed up in an attempt to see the thing but found nothing.

"You must have to develop a skill like that," Alyk said. "I can't remember half my peers at the academy."

"First placement?"

"Yes."

"And already on Prime? Any connections here?"

"No. But now I know Yorek Dhalgrim." Alyk grinned.

Again, it occurred to Yorek—the impropriety of the moment. He should've been put off by this sort of maneuvering. They had come looking for the host, after all. The audacity of it. But it was the way they'd said it that eased him out of his suspicion, their tone lacking any self-conscious calculation. Almost flippant. Yorek trusted his instincts, and he was sure that he liked Alyk. Where was Duncan? Oh, right, probably stuck listening to some assistant to the second chair of some minor committee tell him what great service he'd been to the People. He'd hate that.

"What committee are you on?"

"Currency Quality and Cleanliness."

He raised an eyebrow. "On Prime?"

"I know, right. Managing capital in the capital."

"I would've pegged you as I/EI." At their questioning expression, he added, "Another one of my gifts is reading people. You don't walk around sirring everyone. And, well, you have that ineffable glow of an Intelligence-officer-to-be."

"I did study for it. Among several other placements. This placement is only for two years. Then I'm off to other adventures."

Should Yorek feel unnerved by the near admission that Alyk really was Intelligence? Should he be unnerved that he wasn't unnerved?

"What are you drinking?" Yorek asked.

"Not much tonight. Don't want to embarrass myself."

"I hope I'm not." As soon as the words left his mouth, he felt foolish, and then he felt foolish for feeling foolish. An old man's vanity, no less potent than a young man's. How embarrassing.

"No, you're perfectly poised."

"There you are," came a voice from behind them. Duncan. Yorek was a little disappointed to be interrupted but glad that it was him. He waved Duncan over.

"Ah, the man of the hour. Come, come. Meet Alyk. Recently placed on Prime for, get this, the Currency Quality and Cleanliness Committee."

Duncan extended a hand and shook Alyk's with a face of genuine welcome. "And you're here at this ridiculous party?"

"*Your* ridiculous party," Yorek said.

Duncan's gaze was distant. "Even here, now, with all the evidence around me, it seems impossible, like tomorrow is still years off." He shook his head and turned to Alyk. "Who invited you?"

Duncan was never great at interrogations because it was always clear that he was interrogating.

"Special invite from our committee. They usually send someone to these things, no? I suspected it was some elaborate hazing ritual."

Yorek and Duncan laughed and looked at each other. Duncan's expression was clear: a little young, no? But clear, too, was this: if that's what you want.

Yorek just smiled. "Let's go in. Get Alyk a drink to their liking. Nonalcoholic?"

"Maybe a little alcohol," they said.

With Duncan at the fore, they went in.

————

Yorek didn't come back out to the balcony until three hours later, even drunker than before. The party had died to embers. Lamps along the path into the hills grew brighter with the blackening of night, a river of orange swallowed at its end by the darkness of the land. He watched as people passed through his garden into the street, heading to their houses or to the tram station further on. One person fell over in the grass, motionless until someone came back to retrieve him.

Alyk was gone. A half hour ago. Early morning tomorrow, they'd said. Yorek wasn't fool enough to think he'd found a companion in Alyk, no matter what Duncan's look had implied. He'd outgrown that desire a long time ago. He didn't even hope for it. Not here. Not on Prime.

Bile rose in his throat and he found himself stumbling. People's sake, what had he been drinking? He never got this drunk at these things. When he was a vice-councilor, he'd let himself go once or twice. Duncan was not there then to stare at him disapprovingly. He didn't know when exactly it happened, but his conscience had taken the form of Duncan's face, Duncan's voice, that ever-serious expression: You know that's unwise.

He had replaced Naven in the Dhalgrim seat, but not until getting his act together, mostly.

"You are carrying the weight of many before you," Naven had said. Yorek knew enough to look pensive as he'd heard the words. Now he understood what Naven meant. And he loved that weight, had built an entire life on it. Had resented it, too. For the possibilities it had denied him, the experiences. The universes. So why was he uncertain, now, with all his youth behind him? Why did he hesitate, even in his own mind, to voice the possibility, to accept the inevitability of retirement?

There would be talk, certainly. It would be read as a slight, Yorek passing Duncan over intentionally, hanging on just long enough to prevent Duncan's accession due to his age. Another spar of an old man's vanity: one final year as councilor when many others would have stepped down to allow their vice to serve. An act of cowardice, as well, replacing him without having to replace him. Or maybe it wouldn't be. Maybe it would be seen as a kindness for Duncan. Saving him from a role he wasn't built for. Letting him age gracefully out. What would be the truth? Yorek didn't know. He was tired, he realized, the thought arriving with all the impetuous force of truth. Exhausted.

But tonight, tonight was nice, a welcome respite from the burden of responsibility and the guilt of running from it. A glimpse at a life where there was no push and pull between these extremes. He leaned harder on the rail of his balcony, his legs quivering.

An hour earlier, he'd been talking to Alyk about their proxy. He liked this conversation, talking to travelers about the difference between bodies in different universes. He'd noticed it the first time he traveled and observed it ever since, the way a new body feels strange in an inexplicable way. In some worlds, he was taller or darker or had more facial hair, or it was cut in the local style. Sometimes he had a scar or a near-healed wound or a bad knee that was different in quality to his own bad knee on Prime. Sometimes, rarely, he looked nothing at all the way he thought of himself. He considered his Prime body his real body, the one he was born in, not a proxy made for him to slip into. But he wondered what it was like to be moving between proxies constantly, leapfrogging from one body to the next. What is your body when your bodies are transient? What is your "self" if you're constantly changing?

It was more than just a superficial change to occupy a new proxy. And this was the thing he had recognized every time he traveled, the subtle difference in experience, in thought. He could sometimes feel his brain working differently, altered by the world itself. His body wasn't just different. He was different. His mind, the part of him he considered himself, the kernel of who he was.

That was what he was asking Alyk. Did they like their new body? Did it feel like theirs?

And Alyk, brilliant as they'd been throughout the night, had understood exactly what he meant.

"I've had several bodies," they'd said. "Three since I started at the Academy. Each one was another me entirely. Well, not entirely. The difference is subtle. But every time after, I've noticed that I've been altered a little more until I can't really remember who I'd originally been in that world where I was born. And now, on Prime, I feel like someone else yet again. I can feel, and this is weird, so don't laugh, I can feel the patriotism, the want to be a good citizen, even though I've never been here, in this locality, before now. And it isn't because I'm caught up in the myth of Prime. I've felt that feeling before and would recognize it even if it were more intense now. What I am feeling is the . . . the imperative of this world, the Simulacrum molding me like clay to it. But not just this coat I'm wearing. My soul. I sound crazy, don't I?"

"No, not at all," he said. But he couldn't admit he'd felt that way too. Traveling was his secret. Yorek Dhalgrim had never left Prime without sanctioned approval—that's what any BSR register would show. And there it was again, his use of his name in the third person because Yorek Dhalgrim had ceased to be the whole of who he was. Just a body hung with the adornments of his title and his responsibility. Not who he was. Not all of who he was. "Sounds terrifying," he'd added.

"No, it really isn't. It is beautiful to be so vast."

Alone, standing on his balcony, there were tears in Yorek's eyes. Thank the People he hadn't embarrassed himself in front of Alyk. But why was he crying? Soon he'd be able to live any life he chose. Almost any life. Soon he'd have the opportunity to be vast. All it took was letting go.

Someone opened the door behind him.

Again, Yorek did not look back. "Duncan, go home. I'm fine. I'm just going to bed."

He expected Duncan to argue with him. Sometimes Duncan would have to come to his apartment and pull him back from having traveled overnight, which happened often when Yorek was drunk. The truth was, he was too drunk to travel. He'd gone past the point that allowed his power to activate.

But Duncan didn't argue, didn't say a word. And the hair on Yorek's neck began to stand up. He nearly turned, but a hand caught him around the neck.

And the person whispered in his ear in a familiar, youthful, beautiful voice.

"Thank you for a lovely evening."

Yorek was over the railing before he could speak, was falling, a strangled yell in his throat. His body greeted the stones of the walkway shortly after.

INTERLUDE

Shann and Mëryl sat beside each other, thighs touching, on a stone bench by the east entrance of the Park of Eight Saints, the stairs up out of it to Peace Plaza before them. The wall the stairs ran along was ancient, moss-furred stones rising into the darkness toward the faint sound of the fountain. Voices reached them from up above, Peace Plaza being a popular spot for evening contemplations or romantic conversations, but leaves and branches obscured all speakers.

"I worry there's too much waver in me," Shann said.

"Oh? You seem . . . very dedicated to me."

"Maybe. Maybe I am. But I also feel tempted sometimes. To just . . . let things go. I have to remind myself of why I do this, have to keep it present in my thoughts or it just withers."

"It's hard to keep track of the point of it all while you're doing it," Mëryl said. "It just becomes, you know, work. I understand." She played with the flap of her bag, turning it up then down again. "Whatever the end goal is, you're just one piece, and that one piece isn't the whole thing. I'm not sure anyone can keep the whole thing in view while you're doing your day-to-day work. That's nothing to be ashamed of—it's just the nature of life, I think."

"I guess. I know I have responsibilities, though, duties, to the rest of the multiverse, to the family, to justice and what not, but . . ." Shann waved a hand in the air at this. "I don't know."

Mëryl nodded. "I've been here long enough that I'm not sure I'd feel at home in my own body, anymore. Mëryl, that is. Because Myriel, obviously, she is no more. For me, at least."

"Didn't you want to go back? To see your city burn?"

"First of all . . . yes. I did. I do. But I'd also be scared to. Things change when you're gone, right? You don't arrive back into the same proxy you left. I mean, you do, but years have passed. It's aged. There's no guarantee the things you felt once will still have potency. There's no guarantee you'll still feel like you're you."

"Do you ever feel . . ."

"Selfsick?" Mëryl said.

"Yeah."

"I don't know. Maybe. Maybe I'm just so used to it I don't notice. I know there are some people who think it's a myth, or a delusion, self-inflicted. I've told people that myself, occasionally. 'It's all in your head.' But . . . I don't know. It's not something I've noticed in myself."

Shann nodded and waited for a moment, but Mëryl said nothing further. Shann said, "I think I've started to feel it. The sort of floatiness they talk about. The alienation from yourself. Waking up and not being sure if you've woken up or are still dreaming. Things don't always feel . . . real to me."

"I've heard some people call it life-dreaming."

"I have too, but that's not what it is for me. Not really. I'm not sure I can describe it, but it's a feeling of . . . of falsity. This nagging sense of unreality that's dusted over everything. Like a residue. No, that's not right either. It's not something that's external. It's inside. Or through. Like nothing is . . . nothing's solid. There's no guarantee that if I reach out to touch something, my hand won't just pass right through. Because I'm not sure if someone reaches out to touch me, *their* hand won't just pass right through."

Mëryl put her hand on Shann's shoulder.

"I suppose I asked for that," Shann said.

"Seems solid to me."

"You haven't experienced any of this?"

"Maybe it's just a matter of finding the right body. Who's to say it's Mëryl I'm supposed to be? Maybe I'm not supposed to be anybody since I'm never getting back to Myriel. Maybe I just don't have a real self to be sick for."

"That sounds depressing."

"Yeah. But maybe it's not about the proxy at all. Maybe it's actually about finding the right locality. Some far-off universe, away from all of this, the societies, the intergalactic alliances, the intrigue. Maybe it's not selfsickness we feel, but a longing for a different kind of self altogether. A different kind of self in a different kind of place."

"That does sound appealing . . ." Shann said.

"A kind of place without so much commotion. Without so much traveling."

"You setting the Gowan loose on us?"

Mëryl laughed. "I hope not. A locality free of traveling would be interesting, though. It would solve a lot of political-type problems, I think."

"Is that the different kind of place you're after?"

"Probably not, no. Truthfully, I haven't traveled a lot. Not since I found the Withered Stem. Not more than two dozen different localities."

"Any favorites?"

"I'm not sure," Mëryl said. "That's not how I think about traveling. Maybe I'm not doing it right . . . Although, there was one rather interesting locality. It's a water world; proxies are fish."

"So you've been a fish?"

"I have. Not for very long. And they're very smart fish. Also, fish is maybe the wrong word, but . . . no limbs, no digits, fins, scales, generally pretty fishy."

"What was it like?"

"Wet? I don't know, I was a fish. It was pretty tranquil, actually. Swimming was fun. I stayed in the reef, though, so I probably didn't take full advantage. There are predators further out."

"Well, you've got me beat," Shann said. "I've only ever been a humanoid. I did have some fur, once. Not much, though. And it was gray."

"You would've preferred something more exciting?"

"It was a pretty drab gray. That's what I remember, at least. Maybe it was actually blonder than I'm remembering. Which would make sense, I guess."

"You're a blond? Your real body?"

"Mm." Shann coughed. "Any good candidates for a far-off locality away from Burel Hird and Withered Stem?"

"I don't know any myself. I imagine there are some good choices, but I'm not an explorer, so everything I know is in the context of Withered Stem. The truth is, I like Calyx a lot, but with what's going on now . . . I wouldn't mind retiring to the resort moon in the Klivyn locality. Or maybe even . . . the Grove." She said this as though it were a joke, widening her eyes and wiggling her fingers in the air.

"Is that a real thing or a Withered Stem thing? Or a Settlement thing?" Shann said.

"Withered Stem. It's the closest any Withered Stem gets to religiosity, though. Or maybe it should be called an urban legend? I don't know. It's like the Gowan, though—not real."

"Well, what's it about?"

"When Tanïs was organizing us thousands of years ago, there were always rumors about the Grove. Some people attribute it to her, but I don't think there's any real evidence supporting it, and the official position is that Tanïs hated it, which makes sense to me, as it's kind of antithetical to her ethos: faith in our own innovation and a refusal to rely on external saviors."

"Sure, fine, but what is it?"

"I've also heard some people say that the Arcalumis Society found the Grove or that they were the first to theorize its existence, and we learned about it from them. Or maybe it was from Üt, pre-Withered Stem, a heaven myth that was retrofitted for the multiverse."

"Mëryl."

"It goes like this. The Simulacra is infinite. It follows, then, that within its infinity there exists a locality that is perfect. All is in harmony, all life, all death, and there is no suffering beyond that, which instructs us how to exist joyfully and gratefully. To live within the Grove is not to live opiated by bliss, though, or to take for granted your pleasure, but to be thoughtful, cognizant of the preciousness of life and simultaneously its insignificance. The Grove is the manifestation and the embodiment of the absolute interconnectedness of all life and the richness that proceeds from that knowledge."

"Are you sure it's not a religious thing?"

"It certainly can sound that way, can't it?" Mëryl said. "It's impossible to reach, though. You can't earn your way in through good deeds, nor will the Simulacrum just deposit you there. It is, simultaneously, both distant and close. It is close in that it exists beside us. It *isn't* some far-flung locality, dwelling on the edges of the Simulacra, unlikely and implausible, so many universes away that it may as well not exist. It is among us, a world that is possible, that is achievable, with the appropriate alchemy of will and cooperation and compassion. Yet we cannot travel to it. Among all other localities in existence, there is always one that is closer than the Grove—no locality can claim the Grove is its proximate neighbor. And no matter how the Simulacrum shifts, no matter how the multiverse aligns, that will never change. The denizens of the Grove may journey out as the Simulacra swirls around them, always presenting new worlds for them to explore, but no traveler will ever be able to arrive within the Grove because wherever they are, there will always be a closer locality. The only way to reach it is to be summoned—for someone from the Grove to bring you back."

"Has anyone?"

"Has anyone what?"

"Has anyone been brought back to the Grove? Verifiably?"

"No. In my opinion. Like I said, I don't think it's real. There are people who claim they have been to it, of course, but they're fringe and really do feel culty. That sort of mysticism doesn't sit comfortably in Withered Stem."

"And here I thought you'll feed the worms."

"That's not mystical," Mëryl said quietly. "It's reality."

"Would you really want to go there? Leave everything—Calyx, Withered Stem, me—behind?"

Mëryl looked down. "Would I have to leave you behind?"

"I don't know. What are the rules of your Withered Stem heaven? Do you get to bring a guest?"

Mëryl laughed, the sound breathy, and shrugged. "I never really followed Grove lore. It's only in the last couple of years that I've started to think about it."

"Would it count as defecting?"

"Shann, you're asking me questions like it's an actual place, and there are real answers. It's a fantasy. Whatever rules you want to apply to it, I'm sure there's some nut out there who's made those claims."

"Okay . . ." Shann shrugged and looked down, Mëryl rolling her eyes in response. They sat quietly for a period, neither looking at the other. In her bag, Mëryl's communicator buzzed once more, and though she began to reach in, she stopped herself, placing the bag back down on the ground between her feet.

"If you want to, it's really not a probl—" Shann began, but at a look from Mëryl, she stopped, and when Mëryl pushed the bag beneath her with a foot, Shann looked away, deeper into the park.

———

Night had fully arrived, New Darem's long twilight at last ended, the sky a matte black, rouged around its edges by streetlights and buildings. As a cool wind blew, leaves whispered against each other, branches creaking like some decrepit instrument being tuned, complaining at each movement. Frogs called out, one quite close, its croak abrupt each time it arrived, as though even it was surprised to find itself so near to the path. Amid it all, Shann and Mëryl's silence grew, the sounds of the park filling the space between them.

"Shall we, then?" Mëryl finally said. She stood.

"Can we, before we go, maybe talk a little bit about—" She stopped, then started again. "Mëryl, you know I haven't pushed you, but this is important."

Mëryl closed her eyes and took a deep breath, then turned to go.

"Wait." Shann reached for Mëryl's hand but she stepped away, either not noticing Shann's gesture or not caring. The walk to the edge of the park was short, and Mëryl strode swiftly, holding her bag close against her side. Peace Plaza sat above, the park sloping down into a wide depression at its border, a stone wall demarcating its edge from the rest of New Darem. The stairs up to the plaza rose alongside the wall, 144 of them, one for each of the Eight Saints' tenets, with a landing halfway up, the path doubling back on itself. At regular intervals, marble orbs were set along the path, poised on the slope as though they might roll down, but forever immobile.

They ascended the stairs, Mëryl ahead and Shann behind, the stones so worn their centers were sunken. Night insects trundled along the wall, moths wheeling above them, buffeting the lamps with their wings. The trek was long and the night warm and before long both were breathing loudly. Shann took the last dozen steps before the switchback two at a time, though, passing Mëryl and reaching the landing before her. From the platform, the bench they had mostly recently sat on was visible, along with the path they had walked, a sinuous ribbon of red trailing off through the trees. She stood by the wall, looking out over where they had been, and made space for Mëryl beside her. Mëryl simply walked by her, heading up the final flight, Shann forced to leave the landing behind to follow.

They crested the top stair and Mëryl began crossing the plaza toward the elevated's rails, Shann hurrying after her.

"Could we please just—" Shann began.

Mëryl stopped and sat on the short wall ringing the fountain.

"Yes, exactly, sit. We don't have to talk, we don't have to do anything."

"Okay," Mëryl said.

"Thank you."

Shann sat beside Mëryl. Leaning forward, Shann hung her head while Mëryl sat straight, her hands on her thighs. Behind them, Peace Fountain was lit in soft, white light. It was a complex representation of the flower, all done in stone—a trunkline, from which the water spilled, down over hundreds of individual blossoms, and in the center of the pool was a pitcher, producing a gentle vortex, circling atop coins from wish makers that were caught in a screen. On the edge of the plaza, running parallel to the park it overlooked, was the Boulevard of Eight Saints. A streetcar was rolling past—one of the last lines in the city—the operator ringing its bell at the pedicabs that wove and ducked around it.

It was Shann who spoke first.

"You know I care about you, right?"

Mëryl didn't respond, just kept looking straight ahead.

"And I hate doing this. I hate making you feel this way. I hate how it makes me feel. I hate it all. I wish we could . . . I wish I didn't have to."

Still Mëryl said nothing.

"It just matters," Shann said. "That's all. I know it seems ridiculous that Burel Hird Academy records from a decade ago would make any kind of difference, but . . . It matters, and I believe it matters, so however miserable it makes you and however miserable it makes me, I have to ask you for—"

"Can we not talk about it? Can we just . . . be here? Like this?"

"Mëryl, please."

"I think you would say anything to make me give you what you want, so how can I trust anything you say? And I think I would do anything you asked if it meant I could have you, so how can I trust myself?"

"Mëryl—"

"What do you want me to say, Shann?"

They sat in silence for long minutes. The city was laid out before them, all the way to the harbor at the base of the boulevard. It was as spangled as autumn, lights and colors scaling the sides of buildings up to the fiftieth floor and leaking down out of certain high-up windows from rooms still occupied, despite the hour. Above them, the dirigible had begun its circuit a second time and was passing directly overhead, its motor whirring dyspeptically. The night had finally eased into coolness, relief at long last.

"What's happening?" Mëryl said.

"What do you mean?"

"There's something . . ." Mëryl squinted and stood up, taking a few steps forward.

"Mëryl, what?"

"Look." Pointing down the concourse, Mëryl took another step toward it then stopped, her mouth falling open. The concourse was filled with people made small by the distance, thousands visible as the boulevard unfurled down to the water. They had, moments before, seemed to be revelers, but the noise that reached up to Peace Plaza was rageful, and storefront windows were being shattered. The crowd moved with drowning, desperate force, and around Shann and Mëryl, faces began to light up as personal communicators were consulted. While Shann watched, Mëryl produced her own communicator from within her overstuffed bag, maneuvering it carefully to keep its contents secure.

"No . . ." she said, slumping, letting her hand drop to look at the sky, before consulting it again, continuing to read. "I can't believe this. A cutting is being taken. To another At-Saught world. A polluted, near-ruined one."

"Is there anything you can do?"

Mëryl spread her arms. "I don't know. There's no official announcement, but all of my messages are asking why it's happening or how I could let this go through. I just—I don't understand. I don't understand."

Shann shook her head slowly. "Mëryl, I'm so sorry. Do you think . . ."

"Do I think it was Burel Hird? Of course. At-Saught administration wouldn't make a decision like this at night, and it certainly wouldn't leak the news. As soon as it was decided it would be announced—they value transparency over almost everything else. And it would be decided at noon, during an official confabulation. No, it's the Bureau at work. They must have more agents in At-Saught than I could have imagined to be able to force this through. What they hope to gain from letting this leak, I don't know, but they must see some advantage to it."

Mëryl shook her head, her expression vacant, and sat back down at the edge of the fountain. Cascading through marble petals and frozen leaves, the water shushed the rest of the sounds in the plaza.

It was beginning to empty. Some headed down the concourse, swelling the ranks of the protesters there, while others vanished into the night, getting off the streets while they were still able. The few who remained spoke with companions or in small groups with great intensity—none could fail to know what had been decided.

Mëryl let her bag slip from her shoulder and opened the flap. "Here," she said, withdrawing several thick binders, and handing them to Shann.

"What are they?" Shann said.

"The Academy records. Primarily the August Academy ones you asked for, but a few years from some of the main feeder academies, too. However much information you need, you should be able to get it from here. This is everything to them, Shann. How they choose their leaders, from the lowliest grass clipper to the First Council itself."

"Mëryl . . ."

"They're authentic—I transcribed them myself."

"No, I just mean . . . You had this the whole time." She slid the binders into her own knapsack. "Before we met up, you decided to bring them. I didn't tell you this is why I wanted to meet."

"Yes. Well." Mëryl looked down. "I had an idea."

"Mëryl, if you think this could put people in danger—or you in danger—you don't have to do it."

"Actually, I think I do have to. I think I might not have any other option. Because what else can I do?" She put her head into her hands and spoke into her palms. "What else can I do?"

Shann nodded but said nothing.

"I could go join them," Mëryl said, letting her hands drop and nodding toward the crowd. "Burn the city down. But this isn't even a Burel Hird world. They wouldn't care if the whole universe burned and all its people with it. They just want the flower. Apparently. I had no idea their desire for it was this strong. How could this happen without me knowing?"

Abruptly, Mëryl was crying, and she looked up to the sky, tears running down her cheeks. Shann stroked her back, and Mëryl fell into her, her head on Shann's shoulder. The riot was spreading up the concourse, and as they watched, a bus was overturned and quickly set on fire. Flames glowed dimly within some department stores as well, the broken glass of their storefronts shimmering red and orange in the heat. The few remaining people in Peace Plaza began to cast glances at Mëryl's At-Saught uniform.

"They're going to hate me," she said. "All the people in my neighborhood. They're going to think I had something to do with it. And can I even blame them? I'd hate me. I do hate me. I hate that I didn't stop this. I hate that I didn't even know."

"Mëryl, how could you possibly have known?"

"If I was smarter. If I was better. If I cared more, I would have known."

"I think you know that doesn't make any sense."

"I hate that I didn't do more. I was being safe and conservative and working within At-Saught. I didn't have to. At any point, I could have done more. I thought I'd have more time. At any point, I could have . . ." Mëryl broke down again, new tears wetting her cheeks. Behind them, the fountain turned off, a final stream of water sliding down over its stone into the pool. The surface began to smooth, and in the space where the sound of water had been, there was only the static of the protest.

"I could have done anything," Mëryl said, her voice rising. "I could have sabotaged the mission. Interfered with communications. I could have blown up the Anchor."

"Mëryl . . ."

"Well, I could have tried. It would have been better than fucking filing unfillable requisition requests, or demanding additional impact statements. Every person I ever talk to here is going to blame me, and they'll be right to. They're going to . . ." She sat up, sniffling, wiping at her eyes. "Shann, they're going to kill me. Not my neighbors. The city. They'll realize who I am. Who this proxy is. What she works for. There's nowhere to go."

The mass of people was approaching the end of the concourse, sirens audible but their source obscure. Small contingents of the crowd were attempting organized chants, but the words ran together, half a dozen different phrases clambering over each other, only to be subsumed by the bristled roar of the riot.

Shann stood, Mëryl as well, and though she looked as though she might flee, Shann put a hand on her shoulder.

"It's going to be fine," Shann said.

"Shann, how is it going to be fine? I'm wearing my At-Saught uniform. Carrying my At-Saught bag. How am I supposed to get home? Deïmos, am I going to have to sing?"

"Mëryl." Shann embraced Mëryl, resting her chin on Mëryl's head. "Relax. Breathe. I told you." She took Mëryl's hand in her own, intertwining their fingers. "I'll protect you."

Mëryl nodded slightly, her head rubbing against Shann's shoulder. "You know," she said, "you never did tell me your travel mechanism."

"A kiss. If I kiss someone on the lips, I leave the universe."

The mob had reached the end of the concourse and was splitting, half heading north along the Boulevard of Eight Saints, half heading south. Dozens milled about at the edge of Peace Plaza, though, gathering on its far side, swelling in the direction of the fountain. The shouts were close enough that individual voices could be heard, while the sound of glass shattering came so quickly and so often its sources could no longer be distinguished. Madly twisting shadows fell across the plaza, their shapes conjoined into a shuddering beast of many limbs. The air was thick, an indistinct haze of gray smoke flickering with the whims of the flames, and everywhere was the smell of burning—rubber, fabric, garbage, dumpsters dragged out from alleys and toppled, their contents ablaze, scattered across the pavement like acrid, lonesome pyres. Watching it all, impassive, was Peace Fountain, its marble blooms cast molten by the force of firelight.

"Are you going to kiss me now?" Mëryl asked. She didn't look up, her face still pressed into Shann's shoulder.

"No. No, I'm not going to leave you," Shann lied. "I'm going to keep you safe."

PART FIVE

24

The Grand Royal Security Office for Sassu District, Velellia City, Tekkin-Yut was a squat, broad building that was all rounded corners and sand-dulled metal. It was meticulously maintained, however, and had been recently painted. The blue was bright and even, and the silver accents glinted in the thin light. The interplanetary monarchy that ruled Tekkin-Yut, Shighoa, and a host of minor planets was not, in reality, a monarchy at all—no individual autarch acted as the head of state. When agents of Burel Hird had encountered this locality on the brink of revolutionary chaos and bloodshed, the most expedient way to seize control had been to supplant its current ruler, so the empress had been deposed, and an advisory committee had been formed as an interim ruling power and had taken her place as the monarch.

That interim period had already lasted several turns. Consolidation required a delicate, patient touch and showed no signs of ending.

The public entrance to Velellia's GRSO was staffed by a blue-and-silver-liveried guard, whose ostensible purpose was protecting the building but whose day-to-day activities were primarily acting as a human map and looking strong and handsome in uniform.

"How do, travelers?" the guard said, her teeth shining more whitely than seemed at all reasonable. "Where may I direct you this day?"

A modulated sound came from the direction of Shara's helmet, but Malculm dug a sharp elbow into her ribs, hoping to keep her quiet.

"My name is Blisk Frooby," he said and prepared to swiftly deploy another elbow if necessary. Thankfully, neither Beinir nor Shara made a noise, so he went on with his prepared story. "I'd like to see the Under-Vizier for Special Circumstances about an unauthorized matter-transference operation in the Reemu Valley."

The guard's eyebrows rose halfway up her forehead, but the dazzling smile remained in place. "Well then, you'll need to talk to reception at Interworld Exports Imports." She glanced toward Beinir and Shara then back at Malculm. "Your guards will, of course, be permitted to retain their unique cultural artifacts, but we do have an active dampening field which renders energy weapons inoperable and will deflect any projectiles moving at . . . unsafe velocities. Any projectiles originating from within your sphere of authority, obviously."

"Of course," Malculm agreed.

"Excellent! Interworld is down the hall, to the left, up the ramp, round the spiral, then straight on. You can't miss it!"

"Thank you." Malculm gave Beinir a light shoulder shove then strode through the entrance, the two armored mercenaries barely managing to fit alongside.

———

Once they were halfway up the ramp, Shara said, "Blisk Frooby? Truly?"

"It's a clean cover that will get us in the door," Malculm said quietly. "Now shut up. Aren't you people known as the strong, silent types?"

"You people?" Beinir growled.

"Shh."

A pair of staff officers in ill-fitting, faded cerise uniforms came toward them carrying full crates of scuffed and broken electronics. One of the crates beeped forlornly as the harried officers staggered down the ramp, utterly ignoring Malculm and his captives.

The spiral took them up several levels to a wide, empty corridor leading to a small office with an antechamber. The single functionary at the desk wore a bright yellow uniform tailored perfectly to their fashionably plump body, a matching, perfect manicure adorning the long nails of their four hands.

"How may I assist you this day?" they asked, the sibilant words veering toward a hiss as their forked tongue flashed in the air. The green of their scales was set off nicely by the color of the uniform.

"I'm here to see the under-vizier," Malculm said.

"And who shall I say is calling?" The sibilance had grown stronger, taking on the husky timbre of Citalian consonants. There were no other staff visible in the reception area, but Interworld Exports Imports was usually only a two- or three-person operation.

"Blisk Frooby."

"Ah, yes, Blisk Frooby." The receptionist nodded as if they'd heard of him before, which was exceedingly unlikely. "Please have a seat."

"We prefer to stand," Shara said.

"Of course," the receptionist said, a faint lisp indicating their confusion. "I've just alerted Under-Vizier Yalun that you are here. She'll be with you in just a moment." The receptionist's attention went back to their terminal, the only movement an occasional flick of a shiny, yellow-nailed finger.

The three stood in silence for a moment until a tall, black-scaled Omarian emerged from a back room. The tails of her long suit coat flapped as the under-vizier swept regally into the antechamber, revealing its shiny violet lining. She paused to look over the three visitors as if reading their armor and weapons and body language and then smiled benevolently.

"Blisk Frooby?"

"That's me," Malculm said.

Under-Vizier for Special Circumstances was another holdover from the previous incarnation of leadership in this locality. On another world, the position might be called Senior Officer for Internal Affairs or even Director General of Intelligence. Here, the spies were truly secret, or at least they intended to be. If protocols were being followed, even the Citalian receptionist would believe that this office actually handled importation manifests. But Yalun would know the name Blisk Frooby and would know that Malculm was I/EI and was to be trusted.

"And these are?" Yalun gestured toward Beinir and Shara.

"Interested parties," Shara said before Malculm could answer.

"Is there somewhere we might talk privately?" Malculm said. He gestured to the gilt-edged door the under-vizier had entered from. "The matter is . . . quite urgent."

"Of course," Yalun said, but began leading them down a narrow, dimly lit corridor on the other side of the anteroom. "This way, please."

Malculm froze. Maybe it was all the years of training, or just the bone-deep paranoia of an I/EI operator across dozens of universes, but he was certain that the only thing at the end of the hallway was a prison cell with his name on it.

"Change of plan," he murmured, turning on his heel and linking arms with the two mercenaries on his flanks. "We have an urgent need to be elsewhere."

To their credit, neither Beinir nor Shara hesitated, and the three briskly exited the corridor and then the anteroom. By the shouting emanating in their wake, Malculm knew his instincts had been correct and he broke into a run. Beinir and Shara kept up easily, as the three of them barreled their way back down the spiral toward the ramp.

"We are assailed," Beinir said, just as Malculm noticed the helmeted heads of royal enforcers appearing up the ramp. These weren't ornamental guards like the one who'd greeted them at the public entrance. These were warriors whose uniforms were armored, whose weapons were calibrated to bypass the dampening field, and whose orders were readily apparent. Twelve warriors already, by Malculm's count. Too many.

"This way," Beinir said, veering sharply to the left and increasing his already considerable pace. Malculm followed but immediately tried to halt his forward momentum as he watched Beinir leap over the railing and into the void that was the central concourse.

"No, not that way!" Malculm's shout was roundly ignored as Shara pulled up behind him and, without slowing, scooped him into her arms as if he were little more than a bundle of grain and followed her partner. He screamed, his cloak flying up to cover his face, and for a moment, he was weightless, insensate to the world rushing by beyond the fabric. Then Shara hit the ground in a cloud of dust and a shattering of floor tiles, the machinery in her suit squealing, and Malculm's cloak fell away. He found himself, still in Shara's arms, looking up at several floors' worth of enforcers, ringing the spiral and looking down at them over its railing.

Shara took off at a run after Beinir, and Malculm watched over her shoulder as the enforcers reversed themselves, heading back down the many stories of the ramp they'd just ascended.

Beinir was easily fending off the few who had remained on the ground floor with hand-to-hand combat. His armor was more than formidable enough to absorb the blasts of their sidearms, and he didn't even bother to unsheathe any of his blades as he plowed past two, then three, then half a dozen enforcers. Shara stopped to set Malculm down and did a quick turn of the room. Then, once she was seemingly convinced that the coast was clear, she stepped toward him.

Her helmet showed nothing of her face, but he guessed she was checking to see if he was still busy losing his shit.

"I'm good," he said, and the helmet nodded. The whole thing, from railing to nod, had taken seconds. "Now we run."

Malculm struggled to keep up as Beinir and Shara ran down a winding alley between residential rows. He had neither their stamina nor their power armor leg actuators. Two children kicking a blue ball through a hoop jutting out of the ground gasped as the Kardoraa rounded a corner, and continued past. He managed to wheeze a hello at them, which wasn't received with the cordiality he'd intended. His breathing worsened, his legs grew heavy, and the orders barked from the enforcers grew louder.

Dirt kicked up beside them where an enforcer's blasts failed to connect. A few hit home on Beinir, but ricocheted harmlessly off his

Kardoral armor. Malculm had a feeling the thick cloth he wore wouldn't be much help should one of the blasts find him. He wouldn't be able to keep away, and if Shara carried him, that would likely do nothing but ensure he died in someone's arms.

As Æthelred had essentially died in his. The thought rose unbidden as he fled, protected by the same pair who'd killed Æthelred. And, as it did, so too did memories of Æthelred's annoying habit of sharing unasked-for combat litigation advice between missions. *Limit exposure to liability, prod their argument from a safe stance.* Malculm heard the dead man's voice in his head, more distracting than useful, and he refocused on his surroundings. A family caught unaware by the pursuit scrambled to avoid Beinir's lumbering form moving fast through the crowded space, his armor's power assist sounding off with heavy, mechanical whines.

Shara wasn't far behind, maybe ten paces ahead of Malculm. She turned briefly, beckoning to Malculm with one hand. Malculm followed, but turned abruptly to the right, seeing exactly what he hoped for: a long, sturdy table. Never mind that it was bright yellow in a sea of other loud, clashing colors.

He toppled between himself and the palace enforcers, ducking behind it. A few blasts hit the table, shards flying and scorches marring its surface, but it held.

Shara stopped and turned, ducking behind the table with Malculm. Beinir stopped as well, presumably alerted by Shara's helmet radio.

"What on the seven roads are you doing?" Shara said. "We cannot defeat them, our only hope is to escape before they flank us."

"It's too late," Malculm said. "I can't outrun them. You and Beinir might, but I can't keep up."

"Then I'll carry you."

Malculm shook his head. "I'd slow you down. Look, you can either help me take them out or get out of here with Beinir."

Beinir blanked his helmet's faceplate, showing his confused, annoyed visage through the transparent pane. "Why do we tarry? The enemy is encircling us while we piddle about!"

Shara shook her head. "Malculm is trying his hand at noble sacrifice."

Malculm held up a finger. Two more bolts struck the table, and the voices of enforcers grew louder. "No, that's not what I'm doing. I'm giving you the choice to run or fight. I was honestly hoping you'd stay."

Beinir smiled. "A worthy scrap, this will be."

Shara cursed. "There's too many. We will eventually succumb."

"Maybe," Malculm said, pulling his oversized pistol from his belt. He thought of Æthelred, poised behind a different makeshift barrier in a different universe. "But let's take some shots and see how the judge favors us."

Beinir and Shara looked at each other, confused.

"Just follow my lead." Malculm stood just after two more blasts impacted the table. He quickly zeroed in on the enforcer most exposed, leveled his pistol, and fired.

Instead of a satisfying report, followed by a kick and smoke snaking from the barrel, a loud metallic snap sounded, his pistol falling apart into two pieces.

Beinir flicked his faceplate to opaque and broadcasted, "We die on our feet today!" He charged into the four palace enforcers, several blasts deflecting from his Kardoral armor.

Shara followed behind, seemingly using Beinir as a screen, and surged forward when one of the guards swapped power packs in his rifle. She was an uncoiling snake, striking forward faster than Malculm could process, a wrist-blade finding a home deep in an enforcer's chest.

Malculm felt around for the pieces of his gun. He had no blade, no power armor. No opportunity for sucker punches. Æthelred's voice told him he had one course of action: limit your liability. Malculm stayed crouched behind the table, the blasts gouging more wood out. Two of them broke through. Malculm shuddered at the splintered wood, wondering what it might do to his proxy.

Malculm found the barrel of his pistol, as well as the clip that auto-ejected when failure was detected. A quick readout of the error code his pistol displayed told him the firing pin became misaligned after Shara's leap of insanity. Two more blasts hit the table.

Beyond, Beinir howled, but from pain or fury, he couldn't tell.

Malculm fidgeted with the firing pin, using his thumb to tap it back into place. After a few more taps, the error code disappeared, replaced with a green light. He slid the clip back in, and slowly crept his head above the table, to see how Beinir and Shara were doing.

He realized, a moment too late, that he should have listened to the dead warrior-lawyer's voice in his head. The advice Æthelred repeated until it was seared into Malculm's mind. Expect attacks to come from all angles.

Something large and heavy fell upon him. He found himself on the ground—pinned beneath an eager enforcer who must've scaled one of the buildings to attack from above. There was youth and zeal reflected in his wild eyes, two of Malculm's least favorite things to see.

His pistol remained trapped between his body and the ground while the young enforcer grinned, sitting on top of him.

"Interloper!"

"Hey," Malculm said, wriggling in hopes to free his hand and, with it, the pistol. No luck. "You guys attacked us."

"We recognize an attack when it comes, be it from within or without."

"Let me explain."

The enforcer glared. "I'll not hear your poison." He raised up his blaster, the weight shifting just enough that Malculm's hand could move. Ozone filled Malculm's nostrils as the blaster whirred to life.

A voice screamed in the enforcer's helmet, the words unintelligible. The malice in the enforcer's face was replaced briefly. Confusion. Maybe fear? Malculm didn't have time to process it. He used the opportunity to free his pistol and pull the trigger, the blast hitting the young enforcer in the chest and lifting him off Malculm's body, the enforcer's helmet flying off and bouncing away.

"Code Triangle!" the voice came again, out of the enforcer's fallen helmet. "I repeat, Code Triangle."

The enforcers Beinir and Shara had previously engaged with ran down the road away from them, as did the ones behind them, who nearly succeeded in flanking them. The one Malculm shot stood, slowly holstering his weapon, eyes locked on Malculm. Then he picked up his helmet and limped away with the rest of them.

Soon the alley was empty. Malculm, Beinir, and Shara looked at each other for a moment before running.

———

"Isn't this against your religion?" Malculm asked. He was using a piece of flatbread to scoop up another mouthful of mush from a large, shallow bowl. The mush, like galck, looked revolting. Unlike galck, this was a spicy blend of vegetables, beans, and rich oil, and it was delicious in a completely different way.

"It is not a religion," Beinir said. "And, in truth, the prohibition on outsiders wearing the armor is more guidance than principle. And, if the utility of allowing it should outweigh the value of the precept . . ."

Malculm chewed, not entirely following.

"It's useful that people believe it to be so," Shara explained. "You know, for moments like this."

"Ah," Malculm said, then picked up the faded gauntlet on the table. Even in the dim light from the lantern, he could tell that when it had been new, it would have been a striking, pale blue. In his hands, though, it was as much scuff and scar as it was color, but they had all the component parts for a complete suit that would fit someone of Malculm's height, including the full-face helmet. Wearing it, no one would recognize him as anything other than another anonymous Kardora.

He'd been received with suspicion at the gates of the Kardoral encampment, but after a few words from Shara to the door guard, Malculm had been allowed to follow her and Beinir to this small room. Shortly after they'd settled, a stocky member of the camp arrived with the hand-me-down armor, and wordlessly handed it over to Shara.

"Your clan does not appear to welcome you home," Beinir said, reaching across the table for the bread.

"No." A part of Malculm that was still foolish enough to harbor hope had aspired to do this the easy way, agent to agent, but it was obviously too late for that. He'd strayed too far from the ideals passed down to him in training, too far from the principles he had once believed were inviolable. Was he even Burel Hird anymore? It was a question that he was certain his superiors would also debate if he were to be captured.

The obvious play was to leave. Renqueue was Burel Hird territory, but only barely. It would be difficult to leave the locality, but not impossible. It would certainly be easier and healthier than walking back into the trap that I/EI had become.

But an attempted assassination. On Prime. Even though it was hearsay, improbable hearsay at that, it was the most incendiary piece of intelligence Malculm had ever encountered.

"No," Malculm repeated. "But if there's even a chance that I can stop this assassination attempt, I have to try. This should get me safely to Shighoa." He hefted the helmet.

"Why Shighoa?" Shara asked. "There are detachments going to several planets in this system over the next few days, we could join with any of them."

"I have history with the chief there," Malculm said. If he was surrendering, he wanted to do it to someone he could respect.

"Code Triangle," Beinir said. "Do you know what this means?"

Malculm shook his head. "It means stop immediately. A stand-down order. I just don't know why they called it."

"I still say we should split up," Beinir said. "They will be searching for three of us."

"They're only after me," Malculm pointed out. "Given everything that happened, the assumption will be that you were my paid guards, and, under the terms of the Kardoral Accord, I'm the one who's responsible for your actions."

"You merely desire to wear our armor."

Malculm rolled his eyes, forcing his voice to be light. "I desire to alert my people to a threat that may or may not be real, and I desire to be rid of you, but clearly neither of those are going to be as easy as they should be."

"Why are we helping him, again?" Beinir asked, polishing a boot.

"We aren't, exactly," Shara said. "We're just going to the same place at the same time—and he happens to be the only one with a key for the other end."

"We'll stick with the plan," Malculm said. "We'll join up with the other Kardoraa heading to Shighoa and blend in with the crowd. So, we won't be three, we'll be, what, eight? Nine?"

"What if you're wrong about the Accord," Shara asked, "and the guards recognize us and pull us out of the group? He did beat up a bunch of royal enforcers." She jerked a thumb toward Beinir, who didn't look up from his polishing.

Malculm tore another piece of bread off the shared round in the middle of the table, and ran it around the nearly empty bowl. "You two are capable of handling yourselves. If there's a problem, I don't know— jump out a window or something, that seems to be your go-to move."

Beinir stood, his face dark, and Malculm expected a violent outburst, but he only tossed the oily rag to the dirt.

"The shuttle leaves at first light," Beinir said. "We had better sleep while we may." He padded over to a thin mat near the wall, laid down, and covered himself with a filthy blanket. In minutes, soft snoring emanated from under the blanket.

"Is he always like that?" Malculm whispered to Shara, who was getting ready for bed by her own mat.

"In every world I've known him," she said, not bothering to lower her voice as she settled in. "Sleep well."

Malculm lay in the dark, not sleeping at all.

25

The heat of the early sun warmed Duncan awake, Ecklan's overnight beard oil and the weight of his body next to Duncan's bringing him the familiar mix of comfort and excitement. He lifted the blanket to press in tighter, closing the remaining iota of space between him and his husband, who stirred in his sleep, allowing Duncan to rest his head on the younger man's bicep. Ecklan held a mid-grade seat on the People's Council for Ground Transportation: Mechanical Subcommittee, and his work made his body hard and his rest unencumbered. Many thought them an odd couple, but while Ecklan could wield a sledgehammer as easily as Duncan held a note-taking stylus, he was kind and gentle and believed with his entire being that all the worlds of the many universes shone out of Duncan's eyes.

Before they had met, Duncan never dreamed there could be a love like that for him, and every day since, he reminded himself to not take his husband for granted.

But many days, that thought was lost in the tumult of his duty, and in a battle for his attention, his work always won. And there, amid the warmth of the bed, as the coiled hair of Ecklan's chest tickled Duncan's nose and he breathed in their shared smells, he returned to himself, and remembered that Yorek was gone. Duncan left Ecklan sleeping and went into the bathroom to get ready for the meeting—all thoughts of comfort or excitement were lost to grief.

He dressed mechanically, his arms heavy in their movements, ponderous, his fingers struggling to fit buttons through their holes. A beep from his personal informed him that he was running late. His back ached, a stiffness that had grown worse as he'd aged and troubled him some mornings more than others. He'd never been late for Council in all his years in service, and he knew that he should be anxious. But he wasn't anxious. He was something else entirely, something new. Something monstrous.

He made his way to the council house in a daze. As he walked up the marble hall to the Intercessional Control and Harmony Room, some aide spoke to him as he passed, but the words didn't register. His feet walked as if by their own accord into the already full Council chamber and to the Hérn seat, Duncan's seat, at least for a little while longer. He stopped before sitting, struck anew at the emptiness of the chair next to his.

The chairs in the ICHR had been finely hand-constructed by high-grade members of the Woodworkers and Upholsterers Subcommittee, but they were not grand. Duncan found, however, that he could not keep his gaze from Yorek's empty chair—the absence of it, the absence it held. It dwarfed all else in the room, yet seemed too small to contain the man that had once occupied it. Much too small.

Duncan struggled to breathe.

He realized that he was overwhelmed by a profound sense of futility and inconsequence, feelings that were new to him. Never before had he felt anything approaching despair. Never before had he had cause for it. His life had always enjoyed a clear trajectory, personally and professionally. He had three great loves in his life: the service, his husband, and Yorek. He could still claim two out of three. That wasn't bad; it was more than so many others were lucky enough to experience. So why did he feel so empty?

For the first time in his career, he didn't want to be in the ICHR, in this meeting. He couldn't possibly care less who among his colleagues would be elevated to fill the Dhalgrim seat. The seat that would have been his, had Yorek's death been only a few weeks earlier. But it wasn't the loss of position which numbed him now. All he'd ever hoped for was to labor at Yorek's side, first in the Hérn seat and then in whatever form Yorek would have him, for the entirety of both their careers. At that moment, Duncan's lifetime of service to the People felt like a waste. He wanted to be anywhere in any of myriad other localities rather than this Council chamber.

He stood, fully intending to walk out of the Chamber, to leave behind the pettiness and the maneuvering and the faces he'd read for so many years but could no longer bring himself to look at. When he spoke, calling for attention, his words surprised him as much as they no doubt did the room.

"The death of Yorek is an irreplaceable loss," he said. "He was not just my councilor—my mentor—he was my . . . He was my friend. For many years, he was my friend. And one day, I may come to understand how to—" Duncan paused, waiting for his emotions to pass, or at least subside enough that he could continue. They did not. He could manage only a sentence more, his voice tremulous, his vision blurry. "I would like to ask that we observe a moment's silence in his memory before we go on with the business of this meeting." He sat and hung his head, staring at the space between his knees.

The council members were looking at each other, Duncan knew. Exchanging glances. This wasn't the Duncan they worked with, ordinarily a stickler for the rules of order and not one given to sharing his feelings so openly. The Council chamber was not the place for impromptu eulogies, after all, let alone personal memorials. Grieving and celebrating the life of the deceased had other venues and occasions, bound in tradition and order.

He could make a defense if he wanted to, though. The facts came to Duncan without effort, the precedents, even in his grief, history recalling itself to him as easily as breathing. In the 71st Turn, Maree had spoken extemporaneously for eight hours after her lover had died, and during the Violet Period, Paolea had refused to allow the Chamber's work to proceed until each and every member had spoken about those they'd lost. It had taken four days and was widely considered to have rescued the 59th Turn, and Burel Hird itself, from disaster.

It didn't matter, of course. These were pivotal figures from history—Maree, Paolea, councilors whose work and teachings were still part of the Academy curriculum—whose faces Duncan could look up and see on the wall.

There was silence in the room. No one spoke to second Duncan's request. Maree? Paolea? They were not Duncan. They were remembered, would be still, long after Duncan was gone. They were not faceless. The silence stretched on.

"I, too, have been shaken by Yorek's accident." Trystèsté's voice was abrupt, quiet, but clear, and a red light was illuminated on the table before her. She hesitated and Duncan noticed her struggling with what to say, her impulsiveness having thrust her into the center of attention. Its familiarity was obscurely soothing. "It is easy to forget how fragile and precious a life truly is. Every life. I second Duncan's motion."

Councilor Zeph nodded once. "The chair recognizes an extraordinary motion. Let's make this simple: dissents only, please." He paused, waiting for any opposed to register their votes. No lights flashed on the table, so Zeph said, "Very well. A moment of silence to remember Yorek and a life of service."

Duncan took a breath, which caught in his lungs. The Chamber had never been so quiet in all the years he'd been involved in the Council, first as an academy page nearly forty years prior. The room held decades of memories, nearly all bound tightly to his work with Yorek. He could almost hear the man's voice cutting through the silence: What's with all this melancholy bullshit? Don't you have work to do, people?

The thought made Duncan smile, and the tears he'd been holding at bay spilled out. He'd always worried that it would be Yorek's secret traveling that would finish him. A foolhardy sojourn to a perilous world, Duncan unable to bring him back before a great beast or rogue pirate queen found Yorek at a vulnerable moment. Of all the ways for such a life to be cut short—too much drink and the inevitability of gravity.

Yorek would have undoubtedly found it hilarious.

Zeph cleared his throat and began to speak. "As you all know, I find the rules that forbid Duncan from rising to fill his councilor's place to be arbitrary and ill-considered. Whatever purpose they served at our founding is served no longer. Fifty years may once have been too late to begin a placement, but today it is nothing. And yet here we are, forced to take a vote." He spat the last word out as if it were a curse. "When there's a perfectly good vice-councilor so close to the seat already."

There were a few coughs and awkward glances around the Council chamber. Zeph's views on the Council's age and term limits were well-known, and he'd become less shy about sharing them as he approached the mandated end of his own term. His dissidence was tolerated only because the rules were inviolable, part of Dhalgrim's design—a fact he knew and accepted the same as the rest of them. Whatever his personal feelings, he would cast his vote, and the magnificent, inexorable machinery of Burel Hird would proceed unbroken, as it had for millennia.

It was possible that somewhere, distantly, Duncan understood the results of the election were not contested. All the vice-councilors' Academy and Chamber records were known to the members. A lifetime of test scores, evaluation reports, and suitability assessments open for all in the Chamber to review. While the dossiers stopped short of conferring grades upon each councilor, they could all interpret the data. But as a vice, he wouldn't have a vote on this anyway. It didn't matter. None of it mattered in a universe that didn't have Yorek in it.

He noticed Zeph looking at him pointedly and wondered if he'd been asked a question. That seemed improbable, but he tried to smile. It likely manifested as a grimace, but he couldn't muster the energy to care. "Please, carry on," he said, and Zeph blew a breath out of his nose.

"Indeed. Let us carry on. May I have a motion on the floor to name a successor to the Dhalgrim seat under subsection 73(e) of Article III of the Memorandum of Understanding Governing the First Council of Burel Hird, amended in the Fourth Year of the 9th Turn."

Xelia stood as if they'd been waiting for this moment, which they undoubtedly had been. "Yes, Chair. I propose Priema of the Lirend seat to be elevated from the Chamber to the Council in accordance with the"—they waved their hands vaguely—"relevant regulations."

Sitting next to them, Priema flushed slightly. Likely over her councilor's lack of regulatory specificity rather than on the nomination itself. Legislative research had always been her purview in their collaboration, and ordinarily, she'd never have let Xelia speak so extemporaneously. It came as easily as breathing to Duncan—the observation, the analysis—and passed just as quickly, swallowed by his apathy.

"Is there a seconder for this motion?" Zeph intoned, sounding almost bored. Several green lights illuminated on the tabletop, and Zeph pointed at the one before Melyssa. "I saw you first, Mel. Let the record show that there is a motion by Xelia Sierra, seconded by Melyssa Nandir to promote Priema Lirend to the Dhalgrim seat. Shall we even bother with debate?"

Iskada and Shaddoh glanced at each other, but the councilor shook his head slightly at his vice, and the tabletop remained unilluminated.

"Right. Let's have this blasted vote, then," Zeph said. Six green lights winked on across the table, even before Iskada, a conspicuous dark space before Yorek's empty chair. Priema's chair, now.

"Let the record show that the motion passed unanimously and that I have the honor of introducing Priema Dhalgrim to the Council." For the first time that day Zeph smiled broadly and strode over to the Lirend seat. He pulled Priema up into a hug and said, "Congratulations. You'll continue to be a great asset to the Chamber."

"Thank you, Zeph Estevan," Priema said. "Elevations are always both sour and sweet, and in cases like this, more of the former, I'm afraid." She looked at Duncan, who was only then registering what had happened. "No one could possibly take Yorek's place," she said directly to him, "but I will do my best to live up to the example that he set, the standard he so ably maintained, as established by Dhalgrim Dhalgrim themself." With that, she walked around the room toward him. She dropped a hand on his shoulder, the touch affectionate and soft.

"I know you feel the loss most keenly of us all," she said, quietly enough that only Duncan could hear. "I'm so sorry."

Duncan's eyes clouded with tears, and he leaned back in his chair, uncaring who saw. Across from him, up on the wall, was the bronze sigil of Burel Hird, a figure embracing a globe. The figure was featureless, an abstraction, little more than a parabola with arms, yet at that moment, Duncan could only see it as Yorek. The man who had embraced his life with a verve that amazed Duncan. Who had embraced Burel Hird, who had embraced the People, and improved both for doing so. The man who'd embraced Duncan himself, teaching him how to manage the great, unmanageable machine of their society, showing him what it meant to serve. And he remembered what he'd felt like the first time he walked into this chamber as a member of its illustrious halls, the sense of duty and honor that had filled him, firing his passion. He didn't feel it anymore, but he might again. Someday.

"Thank you, my councilor," he said and gestured to the empty chair next to his. "Please, take your seat."

———

Priema adjourned the meeting quickly, her first act as a councilor and the current chair of Council. She was within her rights to call an agenda or offer a speech, but she evidently felt the somber tone suggested a swift resolution. Once the official business was concluded, a steady stream of colleagues stopped on their way out to offer congratulations and the occasional piece of unsolicited advice. Duncan was rooted to his seat, still craving distance from this place which had once felt more like a sanctuary than a meeting hall, but knowing that his role was to support his councilor. He paid no attention to the conversations, watching the line of councilors slowly shrink until he'd finally be able to escape.

After far too long, only Trystèsté remained to congratulate Priema, her hands twitching in their incessant unconscious motion. Like tame flutterwings. Duncan knew that she and Priema were close—he'd never known the precise nature of their relationship, and he'd never been curious. Yorek had speculated, though, much to Duncan's exasperation. The thought brought another stab of pain, and Duncan must not have hidden it well enough because Priema turned to him.

"You should go," she said gently. "We can meet in a few days for my initial briefing. After . . ." She looked uncharacteristically unsure of what to say, then repeated, "In a few days."

There were no amount of days in any calendar that would bring Duncan solace, and it was not in his nature to shirk his responsibilities. But he couldn't find it within him to demur. He nodded, rising laboriously from his seat, his body still encumbered by grief's narcotic, then slowly walked out of the Chamber. As he exited, he passed under the portraits of councilors dating back to the birth of Burel Hird. Duncan had never much cared about the legacy of the faces, but now that he'd be seeing Yorek's portrait there, the latest in a line that was begun by Dhalgrim themself, he understood the poignancy that many councilors encountered at this wall of paintings.

At the threshold, he stopped and moved to the side. He could go no farther. The corridor he'd walked so many times, Yorek at his side, or he at Yorek's, lay before him. The pearlescent gray of the stone walls, the fluting at each column's crown, the high, bright windows along one side, midmorning sun bisecting the hall: Duncan saw none of it. He was aware only of the cold of the wall—on his cheek, through the sleeve of his shirt on his arm—and a vast, black chasm at his feet.

Though he could not see it, could not bring himself to look down, he could feel it there. Its absence drew him in, the perverse gravity of despondence, and he gripped the wall to keep from tumbling forward. It stretched out in front of him, as wide as it was inevitable, and he knew he would fall, knew he would sink into the velvet darkness of rage and despair and blame, would plummet through depthless—

A voice reached Duncan, and he opened his eyes. It was Darmeth, his tight curls slicked back, shaking, as he waved a hand in Duncan's face.

"Dunca-doodle-doo, let's go. Come share a pot of tea. Tell me about how brilliant Yorek was and I'll tell you how much of an asshole he was."

Duncan tried to smile but settled for a nod. "That sounds—" His voice broke and he paused, then started again. "That sounds nice."

Darmeth made to leave, but Duncan didn't move. He found he couldn't release the wall; his fingers would not obey. They clutched the furrow of a column with such force that his knuckles burned. Without speaking, Darmeth reached out and took one of Duncan's hands in both of his. He patted it gently, the heat of the younger man's grip a comfort that Duncan did not expect, and he let go of the wall. Together they walked slowly, Darmeth still holding Duncan's left hand, down the long slope of the hallway to the teahouse.

The chasm remained, though, just before Duncan, undiminished, and with each step he took, he did not know if his feet would come to rest on solid ground.

26

Priema arranged the pastries on a porcelain platter, then rearranged them. She wasn't nervous, exactly. She'd prepared most of her life to lead, and she'd never doubted that one day, one of the seven seats would be hers. While the other kids at the August Academy were practicing their signatures in the formal, handwritten script of the Council, trying out different seat names, Priema was evaluating her peers for their suitability as a vice-councilor. Six years old, and she had a notebook for each of her classmates.

They had been found, of course—however clever she was, there were few suitable hiding places in her room at the Academy, and she needed them close at hand if she was going to keep them properly updated. She'd been reprimanded by an instructor for her presumption and her egoism and chastised further when she defended her actions. Was it wrong to be prepared?

No, she was informed, it was not, but then neither was it her job to make such evaluations; it was the Academy's. It would be her job, though. She had a clear memory of the room, the adult faces looking down at her, the solemnity of her voice, her certainty so absolute it passed into the realm of knowledge. It very much would be her job.

The only question was which seat she would occupy. Quinn? Nandir? Perhaps even Dhalgrim? Once she became a vice, of course, she'd assumed she'd become Priema Sierra since she was appointed to Xelia's second chair, but Duncan's age made it possible that one of her contemporaries would accede to Yorek's seat. She'd also known she had a good chance of being that person. As she nudged an éclair closer to the edge of the platter, she already felt at home in the office.

Thinking about Duncan caused her to keep fiddling with the plating. She knew he'd work with her if she asked it, knew he'd never undermine her authority or give any indication whatsoever of comparing her to Yorek. He was the perfect "Bureau Man"—as certain externs sometimes inaptly referred to them. He would happily become Duncan Griys and slide onto the Dhalgrim seat's Subcommittee for Internal Clarity and Opacity; he'd do whatever it took to serve. But she wanted more than his service. She wanted him to feel comfortable with her, wanted him to be a true asset, as he'd been to Yorek.

She would never have the relationship with him that Yorek had, but she did hope he'd be able to excel with her.

"Good morning," she said to Duncan, who arrived precisely on time. He stepped through the doorway to their shared workroom with its comfortable chairs and low table, designed as it was to be a space for discussion and debate. His footsteps faltered as he approached. As if an unseen barrier appeared just before the table laden with pastries and tea.

He blinked once, then deliberately walked to the nearest chair and sat, gesturing for Priema to take the other seat.

"It's going to take a while for me to get used to this," he confessed, meeting Priema's gaze evenly. "It wouldn't matter who succeeded Yorek."

"I know," Priema said kindly. "It's uncomfortable for me as well." She gestured toward the table. "Are you hungry?"

Duncan glanced at the pastries. "I am, actually. You wouldn't have anything a little less—"

Priema swapped two plates, bringing forward a scone, unglazed and studded with pieces of smoked cheese.

"Less sweet, precisely. Thank you."

They ate in silence for a moment, then Priema said, "I've read through Yorek's notes on the Vestyl locality situation and—" She paused. Duncan regarded her with a blank expression, his mind obviously elsewhere. Going through the motions.

"Let's drop the bullshit, shall we?" she said, and it took Duncan a moment to register the shift in her tone. Standing, she paced around the small room, its plush carpeting muffling the sounds of her feet. She gazed at the wall, with its portrait of Burel Hird Prime as seen from space, the artist's rendition painting the wilds in vibrant green, the cities picked out in bright blues and yellows. It was beautiful, even if it was a lie.

"Priema, the truth is . . ." Duncan began, then sighed. "I've been talking with Ecklan, and—"

"If you want to follow through with retirement, I would understand. Believe me, Duncan, I would. This is not an easy job, and you've served a long time already. If you wanted to stay on for the transition and then call it, no one would begrudge you your decision."

She turned back to Duncan, who nodded but didn't respond.

"I'm going to be honest with you, though—I need you. We need you. All of us. Not just in the Chamber, not just in Burel Hird. But every single one of us in the transmundi. Because the Chamber has been remiss. We have been remiss, Duncan. Complacent. We have been insufficiently aggressive in our defense of stability and have too willingly accepted an unacceptable gradualism. This society of ours, with its understanding of the limits of freedom and the dangers of permissiveness, we are the only ones who can keep entropy at bay. Who can defend against the chaos and ravages of the . . . the Simulacrum."

Duncan's eyes widened, and he sat up. Good. It wasn't politic to name such things or even use such words, but perhaps it was necessary to make him understand.

"There are universes out there that require our order," Priema continued. "Universes that require our control. People who require our service. This work that we will need to undertake is bigger than any one individual. And to have any chance of success, it's going to take all of us."

Duncan stared at her. With fear? Respect? Loyalty? She didn't know. Not yet.

"I know you feel it, too, just the same as I do. That we must rededicate ourselves to our purpose. To the People, those we serve now and those we will soon enough. So I'm asking you to stay. But"—she held up a hand, staving off Duncan's response—"I'm asking you to put it away, too. The pain. The concern for personal things, for your own loss." She leaned on the word and made him hear it.

Duncan frowned, his brow furrowing.

Priema felt heat in her cheeks and along her back. This was the crux of it, the moment she would secure him—or lose him. When she spoke again, she kept her voice steady, working hard not to rush through her words.

"I'm sorry to ask it of you so soon after Yorek's accident. Truly, I am. I wish I didn't have to. I wish you had all the time you needed. You don't, though. Because this is more important than you and me, more important than Yorek and even the Council itself. This is the future of the transmundi as we know it, and I need to know that I have you, all of you, with me."

She dropped her hands to her side, conscious to keep a loose and open posture. There was a threat inherent in her words, she knew, but that wasn't what she wanted Duncan to hear. She wanted him to hear the plea.

"I know that if I ask, you'll stay on, but it's not enough for you to simply stay on. You know that, too, or I wouldn't say it. Duncan, this is who we are. This is what we do. This is what it means to serve the People. Can we rely on you?"

It was a long moment before he spoke.

"Of course, Councilor," he said, his voice low, even, and full of conviction. "I serve the People."

The tightness in Priema's lungs abated. Good. There was no chance she would be able to steer Burel Hird where it needed to go alone.

"I'm so glad to have you with me," she said.

"Of course," Duncan repeated, his eyes bright and attentive. He pulled out a hand tab and stylus. "Where shall we begin?"

"Are you sure?"

Duncan laid the tab on his lap and smiled. "Priema Dhalgrim, I am ready."

Priema returned his smile and pulled out her own tab, tapping quickly. "I've just sent you a copy of a message I received this morning. For my eyes only, very hush-hush. I think you'll be interested to see what it contains."

Duncan frowned, his eyes darting across the screen as he read. The clenching of his jaw told Priema when he reached the end. "Is this—?"

"The prestige," Priema said, gesturing dramatically with her left hand like a cut-rate stage illusionist.

"So, that business with the Garrison and its rogue agents plotting to take down the Council—it was a long con all along?"

"I actually suspect the Garrison underestimated us, and they had to scramble to find their patsies. It doesn't matter now."

"The Council is never going to agree to this," Duncan said. "The seats have been unchanged since Dhalgrim's day. It is the essence of how the People are served. There's no way that a member of the Joint Adjudication Garrison would also be appointed a single seat on the Council, let alone two. How could they even . . . But this makes no sense!" Duncan's lips were a thin line. "With the petitions halted, they've lost all leverage. They have neither carrot nor stick."

"They have neither," Priema agreed. She turned away, her eyes locked on the portrait of Prime. "Which means they're desperate. Dangerously so."

"When the Chamber finds out—"

"The Chamber is never going to see this request," she said, her voice hard. "This is nothing short of insurrection, and it will be dealt with as such. No hesitation, no mercy."

Duncan said nothing for a moment, and Priema wondered if she'd gone too far.

"I think it's time for a reevaluation of the Garrison's responsibilities. The limb of the bar no longer serves the People, it serves its own agenda. Look at this." She flicked another set of documents to Duncan's tab and waited as he skimmed them. She knew what he was seeing: routine surveillance and access requests that had been sent to Burel Hird outposts in recent months. There was nothing obviously untoward about them, but one of the names would strike him as familiar.

"Malculm Kilkaneade," Duncan said, looking up. "Wasn't he the officer in charge of that debacle on Geçiş? When Trystèsté's pet project blew up?"

"Indeed," Priema said. "He's I/EI. Therefore, he is their responsibility. And yet . . ."

Duncan returned to the records. "These injunctions aren't from Intelligence. They've all come from the Garrison. But why?"

Priema pursed her lips. "Æthelred Æthelred."

"Who?"

"The Garrison's direct representative on the ground at Geçiş. The one Malculm implied made the call that started that whole mess. The one who died."

Duncan closed his eyes. "So this injunction was just their petty revenge? That's . . . shocking. That sort of abuse of power . . . They are acting like children."

"They are also acting well beyond their jurisdiction, I'm sure even their own interpretation of the statutes would have to admit."

"They have no authority to restrict his movements," Duncan agreed. "How could they even imagine this is acceptable?"

"Between this ridiculous act of personal retribution against Malculm, and their blatant power grab for seats in the Chamber, they seem to be under the very mistaken impression that the Garrison is de facto equivalent to the Council," Priema said. "And that cannot stand."

———

Priema sat in the Dhalgrim seat and could feel Duncan's calming presence from his seat next to hers. She met the eyes of each councilor and vice-councilor in turn. "It is my belief that the Joint Adjudication Garrison, in its current form, has outlived its usefulness. The time has come for a change. I've uncovered evidence that the Garrison has been acting outside of their purview, abusing their power, and acting against the best interests of the People."

She gestured to Duncan, who placed a data-slate into the table in front of the Council. Reports began to scroll on the tabletop before each councilor. "I've highlighted the relevant sections," Duncan explained. "As you can see, these clearly show the Garrison overstepping its role."

"These are just some of the examples we have uncovered," Priema went on without pause. "The Garrison has been acting without regard for either due process or proper departmental boundaries. Ironic as it may sound, the Garrison has become a law unto itself, and it is time for the Council to take back its rightful place as the highest authority. I therefore recommend we take action immediately."

Duncan spoke up again. "I agree that this is something that we should give serious thought to. These transgressions are numerous and insidious, and such behavior cannot be allowed to fester."

"And what do you propose?" Iskada asked. "Disbanding the Garrison completely?"

A few murmurs went around the table, but Priema shook her head. "No, we still need the expertise they offer. But the prosecutor-general has to go. And probably all the committee heads as well."

Iskada frowned, but Priema saw Zeph and Melyssa both nod. She turned slightly toward them when she spoke next.

"And I think the organization requires closer oversight. Perhaps as a subcommittee under the office of Practical Transportation Regulatory Administration."

Zeph snorted. "You want to put them under the traffic cops?"

"Not necessarily. I'd say the Nightwatch Board would be an equally reasonable landing spot. Or the Committee for Safe and Congruous Egress."

Now Zeph laughed. "We won't have to fire the generals, they'll all walk out."

Priema shrugged and allowed a smile to play on her lips. "That would certainly be within their rights."

Zeph laughed again.

Duncan sat back as the discussion proceeded, enjoying watching Priema at work. With a minimum of shouting and hardly any recriminations, she maneuvered the other councilors into her way of thinking. Less forceful than Yorek, but also perhaps more deft. In the end, she had her way. The Garrison was stripped of its committee standing. The generals stood down and the adjudicants were to be offered positions far, far away from Prime. The action would be presented as an attempt to streamline administration, which would play well with that small section of the public that followed committee organization news. For that much larger segment of the population for whom such developments meant little, it wouldn't even register. And for the People as a whole, nothing at all needed to be shared regarding this challenge to the First Council's authority.

After the meeting, Duncan hung back, tapping and scrolling conspicuously at his tab, waiting for the ICHR to clear. Once it had, Priema returned to the Dhalgrim seat and sat beside him.

"You did a good job today," Duncan said. "It's possible you've saved the Council, and they don't even know." He refused to meet her gaze.

"We did this," Priema said. "That's not why we're talking, though, is it?"

Duncan shook his head. He swiped on the table slate before him, and the noiseless sound of the recording equipment in the room ceased. The lights had dimmed to their semi-occupied level, a pale white glow emerging from the room's edges. They were alone and unobserved.

Duncan turned his tab to her. On the screen, the Garrison's disbandment order and its concomitant revocation of traveling rights and martial authority were displayed.

"You did this before the Chamber debated," Duncan said.

"I did."

"Before we'd even met."

"I did."

"You did it as soon as you received the message from the Garrison."

"All of this is true."

"Why?"

"If they were desperate enough to come begging for Council seats, they were desperate enough to try and take them. I wasn't interested in waiting to see if they would. The first order will be superseded by today's identical order; no one will be any the wiser."

Duncan placed his tab on the table and for some time said nothing. Priema waited for him to speak.

"We have processes in place for a reason, Priema. It was the Garrison's very failure to adhere to theirs that we rightly punished them for."

"You're not wrong."

"I know I'm not."

"And yet you also knew I'd done it, when I'd done it, and backed me today anyway." She pointed to the access date in the upper right of the screen: the evening before the Chamber meeting.

Duncan nodded but did not look away.

"Why?" Priema said.

Once again, Duncan fell silent. Priema studied him—the furrows of his forehead, the spiderweb of wrinkles at the corners of his eyes, the broad, flat planes of his cheeks, shaved to geometric smoothness. He was studying her, as well, watching as she watched him. She wondered what he saw.

"Duncan, the work we must do will not be easy. I won't pretend to know exactly what's coming, but I do know it will test us. The Chamber, the councilors, they have grown complacent, and worse, comfortable with their complacency. This organ has atrophied. They think peace is mercy, but peace outside the People is cruelty. A peace outside the People is injustice. And if peace is injustice, then conflict is the true mercy.

"Conflict must be the course we chart. Whether that conflict will be bloodless or all-out war, I don't know, but that will be our work. That is the monstrous, glorious weight we must bear. The People must grow. To deny this is to doom those born outside our borders to untold suffering. To deny this is violence. Do you understand?"

Duncan nodded.

"So, let me ask you again. You knew what I'd done. You knew when I'd done it. You were with me still. Why?"

"Priema Dhalgrim, you are a councilor for Burel Hird. That is enough. Together, we serve the People."

Priema put a hand on his shoulder. "Together, we serve the People."

27

The massive walled city of the Palisades was the seat of power on Shighoa, and acted as the royal court for the planetary system. It had been the empress's palace once, but now more closely resembled halls of bureaucracy. Towering silver buildings dotted the skyline above ancient city walls—now useful mainly as tourist attractions—and could be seen from a distance as they approached the southern gates. Beinir maneuvered the rickety skimmer carrying the three of them toward the gates, slowing down as traffic increased. Within the flight lanes, various vehicles headed for the city, mostly huge cargo haulers carrying supplies manufactured outside the walls, but there were a number of passenger shuttles and private vehicles, too. Everything ground to a halt as each vehicle was inspected at the checkpoint.

Earlier, they had docked at the Kardoral encampment in the southern wilds—a landscape rich in minerals and timber, but unusually, and blessedly, unspoiled. The protected mercenary class kept out extractors, both corporate and imperial, but just beyond their area of influence, the scars of mining and logging became apparent.

Beinir had commandeered a small personal transport from the motor pool and he, Malculm, and Shara loaded into the skimmer. It barely hovered with their combined weight, but once Beinir thumbed the throttle, it hummed to life and sped off toward the Palisades.

As they trundled toward the gates, Malculm noticed sleek vehicles lined up outside the regular flight lanes, hovering to one side of the gate. Five of them lined up in formation as Malculm watched. He found himself wishing he hadn't abandoned his Kardoral armor. The overlay would've been helpful.

The vehicles—barges—shone bright in the sun, their polished steel hulls bare. The decks also gleamed, but it took Malculm a while to realize it wasn't because the floors of the vessels were lined with the same polished metal. Those were helmets. Many, many helmets. And the barges, one by one, were entering the city in one of the side gates, reserved only for matters urgent or secret.

Beinir glanced back at Malculm, whose face was clearly visible in his civilian clothes. "I hope you know what you are doing," he said.

"So do I," Malculm said as they pulled up to the checkpoint.

A bored customs agent with a hand scanner stepped up to the flyer. He waved the scanner over the three of them, cocked an eyebrow at Malculm, then said, "Welcome back, sir," and waved them in.

Beinir didn't wait for an explanation and drove into the city. The battered skimmer looked shabby and old among the city denizens' gleaming ground-cars and automated public transports, but they swiftly slotted into traffic and made for the city center.

"That was easy," Shara said. "Troubling."

"I agree," Malculm said sourly. Few things were as ominous as an I/EI red carpet.

———

The Interworld Exports Imports office in the Palisades was the exception to the low-profile rule. An entire floor of one of the gleaming towers belonged to the security secretariat. For a few weeks, Malculm had even worked a desk there, and his feet knew the way through the lifts and corridors. Even as he stepped through the public entrance, he'd expected to feel a firm hand on his arm or to hear his name shouted—to feel the looming shadow of some goon behind him. But there had been nothing but the cool whiff of filtered air and a vaguely electrical smell that somehow permeated the city.

Beinir and Shara were inscrutable in their helmeted armor, but Malculm could sense them both taking note of exits and security measures as they walked toward yet one more anteroom. If they planned to escape, well, that was their right, but this time Malculm was going nowhere. It was the end of the line, one way or another. He'd expected to feel something significant—trepidation or regret—but it was only a cold resolve that filled Malculm, as if the consequences had already been applied once he'd made the decision. What was the career, even the life, of one person weighed against the security of the nine thousand worlds?

The receptionist was human, a man older than Malculm, though he appeared as spry and sharp as someone half his age. He was dressed in a conservatively cut yellow uniform, worn at the joints and seams but still in good condition. He looked up as the three of them entered and smiled.

"Malculm, hello. We got word you were back. It's good to see you again after so long."

Malculm blinked slowly, the calm he projected almost natural. "Nice to see you too, Jenkins." He waited. Nothing happened. He looked at the door to the internal offices. "Is she in?"

Jenkins nodded. "Have a seat, it won't be long." He looked Shara and Beinir over, tapping his chin, and stood before either could move. "Just a moment, please." From a wall compartment, he withdrew what looked like a large blanket and hung it over the settee, carefully tucking in the corners around the cushions.

"Regulations, I'm afraid," he said as he worked, "for any visitors wearing a combat apparatus level two or above, and Kardoraa wear at least a seven."

"Dampening fabric?" Beinir asked. "Shock cloth? What manner of drapery is this?"

"Ah, no," Jenkins said. "Upholstery protector."

"I shall stand," Beinir said.

Finishing, Jenkins shrugged. "Suit yourself."

Beinir and Shara removed their helmets, hanging them from their hips, and Malculm perched on the hard couch, slipping slightly on the cover. Shara fit herself in next to him. "Is this what you expected?" she asked quietly, leaning in close. "Should we be ready?"

Eyeing Jenkins, who had returned to his desk and resumed stamping each paper in an intimidatingly large stack of documents, Malculm realized, with a shock, that he felt a sense of responsibility for Beinir and Shara. Perhaps being carried in Shara's arms as she leaped from a building had that effect, but he wouldn't let them be caught up in the consequences of his mistakes. And, whatever they thought of their prowess, this particular Interworld was not one they'd be able to fight their way out of—he knew its security detail and armory too well for that.

He held his hands out low, motioning for Shara to be calm.

"Don't look a bequeathed cerathern in its top cavity," he said and smiled. Shara nodded, skeptical, then relaxed.

Soon the door to the office opened, and a short woman about Malculm's age stepped out. Her uniform was rumpled, the train of the overskirt tucked into the back of her trousers, and she had half a sandwich in her hand.

"Malculm!" She beamed and waved him over with her sandwich. "You've got an army with you, I see."

"Not an army, Fatima," Malculm said, standing. "Why would I need an army?"

She furrowed her brow in response. "You wouldn't. Come. Let's talk."

Malculm relaxed when she gestured for him to follow her back into her office but hesitated, glancing at Beinir and Shara.

Fatima rolled her eyes. "Bring your meat slabs too, if you want. I just had my sofa replaced, and it's not graded for power armor, so they have to stand."

"Your people do trouble over their furniture," Beinir said as they filed into the room.

Fatima snorted. "If you had any idea how paltry my decoration budget was, you would not be saying this."

———

Though Fatima was officially the Grand Vizier for Special Circumstances, she preferred her Burel Hird title of I/EI Committee Chair for Renqueue. This locality, and her permanently disheveled appearance, belied a mind that was among the sharpest Malculm had encountered, though she used it primarily to find clever ways to reduce her workload. An underperforming committee chair for an outer locality was hardly top brass, but she would be the best chance he had of getting a warning through to Prime.

She closed the door behind them and flopped into the chair behind her desk. "Well, you've had a time, haven't you, Malculm?"

He nodded, lowering himself slowly onto the visitors' couch, and looked around. Beinir and Shara staked out spots to either side and scanned the room for threats as Fatima watched, amusement on her face. It was only the four of them, though; no goons lay in wait, no enforcers crowded together in concealed closets.

"I must confess," Malculm said, "this is a rather different reception than my last visit to Interworld."

"We're a rather different Burel Hird."

"Have several centuries passed without me noticing?"

"Har har. There's been an administrative shakeup, and it would seem you, at least, are one of the beneficiaries."

"Oh. You were being serious?"

"I was. It was led by Priema Dhalgrim, apparently. Her first act as councilor."

"Priema Dhal—? Right."

"I wouldn't presume to know what goes on at that elevation, but one rather doubts it was a question of 'efficiency and departmental streamlining,' given where the Garrison ended up on the org chart."

"What does the limb of the bar have to do with anything?"

"Yes, well, that is where things get rather knotty." Fatima pursed her lips and sat back in her chair. "It was the Garrison that injuncted you."

Malculm's eye twitched. "Come again?"

"As you may or may not have noticed—that was a joke—there was a flag on your movements. It originated in the Joint Adjudication Garrison. That flag, along with a great many other similar markers, has been expunged."

"Expunged . . ."

"And just in time, too," Fatima said. "I had to call in a Code Triangle for you. Best I could do from here. It was a good thing that enforcer you shot in Velellia survived, or we'd have a bigger mess on our hands."

Malculm took a breath. "Fatima, wait . . . Pretend, for a moment, that I'm a complete fucking moron, and explain to me how the ever-loving fuck the Garrison was able to injunct a duly chaired officer of I/EI without I/EI high seats raising so much as a peep."

"Like I said, hard to imagine there's not more going on than just an efficiency audit, but we're certainly never going to learn the full story." Fatima laughed and ran a hand through her hair. "The 90th Turn has already brought its share of surprises."

Malculm finally registered the mourning pink in the room, the thin rose sash at Fatima's shoulder, the vase of dyed lilies pressed against the window. It was the color of failure. He was too late, the plot had been enacted. But how could it possibly be? That some extern killer could infiltrate Prime when Malculm, who was Burel Hird himself, privy to a deep knowledge of its security protocols, had barely been able to sneak into a Vorren four edge world like Renqueue? It was absurd. There had to be more to it, maybe even . . . He looked at Fatima, who was clearly waiting for a response. He couldn't trust anyone anymore.

"The '90th Turn' . . ." he said slowly. "It's going to take some time to get used to that."

"Tell me about it! I've had to rewrite at least a dozen forms already. Yorek's been in the Dhalgrim seat—shit, was in the Dhalgrim seat, for the entirety of our careers. It's going to take longer than a week to make the shift."

"This Yorek died?" Shara said.

"He did," Fatima said. "An accident. A tragic accident. He served well and had almost finished his term. The People are poorer for his absence."

"That must be who—"

"Yes, it is!" Malculm stomped on Shara's foot as quietly as he could manage. His heart raced. "That is indeed who I was telling you both about. Regaling you with tales. Of his brilliance. Remember?"

Shara and Beinir stared at him.

"The gambit in the Novy Urk locality?" he continued. "The negotiation with the Ajjenet emissary? Holding our ambassador for three days to ensure we didn't lie to the emissary? A masterstroke."

"You told them about Novy Urk?" Fatima laughed, incredulous. "But . . . why?"

"Because we've gotten to know each other and I've learned how much the Kardoraa appreciate stories of restraint, of the canny withholding of crucial information based on changing circumstances. Right?" He turned to the Of Tala.

"Yes, we do," Shara said, her voice tentative. "Don't we, Beinir?"

"Certainly. I relish a tale of . . . negotiation!"

"You see?" Malculm said. "A negotiation just like Yorek engineered."

Fatima laughed again. "I wouldn't have expected such enthusiasm for bureaucratic maneuvering."

"The Kardoraa contain multitudes," Malculm said.

"Malculm, why are they here?"

"Because I came to surrender, and I didn't want some trigger-happy Shighoan splattering my guts against a wall trying to impress their superior. I saw the barges coming in. I thought this might go differently, though I was flattered you'd called in four battalions for me."

"For you?" Fatima snorted. "We've been trying to stamp out the monarchists since the 88th Turn. This is just another flare-up. We've been Vorren four here since . . . Hold on, you hired Kardoraa as bodyguards?

Good luck getting ret-comp for that. You're more likely to get an ERC visit."

"No. No! Certainly not. I wouldn't hire them. I wouldn't do something like that. They're . . . friends." Malculm stood, Beinir and Shara flanking him. "They're friends doing me a favor." Malculm put an arm around each of their shoulders, their pauldrons rough beneath his touch. He could almost hear Shara's eyes rolling.

Fatima shook her head, her expression amused. "This has been unexpected and educational, Malculm. You're not the same man you were the last time you were here."

"It's the 90th Turn, Fatima. New Burel Hird, new Malculm Kilkaneade."

"Yeah. About that." Fatima stood and stepped in front of her desk. "So, you have a C53 to fill out. You can grab it from Jenkins on the way out."

"Back pay? Well, that's a pleasant surprise."

"And an X stroke 37 . . ."

"What?!" Malculm fell back onto the couch, his hand on his forehead. He thought he'd known what he was choosing when he came here, but the situation had evolved without him. He needed a second, a moment, to think. At least he knew what Fatima expected to hear at a time like this. He let his training do the talking while he allowed the new information to filter into his brain.

"I know. Sorry. Padre's still pretty pissed."

Malculm slumped in his chair. "I knew it would be bad. I wasn't expecting full abdication." He bowed his head and stared at the lines in his hands. "I'd be starting my entire career over. From the bottom."

"A provisional full abdication. There's no guarantee it'd stick."

"There's no guarantee it wouldn't."

"Keep your nose clean, and after three or four years on toothbrush duty, you'll be right back in the thick of it."

"Shitship, Fatima, are you serious?"

"I . . . Listen, you got dealt a garbage hand. The Garrison screwed you over, and how, but an X stroke 37 is about the best you could've hoped for. Assaulting Padre, Malculm? Kidnapping? Your situation was bad, but you panicked, and if you'd just sat and stewed on Engine, we wouldn't be here."

Malculm groaned.

"Hey." Fatima sat on the edge of her desk and crossed her arms. "I can't do anything for you in I/EI, but if you want out, I can find you a soft landing spot. It'd be the end of the line with Intelligence, but . . ." She spread her hands. "Up to you. Only if you want it."

Malculm sank back into the couch. Against its plush cushions, the muscles of his neck and shoulders were hard, and he took a long, slow breath, trying to release the tension. Shara tried to catch his eye, but he ignored her. Fatima tactfully stood and went to the window, finishing her sandwich.

He was free. If he wanted it, he was free. But he'd failed, as well. Yorek was dead—the Tala's assassination plot, he was sure of it. Coincidence was a euphemism for conspiracy. Dima had taught him that, and he believed it still. There had been a conspiracy, a plot, and the leadership of Burel Hird remained unaware of it. Or even . . . The maneuvering for power in the First Council was ruthless, but ruthless enough for a councilor to be complicit? It was dubious at best. And yet, so too was an extern infiltrating and assassinating the Dhalgrim seat of the First Council. He'd been unable to prevent it, but there was still a chance he could solve it. It would be difficult to unravel while on toothbrush duty; it would be impossible to unravel if he was outside of I/EI.

He inhaled again, feeling his chest expand, listening to the air in his nose. He heard the tides of Geçiş, the pneumatic hush of the subway on Engine, the gasping of Padre and Gervin when he'd punched them. He breathed out and heard the air leave Ronni's lungs when he hugged her, the hiss and roar of the rosantans, the rattling breaths of the dying proxy he'd left behind.

"No," Malculm said. "No, let them thirty-seven me. I've come this far. I'll take them both, the C53 and the X stroke 37."

Fatima turned from the window. "There he is!" she said around a mouthful of sandwich. "Good man. You'll be back before you know it." She swallowed and licked her fingers clean then clapped her hands together, the sound loud in the small room. "Now, though, if you'll excuse me, I need to persuade a Citalian baronet that they'd benefit from an additional layer of Interworld security. Jenkins will have everything you need." Malculm stood once more, and Fatima came to him, placing a hand on his shoulder. "It was good to see you, Malculm."

"Likewise, Fatima."

"Good luck out there. You've had enough bad luck to last a lifetime."

Malculm smiled, but felt how weak it was. "Several, by my count," he said.

———

"Why did you not let me tell her?" Shara punched the table they sat around, the sounds of the Kardoral encampment outside their tent momentarily silenced. "Your Yorek was the victim of this plot, he must have been. I thought the reason you came here was to tell someone."

"Yes," Malculm said.

"Then there has been a crime! They must know of it."

"Yes."

"And yet you did not let me tell her! You spun an absurd story and expected us to simply go along with it. Why?"

"Which of the seventeen reasons would you like? A semi-disgraced agent, already on the shit list for assault and kidnapping, shows up with two mercenaries from a fanatically mystical society—"

"Mind your tongue," Beinir said.

"—talking about an assassination that's already happened? It would have been career suicide. I wouldn't even have been able to finish the sentence."

"We effected escape from just such a situation not three days ago," Beinir said.

"That was Tekkin-Yut," Malculm said. "This is Shighoa."

"You treat this like a game," Shara said, "and us like its pieces. What happened to 'Come what may'?"

"That's not—"

"I'm taking a walk," Shara said. She stood without waiting for a response and left, slapping the tent's flap aside with such violence that the leather flew up and landed on the roof outside. Beinir walked to the entrance but only fixed the flap, letting it fall back into place, then returned to the small table Malculm sat at.

"Is she all right?" Malculm asked.

"No, I do not believe she is."

"I wasn't trying to offend, but I really don't think it would have been a good idea to tell Fatima—"

"It was not you that set her off."

"You're not going to go after her?"

Sighing, Beinir looked away. "I am coming to believe that may not always be wise."

Malculm shrugged. "Whatever you say."

"You have had trials of your own, I think," Beinir said. "More than we knew."

"How very observant."

Beinir poured them drinks from the skin on the table. The liquid was a cloudy blue, and Malculm stared down at it while Beinir drank deeply.

"Being left out in the cold by your kin," Beinir said, foam on his lip, the glass still in his hand, "your clan, those meant to support you— that can change a person."

"I don't know."

"It should change a person."

"Maybe."

Beinir set down his glass, then looked away. When he spoke again, the words came slowly. "I have heard it said that, at times, perhaps one creed might be exchanged for another. If the first no longer suits."

"Have you heard that?" Malculm asked.

"There are tales. The first Butcher of Tala is one of those. It is certainly not an impossibility—if one were so inclined to make such a change." He lifted his glass and drained it, then poured the last of the jug without asking.

To the side of the room sat Beinir's cot, his helmet resting on a pillow. Streaks of green and rust told its story. Malculm thought of the borrowed armor, its own history written in scratches and dents painted the color of the sky in summer on his home planet. He hadn't even thought of that world, that universe, in years, but he still remembered the sound of the festral birds on the longest day, the heat of the sun on his back.

Yorek Dhalgrim was dead. Murdered. One of the seven most powerful, most important, most righteous people in Burel Hird—and Malculm had failed to save him. And Malculm alone knew of that failure. Before him, a vast, terrible vista opened, a future of cowardice and mediocrity. He could simply do nothing. Burel Hird was strong. No single councilor held such importance that their loss couldn't be dealt with. No one even noticed a crime had been committed. And to announce that one had been, when he had few details and even less evidence, how would that help anyone? And when his discovery could be so easily misconstrued as the rankest individualism? It was indefensible.

Or there was Beinir's offer. To abandon Burel Hird altogether and turn his back on everything. He almost laughed. What could he possibly endure that would drive him to such an act? And yet. Seductive in its ease, its anonymity, Malculm wondered if he was actually considering it. Surely not. His purpose, his life, had been taken from him, and he'd violated every oath he'd made to the People to cross the transmundi and search for a new purpose. Dammed up within Malculm, beneath this body's hazy memories, was his true history. No matter where he went, no matter what proxy he occupied, he carried it with him always. He heard again the call of the festral, felt the tall grass tickle his knees beneath his short pants. He heard again the wash of Geçiş's tides.

Someone out there, some society, had believed they could strike at the heart of Burel Hird with impunity—and done so. Or, more chilling still, was it someone within Burel Hird who had believed it?

He didn't know. He knew so little. It was the not knowing that infuriated Malculm. It was the not knowing that would keep him Burel Hird.

Beinir was watching Malculm, his face open, though without expectation.

"Did any rely on this first butcher?" Malculm said.

"Rely?"

"Were there trillions upon trillions of people, scattered across nine thousand universes, all of whom, whether they knew it or not, relying on this butcher to uncover a conspiracy at the very heart of their society?"

"I do not recall such a part in the tale, no."

Malculm nodded. "I thought not. There may be times when one creed should be exchanged for another. But there are times, as well, when perseverance is called for. When that exchange would be little more than betrayal. When one is called on to spend several years cleaning grout with a toothbrush in service of a greater cause."

"Is this a literal—"

"Sometimes, yes."

Beinir nodded. "I understand. Perseverance is a virtue that does credit to its possessor. Who could begrudge another their perseverance? No roamer, certainly."

"No roamer," Malculm said, and laughed, taking a drink, letting the bitterness linger on his tongue until it became a comfort. Neither spoke. From outside came the sound of a Kardoral worship song, bidding farewell to the setting sun, the notes long and slow, pitched first deep, then high. It unnerved Malculm, but, with a jolt, he realized that this, too, had become a comfort—the alien somehow, by its very alienness, soothing. He sat and listened, fortified by the strange harmonies, until the prayer had finished and darkness crept in through the flap.

"Still," Malculm said, breaking the silence. "Tell me of this butcher."

"Oh?"

"Please. I would be happy to hear the story."

"This is a tale," Beinir said, grinning. "One for the ages. And oh, the weapon . . . ! A gunknife!"

"I'm having trouble picturing that."

"Well, it is truly more of a . . . Och, be silent and hear this tale."

As dusk came for the camp, Beinir began, and continued long into the night, until the nightbirds had returned to their roosts and the tree-dogs had given up their hunts, until the air had grown cold and the moon brilliant, until the damp had slicked the grass, the speeders, the tents and their ropes, until there were only the sounds of Malculm's laughter and Beinir's voice, the next day only hours distant, but as far off as Malculm could imagine.

28

"Well, I guess we can call that pulling a Madds, huh?"

As good as his word, Reg and Maddalena were in a balloon over the Ghastly Sea. They stood in the lower gondola, the aeronaut above in the upper gondola, working the flame and the rudder. The promised whales had not revealed themselves, however.

"What's that?" Maddalena said.

"Starting a planetwide riot just to get some school records."

"I wasn't trying to start anything that big. I just needed Mëryl to think a cutting was being taken."

"And is one being taken?"

Maddalena shrugged and Reg laughed, shaking his head with obvious pleasure.

"Ironic," he said. "Trantin wanted his own job, and some no-name is going to swoop in and cement her own legacy instead."

"No-name? I'm Maddalena Vaish."

"Not by blood or marriage, you're not," Reg said.

"I'm on the rolls, aren't I? And wait, why does anyone aside from you know?"

"Maddalena, I have told positively everyone. How could I not?

Everything about what you've done is delightful. The scale of it, the te-merity, the absolute unmitigated success. Incredible. You'd been working on getting that stuff for how long? And then, when the pressure was on, you did it in a day."

"The setup took a few days as well, actually."

"Still. And the style? The panache? Madds, there were worldwide riots. Every city, every town, there were people out in the streets because of you. And the rumor is the At-Saught office on the southern conti-nent was straight-up burned to the ground."

"Yeah . . . It was all a little much."

"'A little much,' she says. A heist for the ages, and she wants to go smaller."

"If it could've gone smaller I would have preferred that, yes. I'm not in an occupation that rewards bravado."

"Perhaps not, but you are in a family that most certainly does."

"Now I'm Vaish, huh?" Maddalena snorted. "Funny how that works . . ."

"Could it work any other way?"

"For quite a few Vaish, I think it does."

Reg shrugged. "You're going to resent them for their bloodline?"

"I'm going to resent them for their complacency."

"Oh pishposh. Now isn't the time for any resentments at all. You've won a great victory for the Vaish family and a great victory for all of Firmāre. We can soon expect closer ties between Burel Hird and ourselves, and if not closer ties, then at least a more remunerative re-lationship."

"The operation was a success, then?"

"It will be, yes. Alyk is being dispatched today."

Maddelena stood suddenly, holding her hands out to steady herself as the gondola swayed, responding to her movement. "Today?! Reg, there's no time! Frankie Two-Eyes confirmed the data a week ago, how could you possibly . . . What is the delay? The entire point was the timing of this thing. We can't wait, there can't be any hesitation here, if it's not done quickly then—"

"Madds."

"—it doesn't work at all. Did you not explain their idiotic rules properly? Is this your failure or Trantin's? I practically—"

"Madds."

"—destabilized an entire planet to ensure a successful operation would be accomplished in an appropriate time frame only to find out the sheer incompetence of my superiors—"

"Maddalena."

"What?!"

"I'm messing with you. It's done. Alyk was summoned back to Gora yesterday. Yorek is dead."

Maddalena said nothing and slumped into her seat.

"As it turns out, there was neither failure nor incompetence. Everything went exactly as it was meant to."

"Hm."

"They will have already named his replacement. We don't know yet if it was indeed Priema, but that seems likely based on what you brought us. We'll find out soon enough."

"Yes, well."

Reg raised an eyebrow at Maddalena.

"Don't expect an apology."

Reg nodded, then waved his hands magnanimously. "Consider it forgotten. You've earned some leeway here, I think."

Maddalena's palms were burning, and she realized she was gripping the rope around the basket with all of her strength. She released it and rubbed her hands together. Delicious heat bloomed in her palms as blood flowed through them once more, her fingers tingling gently as feeling returned.

The day was crisp, if overcast, clouds the color of misery, the sea a pallid mirror. When the sun broke through to fall on her skin, it quickly became too hot, but as soon as it vanished the chill returned and Maddalena longed for its return. They were high enough that the only smell was a faint, indistinct saltiness, swelling and ebbing with the breeze.

"I thought we were supposed to be seeing some whales," she said.

"We might be too late."

"You woke me up before dawn so we could float over the ocean in an unheated basket and we were too late?"

"Technically, it's called a gondola."

"Reg."

"I'm not a whale expert, Maddalena. This is when they told me we would have the best chance. This is when I saw them when I last went up. Look." He pointed, so far as Maddalena could tell, in the direction of the rising sun, just then appearing between cloud banks.

"What?" she said.

"A whaler. See? Due west."

She raised a hand and narrowed her eyes and, amid the glare and the glitter of the water, was able to make out the small shape of a ship in the swells, its sails the dark purple of Gdercc's standard. In the vast emptiness of the water, it looked fragile, precious, something easily misplaced, easily lost.

"I see it."

"They had the same thought as us," Reg said. "Coming up empty, too. The best time to get the whales is when they dive. Still groggy after waking up. You need to be close enough to their landing spot to harpoon them before they dive but not so close that they see you and land on you, crushing the ship. Dangerous work, not even considering the other beasts in these waters. One in five crews are lost each year."

"Those are bad numbers . . . They should find a new line of work."

Reg shrugged. "It's who they are—their nature. In Gdercc, they whale."

"Sounds like in Gdercc, they die."

"Just so. But, as I said: their nature."

"Hmm. So what now?"

"I thought we might make a quick detour and see what it is we're doing here." He whistled and called out: "Kbousch!" A head appeared over the edge of the upper gondola. Reg made a series of hand gestures, and the head, Kbousch's evidently, nodded, then disappeared. They began to rise, the wind taking them in a different direction, toward a small cluster of islands.

"I meant with Burel Hird."

"Ah. So quickly your thoughts return to work . . ."

"My own nature, I guess."

"I don't doubt it. Well, now we establish some contracts. That's the hope, at least."

"And that 'we' there is . . ."

"Vaish. For now. We'll see how long it lasts before it's all of Firmāre. Once Pasces Gahn gets wind of what we're doing, I'd say we've got a week before they're undercutting us. Their nature . . ."

"And what exactly are we providing with these contracts?" Maddalena asked.

"Whatever they need. Our relationship is just beginning—we're bound to figure something out. They're spooked by Of Tala, so maybe there's an angle there. And they may have remarkable knowledge of their own localities, but every good authoritarian regime needs intel to properly expand, and we've certainly got our fair share of that. And hey, who knows? Maybe we pull a Madds and start a planetwide riot. Maybe we persuade them of the need for some additional security."

"Good luck getting a Bureau world to riot. Hell, good luck figuring out a way to increase security on a Bureau world. And I thought pulling a Madds was starting a planetwide riot specifically to secure some report cards."

"I think we can broaden the definition to include any and all planetary riots meant to accomplish some ancillary goal. Rioting not for rioting's own sake."

"Who exactly riots for its own sake?"

"Is that not Harraka's entire purpose?"

Maddalena rolled her eyes. "Maybe I've spent too long impersonating them, but I feel pretty confident in saying that for most of them, it is not, in fact, their entire purpose."

"Starting to develop some sympathies, are we?"

"I am not. There are some striking similarities between Firmāre and Harraka, though. An interest in freedom, in movement. We just define those things differently."

"You know, I've never actually gotten the chance to give a member of Harraka the 'We're-not-so-different-you-and-I' speech. It's one of my favorites. Did I ever tell you about the time I tried to seduce a Vhyx witch by convincing him that, ultimately, depending on how you think about it, his worship of—"

"Yes. Many times."

"It was on a moon base, did I tell you that? The moon base part? And not, like, a developed moon base, a real old-school galactic explorer, frontier type of—"

"Yes. I remember the moon base. And the mining explosion," Maddalena said, preempting Reg, who had opened his mouth to speak.

"Well, then, I guess I've imparted all my wisdom to you."

"I guess so."

They stood without speaking for a moment. From above came the sounds of the balloon's operation: the gasp of the flame, the creak of rope, swirling voices like a pedal point, and a steady hum beneath it all. A breeze was at their backs, ruffling the tattered sleeves of Maddalena's tunic and making the thin hair atop Reg's head stand up straight. The leather of her belt squeaked quietly as she shifted, the bandolier across her chest complaining more loudly as she adjusted it. She became aware of the folded recourse strapped to her back and the discomfort of its weight.

"It's not masquerading as Harraka that got to me." She had begun speaking without thinking and she didn't quite know what she was going to say. "It was the coat. I'm always so . . . chatty. I hate it."

Reg laughed. "Of all the things that can go wrong when traveling, I think 'enjoys talking' is a complaint only you could make."

"I can't control it. That's what I hate. I can't control how nice it feels to talk. How nice it feels to talk with her."

"Maybe she was recruiting you."

"In a sense . . ."

"Maddalena, you didn't give anything away, did you?"

She sighed. "No, Reg. 'I was the very soul of discretion, a model of restraint.'" The words came like a schoolyard chant, singsong, and she rolled her eyes as she recited them. "'I was—in essence—shadow, the murky—'"

"Yes, I get it."

"Then don't insult me."

"You were the one bemoaning how chatty your coat was."

"Reg, I can be chatty without giving myself away. However different a coat is, I'm still me. I still know what I'm doing." Maddalena knew her annoyance was not proportional to Reg's comment, but she couldn't stop herself and wasn't sure why.

"I know," Reg said. "Of course, I know. Brain chemistry can be . . . unpredictable, certainly. I've experienced it myself. I meant no offense."

Maddalena nodded. "Thank you. I appreciate that." She opened her mouth to speak but no words came. Something within her churned slowly, like low-grade nausea, some unnamable imbalance.

"But?" Reg prompted.

"I don't know. But I miss it, I guess. That's all. I just . . . miss it."

"Miss what? Chatting?"

Maddalena nodded.

"Or chatting with her?" Reg said.

"Just the talking." She paused, her brow furrowing. "I think."

"Well, here we are, talking now," Reg said. "I'm happy to talk as much or as little as you'd like."

"Hmm."

"How's it feel?"

"Different. Worse."

"Well, I'm sorry I'm such a poor conversational partner! I'll have you know many of my operatives find my anecdotes and my insights to be—"

"It's me, Reg. It's this coat. It's all of my coats. Except for the Calyx one. I just . . . She said something about how she couldn't trust herself. And it made me wonder about why I trust my own self when I don't really have a self to trust. Everything is filtered through a coat. We pretend like it's just something we put on and it doesn't change who we are, but . . . the traveler? The body? They're inseparable."

Reg nodded at her but didn't respond. His expression was unreadable.

"There's no moment where we don't have a body to . . . to mediate what we're feeling. We don't get to just think. What I feel now, about how nice it felt to talk as Shann, how do I know that's not responding to this coat's loneliness, the lack of fulfillment in her life? I don't! I can say it's not, can say that it's wholly my own feeling, but even that thought can't be its own because it's an outgrowth of all the physical, chemical things happening in this body right now."

"Does it make you doubt what we do? Or question the work?"

"No, Reg, this isn't about fucking Firmāre. It's about me, it's about bodies, it's about travel itself. The thrice-cursed Twisted Jynx. And I guess it's about how I talked with Mēryl about this sort of thing and how much I liked doing it."

Reg nodded again, but more slowly, and Maddalena closed her eyes. The motion of the gondola was abruptly queasy-making and she thought, for the first time, of just how high up they were. She opened her eyes, and for a moment, there was no sky and no sea before her, just an uninterrupted tableau of grays, and she was weightless, adrift in the gray, falling and floating all at once, the horizon flattened into turbid vertigo, all of existence just this inscrutable expanse. And then it was gone—she was oriented once more, planted firmly within the basket.

"It sounds like you need to be yourself again," Reg said. His voice was quiet and soothing—he was placating her as though she were a wild animal: unpredictable, erratic. "It sounds like you need to come home."

"Yeah. Maybe. I guess." Maddalena rubbed her hands over her head and opened her eyes wide, blinking vigorously. Her hair was close-cropped and spiky with salt—typical for Gdercc but something she wasn't used to. And yet, it felt natural, the haircut she'd had for years, just as much as it felt alien. She let her hands fall to her sides and sighed.

"You should prepare yourself for quite the welcome, though."

"Oh?"

"Truly, Maddalena, Trantin is pleased. Impressed, even. And your father—"

"Stepfather."

"—is so proud. Vilrona Pon Tetch, too. She's been telling everyone who will listen of her daughter's great ingenuity. Give it another couple of weeks, and Kasahvi will be forgotten entirely—not a soul alive will associate you with it. Not after the success of Calyx."

"Hmm. What a relief. How much does it turn your mouth to say my mother's name?"

"She is Vaish. That she chose to keep her lesser family's name after marrying Eedin Vaish makes me think no less of her."

"Of course not. And my mo—And Enora Haight?"

Reg looked out at the water. His mouth was a thin line, his stomach pressing through the bars of the railing and hanging out over the edge of the gondola.

"I'm not sure any success you achieve could ease her circumstances."

Maddalena looked down. The water beneath them was choppier than it had been, lines of yellow-white froth like ruined capillaries atop its surface—they had approached the islands. There were six of them, small but thickly wooded. A squat lighthouse sat on the furthest, little more than a hump emerging up out of the evergreens. The nearest—the largest of the six—had a clearing in the center, visible from their vantage, though it would have been hidden from water level. Within it, something was being constructed, thick ribs of wood curling toward each other and the faint sheen of whalebone, though Maddalena couldn't tell for sure what it was. Behind them, Gdercc was a bluish-green furl in the water, barely distinguishable from the sea around it. Only the Lighthouse of Gvynni and Helioc's Spire could be identified, thin needles each against a backdrop of clouds.

"The Knuckles are set aside for another three years still," Reg said, "reserved by the duchy for timber for shipbuilding. Liszel knows which palms to grease and which throats to slit, though, so here we are."

"Then in three years someone's going to be displeased to find a big hole in the center of their tree farm . . ."

Reg shrugged. "With any luck, this world will have changed by then, the duchy, perhaps, no more."

"Are we establishing a foothold here? Taking over any local operations?"

"Nah." Reg shook his head. "Not a lot here that offers much hope of profitability. I've talked to some agents who think there's a tourism opportunity with the sea monsters, big game hunting, and whatnot, but I don't see it."

"What, then?"

"Contracts, contracts, contracts. We're giving them a bit of technology. Rigid-body airships."

He pointed down at the clearing and Maddalena could see the construction for what it was: an inchoate dirigible, several dozen workers already swarming it like sea lice on salmon.

A number paused to watch their balloon drift by, but a barrage of curses made delicate and absurd by the distance returned them to their labors.

"We've got three or four agents here at a given time. I'll tell you, it was something else watching those knife jockeys learning principles of aerodynamics and materials science for this. We tried to get some Withered Stem eggheads out here, offered them the chance to examine some 'novel megafauna' in exchange—you got to use their language, right?—but no dice."

"What do they want airships for? Gdercc, I mean. Liszel."

"That's up to them. Up to her. Maybe they hunt the whales while they're asleep and floating—minimize the number of people down in the water."

"Makes sense."

"Maybe they learn to make the trip to Tkerry without spending twenty days on the open ocean. It'd save a lot of lives. The point is to let them dream big. Liszel was practically salivating at the thought of transforming this world, with her as the baroness of the skies."

"And what does Vaish get in return?"

"The same thing we always get from these rustic worlds. They let us bring a tracker 'round, the tracker does their work, we bring some kids back with us. Kids with traveling abilities."

Maddalena blinked rapidly. "What?"

"Yeah. You know that's how all this goes. Withered Stem might be able to make their own travelers, but we can't, and the work must go on."

"I really didn't know that's how all this goes. This isn't part of what I do."

Maddalena leaned forward against the gondola's rails, her mind moving slowly. She didn't believe the things she'd said as Shann, didn't believe in the unique monstrosity of Burel Hird's system. At least, she didn't think she did. The children of their academies had been an abstraction, and how they arranged their society was their own business. There was something different about her society doing it, her own family, even estranged though she was from her identity as Vaish. Something implicatory. She didn't like it—it refused to fall from her mind.

"We're really taking kids?" she said.

"Ech, you make it sound so sinister. They're not really kids. Adolescents. Can't tell if they're travelers if they're literally children. Just kids to me. And they'd leave eventually, and almost certainly by accident, traveling without understanding what traveling is. They'd leave their parents behind and get completely terrified in the process, probably get themselves killed."

"Not everyone who can travel ends up traveling, Reg, you know that."

He waved this away. "Most of these parents won't even notice, anyway. Not being attuned to Ol' Wryneck at work, they won't realize their kiddo is an empty coat. We rescue some talented young people from these dismal backwaters, and they don't have to deal with the terror of navigating the Jynx's roost on their own. Everybody wins."

"You have a different definition of victory than I do."

"I most certainly do not. Victory is profit, Maddalena—we're Firmāre; it's axiomatic—and all will profit. The Vaish receive a new generation of travelers, ready to spread our venture across the Simulacra and bring us untold riches. And that new generation, those lucky young people, get the honor and the pleasure of being Vaish."

"You can't truly believe that, Reg."

"Do not be so foolish as to presume your experience is the only one possible, or so arrogant as to believe that you understand the lives of all Vaish's children."

Maddalena raised her eyebrows. She wanted to respond, but something in his tone—its level, understated ferocity—stopped her. For long minutes there was only the wind and the ropes to fill the silences.

In time, Reg said, "The parents are an externality—some will notice a change in their children, and their lives will be diminished. For the children themselves, though, there is only improvement, to say nothing of the advancement of Vaish's interests, and, in the end, the calculus is clear." He fell silent once more and pushed away from the railing, walking around the gondola to the other side. Maddalena followed him, though she didn't speak.

"Ah!" Reg's expression brightened. "There. Look. We're not too late." He pointed to the horizon, back toward Gdercc, though farther north. A dark speckle hung in the air, and Maddalena squinted, trying to make out what it was.

"Whales," Reg said. "We'll get to see them yet. They're getting a late start to their day, it would seem. No matter; they won't all dive by the time we get there."

Maddalena shielded her eyes, though this did nothing to improve her vision.

"Are those whales?" she said.

"In Gdercc, whales are profit, and I know profit when I see it!" Reg whistled again, and once more, Kbousch's head appeared over the edge of the upper gondola. Pointing in the direction of the speckle, Reg spun his other hand and Kbousch looked up, gazing at the horizon. His shoulders twitched, a shrug perhaps, and he nodded, withdrawing. A moment later came the faint hiss of flame, and they began, almost imperceptibly, to rise.

"What if the winds don't take us back to Gdercc?" Maddalena said.

"We've got four charged propellers. If need be, we'll use those. The winds here, though, are very consistent. We'll be able to make a loop."

"Floating over the ocean in a world of giant sea monsters just seems like asking for trouble."

"Madds. Really. It won't be a problem. Kbousch won't do it if it's too dangerous. I'm not paying him enough to risk his life, or his crew's life, for me." He laughed, the sound oddly drowsy, and rubbed his beard. "This is what he does: whale spotter. He can be relied upon."

Maddalena looked again, but no more was revealed to her. The spot Reg had pointed to was a discoloration, perhaps a cloud darker than the rest, or some other phenomenon unknown to her; it looked like nothing.

"Are you sure?" she said.

Reg nodded sagely, spreading his arms wide as he yawned and shaking his head. His jowls swung for a moment after he stopped.

"I am sure," he said. "Profit, Madds, profit. I told you: I can see it, no matter the distance."

Maddalena leaned on the rail as the balloon drifted in the direction of the darkness.

The wind stiffened, bringing with it scents of cut wood and tar and something acrid, something caustic, and Maddalena's eyes watered. She rubbed them, but the wetness remained, and her vision swam. The basket swayed gently, the world a half degree off, first one way then the other, and though at this height the air should have been clear, the smell and the motion brought only a nauseated uncertainty. What it was they were floating toward, Maddalena couldn't tell, and though she squinted till her face ached and her brows burned, it remained obscure; so far as she could see, it was only a darkness, as indistinct as optimism, grays on grays on grays.

ACKNOWLEDGMENTS

Transmentation | Transience was written by five people, but many more were instrumental in creating the book you have just read. Thanks to our agent, Kim-Mei Kirtland, for taking on not only these books but this entire project. Our editor, Diana Gill, and the team at Blackstone Publishing were faced with the novelty of dealing with a five-headed hydra of an author and met the challenge with unflappable composure. We're especially grateful to Josie Woodbridge for her enthusiasm and Josh Stanton for being such a champion for the larger Many Worlds project.

Thanks to Kathryn English for designing the glorious cover, to Cole Barnes, Levi Coren, and Lydia Rogue for fastidious copyediting, to Sarah Bonamino for wrangling publicity, and to the exceptionally talented Dion Graham for the audiobook narration.

This book is part of a larger whole, and so is its author. We are deeply thankful to the other members of the Many Worlds collective for supporting us in this intense and consuming project: Justin, Maria, Betsy, Bonnie Jo, Cliff, Elliot, Ted, Shiv, Jendayi, Smriti, Liz, Rebekah, Mark, Veronica, Rafeeat, and Misha.

Immense gratitude to our early readers: Betsy Aoki, Carrie Blackburn, and Steven Ensslen.

Thanks to our families and friends who put up with us. Our partners:

Caroline, Anju, Steven, Carrie, Alisa. Our kids: Travis, Wren, Asher, Caleb, and Gabriel. Our pets: Sgt. Snuggles, Gordo, Trotsky, Executive Officer Woofers T. Woofington (XO), Clem Fandango, Corra, Kiba, one owl, and a bale of transient mud turtles.

And thanks to the magic of modern technology for letting us dark-lies actually talk to each other.

To everyone else who supported us, our gratitude is endless.

To our faithful Episcopal censors: We appreciate that you've allowed us this much latitude in telling such a tale.

And, most importantly: you. The reader. May the Simulacrum pre-serve you precisely as you wish.